FREEMAN WALKER

FREEMAN WALKER

DAVID ALLAN CATES

UNBRIDLED BOOKS

Unbridled Books
Denver, Colorado

Library of Congress Cataloging-in-Publication Data

Cates, David Allan.
Freeman Walker : a novel / by David Allan Cates.
p. cm.
ISBN 978-1-932961-55-3 (hardcover : alk. paper)
1. Freedmen—Fiction. I. Title.
PS3553.A84F74 2008
813'.54—dc22   2008017456

1   3   5   7   9   10   8   6   4   2

Book Design by SH • CV

First Printing

For Mom and Dad—your songs and stories
made air to breathe and fly on

BOOK ONE

I know how men in exile feed on dreams of hope.
—Aeschylus, *Agamemmon*

LOVE

WHEN I WAS A boy I had little interest in freedom, but my father did, so when I was seven years old he freed me, and I was sent across the sea with a change of clothing in a little black maw and a rolled-up copy of the Declaration of Independence that I could not read.

That's true, and so my story begins.

Or I could begin earlier, say, at my conception. *There,* you might say, if you were the kind to say it, *is the Original Sin. The cause of it all!* Because my father was the legal owner of my mother, you presume her consent, being unnecessary, was not given. But that would be like saying that songs, being unnecessary, aren't sung.

(Your father, after all, might have taken your mother by force, but do we presume it?)

Of course I'm aware that the Sweet Grass Farm, like the rest of the world, was a place of pain and difficulty, indeed horrors of human suffering—but these horrors happened to other people and not to me. Mama and I lived in a cabin along the river bottom. Our job was to tend the dairy cows, milk them, make butter, and take care of the calves. My parents loved one another and they loved me—I knew that the way a child knows anything, in my body—and I loved them, and was happy for a while.

But all happiness ends. What is unique is the cause. In my case, it was my father's love and aspirations for me, his only son, combined with his obligations to his legal wife and his desire to please my mother that moved him to *strike the fetters from my limbs,* as he said, and send me to England to study.

The first hint that the day of my new life had arrived—that I was being conceived again—was the carriage. My father was a walker. He rarely even rode a horse. So to see him arrive at the cabin that morning in a carriage pulled by a splendid team of grays was indeed different.

Excited, I ran to greet him, and there received the second hint: a package with new clothes. He lifted me up onto a large flat sitting stump in our yard and helped me dress. I remember his big fingers doing a lot of buttons on the shirt and trousers, but mainly I remember him slipping on the boots. I loved how they looked and smelled, shiny and tall, and I loved how they looked like his boots, but I hated how they felt to stand in. They separated my feet from the earth with a thick sole and heel, and boxed in my toes and weighed down my step. They felt as unnatural to me as a mouth full of cotton.

Nevertheless, enjoying the novelty of the occasion, I happily stepped up into the carriage and took my place across from my father on a soft leather seat. He was dressed in an identical black suit and wore a high beaver-felt hat. He held another one on his lap, which he handed to me. It was a miniature version of his, and I took it with more pride than you can imagine. I put it on. I tilted it at just the same angle as his. The carriage smelled of oil and smoke, and seeing me sitting across from him, booted and hatted just as he was, my father smiled at me in a tight, uncharacteristic way that might have been my third hint.

But what happy child can anticipate losing everything he's ever had? Especially wearing such a respectable hat and hearing the driver click his tongue and feeling the team suddenly lurch forward? Here I must have asked where we were going, because I remember him saying, "To say good-bye to your mother."

Which still did not make me worry. I assumed we were going on an errand, on an outing, and I imagined myself waving from the carriage and Mama looking at me wearing my hat with the same pride and love I sometimes saw in her face when she looked at my father. I imagined all of that, and hoped for it as the carriage followed the trace down to the run where the cattle lolled in the cool shade. Auntie Luck told us Mama was in the field, but when we went there we were told she was in the woods on nature's call. We waited; she did not return. I begged my father to direct the carriage one last time to the cabin, where I was sure she must be by now. I wanted to see her face when she saw me step out of the carriage and walk tall in my new boots and hat.

As we approached, I thought I saw smoke rising from the chimney. We stopped, but instead of making the dignified entrance I'd imagined, I jumped off the carriage and ran through the grass to the cabin door. I opened it and waited a moment while my eyes adjusted to the dark. Was that her bent by the fireplace stirring coals? Before I could call out, she disappeared and the coals turned to ash. My heart dropped and I was about to turn, but she appeared again suddenly, this time standing at the basin, her back turned.

Mama? I didn't recognize my voice. I was not unaccustomed to seeing spirits, but I was used to them being dead. And just that morning, my mother had been alive enough to tickle me awake.

Look at me, Mama, I said, but she disappeared again. I could smell her, though—so she was close, or her ghost was. Then I saw her on a bench before me at the door shelling peas, her brown face bent over her work.

Mama?

She wouldn't look up. Her fingers worked the pods. I wanted her to look up and see my new stiff white collar and black suit, see what she'd call my tall *civ'lized* hat and tall *civ'lized* boots, see how much I looked like my father.

Look at me, I said again in my new voice.

Finally she did, but her eyes were black and empty. She touched the scar where her left ear should have been. I'd seen the scar but never until that moment understood that there used to be an ear there, that once upon a time she'd had two, just like me.

Where'd your ear go, Mama?

I ran, she answered, and I pictured the ear coming off by the sheer speed of her running.

Ran? Where?

"Not here?" It was my father, and at the sound of his voice—he sounded terribly sad—Mama disappeared again. The bench was suddenly empty, no bowl of shelled peas, either. Where had she gone? Had I merely imagined her? I felt his hand on my shoulder, then on my hand. I looked again at the empty cabin but felt my father pulling me away. I glanced up at his face, at his long dark nostrils and the cloud of anger on his brow, his slit-mouth deliberately calm. I was disappointed that Mama wasn't there to see me in my civilized clothes, and we hadn't said good-bye, but I couldn't have suspected then what I do now—and what most likely my father knew—that his legal wife, out of respectable spite, had sent my mother on an errand hours ago.

He asked me to close the door and come along. Asked, not commanded, and that was a crucial difference. Because regardless of the fact that I was a seven-year-old boy and did not have a choice at all, it was with my own hand, the one not being held by my father and master, that I closed the door on the old-wood-and-mildew smell of the cabin. Closed the door and turned away from the phantom flesh of my mother.

We got back into the carriage and the driver clicked his tongue and the team began to trot. I watched my father's face as he turned to look out the window at the passing trees and fields in the glaring light of midday. I was waiting for him to tell me something but for a long while he seemed unable to speak. He was not, generally, a distant man. He was playful and quick to wrestle, to tickle, to kiss me. He was a flesh-and-blood body to me. When we walked in the woods, he held my hand. When we sat in the shade, I sat so close his sweat was my sweat, his smell was mine. I can still see his green eyes lively as new leaves and the full flush of his cheeks beneath his thin blond beard. When we played *whaler* in the creek (I was the whaler, he the whale) he'd throw me in the air and I'd laugh to see water roll off his big white back and monster head.

But that moment, in the carriage, I saw his face as I had never seen it before and his sadness scared me. Maybe because of that fear, and maybe because after too much silence I was suffocating for the sound of his voice, and maybe because when he finally did speak he deliberately touched each of his fingers and thumb before each sentence, and maybe because he used the pronoun *we,* which served to intensify our intimacy as the horses broke into a gallop and the carriage began to sway—maybe for all of those reasons I have never forgotten what he said to me.

"We," he said, and he touched his little finger, "all suffer."

Then he touched his ring finger, bent it back almost ninety degrees before straightening it again. "And we are all going to die. It's a law of nature. You know these things already."

He swallowed. I swallowed. I watched him touch his middle finger and pause as though he found this one the most difficult to contemplate. He blinked rapidly, nodded beyond me to the passing world out the window, the world we were leaving behind—my mother?

"We are not in control," he said.

I could not take my eyes off him. I tried to swallow again but my throat felt dry and swollen. I was dying to unbutton my collar but dared not.

"It will take becoming a man," he said, "to learn these last two. First—" He touched his pointer. "We do not live for ourselves." Then he made a fist and shook it slightly as if he were holding something precious that he could feel and did not want to let go.

He lifted his thumb and whispered, "But we are free!"

I blinked back tears, swallowed hard, and turned my gaze to the window. That's when he explained where I was going: to the port, to board a ship that would sail with the tide at dawn. I didn't know what to say. The sky was a magnificent blue and the breeze bent the crowns of the trees along the road. *Sail with the tide.* I had only the vaguest notion of what that might mean.

He pulled some papers from his pocket and showed them to me, although I could not read. One was the rolled-up copy of the Declaration of Independence. He slipped it into my pocket and said it was civilized law—the law of men aspiring to be divine. He said I should keep it and learn to read it. Then he showed me other papers that were folded in an envelope.

"Men's law," he said.

I started to take the envelope but he said he'd keep it for now and give it to the captain. Before he slipped it back inside his coat, he pointed to the two words on the envelope: "James Gates," he said.

I had always been Jimmy. He had always been Mr. Gates.

"James Gates." The words felt odd in my mouth.

"Because you're my son," he said, and smiled.

I wanted to smile, too. He must have sensed my confusion, for he patted the papers in his coat pocket. "Your free papers," he said. I might have asked why I needed those, why they were mine, because he said a word that I don't remember ever having heard before, at least not applied to me. I repeated it, feeling my tongue slide easily across the surface of the sound, closing it with my teeth and lip.

"Slave?"

He looked at his watch, seemed for a moment to be calculating the time, and said he'd show me.

So before we boarded the ship he took me to a crowded market. He held my hand as we pushed our way through more people than I had seen in my entire life. I was overwhelmed by the smells and colors, by the sound of so many voices and the sheer variety of the human face. Who were these people? Where did they come from? Were they also going to *sail with the tide* at dawn?

To abate my confusion, I looked straight up at my father's face, his slit nostrils and long thin nose and the blue sky beyond his head, and that was how I kept my balance.

Soon he halted and lifted me by the armpits up over his head to his shoulders, where I straddled his neck and peeked around the sweat-stained crown of his tall civilized hat to see a barely dressed—naked, really—Negro man and woman and two children on a raised wooden platform. Chains connected shackles from their necks to their ankles. I'd never seen shackles before and they terrified me, as did the man pointing to the people wearing the shackles with a long stick and calling out numbers to other men who called out more numbers.

I focused on the children, a boy slightly older than I, and a girl a bit younger. The girl had scabs on the right side of her face and the boy had long muscular arms and black skin shiny as tar, an empty socket where his right eye should have been. The two of them sat in the heat and stared with three spooky yellow eyes at something above our heads.

"Your mother," my father said, "was auctioned away from her parents as a girl, and that's why—"

He squeezed my ankles hanging down on each side of his neck and then turned and walked away through the crowd. I was confused. Was he thinking what I was thinking? Of Mama running, of her ear flying off? From his shoulders I could see down the long street to white gulls flying arcs over the blue harbor.

Just before dusk he said good-bye to me on board the ship. The pier smelled of fish and tar. He assured me that he'd come to visit at the end of the school year but that seemed so far in the future as to be irrelevant. He told me that miserable as it might feel to leave, staying at Sweet Grass would in time make me more so. He said this country was diseased, and he was sending me away to save me. He said he used to think civilization moved west until he'd been to the jungles of Mississippi to visit his brother and seen the horrors of what men do to other men when they can, when there's nothing to stop them. He told me the school in England would take care of me—I'd be taught to read and think, and have a chance to become the free man God meant for me to become. His kiss on my forehead left a wet spot that I resisted wiping even as I stood at the rail and watched him hand my papers to the captain, walk down the gangplank, and disappear across the crowded dock.

It was the close of a hot July day, not unlike the day before or the day that surely followed. Yet when the cool spot of his kiss finally dried, I found myself separated from everything I loved and everyone who loved me.

ON BOARD SHIP I was given my own compartment and then left alone to mourn. In the dark I could feel the pitch and roll of the ship, hear the creak of the timbers and the occasional shouts of the crew. The first morning I dared a peek out on deck, but the sight of the gray sea and the sky forever in all directions frightened me and I quickly threw myself back onto my bunk. I slept and cried all day and night and day and night again. My grief must have alarmed the captain, for he sent for me to be picked up by the ears and carried into the dining area. When I refused to sip the wretched soup, an old man with the dirtiest fingers I'd ever seen pushed rancid chunks of cod into my mouth while he proclaimed over and over again that a boy like me ought to be grateful.

This happened often enough during the voyage that for many years afterward I confused the words *grateful* with *nauseated.*

The difficulty of this trip cannot be underestimated. It marked me forever, and even when I say or write the words *ocean* or *ship,* I think of that experience and feel again the yawning solitude that swallowed me. I didn't want to cross the sea. I didn't want to study—whatever that meant. And what good was freedom if I had no control?

We all suffer. My father had assumed I already knew this. But I didn't. I was a child. I only knew that *I* suffered.

I arrived so ill that I remember nothing of my transport from the ship to Hodgson Academy, a half day's carriage ride from London. I remember only waking from my fever on a comfortable bed in a small white room with a table, a chair, and a lamp. Here I was brought regular meals and a change of sheets by a woman with what I assumed must have been a great fear that if she moved her mouth to speak, or smiled, her hard white face would crack like an egg. In silence I was served, in silence my bed was changed, and in silence I was peeked at and prodded for signs of the lingering disease of my diseased country. Night followed day followed night. Had I dreamed water as far as I could see, water that touched the sky? I remembered the plantation and its grasses and trees, the cool stream where I played with my father, the taste of bare dirt outside our door and the salt on my mother's skin, the sound of voices, dogs, cows—the smell of my mother and the cabin: these things had been separated from me by ocean and by time. How much? I didn't know. Did it matter? Once I closed the door on the cabin, the door was closed. It happened—or did I dream that, too?

All I knew for sure was alone in that room I sometimes felt a wind race through my empty body, around and around, and I was afraid if I opened my mouth the wind would pour out and my scream would fill the world. I hated freedom, and I wanted to suffocate, to waste away with hunger.

But not quite. It has been my experience with despair that even if in our conscious mind we race to embrace it, there is something deeper inside us, and wiser, that will do anything to maintain hope.

For me it started with my body. Specifically, with the food I was being given to eat. Healthy again, I had a huge appetite—and I really liked toast with orange marmalade. I had never had either before, and I loved the smell and look of the marmalade, and I loved spreading it so thickly that the toast became simply a platform on which to hold all the marmalade. I was given a boiled egg every morning with salt. And pieces of chicken or beef or pork with my rice or boiled potatoes in the evening, with butter, and more salt, and a pot of tea, all for me, with biscuits, always with biscuits. And because there wasn't much to do but eat, I looked forward to each meal with passion. At first I ate my meals fast, in as few bites as possible. I was afraid the woman—Miss Crinkle, I called her, for the many tiny wrinkles in her face—would take my plates away before I was finished. But after a few days, when I realized she would not come back until the next mealtime, I began eating very slowly, holding each mouthful for as long as I could before swallowing, trying in vain to draw out the meal until the next one came.

But I couldn't, of course, so in the too quiet time between meals, I restlessly paced my room. I could walk the loop of my room with my eyes closed, counting breaths, counting steps. From one corner of the room to another. From that corner around the bed and past the night-stand to the other. And from that corner past the door to the first corner. Over and over again. I learned when to shorten or lengthen my step to avoid a creaky board, how to make the entire loop without making a sound or bumping against a table or bedpost or wall. Or where to step so that each footfall caused the floor to creak. I began to know my steps, and my breaths and the dimensions of my space, and from those truths I could invent the rest. Soon there was no difference between what I remembered and what I dreamed, between what I saw—the pale woman who brought me food and took away my waste—and Mama's laughing face behind her, Mama standing at the door with her back turned, Mama carrying a wooden milk pail on her head. I could hear her breathe in the dark behind me, in front of me, and I could hear her laugh joyously, and often laughed with her. She was here, there, touchable like a warm meal, or visible like a ray of light under the door. Home was a warm cabin I could imagine, my sunny memories sometimes as real as the cold room I occupied. Mama was at once a dream, a memory, and someone who actually lived and breathed with me. In. Out. In. Out. My nostrils filled with the smell of her flesh. I imagined we were breathing at the same time, and even breathing the same air. In. Out. In. Out. And so like that, exhausted from a day of walking, I'd fall asleep with the feel of her fingers in my hair.

During such moments of happiness, I began to make assessments. Childish as they were, they formed the shape of my ambition. If I could conjure the past, certainly I could conjure the future. And if love had sent me here, might not love send me home again?

I SET MY SIGHTS on the only human being I knew: Miss Crinkle. Her thrice-daily food deliveries were like visits from the dead. If I said before she was *silent,* let me correct that. She didn't talk, but she did make odd groans deep in her throat like a spirit, or an old dog. I tried speaking to her. I said *thank you* and *good morning,* but she didn't even turn her head. I asked if she had grandchildren. I asked if she made the toast herself. I asked what the weather was like outside but she only clamped her wrinkled face between her two palms and let loose a moan as though she were freeing the very wind from where it had been caught in her throat.

Did I say she frightened me? Did I mention I had nightmares in which we had entire conversations where she would only make that fierce sound?

Indeed. But we all risk death by monster rather than stay home alone. Especially if beyond the walls of your room you sometimes hear other children laughing.

One night I lay in bed and determined I would sing for her in the morning. I could not sleep with anticipation. I waited all night until I saw the yellow lamplight under the door, which for me was dawn. I heard the sound of her shoes, and the key in the lock, and I leaped up to a standing position on top of my bed when the door swung open. And as the light of her lamp filled the room, I spread my arms and opened my mouth and began to sing "O Thy Joy Has Come to Me."

She might have paused—how could she not have? The sudden volume must have startled her. But if so, I didn't see it. I watched her carry the tray with my toast and marmalade and tea and set it on the end table, and then she turned, without looking, and walked over to the corner, where she stooped to pick up my chamber pot, and then she let herself out, closed the door, and locked it.

More miserable than ever, I spilled my tea and threw my precious toast against the wall and waited for her to come back at midday. I stood on the bed again like a little emperor, silent this time, with my arms folded, and watched her stoop to sop up the spilled tea and scrub the wall where the toast had stuck. I tried to satisfy myself with the fact that at least I had delayed her. Rather than come and go, she'd come and gone, and come back with a mop and bucket, and only after cleaning did she go for good.

So I tried the same thing with my dinner, tossing it all over the room, here and there, sticking it to the walls and ceiling. As you can imagine, this was not an easy sacrifice. I waited hungrily (and guiltily) for her to come back in the evening. When she did, I was once again up on the bed (closer to her eye level, was my reasoning) and I immediately spoke.

"I'm terrible sorry, ma'am, for the accident."

She ignored me. She surveyed the mess to determine tactics, left, and returned with the appropriate cleaning devices. I stood on the bed and watched the back of her neck as she scrubbed. She was an old woman, and I could hear the difficulty in her breathing as she worked. No sighs, but a change of breath, at least. I asked her if she had a dog, for I could hear one barking just then, and it scared me. I asked her if she liked molasses on sweetbread, my favorite back home, and then, scratching myself and lowering my trousers sufficiently, I asked if she wanted to see my do-jiggy.

No answer. Not even a turn of the head. I watched her on her knees scrubbing, and she didn't even pause. I moved close to the edge of the bed, struggled slightly with keeping my balance on the soft mattress, and did what comes naturally to a boy standing on the heights with his pants lowered. I pointed toward the ceiling and peed a pretty yellow arc onto the floor. She paused in her scrubbing when the room filled with the smell, but she still did not look at me. When she finished in the corner, she cleaned up my puddle with a mop, and then she left me again, closing the door with a firm click, no more loudly or angrily than any time before.

That night I thought of defecating on the floor in front of the door so that she'd step on it when she walked in—then of standing on the bed and urinating on her when she knelt to clean it up.

But in the morning the door opened, and again I was petrified by her presence—this time with shame, not with fear. Shame likes company, though, and so I also began to feel anger. When she came in I concentrated all of my loathing in the hope that she would feel it and so do something that might make me stop hating her. I stared at her coldly but she didn't seem to notice. So I unleashed a torrent of all of the worst words I had ever heard anybody speak, and she still refused to look at me. Oh how I hated her! And for a few hours hate was my companion. I paced the room and hated Miss Crinkle. I wished her dead. I thought about killing her. How? Beating her with my pillow, suffocating her, pounding her with my fists, stabbing her with a fork. *We are all going to die,* my father had said. So why not her? Why not now?

Why not, indeed.

Because the very next morning, to my horror and amazement, as she stooped to get my bedpan her face contorted, and her lips parted and issued a horrendous groan before she collapsed.

I sat up in the bed and looked at the floor where she'd crumpled in a pile of dress and hair—her gray hair had come all undone and splashed about her face. I believed I must have been dreaming, so unreal was the scene. I walked over to her, stooped to touch her head, and pushed the hair off her ashen face. It was the first time I had ever touched a white woman's face or hair. I looked at the spittle in the corners of her mouth, and I laid the flat of my hand on her forehead. The hundreds of wrinkles seemed to have relaxed and the heat was already leaving her cheek. She wasn't breathing, yet for a few moments she seemed conscious. There was a question in her eyes, and I could have sworn she looked at me for the first time. Did she know I'd wished her dead? Yet there was no anger in her look, no reproach, as the light in her eyes blinked out.

After the initial shock, I felt afraid. Who would bring me my food? Would I ever see anybody again? And would they know I'd wished her dead?

I crawled back up onto my bed. The door was open—why didn't I go out? Perhaps I heard the dog barking. I must have been very tired because I fell asleep instead.

When I woke the body was gone and the door closed. There was food on my tray that I ate without pleasure. That night I couldn't sleep. I paced the room with the restless step of a murderer. I walked and breathed, and stifled the desire to scream. For what? Perhaps I had only dreamed her dead body?

Regardless, I carefully stepped over the spot where I had dreamed her.

I felt my body get hot and then cold, and my brow sweat profusely. Suddenly I felt fine again, and I kept walking. Then I felt the chill return. Was that her spirit? So be it. I was too light-headed to be afraid. I remember feeling as though I were walking differently than usual. Walking just a few inches above the floor, but a new blast of sudden cold shook me to my bones and I lay down in bed. I curled up under my covers to get warm but her cold ghost was there, too.

Is this what it felt like to be a killer? Is that what I'd become?

Despite my chill, I can't say I lay awake over it. In fact, for a brief moment before drifting off to feverish sleep, I admit the possibility thrilled me.

I WOKE UP IN a pool of wet sheets and a young woman was in my room with a stack of clean ones. I slipped off the mattress and watched as she made my bed. She had hair like orange rust, eyes green as grass, and freckles like flecks in cream. She kept her eyes averted, but she did not terrify me. I could see the slight flush of her cheek when she became aware I was watching her. I seized my advantage and ran past her as fast as I could to jump up on the bed.

I said, *"Yiiiiiiiii,"* and jumped so high I thought I might touch the ceiling, and this caused her to look at me with wonder. She stood with a hand on her hip for a moment and watched me and I thought I saw her lips change shape. A smile?

Again, I yelled, *"Yiiiiiiiiiii!"* and she reached for me. I avoided her and kept jumping. She lifted her broom and tried to sweep me off but I jumped to avoid the broom. Despite ourselves, both of us were laughing. She lifted the broom higher and swung this way and that until she finally managed to cock me alongside my head, which caused me to lose my balance and fall to the floor. Unfazed, I wriggled over to try to look up her skirt.

She shrieked, stepped back, and picked me up by my nightshirt and tossed me onto the bed. I bounced once or twice before coming to a thumping halt against the wall. Then she wagged a chubby pink finger at me and accompanied it with a sentence of such music I had to repeat the sound over and over again after she'd walked out and locked the door before I could find the individual words and the meaning became clear.

"You wee monkey," she said, "is this how the niggers behave in America, jumping and shrieking like banshees and poking their wee mugs where they're not supposed to be?"

A long way from love, I suppose, but it was a start.

The next morning I lay waiting for her, curled up in bed and pretending to be sorry. She looked at me as soon as she came in the door. I told her I was sorry I'd misbehaved. I told her I'd had a fever the night before and felt bad about the dead woman. I almost admitted to killing Crinkle but dared not. I told her I'd been in this room a long time. I started to cry.

She stood with her hand on her hips, suspicious. But my tears were real—they surprised even me. She sat down. Told me not to worry about Miss Crinkle—Tennyson, actually, Miss Tennyson.

"She's happier dead, I'm sure," she said.

"Happier?"

"Deaf and dumb her whole life long, the poor dear."

"What?" I was having a hard time understanding her.

"As a doorknob!" she said.

I loved the way she smelled. I loved looking at her orange hair and skin like cream. But I couldn't understand her when she talked.

"Deaf," she said again, and pointed to her ears, and shook her head. "No hear! No talk!"

Oh! A light went on. I felt a weight lift. Miss Crinkle had never heard a word I'd said. She couldn't even hear herself moan and groan.

"Why am I here?" I asked this woman whom I had already begun to love.

She smiled. "Poor wee monkey," she said, "you must be awfully lonely. Ten days here already? Well, there's been a plague of sorts about and the school doctor's ran away with his wife's sister to France and I suspect when you arrived ill from America they didn't want to infect the others."

I didn't speak, I didn't know what to say. My eyes were overrunning with tears. It wasn't my fault my country was diseased.

"Be patient," she said, and she put her arm around me and gave me a quick squeeze. "You'll be out with your mates in no time at all."

I didn't know what *mates* were, but even if they were alligators I was still pleased they would be *mine,* and pleased I would be *out* with them.

She gave me a quick squeeze, called me her wee monkey again, and said a prayer for me when she tucked me into bed that night. Sitting on my bed and bending over me, she asked me about my one green eye and one brown, features to which I'd given little thought. My father had green eyes and my mother had brown, so why shouldn't I have the two colors? But Bridget—for that was her name—told me she'd seen perhaps a few thousand people in her life and never one with eyes like mine. She asked me how many people I had seen, and she asked me to try to count them, and asked if I had ever seen a person with two different-colored eyes, and I had not, and soon lost count anyway, never having learned how to count past nineteen.

That neither of us had seen another like me was proof then, she said, that two distinctly colored eyes must be a sign for something. She didn't know what, and yet it was true, and I might learn only as I lived what it was a sign for. She ran from the room and brought back a hand mirror and turned me this way and then that, holding the mirror for me, and said from one side I was practically a white boy except for my hair. It was the first time I'd seen myself that close, both sides like that, and when I said so, Miss Bridget left the mirror with me that evening. It provided some mild entertainment for the next few hours as I moved it from side to side to see the texture and pigment of my eyes and the pores in my skin as well.

The next day Miss Bridget told me she was not from this place either, but from an island country nearby that had been conquered a long time ago, and her people made to suffer for it. She said her parents had died when she was young and she'd been working in other people's homes since she could remember. Most recently she'd been employed by a Mr. Ryan back home, but he'd left for America, and so she'd lost her position. Being a good man, he'd found her a position here at Hodgson Academy, a place so foggy even the faeries lost their way.

"Foggy?" I told her I'd been confined to my room and not yet seen outside.

"Not once?" she said.

I shook my head. She studied me, laid her creamy hand on my face.

"I don't believe you have the pestilence anymore," she said.

I was glad about that and I told her so, and I told her I was even gladder that she didn't think so.

"Then I'll be having a surprise for you tomorrow morning," she said.

And she did, although it wasn't on the tray when she opened the door. Nor in her apron, either, at least that I could see, and for a brief moment after a long night of anticipation I felt disappointed. I thought she'd forgotten. But she hadn't. She set the tray down with its toast and tea, but instead of picking up the chamber pot, she took my hand and walked me out of my room and through a large, cavernous hall trimmed with dark wood. I was so shocked to be suddenly out of my room that I couldn't speak. We paused by a tall window and she urged me to slip behind the heavy drapes. What followed was a pleasure I cannot fully describe. She opened the window for me, lifted the sash slightly so I could smell the fresh air. I was too short to see over the sill, so she bent down and lifted me. The feel of her arms and hands, and the brief moment of being squeezed to her bosom, followed by the touch of new air on my face and the sight of a dawn sky over a grassy garden surrounded by tall trees—all this was a kindness I'll never forget.

"World," Bridget said, as though speaking to the great beyond, "'tis James."

"Jimmy," I said.

"Jimmy," she repeated. "He's wee indeed but a strong and healthy ragamuffin and not too brown for all we call him a monkey. He's whiter than many a one and yet not as white as you would say. Jimmy, say hello to the world."

I don't know that I spoke. I stared and blinked, and felt the air on my skin. I watched the faintest touch of color spread across the sky behind the trees.

"Do you like it much, Jimmy?" she said.

"Very much," I said.

AND SO I WAS held to a woman's breast, newborn again into a world so different from Sweet Grass—so beyond what I would have been capable of imagining just a few short months before—that I'm sure I would have believed anyone in authority who might have told me that either Sweet Grass or Hodgson Academy were dreams. For how could the same waking world hold both?

But if dreams have purposes, one must be to remind us that what we see in the daytime is only partly true. I lived at Hodgson and dreamed of Sweet Grass—and so I knew the world was bigger than my bounty. And if I ever returned to the shacks and fields of Sweet Grass, I knew I'd carry the dream of this good life, its distinct colors and shapes, stone buildings with sealed rooms and glass windows, a world with measured and counted hours, bountiful food and companionship, and grown people who dedicated their days to teaching me to read, to add and subtract figures, and to recite accounts of Egypt and Greece in stories as beautiful and strange as the fancies Mama had told me about spirits.

I had never spent time with white children before, and although I don't remember walking into the school or being introduced, I remember sitting at my desk in the back of the classroom and studying the variety of my classmates' hair, the color of flame, or cream, or various kinds of wood. I remember the light from the high windows falling on the skin of their hands and necks as they bent over their studies. And because my features and hair were a novelty to them, I remember their furtive glances back at me, their curious multicolored eyes.

One of the other boys raised his hand and asked if niggers spoke Arabic, and if that was why I talked so funny. Our teacher, Mr. Collins, took the opportunity to tell us the story of how sugar from the Indies was shipped to England and African people were shipped to the Indies, and there was tea in there somewhere, and the Africans were sold as slaves in America for the cotton brought back to England, but the gist was that we were Negroes or Africans and not Arabs or niggers.

Mr. Collins looked at me when he finished as though waiting for my confirmation, and I was so lost I could only say, "No sir."

"No sir, what?" he asked.

I swallowed. I could feel all of the boys' eyes aimed at me.

"No sir, you're right, we don't speak Arab."

The class laughed. "Arabic," he said.

Confused, I said, "That neither," and everybody laughed some more.

But it was a laugh without malice. In fact, when the teacher explained that I used to be a *slave,* their pink mouths opened wide and formed rows of O's. And when he pronounced me a *freed slave,* the expressions of admiration could not have been greater if he had said I was a former pirate.

Mr. Collins was asked if there were other Negro slaves with one green eye. He looked at me, and I shook my head no. Then the same questioner asked Mr. Collins if I had been set free *because* I had one green eye—did a slave have to have two brown eyes to be a slave?— and Mr. Collins again said no, that one never knew or could scarcely guess what it was that caused God to dim the soul of a human being to such an extent as to make him think he could own another human being, or that caused that same God to enlighten that man's soul sufficiently so he could see to free one of his slaves, and if—

"It was my father," I said, interrupting him.

All eyes turned to me again. I felt my face get hot with blood.

"Your father?" Mr. Collins said, raising his eyebrows and waiting.

"Who freed me," I said.

Mr. Collins suddenly smiled as though I'd shone light on him and he was beaming it back at me. "Our Father, our Lord," he said.

"No," I said, and his smile disappeared, light out. "It's Mr. Gates's green eye I got," I said, pointing to my right one. I turned and pointed to the other. I could feel every single eye on me, and I took my time to say, "Mama's brown one."

Mr. Collins blinked slowly. They all did. The room was absolutely silent. Then Mr. Collins nodded in a way that conveyed that he both understood and did not understand, as though what he'd just heard was perfect proof of how things that seem true often aren't, and things that seem untrue often are.

"Oh, the mystery," he said, quietly, almost under his breath, an expression I grew used to him saying in these moments when there was nothing else to say. The other students took it as an end of the discussion. They seemed to collectively exhale before their heads swiveled away from me toward the front of the class.

"Oh, the mystery," I said under my breath, intrigued by Mr. Collins's accent and the strange power of his words. All the students' heads turned back to me. Apparently I'd spoken more loudly than I'd meant to. And in a way that sounded very similar to Mr. Collins. I might have been mortified, but in all of those eyes I saw delight. Even Mr. Collins looked at me with admiration. For a moment it was silent, and then sudden laughter broke the tension, and it felt as if I were bathing in warm waves of love.

There are more scenes I remember from my years of school—but this one still stands out most vividly because the two things I learned that morning correspond with the two big things I learned at Hodgson. The first was *Oh, the mystery.* Mr. Collins said it with wonder and sadness and love, and so I learned that even teachers thought the world was mysterious, and could be struck dumb or sad and amazed by their inability to understand.

And the second thing I learned was that I could make people laugh.

In the days that followed, my accent and novel background provided great entertainment for my classmates, an entertainment I enjoyed providing. I was asked all sorts of questions regarding the difficulties of slavery—ironic for a boy who hadn't even known he was a slave until he was being freed. I was asked if I'd ever been whipped? (No.) Had I seen others whipped? (Yes, I lied.) Had there been much blood and wailing? (Yes blood, no wailing—in fact it was quiet except for the cut of the whip and the harsh breathing of both whipper and whipped—I was a good liar, even then.) Why had the man been whipped? (I didn't know—lying or stealing, probably.) Where did I see it? (Sitting on my mother's lap. We had taken a walk and stopped in the shade and one fellow came past whipping his slave, who was wearing chains.) Did I think it would have been better to have been a slave in Egypt, Roman times, or America? (Because I did not know what Egypt or Roman times were, I said America.) Had I seen lions in America? (No, but a bear, yes.) Was it true full-grown adult Negroes smelled like tigers? (This asked with such glee that I was tempted to say yes but had to admit I didn't know, as I'd never smelled tigers.) Never? I was asked again, as though that fact, coming from an ex-slave, was extraordinarily disappointing. (Well, maybe once or twice.) Had I any brothers or sisters sold off before my eyes? (No.) Ever seen families torn apart by slavery? (I imagined *torn apart* as in torn apart by claws, and so I said yes, I'd seen a slave girl who'd lost half her face to a tiger and a boy who'd lost an eye.) That impressed everyone so much that I added that my mother had lost an ear, sliced off by a tiger's claw when she ran.

Soon enough, though, my novelty wore off and my classmates and I were playing together as though our mothers had been sisters. I kept my hair short, not to make less visible my mother's blood but because their hair was short and combed and I wanted to look like them. I was given the gift of mimicry and fairly quickly even spoke as they did. And for all we soon remembered, I always had.

School, then, was a place of comfort. The beds were warm and the food filling and good, and I was cared for and treated with kindness. I learned to read and was often praised for my diligence and intelligence. I was rarely alone, but when I had a chance, I would study my little rolled-up copy of the Declaration of Independence because I thought that if I learned *civilized law,* my father would be proud of me—would remember how much he loved me—and so take me home to see my mother again.

In its words I searched for a reason for my banishment, and was encouraged by the first sentence, which says sometimes it is *necessary for one people to dissolve the political bands which have connected them with another,* and that *a decent respect to the opinions of mankind requires that they should declare the causes which impel them to the separation.* But I understood little of politics, or what followed in the document, and remember being especially puzzled by the fact that I'd been sent to be free in England, of all places, whose monarch (the document asserted, though I had yet to meet him) was the source of *absolute tyranny.*

At Hodgson I learned to write letters. I knew Mama couldn't read but I trusted that my father would read them to her. I have no notion whether or not he did. In his monthly letters to me, he only thanked me for mine and said my mother was well. I continued writing nonetheless. I wrote of my days, of what I ate, of my studies. I did not complain, as I had little to complain about save the ache in my heart. I reported my good marks in my studies, and felt that if I did well enough, and put my very best face forward on the page, perhaps I'd be able to go home again.

But in the spring, despite my earnest efforts, I learned that illness (from the *diseased* country?) had postponed his visit, and so another year passed, and another and another, and it wasn't until after my fourth year of schooling that I received a letter from him informing me of his imminent arrival. I don't think I can describe properly my emotion at receiving such news. Part of me didn't believe it, but the part that did hoped beyond hope that he would arrive and see what marvelous (for I was always at the head of my class) progress I had made, see that even though I was still a boy, I'd miraculously become the free man God meant for me to become. Overjoyed, he would decide to take me home again to my mother—or even better, the most optimistic part of me hoped beyond hope that he would bring my mother with him and we could all live disease-free at Hodgson.

His letter didn't say. It said simply, *I am to board the ship* Wilton Mare *on the First of August and expect to help you celebrate your Twelfth birthday on the First of October.*

I received the letter after he had already set sail. I lay in bed with the envelope in my hands and imagined him in the same cabin I had been in when I'd crossed the ocean. I imagined the sad sea spreading out forever, and the big sky, and the toss of the waves, the snap of the sails, and creak of the timbers as he lay in bed at night. And because I did not like thinking of him alone, I imagined Mama with him, too, although I'd never seen them together anywhere but in our cabin and on the bottomland below it. I imagined them standing at the rail of the ship looking outward, thinking about me. I imagined them holding hands as they sometimes did when we'd go down to the run to picnic in the afternoon. I could imagine the shapes of their bodies, and the heat between them that I could feel when I squeezed between their thighs, but I could not see their faces, and I worried endlessly that I would not recognize them, or that they would not recognize me.

But days before he was to arrive I became ill with fever again and was removed from the other children to a back bedroom, where I lay alone again, dreaming and fretful through the night, into a day, and into another night. Strangely, words from the Declaration of Independence kept running through my mind. I cursed England for having *plundered our seas, ravaged our coasts, burnt our towns, and destroyed the lives of our people.* I dreamed of *the large armies of mercenaries completing the works of death, desolation, and tyranny.* I imagined *our fellow citizens taken captive on the high seas to bear arms against their country, to become the executioners of their friends and brethren,* and most frightening of all, I dreamed of *the merciless Indian savages, whose known rule of warfare is an undistinguished destruction of all ages, sexes, and conditions.*

One evening, awakening from a fit of fever, I overheard a discussion between the rector and Mr. Collins about whether I should be sent back to isolation. The word *isolation* frightened me so much that I conjured old Miss Crinkle's face—and as though she were God I prayed to her. I told her I would do anything if I could get well and rejoin the other children. I told her I would learn by heart the law of men aspiring to be divine. I told her I would give up anything.

And then I conjured my father's face and green eyes and longed for him and hated him, too. I saw him standing at the rail of a ship in a storm. With my mind's power, I lifted his booted foot over the rail and then lifted his hands as though to touch the tempest itself. He straddled a wooden rail and, reaching for the heavens, teetered one way and then the other. I played with the image in my mind and found I could make him lean farther toward the deck, then toward the sea, his hands still reaching upward and his face aimed at the storm.

Then, just to see if I could do it, I tilted him so far toward the sea that he lost his balance and his body carved a graceful arc, backward, into the foam.

By the time morning broke, so had the fever.

If my spirits soared with my improved health, imagine the crash a few days later when I was told that the ship on which my father had been crossing the ocean had sunk, and he'd drowned at sea.

I DON'T REMEMBER the pain of his death as perhaps I should. For three years in a row he'd said he was coming and then changed his plans, so in the fog of my grief perhaps I was able to fold the horror of his drowning into the more mild disappointments of the past few years. I'm only speculating. But I do know that the immediate sadness I felt for his loss was absorbed and overshadowed by the knowledge that without support from home (my father's property, including my mother, had gone to his widow) I would be forced to leave school and sent to a London workhouse.

Again I would be cast out. Again I would be alone.

During my years at Hodgson, I had learned to read and write, and to add and subtract, and to feel comfortable and happy with my companions. Because we lived and studied and slept and ate together, we had become each other's family, and there was a lot of talk about *being in it together through the thick and thin,* or *being blood brothers*—the kind of things boys say when their connection with one another is deep. But as soon as my father died, the camaraderie of fifteen hundred days of playing and wrestling and studying together—fifteen hundred days of alliance against the forces of benevolent rule imposed on us by the rector and teachers—a thousand and a half days of mutual affection engendered by our mutual loneliness, affection I had believed was enduring—ended.

Again I was cast out, again I was alone.

And again it was my fault.

Because we cannot forgive ourselves for being powerless—*We are not in control*—we conjure our own power even when we have very little. We find patterns in our lives, and turn antecedents into causes when it suits us. If times stay bad, we believe in our bones we might have changed things if only we'd tried harder. And if they do indeed change, we are quick to take the credit or blame.

We are free, aren't we?

For the second time in three years I'd willed somebody dead and my circumstances had changed. If later I'd do worse, perhaps this was the start. For the time being, however, I refused to be haunted by ghosts, or madness, or a world bigger than anything I could ever conceive. So two feelings began to emerge that would serve both to keep me temporarily upright and to guide my strategies into adulthood: First, I began to fear my deepest desires. And second, I began to think of myself as a heroic figure.

On the morning of my departure, the sky was gray and the wind chilly, and crows gathered on the still green lawn amid a swirl of falling leaves. All the boys came out to wave to me—as though I were off on a splendid journey. Mr. Collins seemed the only truly sad one, and I didn't like him for that. Because in his face I saw all my fears and sadness, too, and I didn't want to feel those things. I wanted to leap on top of the carriage and salute, so that was what I did. Even as the team of horses lurched us into motion I kept my balance, to the delight of my classmates, and heard their cheers erupt and fade, erupt and fade. I was frightened and also strangely exhilarated. I carried the immensity of my new sense of power awesome in my breast alongside my sense of powerlessness. Oh, the mystery! I had hated my father for sending me away, and loved him, and I loved my mother and hated her for not being home when I came to say good-bye. I hated myself for closing the door to the cabin, and I hated her for loving my father and him for loving her, and I loved their love for one another, and I hated my father for dying and not rescuing me, and I hated myself for sacrificing his life to keep me well—

And yet I loved being well!

The carriage rocked beneath my feet. I felt strong. A new gust of wind sent more leaves swirling across the lawn, giving me goose bumps of glory before a wall of trees rose up on the side of the drive and Hodgson Academy disappeared forever.

Or I did.

BECAUSE I WAS CERTAINLY a more humble boy just a half a day later down a road that crossed a boggy bottom and followed the river into the heart of a London slum, when I was shoved off the carriage by the teamster's brawny fist and watched my shiny civilized boots sink ankle deep in mud.

I stooped to grab the handle of my small trunk and drag it to the big front door of the Sunny Side Saddlery, where Mr. Collins had assured me arrangements had been made for my placement. Up and down the narrow street were more people than I had ever seen in my life, more people than I could count, a stream of movement that I could not see the end of. The air was foul with rancid grease, human and animal excrement, and coal smoke.

I gulped down my fear and knocked on the door, determined, as I watched the carriage drive off, to do as Mr. Collins had advised, and "make do."

While I waited for the door to open, I touched my front pocket where I carried both the rolled-up copy of the Declaration of Independence that my father had given me and the envelope with my free papers. I wanted to take them out and touch them again, if only to hold something that his hands had held, but the street was crowded and I felt jostled from behind. I thought about *life, liberty, and pursuit of happiness,* and if these were truly *inalienable* rights, why were they so easily taken away? Why did my father die? Why was my mother a slave? And why was I unhappy?

Because *we are all going to die; we are not in control; we all suffer.*

Or was it because I had sacrificed him and closed the door on her?

We are free!

Again I knocked on the door and again I felt pushed from behind. Next to me an old woman squatted on a wooden block to keep herself out of the mud, and between her feet she guarded a pot of ashes that looked cold enough but might still have given some warmth, for she dangled her gnarled fingers above it. Across the street shrieks of laugher spilled out of a gin house, and a woman with sickly yellow skin passed just in front of me. Her hair was matted and her gray eyes crazed, and two tiny, big-eyed children walked alongside hanging on to her dress, it seemed, for dear life.

I held my little trunk and knocked again and waited for the door to open. Behind me a boy lost control of his apple cart and the cart tipped and the fruit spilled across the street in a spreading pile. What happened next shocked me. It was as though the chaos of the street were suddenly organized by the opportunity to plunder. All passersby within sight of the overturned cart suddenly stopped their activity to run to fill their pockets and aprons and hats, and any other container they found handy, with apples. The boy stood shouting and waving his arms, which had only the effect of gathering even more of a crowd. In the frantic grasping for fruit, I could see a kind of grotesque mob joy—the joy that comes from unearned bounty—a perverse dance of riches. Entranced, I didn't even notice how I was knocked down, or by whom. I only felt the old woman suddenly under my head and shoulders and her pot of ashes in front of me. I'd fallen onto her bony lap, and immediately felt her arms cradle my head. And so I was lying when I looked up and saw the door of the workhouse open slightly and the head of a man with a shiny pate and long gray beard poke out from the opening.

"Who's there?" the man called into the din.

The old woman smelled of something horrible, yet the harder I struggled to free myself the tighter she squeezed my head in her bony arms. She said, "If this be the babe you're looking for, I'll let him go for a shilling."

There followed a struggle during which I thought I would be pulled in two. The old woman held my head and the bearded man pulled my legs. Being the stronger of the two, the man pulled not only me but the old woman up off the ground—her still clinging to my head—and all the way to the threshold of the open door.

Still the tenacious old woman would not let go, and my face was contorted in her grasp, my hair pulled, until finally, I suppose, because of the fortuitous arrival of a visitor, who must have given the old woman the coin she was so diligently demanding, my head was released.

The door closed behind me and suddenly I was in a quiet, dark hallway, dangling upside down, with my feet in the bearded man's hands and my head toward the floor.

"It's how she lives," I heard the other man say. His speech was both accented and slurred, and even upside down I could tell he walked with a limp.

The bearded man continued to hold me like that. Was he going to shake me down? Had he forgotten about me? I struggled to make him let go, but his hands on my ankles had the grip of iron.

"My trunk," I finally managed to say. "It's in the street."

"Mon dieu," the visitor said, and the door opened again, and the bearded man let go of my ankles. I caught myself with my hands and struggled to stand upright again and make a dash for the trunk. But I paused. The street was back to its original moving chaos: men and women and children, horses and dogs, and a pig on a leash. Everything looked the same but the specifics. The boy and his cart, for example, were gone. As were the apples, the smelly old woman and her pot of ashes—and of course my trunk with its precious books and the few pieces of clothing I owned in the world.

SUNNY SIDE SADDLERY was a private work home on the banks of the Thames where eight parentless waifs and I cut and softened and stretched and molded and sewed leather into bridles and saddles. The first months of my time there were as bleak as any in my life. My twelfth birthday came and went without notice, and then winter followed quickly and brought its perpetual darkness and cold. When we did manage to warm up with enough wood or coal to stoke the fire, hundreds of flies would emerge from the woodwork and cluster on our one grimy window. The food was bad—gruel thickened with various crawling insects—yet we worked long hours in bad light, half out of our minds with both fatigue and the strange effects of chemical fumes while Mr. Perry, the man with the bald pate and beard who'd pulled me from the street woman's arms, paced back and forth telling and retelling the story of his life (as though this time, finally, it might make sense) to a lanky Frenchman named Le Chat, who limped the floor besides him sipping brandy from a pocket flask as though condemned to it.

Mr. Perry's story went like this: he was been born in Newfoundland and there blossomed into manhood on grog, codfish, and a passion for poker. Running from a bad debt, he slipped away from the banks and took to the world at large. It seemed he'd been everywhere with everyone—in opium dens with thieves, in cabarets with ballet girls, on tropical islands with bare-breasted women, in jungles with crocodiles and snake charmers. He traveled the world until almost twenty years ago he found himself in the town of David, Panama, where he fell in love with an Indian girl, whom he married on sight. He adored her as the perfection of beauty, and she, in return, adored him as all that was chivalrous and fascinating, until one sad day Tragedy struck.

"Aaaahh," he said, "happiness is but an illusion that lasts precisely until savages emerge from the wood to slay your pretty wife."

Mad with grief for her, his sugar investments drained of profit by his gambling debts, Mr. Perry learned that a distant relative had died in England, leaving him *T'is wretched business,* he called it, this saddlery in London.

When I arrived, he'd been there almost a decade, still licking his wounds and still claiming to be gathering himself for a new leap.

Besides making saddles, we boys were assigned other tasks. Mine, as the youngest, was to empty the chamber pots onto the mud that lay outside our back door when the tide was out. The smell of the flat, decorated with the defecations of a thousand neighbors, the haze of flies that such a scene attracted on warm days, and the general coal-fouled air of London produced such a stark contrast to the pastoral world of my past as to cause me to doubt reality. Although I am sure that as a boy I did not think, *This is not the real world!*—I know I felt that way and I was forced to populate it with figments I conjured from thin air—friends from Hodgson, my parents, my own inventions. Hodgson had taught me to speak like a schoolboy, and my new colleagues derided me for it, so I stayed quiet for a long time, weeks perhaps, deepening my isolation. I invented a game where I could lift myself out of my body and look down on myself hunched over a piece of leather at the long candlelit table where I worked with the other boys. I studied the tops of our heads and wondered at the personal sorrow of each and every one of us. Invariably I would find me, of course, the top of my hatless head, the one with the Negro hair cut so short nobody knew, the one who still had a living parent, and I wondered dispassionately who I was, and who I might become. From this height, my world became scenery in the play of my life, and it gave me confidence that when this act ended another would begin. I didn't know what would come next, but I knew something would, and in this way I avoided despair.

Then one night I lay shivering on my straw tick. The salt smell of high tide wafted in our window, threatening to make me weep with loneliness. And while I'm sure I meant to merely think the words, I heard them escape my lips in a voice identical to Mr. Perry's.

T'is wretched business! I said.

Across the dark room I heard my colleagues giggle at my mimicry, so I continued the speech we'd all heard a hundred times. *T'is wretched business is only a game I'll be playin' til ta woe has settled fully into me flesh, and I emerge a bright new creature, with a bright new plan!*

The idea of old Mr. Perry as a bright new creature sent us into hysterics.

THE FRONT OF THE saddlery faced the street and the back was supported by pilings over a place in the estuary where the high tide eddied. While the other boys slept on straw ticks in the big room on the street side, Mr. Perry soon moved me to sleep in the closet directly over the pilings. There were two reasons for this. The first was because on Saturday nights after coming home from another losing night at cards, he liked to kneel beside me in the dark, stinking of gin, and weep while he stroked with gentle hand my face and head.

The first few times it happened I lay awake petrified, and I passed my Sundays in a fog of fatigue. The other boys speculated that I reminded Mr. Perry of his Indian wife, a thought I preferred not to think. In subsequent weeks I gained some relief by imagining my drowned father forgiving me, but the comfort of ghosts is limited, especially to a murderer. Nevertheless I had an advantage over Mr. Perry. Or at least I felt more fortunate. Because while he might have been imagining his dead wife, I soon learned that by picturing the warm face of my living mother I could begin to relax beneath his fingers and sometimes drift to sleep.

The other reason I slept in the closet above the pilings was so I would be awakened by the bump of things floating by in the rising tide. When I heard or felt a floater strike the piling below me, I was to get up and go to Mr. Perry and the two of us would use a grappling hook and line to pull it in. Sometimes it was a log we could sell for timber. Sometimes a broken boat from which planks could be scavenged. Sometimes a dead horse or cow, which we would haul up out of the water by means of a block and tackle, and if it were not too decomposed—or even if it were—we could sell the meat to the butcher for a few shillings. But not uncommonly we pulled out of the black water a bloated man or woman or child. If the body still wore clothes, we'd check the pockets for money, take whatever seemed of value, and then launch the body back out again to be taken away in the current.

We're milkin' ta ol' codfish! Mr. Perry would say, jangling the coins in his hand.

He always shared the profits with me, and urged me to be *grateful.* I assured him I was, for you'll remember my confusion of that word with *nauseated.*

37

Nevertheless, the money did serve as incentive for me to wake him when I felt the bump of a floating object, and to not protest my unique sleeping arrangements. As my pouch of coins grew, so did my esteem among the other boys. To stem the tide of their envy, I took to buying periodicals and books, and in the evening, especially in the summer when the light lingered late in the sky, I'd sit in the window and read aloud for their entertainment. I read serial stories and used my gift of mimicry to create different voices for the characters. (I also learned to use my one brown eye and one green, and by turning profiles to play different characters.) We took great comfort in these partial hours stolen before the light grew too dim for me to see the words. We imagined ourselves enduring long journeys in small boats, stumbling across deserts, or scaling peaks. We lifted our swords and saw our enemies flee before us like rats at daybreak. We imagined our beloved and their faces lit the darkness, and we basked in their love and light as we pulled them out of harm's way into the safety of our strong arms.

We do not live for ourselves, my father had told me. Although he'd said I wouldn't truly understand until I was a man, the stories gave me glimpses. Depending on the tide, we lay awake at night smelling either our own shit or the encroaching salt sea of our grief—so we needed more than ever to cry sweet tears for innocent maidens, and to shiver proudly at the brave deeds of our heroes. If our lives and the lives of our neighbors were indeed *wretched,* and if we often heard outside our window the wails of gin-soaked rage, if all of us were indeed *only playing a game until ta woe had settled,* well, we needed to be ready.

For what? Personally I had a vague notion of a great struggle in my future that would determine my fate and the fate of many others. I didn't picture anything specific—but the struggle would bring an as yet unimaginable hardship that I anticipated with foreboding as well as excitement. If my current misery were to make any sense at all, I had to see myself as training for an even more difficult adventure. I had to see myself as waiting for my big black stallion to arrive. Every saddle I made was practice for the one I would make him, for the one I would sit in when I found my mother, rescued her from slavery, and lived with her again in happiness.

I continued to write to her, although I did so with discretion, as the rest of the boys at Sunny Side were orphans and I did not wish to distinguish myself. Writing to her was a private comfort. Although I never received an answer, I calmed myself by telling her things that were in my mind and heart. I felt less alone writing the letters and imagining my mother's loving face listening while Auntie (who couldn't read either) read her my words aloud.

The months and years passed this way. I will not deny the occasional day of rage when I never heard anything from her, rage at her powerlessness and at mine. Rage at my dead father. Rage that I tucked away like a fearful, secret weapon. But most days I was sustained by gentler feelings. Our lives at Sunny Side were sheltered—we worked by day and slept by night, and ventured onto the street only for necessities.

Alas, some ignorance ends, and so its peculiar sustenance.

Five years after my father's death, when I had just turned seventeen, a letter arrived from America addressed to me. It had been sent to Nigger Jimmy, Sunny Side Saddlery, London, and the date on the letter indicated that a year had passed since it had been written.

Dear Jimmy, it said. *Your Mama Jennyveeve was sold years ago to a slaver near Centreville. Don't write here no more as she ain't never come back nor will.*

It was signed, *Mr. G. R. Norton,* a name with which I was unfamiliar.

THIS NEWS SENT ME into a bitter melancholy as gray and deep as the sea I'd crossed when I was first set free. If my mother was no longer at Sweet Grass, where was she? And if I had lost her, who loved me? And if no one did, who was I?

And what about my idea of the future? If I didn't know where she was, how could I set her free?

I tried reading the Declaration of Independence again, but it only drew me further toward despair. Why did I have no *right to happiness,* only a right *to pursue* happiness—isn't that a torment? To have the right, without the means?

Civilized law, my father had said. But how could *men aspiring to be divine* invent such a torture?

I spiraled downward, and if it weren't for my special relationship with Mr. Perry, I might have been tossed out into the street. For I'd sit at my work station and do nothing but stare through the dirty window at the putrid river. I was alone at the saddlery by then. In recent years my colleagues had come of age and drifted off—out of the workhouse to the army, the navy, or the merchant marine. I dreamed of where they were and what they were doing. The saddlery was limping along. Mr. Perry had gambled it away, and Le Chat had taken possession of it piece by piece, and he didn't seem to care if he made any money or not. I'd gaze and dawdle, and finally I stopped getting out of bed altogether. I stayed upstairs in my closet, and I dreamed of death. I wondered how long it would take to drown if I were to jump into the river.

I don't know how long this lasted. Mr. Perry visited numerous times, so perhaps weeks passed, or perhaps he came to see me more often. I don't know. I do know I tried to conjure my mother, as I had always done. Yet knowing she'd been sold, and knowing that for years I'd been fool enough to commune with a mere figment, made imagining her difficult. I was stripped of my ability to cope, so Mr. Perry's touches became an exquisite torture that illuminated a broad path toward self-destruction.

Why didn't I take it? Again, the antidote to despair began with my body.

I'd grown tall, and my lean limbs bristled with strength. I could run fast and jump high, and a physical restlessness began to rule my days and nights. In the growth of my body, I felt new power. My hands, my shoulders, my thighs . . . I could lie in bed and feel the pulsing demand . . . for what?

Gradually my mind turned from the river and its cold death to something else. I went back to work making saddles. And on three consecutive evenings, I was awakened by a bumping on the pilings beneath my bed and Mr. Perry and I fished out a couple of good logs and a dead horse. But instead of using my share of the money for books, I visited the prostitutes across the street.

One in particular. A stringy-haired girl not much older than I who talked like Miss Bridget but whose name was Nancy. Her room was a tiny closet much like mine and we lay on a mildewed pallet soaked with the moisture of countless bodies. But I liked the smells there. I liked the smell of the candle, and of her often unwashed skin. I liked the smell of our sex and our breaths, and her hair. As often as I could afford it, I made the trip across the street and handed over my money and cleaved into her until I felt myself disappear. I have no certainty of her feelings, of course, and I distrusted mine, but she tolerated me with grace and even, on occasion, with affection. I liked her pale skin and the blue veins in her hands and temples and breasts, and I liked the look of her tiny shoes against the wall, and the clothes she took off folded neatly on the stool. And how her thin arms wrapped around my neck, and how her lower lip quivered when I plunged into her, and her chin would lift, and her eyelids drop wantonly. I liked to open my mouth against her neck and close my eyes and taste her salt—and there, like that, I could be quite certain there was no suffering that I could not endure as long as I could do this.

Even after climax I stayed close. She'd hold perfectly still, and I would, too, entwined in her arms and legs. She breathed quietly through her nose. She turned her face and neck to accommodate my kisses.

Although her general state was one of silence, she never hesitated to say in her pretty accent whatever words, fair or foul, I asked her to say, and sometimes just saying the words seemed to animate her and she'd begin to talk and tease.

Once I asked her to call me her wee monkey.

She petted my head. "Me wee monkey," she said. "Why me wee monkey?"

"Because I'm a nigger," I said.

"Nigger?" she said. "Is ye?" We were lying on our sides. She raised her head to look at my face in the candlelight. "From this side, I suppose one could say so. Or not. I thought ye might be a Spanish."

"When my hair is longer it shows," I said.

She rubbed her hand over my head. "What's it like?"

"Curly." I pulled her close to me on the bed and pushed her hand down between us. "Like this."

She smiled. "I mean what's it like being a nigger?"

"Oh," I said. "I don't know."

"Then how do you know you are one?"

"My mother's a slave," I said.

She laughed in my ear. "And mine's a good Irish wife!"

I didn't speak. She took my hand in hers and kissed the tips of my fingers where they were cracked and stained brown from work.

"And yer da?" she asked.

"Drowned in the sea."

"Ahhh," she said. "Then maybe you're drowned, too?"

I stayed quiet. I could hear her breathing in my ear.

"He freed me before he died," I said.

"Why would he do that?"

"So I'd be free. A free man."

"Man ye are." She squeezed me gently.

"I've got papers to prove it."

"Sure you do," she said. She held me in her hand, eyes locked on mine, until I began to grow again.

"Is that the wee monkey, then?"

"Big monkey," I said.

She rolled onto me, and her hair covered my face. "Free man," she whispered, "big monkey."

THOSE WHO CATEGORICALLY CONDEMN vice have never been saved by it. Regardless of the wretched life Nancy lived or was destined to live—and regardless of how you might judge the value of my life—Nancy did save me. She held me when I needed holding, said the words I needed to hear, and so prevented me from tossing myself into the freezing Thames.

Maybe the problem comes from choosing the wrong vice, like Mr. Perry. His was me, I suppose, and the gambling table—and we both took him down in the end.

But he might have gone down sooner without us.

What do we know? Do we even get to *choose* our vices? I suspect they choose us.

Like all gamblers, Mr. Perry believed in his bones that a big win was just around the corner. Yet whenever he won, he was quick to desire an even bigger win, and he'd keep playing until all of his winnings had been lost. So it wasn't really a big win he wanted, it was the *idea* of one. It was the *next* one. It wasn't rebirth as *a bright new creature* that he wanted, it was the *anticipation* of that rebirth.

He continued to play. He continued to lose. And he continued to talk about winning. The more he lost, the more obsessed he became with the big one, the big win, the one that would change everything and allow him to sail off into the sunset, to start something, anything new. He'd dug himself a hole, and the deeper he dug, the more desperately he talked of escape.

Which brings me to Le Chat, the lanky Frenchman who'd ransomed me my first day from the smelly bosom of the street woman, and who daily limped the floor sipping from a flask of brandy while listening to Mr. Perry talk. A wiry fellow who often wore nankeen trousers, glazed pumps, and a Panama hat, he didn't speak much, so his story dribbled out in odd pieces I later put together. He was born in Paris, joined the army at sixteen, and saw action for the first and last time at Waterloo, where a wound took away the full use of his left leg. After the war he moved to Marseille, where, *profuse with claret and absinthe,* I heard him say, he spent what he called his *frolicsome years.*

"Running over with song and festive at all hours," he said, "I was the brightest star of whatever luminous cluster I was a part of!"

Lugubrious and self-pitying, drunken and lame, Le Chat as *a frolicsome bright star* was amusing to imagine.

But it was in Marseille that he made his fortune selling Dr. Le Chat's Electric Skin Softening Oil. Until, he claimed, members of the Vigilance Committee of Louis Napoleon, jealous of his growing wealth and social brilliance, hounded him out of France.

Waving *adieu* to his homeland, he sailed to this land of Alfred and Shakespeare, as he called it, secured a room in this historic district, and continued his tireless efforts (from which he always seemed to be resting) to restore his good name and return to Marseille.

I developed a different theory as to why he'd been chased out of France, which explained why he took to financing Mr. Perry's gambling debts and why, despite his wealth, he lived in a wretched little flat down the street and spent his intemperate days with us.

He was in love with Mr. Perry.

But Mr. Perry was in love with his dead wife, whom he somehow confused with me, and I was in love with my mother, whom I hadn't seen in ten years and couldn't even be sure was alive.

Love, love, love. No wonder we all needed vice, vice, vice.

I LET MY HAIR grow long to see what it would look like, and, woolly and black, it didn't disappoint. I began to like rolling it in my fingers when nobody was around. Because I was spending all my extra money across the street, I began reading aloud the decade-old newspapers I found stacked against the walls to keep the wind out of Nancy's closet. Specifically, I read reports about a time when thousands upon thousands of Irish starved because of a potato blight, and the English did nothing to help, and so certain Irishmen rebelled against the crown in an effort to gain their country's independence.

One of their leaders was a man named Cornelius O'Keefe— O'Keefe of the Sword—and I read and reread his speeches, and I committed to memory his statements on liberty: *I am not ungrateful to the man who struck the fetters from my limbs while I was yet a child*—my father's very words!

And on war: *There are times when arms alone will suffice. And the King of Heaven bestows his benediction upon those who unsheathe the sword in the hour of a nation's peril!*

These brave young Irishmen defied the crown and rebelled, but the rebellion was foiled, and O'Keefe and his fellow conspirators were caught, tried, and convicted. Before sentencing, O'Keefe was given the opportunity to speak for the last time. The words he said grew in my mind to epitomize courage. I imagined him standing on a raised block before a panel of somber judges, a lone man with perhaps a spot of sunlight coming through a high window to illuminate his face. Waiting to be sentenced to certain death, and speaking to those who would sentence him, he made this tender articulation of self-sacrifice: *My lords, you may deem this language unbecoming, and perhaps it seals my fate. But I am here to speak the truth whatever it may cost. I am here to regret nothing I have ever done, to retract nothing I have ever said, and to crave with no lying lip the life I consecrate to the liberty of my country. Far from it, here—even here, where the thief, the libertine, the murderer have left their footprints in the dust—here on this spot I offer to that country, as proof of the love I bear her, and the sincerity with which I thought and spoke, and struggled for her freedom—I offer the life of a young heart.*

It thrilled me to contemplate making a similar kind of statement if ever I faced death for something I loved. I wanted to weep for the beauty of such courage. But O'Keefe went even further. Just in case anybody thought he was pandering to the sympathies of his persecutors, he said, *On the other hand, my lords, if you will be easy with us this once, and spare us the gallows, we promise on our word as Irish gentlemen, to try to do better next time. And next time—sure, we won't be fools enough to be caught!*

Imagining such impudence made my blood pump hard and fast. Could I ever be so brave? Why not? Just a few months ago I'd been contemplating throwing myself into the Thames. If I could die for nothing, why couldn't I die for something?

And then, as if to validate such courage, the Queen of England showed mercy and, rather than hang him by the neck until death, she banished him to the far reaches of the earth, to Van Diemen's Land, for the rest of his days. Yet he'd escaped from there, I learned, and made his way to New York, where he had became a celebrated lecturer—a hero to the Irish and all who yearned to be free.

I reread the Declaration of Independence and an inspired patriotism grew within me. I was an American, after all, diseased or not. And I was becoming a man and knew I could no longer live in my mind. The scene I'd known would change when I'd first come to Sunny Side Saddlery was now changing. To what, I did not know. But inspired by O'Keefe's soaring rhetoric, I found the hope that I, at least, if not Mr. Perry, might someday *emerge a bright new creature* and go home again. I would search every corner of my country until I found my enslaved mother, and then I would fight to free her.

That was it. I would become a warrior.

I began to think strategically. What did the warriors I read about have that I did not?

Means, perhaps? I had no money to travel home.

And the willpower to change bad habits? Perhaps that, too.

But it is rarely only willpower that changes habits. Habits change when something unexpected happens that knocks us out of our groove. That forces us to respond, to act without opportunity to think, or prepare, or deliberate—and when we act, well, it is only naked us, after all, naked us stripped of the cloak of habit.

In my case the something unexpected was Nancy being ill on a Saturday night and so causing me to go with another—a bigger, fleshier woman named Joyce. I burrowed into her and would not pull out, and when I grew again, I pushed into her more, and she seemed vaguely bothered by my efforts. I could not suck her neck because it smelled so strongly of garlic, so I attached to her nipple and to my surprise got a mouthful of sweet milk. She pushed me away.

"That's for me babe," she said.

Embarrassed and angered, I said, "I paid for you."

"Not for that," she said.

I ignored her and pinned her down. She fought under me, scratched my face and back and head, tried to gouge my eyes, but I endured the pain and drank first from one breast and then from the other until she had no more milk to give and I felt her body go completely limp beneath me.

"What kind of man are you?" I heard her ask.

I detached from her and sat up drunk on cruelty and mother's milk. I could feel blood trickle from the scratches on my face and neck and head. She lay on her back, her hair spread around her head like a dark pool. She sneered and her face contorted in anguish and mirth.

"I see you now," she said, and gave a scornful laugh. "You're just a cross-eyed babe yourself and you want for a mum."

Her words stung, and in my embarrassment and sudden rage I slapped her. She put her hands to her face and rolled away, curled up. I raised my tingling hand to strike her again. And I might have, I would have, if she hadn't spoken again.

"Go away now," she said, and the tone of her voice drained me suddenly of my mysterious wrath. "Go," she said again, and so I lowered my hand, dressed, and left.

Later, the heat of that violence still racing in my veins, my scratches scabbing and my unwashed blood dried on my skin, I lay on my straw mattress back in my closet. I heard Mr. Perry come home singing joyfully. As usual, I lay curled on my side with my back to the door when I heard it open. I heard his breathing change as he lowered himself to his knees behind me. I must have looked the same to him, lying like that in the dark. How could he have known that I'd sacrificed the smooth skin on my neck and the back of my head to the nails of a desperate whore? How could he have known what was racing through my heart and that, instead of a gently curled boy, he was about to touch a tiger crouched and ready to spring?

It seemed forever waiting for that first touch. I knew where it would come, of course. On the back of my neck. His fingers would linger there a moment, and then slowly move up the back of my head, sending tingles down my spine. He would stroke my head slowly, and soon I'd become aware of something else. I'd feel the floor begin to move slightly, hear his rapid breathing. His fingers would stay on my head, stay steady, smooth, while his other hand pleasured himself. That was how it would go. His gentle petting of my head and hair. Our mutual thoughts of someone else . . .

But not this time. This time he paused behind me. I knew he was kneeling and I could hear him breathing. I waited for what seemed an eternity there in the dark. Was he weeping? Praying?

"I've won it, Jimmy," he said. "The big one! And before I could lose it all a fire broke out below and we all ran into the street."

I stayed still, controlling my soaring emotions, and when I didn't move, that was when I felt his fingers finally touch me. It was as though he'd flicked a switch and unleashed a physical power I could not control. For I honestly had no plan in my head. But feeling his fingers suddenly on my face, I spun and took his hand with such force that I felt his bones crunch. He sucked in air and I watched the outline of his body shrink.

"I need it," I said.

I heard him wheeze with pain. "I've little with me," he said.

"Liar."

He reached into his pocket with his free hand and turned it inside out. A few coins jingled out against the floor.

"I need more," I said, and squeezed until his body collapsed and he was crippled beneath the pain of my grip.

"Jesus, Jimmy, I've given most of it to Le Chat!"

"How much?"

"Enough, Jimmy. Enough to change everything."

"Get it back."

"How?"

I thought I heard him sob. I put both of my hands around his one and squeezed as hard as I could and watched his old frame begin to writhe on the dark floor in front of me.

"I've loved you, Jimmy, you know I—"

I squeezed harder to shut him up, but it didn't work.

"Jesus, Jimmy," he gasped. "You only had to ask."

A FREE PERSON CAN betray someone. A free person has that choice. To scheme or not. To lie or not. To steal, to flee. These are all choices of free men and women, and so I made mine.

Lying was easy. I loved my imagined future as a warrior hero even more than I loved the truth. Not even close. So I told Mr. Perry I'd meet up with him later and split the loot, although I had no intention of doing that. A ship was sailing that night, and my scheme on the night of the plan was to go directly from Le Chat's to the ship—I'd already reserved a space in steerage with my own few coins.

"And the rest?" the captain had asked.

Enough, Jimmy—enough to change everything!

"I'll have it," I told him.

That night I skirted quickly out the door past cries from the gin house across the street, around the corner and through a pack of children running wild in rags. I stepped around an old man pulling a squeaking cart that carried the stinking dead. At the next corner under a gaslight, a sick dog walked a circle, around and around and around like a drunk. Was it walking after death, or was death walking after it? That was what my mother would have asked. If you knew the answer, you might know your fate. But you also might not. You might need to know if the dog was black or brown or spotted, male or female, and in the dark, passing quickly, I didn't see. *Oh, the mystery!*

I climbed the stairs to Le Chat's flat and opened it slowly—Mr. Perry had left it unlocked—and stepped into the darkness. I could hear nothing—and then movement on the bed. A throat cleared. A cough. I stood perfectly still until my eyes adjusted to the dark and I could see a lump under the blankets move.

This was not the plan. They were supposed to be out. They weren't supposed to be back. But I was in now, and I knew no way to go but forward. I crouched and slid on my belly across the floor, and then slowly, slowly, under the bed. I could taste dust and my heart pounded so loudly in my ears I was sure they'd hear it. And sure enough, one of them woke, for the mattress swayed with his weight and then a pair of bare feet swung down to the floor. It must have been Le Chat, because he limped across the room to the window, and he lifted the sash and stood in front of the open window. I could smell his urine in the fresh air. Then he limped back to the bed, lay down, and made a cat-like noise—was this the sound of frolicking? Indeed. I heard a murmur and then . . . something else. How long could Mr. Perry endure it? I expected at any minute he would bolt, and then where would I be?

I've loved you, Jimmy, you know I—

I slid my hands frantically over the floorboards searching for loose ones I could lift with my fingers. I had a knife on my belt, and it had somehow slipped under me and poked my thigh and hipbone, but I dared not lift myself to move it, free it, for fear my movement would be felt under the mattress. To calm myself, I imagined I was rescuing somebody—which of course I was. I took a slow hero's breath, and slid my fingers once again along the lines between the boards until I found a widening. I wedged in my finger and the board moved. I stopped breathing, then deliberately started again. I tilted the board slowly onto its edge and put my palm under to slide it off. Above me the men moved more briskly on the mattress. I reached into the hole and pulled out a sack of gold coins the size of two fists. I squeezed it hard to keep the coins from clanking together, and also to keep my hand from shaking. Still on my belly, I wormed my way slowly out from under the bed toward the door. I felt that at any moment I'd be seen or heard and so I prepared myself to leap up and kill. I had a knife and would use it. I would not be denied now. I didn't want to kill—but I knew I could, and I knew I would!

I didn't have to. *We are not in control.* The bedposts moaned, the mattress sighed, and indeed I was grateful for the nauseating sounds of love. I stood quickly at the door and slipped out with the gold, took the steps four at a time to the street. A yellow fog lay over the top of the buildings. I ducked into an alley, and then another and another. I jumped over street sleepers, past dark groups of laughing men and a closed carriage pulled by a galloping horse. I turned the corner and narrowly avoided the grasp of a drunken woman leaning against a building. I heard my feet in the street and felt the air burn my lungs as I ran past mad laughter toward the smell of high tide.

At the harbor I boarded my ship and stood breathless at the rail while the gangplank was raised. I was doing what I had dreamed about for years, going home again. I thought I should feel overjoyed, but as the dull lights of London slid backward into inky darkness, I felt oddly disconnected and lost. I knew I stood where I stood, on this ship, as a direct result of my decisions, my actions—and yet instead of pride I felt as powerless and sad as I had the first time I'd boarded a ship, my hand in my father's, to sail away with the tide.

BUT MY MELANCHOLY WAS fleeting. On the third day out we got word from a passing schooner that Fort Sumter had been attacked and the war between the states had begun. I thought of O'Keefe of the Sword, and of his call to arms—*when politics call for a drop of blood, for many thousand drops of blood*—and on that long ocean voyage, I dreamed myself a warrior. Each night I gave thanks to Providence for dropping in my lap a righteous war: a fever to burn my diseased country to health. Not only would I find and free my mother but I would now have an opportunity to fight for an even greater cause. I would make available the strength of my arm and the courage of my heart for the just cause of freedom for all.

In this determination I grew happier than I had ever been. In the evening I stood on the deck and watched the sun set into the sea off the bow—the sea that now contained my father's very bones. I watched wild colors grow upward from the horizon, fill half the sky and the surface of the water before me, and then begin to shrink and fade. Just before the stars came out there was a moment of twilight when all that separated sea from sky was a thin silver line. It was then that the nature of things stood before me as clear as they had ever been. I wished Mr. Collins were there, for the mystery was revealed, or so it seemed, and I was part of the mystery, part of creation, no longer separate. I was my father and not my father, my mother and not her, too. My freedom was everyone's freedom, and everyone's freedom was mine and all of us were endowed by our Creator with inalienable rights.

Inalienable because if they were denied I would fight for them. I would kill for them. Die for them.

I breathed all of that new sea air and felt the euphoria that comes with having a purpose, and with having what in my youth I could only imagine to be a realistic chance of success.

Then night fell, full night. Looking west into the darkness across the broad belly of ocean toward the still submerged dreamland of my past and my future, I felt for the first time what I imagined my father must have hoped I'd someday feel when he kissed me on the forehead and sent me away to be free.

WAR

THE SHIP LANDED IN Philadelphia in the rain. I was wearing a
brown wool suit I'd bought from a merchant on board, a suit I'd
bought for this day, as nice a piece of clothing as I had ever owned, but
with no adequate raincoat—or a raincoat of such condition that it
would have negated the positive effect of my new suit. So I was forced
to stay belowdecks in my steaming quarters—my heart racing with
joy—until I could hear the rain stop and I could finally emerge from
my shelter and get my first glimpse of the dock gleaming in the new
sunlight. Men with floppy hats pushed carts of cargo from ships to
wagons harnessed to teams of gleaming, wet-backed horses. Arriving
passengers and their greeting families formed clumps of adults surrounded by racing children. I heard shouts and laughter, took a deep
whiff of harbor—horse manure, tar, and decayed fish—set my top hat
on my head (tilting it just as I'd seen it worn in London) and set forth
down the gangplank.

If I'd had a glimpse of clarity aboard the ship, it quickly dissolved
on shore. For one thing, in all the common activity in the immediate
area, I saw no evidence that anybody else was feeling the same warrior
spirit I was feeling. When I had imagined this moment of homecoming, this moment when I stepped onto the solid land of America, I'd
thought I might shout that I was back! Shout out that Jimmy Gates

had returned to his native soil and stood ready to give his life for the freedom of his people—both black and white! Ready to kill and die for civilization, for the law of men aspiring to be divine!

But there was not one soldier in sight. Not one cannon, or sign of arms. Where was the war? Could it be over already?

The truth was, that was my biggest fear—that in the weeks or months that it would take me to find my mother, buy her, and bring her north again, the war would end, and I'd miss all of the good fighting. But I hadn't counted on it ending before we even reached shore.

I crossed through the crowd on the dock, made my way onto the street, and began to walk faster. But before I could even ask anybody which way to Maryland, the sun retreated and rain began to fall again, so I stepped into a barroom with a sawdust floor and worked my way through the crowd to a small table in the corner. I didn't notice that the bar was full of white people. For years I had been the only person in any given room with Negro blood. It was only when a Negro waiter approached and I tried to place an order that I grew aware. This fellow, not much older than I, was dressed in a white cotton shirt that contrasted beautifully with his gleaming black skin. He had a face I wanted to stare at for the variety of joyful feelings it inspired in me, but when he saw me he held up a finger as though to say he'd be right with me and then disappeared into the kitchen.

I sat down and removed my dripping hat and set it on the corner of the table. I carried only a small tote sack, which I set on the floor between my feet, and I felt my pockets for money.

Just then the waiter stepped back out of the kitchen. Squeezing politely between patrons, he stopped suddenly and stared at me, at my hat on the table, and then at me again. His yellow eyes narrowed, and he raised his right forefinger and shook it back and forth.

"What?" I asked.

But he'd turned and was making his way to the bar to fetch a tray. When he passed again, he gave me the same puzzled and vaguely disapproving look. Did he think he knew me? I looked around the crowded room and nobody else had given me a second glance, but the third time he passed, with tray empty this time, he very specifically pointed to my hat.

"Do you like it?" I said, feeling proud of it, and of myself for choosing it, and flattered by his attention.

He stepped very close to my table, so he loomed over me, and he studied my face as I studied his for his intention. My heart beat loudly in my chest. Had somebody I used to know been expecting me? Was my homecoming going to be celebrated with camaraderie? He looked from my green eye to my brown, and suddenly seemed amused.

"Put on the hat," he said. And for the next part he leaned slowly down until his face was next to mine, and he whispered so close to my ear I shivered. "Otherwise you look like what we both knows you is."

Suddenly all the pride I'd felt coming home drained away and into that place flooded shame. I wanted to flee. But fleeing would have increased my shame. So I coolly lifted the hat off the table and set it on my head.

"What can I get you, massah?" he said, drawing out the last word with clear contempt.

I turned so my chair was facing the door and my green eye was visible from the barroom. "Beer and biscuits," I said, although my appetite had vanished.

Hearing my voice, my accent, the waiter nodded in admiration, dipped his head and shoulders in mock humility, and pivoted to disappear into the crowd.

Out the open window, I could see the rain had ceased, and so before he returned, I set my cap at the correct angle and stood to leave.

But before I slipped out of the bar and onto the street, I had to ask somebody about the war—was it over?

I paused in the threshold in front of a silver-faced man wearing the same kind of hat I wore. I let him take me in quickly with a glance, and he nodded and lifted his hand to touch the brim of his hat. I did the same.

"Pardon me," I said, "is it true what they say about a war between the states?"

He must have heard the foreignness in my voice, because a smile of condescension appeared first in his eyes and spread downward to his tiny mouth. "What do they say?" he asked.

"That it has begun."

"Not quite," he said.

"Is it all over, then?"

"No sir," he said. "Folks is still picking sides."

Relieved, I thanked him and slipped out of the bar and onto the street, and swung my tote up onto my shoulder. I still didn't know where Maryland was, but I looked both ways down the street, made a guess, and began to walk.

WHEN I FIRST WENT to England and sat in a classroom with white children, I studied their faces and skin and eyes and hair. Now, as I made my way through the crowded city, I found myself studying the other Negroes I saw. My experience with Negroes had been the experience of being with my mother, and with a few uncles and aunties—that was it. I think there were five altogether at Sweet Grass, and I was the only child on the farm until another was born shortly before I was sent away. I turned a corner and soon found myself in Negro Town. I watched the way they walked and held their heads, and listened to the way they talked. It shocked me to hear their loud voices, and accents I didn't understand. Not the mellow accents of the plantation, but something harsher. I noted the way people sat in windows or on stoops. Listened to the chanting games of the children. And the big voices of the women as they called to each other across the street. They claimed air and space, these women. They walked with a swaying certainty of flesh. Did my mother walk like that? Talk like that? I recognized her laughter across the street and recalled the sound of her song across the yard or pasture. Inside these houses, food was cooking, for I recognized smells I could no longer name but that still made my mouth water. I could not help smiling, and I wanted to talk to somebody, to pause, to linger, to ask somebody something, but I didn't know what.

Partly I was afraid. I wanted them to know I was of them, that I'd been born here, and my mother was still a slave here, but I was afraid of their doubt and their wonder at my accent. I was afraid of being treated as the waiter had treated me, and so soon I was quickening my pace.

Then something happened that had never happened to me before. As I approached a couple on the narrow sidewalk and prepared to step down into the mud so that they might pass, they stepped down first, and kept their eyes averted.

I felt dumbfounded. I wanted to tell them I wasn't white—but that wouldn't be true. I was white. So maybe I should have said I was Negro, my mother a slave. But I didn't. Why should I tell a complete stranger on the sidewalk who my mother was?

"Thank you," I mumbled, and resumed walking. It was getting hot and muggy, and I felt sweat dripping down my cheeks from my hat brim. The sidewalk was narrow on this block, so it happened twice more before I reached the next street. Negroes walking toward me

stepped off the sidewalk into the muddy street. The experience, combined with my utter lack of poise (I raised my hand to tip my hat, lost
control of the cloth duffel I was carrying, and almost dropped it), made
me feel very alone.

I tried to comfort myself. So what if people thought I was white?
Wasn't I half white? And doesn't everybody have real qualities that
others cannot see?

Of course. Then why did I still feel ashamed again? In the barroom
I'd been ashamed that the man had seen my mother's blood, and here
I was ashamed that people could not see it.

No, that wasn't exactly true. In the bar I'd felt ashamed that the
waiter thought I was pretending something that I was not pretending.
I was ashamed to be looked at as a fraud. And here on the sidewalk I
felt ashamed for a similar reason, because the people saw me for something that was only partly true. And also I felt ashamed, I have to admit, of being glad for having made it the length of that muddy street
without soiling my newly polished boots!

So far all I'd felt in America was shame. Me, the dandy with the
clean boots—the greatest of all democrats! I laughed at myself—I had
enough self-awareness, at least, for that. And I remembered—how
could I have forgotten when just a few hours before I'd been half expecting (hoping!) the ship would dock in the middle of a battle—I remembered that the war between the states had begun, a war for the
free union and against a slavery-dependent confederacy, an institution
that still claimed the relatives of most of these people around me, as it
still claimed mine. So why did they seem oblivious?

Finally a question I could actually ask occurred to me.

A young blacksmith sat resting on a bench outside his shop. His
skin was coal black, and I was struck with the odd sensation of wanting
to touch his bare arm.

60

"Excuse me?" I said.

I think my voice startled him, or the fact that I had paused to speak.

"Would you be so kind as to tell me the quickest way to Maryland?"

"From here?" he said.

"Yessir," I said.

"From here," he repeated, and furrowed his brow in imitation of thought. "Merry-land. You goes down as far as this road goes . . ." He paused again and furrowed his brow. I waited. He looked down the road as if he'd be able to see the answer if he looked hard enough.

"You go down as far as this road goes," I said, repeating his words. "And . . ."

"And den I s'pose you just keep right on."

"Keep right on?"

"Keep right on g'won," he said.

"And then I'll be in Maryland?"

"Not dere."

"Not there?"

"No suh," he said.

"Then where?"

"Suh?"

"If I take this road, and just keep right on going, where will I be?"

"Not dere, but head'n dere."

"You're very kind, sir," I said, and tipped my hat. He nodded a *you're welcome,* and I moved down the street, certain he hadn't the slightest idea where Maryland was. Or maybe even what it was.

I stopped and asked an older man with yellow eyes and chocolate skin thin like paper. But this time I tried an experiment. I took my hat off and stood before him and let him look me up and down very carefully. Finally he blinked. Apparently he'd seen what he was looking for.

"What you want to go to dere for?"

"I beg your pardon?" I said.

He said, "You can take da nigger outta da plantation, dress him up purty, but dat don' foo' nobody fo' long roun' heah. Don' foo' nobody down Mary-land way, neither."

Satisfied that I seemed to be able to change races by putting on or taking off my hat, I put my hat back on, very deliberately, and set it at just the right angle.

"I'm not trying to fool anybody," I said, pausing. A yellow dog crossed the street behind him chasing a rooster, and they both were nearly run over by a white man galloping by on a black horse. We both turned to watch him pass, and then I said, "Been in England for eleven years, but I was born in Maryland. There are people there that may know where my mother was taken."

"Taken?" he repeated.

"Yessir."

"Taken?" he said again, and looked at me steadily. I could feel sweat dripping down my back under my suit.

"Sold," I said. "To a trader." When he heard that last word his eyes did something that made me feel as if a big wind had blown through me and I could feel how little of me there was—and of that, how little I understood. I was home, but felt in a foreign country. I wasn't an American anymore. Nor was I an Englishman. Englishmen didn't have mothers who had been sold. Nor did white Americans. So I wasn't white—but it was just as clear that I wasn't Negro, not like this man. I was free, and I touched my free papers in my chest pocket as if to remind myself. But what was "free"? I was a man, but felt like a boy. I wanted to be a warrior—and just a few hours ago I'd felt like one—yet in order to be a fighter, the world has to be clear, and this man's gaze had confused me. Did I think I'd get back to the farm and somebody would tell me exactly where I could find the trader—and even if I could find him in Centreville, would he tell me where he'd sold my mother? And to whom? Would he even remember? Absurd. Not only finding her, but buying her. *Buying* her? Keep my hat on and bring her north—but to where? Then join the army to fight the slavers of the South. What army? The only troops I saw in uniform were two white men sitting across the street outside what must have been a supply de-pot, asleep with their boots up on the lower tier of a house-sized stack of hundred-pound flour bags that a crew of shirtless Negroes was heft-ing, one by one, to load into a line of wagons.

Then the old man was smiling at me kindly. I don't know why. Mercy?

"Dat way," he said, pointing.

And so under a bright white sky heavy with muggy heat, I began to walk.

TO WALK. TO BREATHE. To move and not to think, but to let thoughts come. Not to feel, but to let feelings settle. If I can't precisely say walking brings clarity, I can say there are few confusions or feelings that can't be walked out of. All that is important, after all, is the next step. Something you know how to do. Take a step. Take another. The feel of the earth under your feet calms you. You look at the blue sky or gray sky, or puffs of little white cloud. You let your eyes play across the different shapes of trees, and the thousand shades of green, and the in-finite variety of lines caused by the intersection of earth and sky. You see the yellow, red, orange, and purple blossoms. Pink blossoms. You listen to the buzz of insects, the call of roosters and barking dogs (for which you always carry a stick). You hear the cows bawling to their calves and their calves' bleating answer. You hear the horses whinny across fields and children laugh in the shade by a stream, splashing in the water, or a woman's voice across a yard, or the ring of metal on metal from the open door of a smithy's shed, the whistle of a man carrying a shovel down the road, the song of the masons as they mix their mud, the hymns from the churches and juke joints and the sound of hooves behind you and in front of you, and the squeak of wagon springs, and birdsong—all the many familiar, unnamed birds. Little blackie. Little purple chest. Pointy wing. I breathed deeply the new air over every hill, around every bend in the trail—mint, pine, apples, swamp—filling myself with a world I'd forgotten during my years along the Thames.

It took two weeks to get back to Sweet Grass. If I'd known the way and could have walked straight there, I might have arrived in half that time. My suit grew dirty and lost its crisp hang, but I kept my hat on and found I was spoken to with friendliness and respect—while more often than not being given incorrect directions. Nevertheless I was reassured over and over that I wasn't missing the war—that it hadn't started yet for real, and that they were just now beginning to recruit ninety-day volunteers.

It was late May and early June and the days not too hot but the nights balmy and just right for sleeping in long grass under the stars when it was clear or curled up in barns or under shed roofs when it rained. In the evening I'd find a place to sleep along the road under bushes and sometimes I'd be awakened in the dead darkness by dogs barking, or mules braying, or roosters crowing. And who knows what would start it, but the barking and braying and crowing would spread to the dogs and roosters and mules a little farther away, and then even farther, and then even farther. I'd lie on my back and look up at the

stars and imagine myself in the middle of an unlimited number of con-
centric circles of dogs and roosters and braying mules that spread out
around me across the broad dark land ending only at the mountains
and the sea, and at the wilderness of forest and ice in the north, and the
jungles of the south. These sounds were the sounds of my country, the
sounds I'd heard just past my mother's heartbeat, and feeling surrounded by them at night again felt as if I were cradled again in the
great palm of my American home.

In Maryland I saw my first troops, Federals under the command of
General Butler, who was forcing the state to join the Union. I stepped
off the road to watch them pass, and I longed to join them. I looked at
their muskets with envy, and their uniforms, and their belts and boots
and the way they walked in a long, long line. Each man taking his own
steps, but each a part of a line that had no end.

The man who will listen to reason—O'Keefe of the Sword, the Irish
revolutionary, had said—*let him be reasoned with, but it is the weap-
oned arm of the patriot that can alone prevail against despotism.*

In the days after seeing that massive army—it took most of one day
to pass—I often imagined I too was walking in a file with ten thousand
companions in crisp royal-blue uniforms, all of us armed and ready to
fight enemies of freedom.

When in the course of human events, I thought, as I walked, imagining a glorious battle that we'd win, of course, because a just God would
reward our courage and righteousness and fervor to fight for that with
which He the Creator had endowed us.

That all men are created equal, I thought as I walked, and that *whenever any form of government becomes destructive of these ends, it is the
right of the people to alter or to abolish it.*

Alone, to the rhythm of my own footsteps and words along the
dusty or muddy roads of Maryland, circling around and then, finally,

homing in on the farm where I was born, I thought again of what had made me, what had brought me here: a father's hope, a mother's love.

We hold these truths to be self-evident.

And so, like that, step by step, I dispatched the confusions of the city and managed to recapture the happiness I'd achieved on the sea voyage.

BUT NOT QUITE—because I hated the way I felt with my hat on. For although white people tended to treat me as white, every third or fourth Negro seemed to see right through me. They'd wink, or scowl, and make me hurry my pace.

One day I said the hell with it and took my hat off. I decided I'd be a Negro proudly, whether anybody wanted me or not. It was midafternoon, and very hot, and I sat resting in the shade when I happened to glance up from my reading to see two small spots on the top of a distant hill. Those two spots grew as they approached to become two dusty men standing on the road in front of me. There was no place to hide, and the tree I was under was the only shade, so they looked at me for what seemed a long time before they asked if they could pause there for a bit, and I said, sure.

I glanced at my hat lying in the grass next to me but it was too late. My mother's hair had grown (I'd not cut it, as I was half afraid that when I found her, she might not recognize me) and my skin had bronzed in the sun, and as soon as my fellow pilgrims sat down and saw me up close, their demeanor changed from a stiff politeness to a slack-jawed insolence. They looked at me without modesty. One let his gaze linger way too long on my face. He was the skinnier one, and his eyes were bloodshot. The other had eyes so shiny and green they seemed to jump out of his sunburned face. He must still have had some sense of shame—or something else on his mind—because he had no interest in gaping at me.

"What's that you're reading there, boy?" the skinny one asked.

"The Declaration of Independence," I said.

They both looked at me. My accent had surprised them, but when they turned to look at each other, the surprise changed to amusement.

"Let's hear you read some in that pretty voice of yours," the skinny one said.

Not feeling as if I had a choice, I did. I tried to read it well because I naively thought they'd be as inspired by the words as I was. I could feel their eyes on me, and read clearly and slowly the part that habitually gave me goose bumps—*but when a long train of abuses and usurpations pursuing invariably the same object evinces a design to reduce them under absolute despotism, it is their right, it is their duty, to throw off such government.* As I read, my voice began to tighten with emotion, but I could feel my companions looking back and forth between each other, and I knew they weren't paying attention anymore, not to the words, anyway. I paused, licked my lips, and waited. I didn't dare look up from my little scroll.

"Well, well," the skinny one said. I waited, my eyes down. I heard frogs in the run and crows across the field behind us. "A trained monkey," he said, and kicked the paper out of my hands and I watched it land about five feet away just beyond the limit of the shade in the middle of a fresh cow pie.

I was indignant, and used every bit of my self-control not to show it. "That was a gift from my father," I said.

"And was *your faaah-ther,*" he said, imitating my accent, "a trained monkey, too?" Without waiting for an answer, he freely picked up my jacket from where I had been using it for a pillow. He held it dangling from his filthy fingers, and I thought of the money I had sewn into the lining. I wanted to pull it away from him but didn't want to trigger his suspicion.

"Well?" He snickered and dangled the coat like a bullfighter trying to get me to charge. I glanced quickly to his green-eyed, red-faced companion. He wasn't particularly interested, and I judged that unless I forced a confrontation, he would not join in the meanness.

"Well, what?"

He shook the coat again. Could he feel the money in there? "Was he a trained monkey just like you?"

"He was a white man," I said.

The green-eyed one had been looking down the road thinking about something else, but what I said suddenly interested him. "A white man?" he asked.

"Yes."

"An abolitionist?"

"What?"

"Your daddy."

I shook my head. "Slave owner," I said.

The skinny one gave me a long look, then snickered and tossed the coat back where he found it. "Funny how you can put cream in the coffee but it always gonna be coffee, ain't it?" He smiled brightly and I noticed his teeth were unusually straight and white. "Ain't never gonna be cream. No sir."

Then he did something that turned my outrage into fear. He reached around behind him and pulled out a pistol and touched the open barrel to my chin.

"How much do you suppose we can sell this here runaway nigger for?" he asked.

The green-eyed one reached down and picked a stalk of timothy and chewed on it. I thought of my free papers. They were in my shirt pocket.

"I'm a free man," I said. "I've got papers."

The skinny one slid the pistol from my chin up to my temple. "Hear that?" he said to his companion. "He's got papers!"

"Lemme see 'em," the green-eyed one said.

I slowly lifted my hand and fingered the envelope out of my chest pocket. I closed my eyes and swallowed hard. I could hear cows bawling in the distance. I could hear the mad song of a meadowlark. I listened to the sound of my breathing and the sound of filthy fingers unfolding the papers he couldn't even read. I had a horrible feeling that he might tear the paper, or destroy it. I felt as if everything I had of value was in his hands. The skinny one pressed the pistol to my head, but for that short moment I was more afraid of losing those papers than I was of a bullet.

But when I opened my eyes again he was handing the papers back to me. I took them, folded them, and slid them back into the envelope that my father had put them in so long ago. The pistol on my temple again became my primary concern.

"Well?" said the one with the gun.

"He got papers," the green-eyed one said.

"Papers burn."

"We ain't got time to be selling niggers," the green-eyed one said.

I looked past them at the shallow green valley that spread out below us and watched small cloud shadows pass briskly over the land. The green-eyed one reached back from where he was sitting and retrieved the Declaration of Independence scroll from the cow pie. He wiped it on the grass to clean it, and seeing how that didn't work well, he used his filthy hand. When that didn't work either, he just shrugged and handed me the manure-stained paper.

"Read some more," he said.

I could feel the gun against my skin, very gentle, and then heard the hammer cock.

Green eyes kept his eyes shining at me like lights. He licked his lips. Nodded sharply. "Where you left off," he said.

The paper was smudged badly, but I didn't need to still see the words I'd memorized long ago. I swallowed and said very carefully, *". . . it is their duty, their right to throw off such government, and to provide new guards for their future security. Such has been the patient sufferance of these Colonies; and such is now the necessity which constrains them to alter their former systems of government—"*

"There, Johnny," the green-eyed one said, and he seemed genuinely pleased to have heard the words. He turned to the skinny one, who held the pistol remarkably steady. "I told you."

Johnny looked at him. "Told me *what?*"

"That after enough patient sufferance, we have a *right* to rebel."

I looked down at my manure-stained *civilized law.*

"Let's go," the green-eyed one said.

Johnny glared at me. "I like resting here in the shade, even if I do have to poke a fancy nigger in the face with my gun."

I felt my blood heat and contemplated something foolish. "Then you stay right here," I said, "if you like it so much."

His eyes narrowed. "What?"

"You stay," I said, "I'm leaving," and I leaned away from the pistol so it no longer touched my head and I stood up and turned my back and began walking across the sunny field toward the valley below. I walked as tall as I could, as bravely as I could, but I didn't feel that way. I felt small and frightened, and when Johnny fired his pistol and it kicked up dirt at my feet, I lost control of my bladder. But they couldn't see that, and I kept walking, and I could hear John's laughter and half expected the next shot to hit me in the spine. The next shot hit closer, just behind my boots but I didn't change my pace. I kept my hat in one hand, my jacket in the other, and walked as straight as I could, as deliberately as I could, and resisted with every fiber of my being the urge to break out into a run. Across the long meadow was a copse of trees and after what seemed an eternity I finally arrived in its cooling shade. When I felt sufficiently out of sight, I threw myself onto my knees, pressed my face into the wet soil, and wept with shame.

AFTER THAT I KEPT my hat on, mostly, and I traveled at night. I felt like a fugitive in my own country, but I also felt—*Oh, the mystery!*— an unreasonable happiness. The cruelty of the man under the tree simply reinforced my certainty that my mission, my goal of being a soldier, of dying for my country, was a good and worthwhile ambition. I felt sure a heroic life and death lingered out there in the glorious future— even as I crept fearfully along the edges of moonlit fields and slept by day in the thick brush along winding runs. I scooted along sunken roads, skirted the edges of forests, and, armed with nothing but a long stick to ward off dogs, crouched behind stone walls to steal chickens. After six years in a London slum, I was overjoyed to be in the country again. I've described how the sounds made me feel, but I was drunk on the air as well. Despite my fear and constant vigilance, each stolen breath brought pleasure. It was early summer, and I smelled new grass and wet manure. Dew drying on last year's pine needles. Blossoms and soil and sap. I liked the sound of water, and wind, and even walking in the dark of night I believed I could distinguish the soil of Maryland from the soil of everywhere else simply by how it felt under my feet. Even with my eyes closed, this land felt like home.

And then one night, I was home. I turned a corner, and from under a row of trees that formed a shady tunnel in the day, I could see my father's big white house at the end of the lane. Before I approached I stood still for a long time. No dog barked. No light shone in the window. Hearing nothing, I crept closer. The edges of the lane had not been trimmed, the drive was overgrown, as though nobody used it anymore, but there were fresh wagon tracks through the tall grass. Even in the moonlight I could see that the house looked shabby. It needed paint and the shutters hung crooked. I circled around it from a distance, and then, when I was upwind, a dog began to bark in the dark house. I froze and stood perfectly still for a long time. I assumed whoever was in the house was now looking out one of those dark windows. The dog barked madly and wouldn't stop. I waited as long as I could stand it and then moved, very slowly, down into the woods and out of sight of the dark empty windows of the big house.

The dog's barking grew fainter and then stopped. My mother's and my cabin was along another lane that led from behind the house down to Rooster Run, which I followed in the dark, my heart pounding madly. This was the place I'd dreamed of so often, and it no longer existed. No smell of smoke. No sound of laughter or music coming from any of the broken cabins I passed on the way. No murmur of voices. Nobody here. When I got to where my mother and I had lived, I noticed the roof had caved in and willows clogged the yard between the run and the front door. Too thick to see anything, too dark. I found a place to lie down and wait for morning, but my heart raced. I could feel it beating against the grassy soil. Maybe it would break with sadness, I thought, break for the memory of so many things lost. My childhood. The love of my parents. Where were those things? Still here? Still in the wind? In the smell of the land? I knew my father was dead, and I knew my mother had been sold, but until now their loss was something I'd known only in my head—in my heart they had still been back here.

Yet here I was, and they weren't. They were gone.

I curled up in the grass next to the collapsed cabin wall. I tried not to think about snakes under the wood. I just knew I needed to get close to the smell of the old wood that had been the cabin walls.

I slept, finally, and in the morning walked through the dewy grass to the big house and knocked on the front door. I could smell food cooking. Eggs? But I hadn't seen any chickens. If I had, I would have figured how to steal one before I left. I hadn't eaten in a couple of days and my stomach had formed a solid knot. Inside, the dog began to bark. Not just bark, but throw itself against the door. I fought an urge to flee and knocked again. Finally an old woman cracked the door and peeked out at me. I could see by her one dark-blue eye visible though the narrow opening that she was my father's widow.

"Ma'am," I said, and took my hat off.

"Niggers around back," she said.

The dog barked madly and I swallowed my fear. "And sons of the master?"

She didn't shut the door. She kept it open slightly, and through the crack I could see she'd grown a goiter on her neck the size of a fist. Her eye blinked as she looked me over. I was weary from the road, and not clean, but my suit was still a good one and she took it all in. Did she know I'd promised God anything to stay out of isolation, and so sacrificed her husband, my father? Of course not. I swallowed my panic and waited for an answer.

Her eye blinked again. "He ain't here," she said.

The dog in the house threw itself at the door and pried its snout into the opening. All she would have had to do was open the door just a crack more and the dog would have burst out and ripped open my throat. Instead she used her knee to push it aside.

"I know," I said, swallowing my fear. "I'm sorry." I said this out of a sense of formality. But when I said it, I felt it. Sorry not for her, but for myself. I paused to regain my composure. The dog barked madly, and again her eye blinked.

"What do you want?" she asked.

"Do you know where she is?"

I remembered then how one of her dogs had mauled a Negro man on the back steps. By the time the dog was pulled off, its face was bloody and so was the man's. Who knows how old I was when I saw it? Two? One? Too early for context. The vision of it caught me unaware—it was something I'd completely forgotten, but now it emerged as real and horrifying as if it were happening in front of me. I felt as if I were waking from a bad dream with the horror still present there in the dark room. I swallowed hard and used all of my courage to keep my feet still.

Her eye had come to rest on my green eye. "He left his mark, I see," she said.

I didn't say anything. I stood up straighter, though. I was a man, and could feel his mark both outside and in.

"What you fixin' to do when you find her?"

Finish what he only started, I thought. Free her, and after that, fight for the freedom of all. I didn't say any of that, though.

"Buy her," I said.

Again the barking dog threw itself at the door. As though she could smell my rancid fear, she wrinkled her tiny nose and turned and said, "Butch," and the dog suddenly stopped barking and retreated out of sight. The silence was a relief, but I didn't like not knowing exactly where Butch was.

"I only know what I heard," she said.

I stood and waited. I could hear robins behind me on the lawn. It was already getting hot on this side of the house, and I'd begun to sweat, but there must have been a high breeze because the willows hissed and danced along the lane.

"When Mr. Gates died," she said, "a fellow by the name of Norton took over around here."

"He's the one who wrote me."

"I give him your letters," she said.

I tried to shake off my irritation. If I hadn't suspected the dog was sitting like a lion behind the door, I might have pushed open the door and grabbed her by the goiter. Over her shoulder, in the kitchen, I could see a white chicken fly up and perch in an open kitchen cupboard. The dog must have been chasing it, for he positioned himself below and began again to bark. She turned her eye away from me and yelled, "Butch!" The dog quieted again and the chicken seemed to settle safely in. She looked back at me and said, "Too many thieves—" Hungry as I was, she didn't have to explain.

"Where's Norton?" I asked.

She shook her head.

"And the trader's name?"

Again she shook her head.

We looked at each other. I felt sweat drip down my back under my shirt. I'd seen her almost every day, as a child, but I'd never really looked at her. What did she have to do with me? By the way she was looking at me through the door, by the way she'd been looking at me ever since she opened the door, I understood that she had always looked at me. She'd watched my mother carry me on her back as an infant. She'd watched me crawl in the dirt outside the cabin, toddle along behind my mother and the cows. Watched me haul buckets of butter and water and watched my mother's every move, my mother, who'd had what she apparently had not been able to have, a child by my father.

"Why didn't you write me right away?" I asked. "You let me think all those years—"

She sighed deeply. That and the feeling in my own throat cut me off. Surrounding us was silence. Where was Butch? I half expected him to come running around the corner behind me.

"Spite," she said matter-of-factly.

I stared at her face—half of her face, and half expected she'd continue, but she didn't. I'd asked a question and gotten an answer. I put my hat back on and turned to go. I was halfway across the yard before I heard the door close behind me. Then I heard it open once again and I spun around, looking for a stick or a rock. I expected to see Butch coming my way fast, but what I saw was her entire gray head sticking out of the crack—both eyes full on me. "Family might have been named Simpson," she called.

"What family?"

"Trader's. Down around Centreville."

I stared at her. From this distance, except for the fact that she was upright, she looked close to dead, her skin almost see-through. I touched the brim of my hat, and she closed the door for the last time. Centreville. I breathed deeply. Family named Simpson, maybe. A traveling trader who'd bought a slave named Jennyveeve from Norton at Sweet Grass six years ago. I turned so the morning sun was on my left, tilted my hat that way, and headed south.

TO BE SAFE, I continued traveling at night, cleaning myself up in the morning to come into towns and buy food if I needed it. I walked generally southwest across Maryland and into Virginia—one hour being a white man, the next a free Negro—asking for a town called Centreville, a family named Simpson, a trader named Norton. One day I'd stop bareheaded at a slave shack, tell them about my mother being sold away, and the next day I might find myself sitting with white men in a town square telling the story of my education in England, my poor dead father, and my mother left alone with only me to see her safely through these troubled times.

In those weeks there were a lot of men on the road. Lone traveling men like me, and clumps of marching soldiers as well. I'd seen large groups of Yankees for the first time in Maryland, and then again as I slogged through swamps and foggy meadows into Washington, row after row of marching soldiers. The magnificent Army of the Potomac! The uniforms. The white tents filling fields on both sides of the road. The men and weapons and mules. There were no Negro units, so I knew I would have to fight as a white man. But that did not disturb me. It seemed natural that one side of me would fight for the other side of me.

The storm cloud of war had been building over Virginia, and beneath it gathered masses of armed men. In just one morning I stepped off the same road twice to allow two great mounted cavalries to pass, one from the South and one from the North. So it was no great surprise that this was where the war's first lightning would scorch the earth. But what did surprise—*shocked,* actually—was that the first great bolt ripped straight down from the sky and hit *me.*

I WAS AWOKEN out of a sound sleep in the dark before dawn by the sound of thousands of soldiers marching a few feet from my bed of leaves. Mistaken for a straggler, I was kicked to my feet and before I knew it was walking through a dense forest in the dark with a brigade of Irish soldiers. I kept my mouth shut, both sleepy and eager to be included. By dawn, as the sky lit our way and each other's faces, it became clear I was not much like those with whom I marched. These men wore bright-red uniforms, carried muskets on their shoulders and long knives in their belts—I was unarmed and wearing my brown wool suit and a top hat, and just plain didn't look much like an Irishman. (I had never seen so many Irishmen together, and their faces were amazingly similar.) They were the fighting Irish Zouaves, I was told, part of the Union Army, and unless I was a spy, I was welcome to march with them for the day. There'd be shooting soon enough and I could pick up a gun dropped by a dead rebel. Not to worry, they assured me as we pressed onward in single file through the forest, not to worry.

But by midmorning many of us were tired and hungry and there'd still been no sign of the enemy. We paused by a muddy run to drink. I'd just lain down in the shade to rest, my face wet with stream water, when a shout rolled down along the line. Somebody waved a green flag, and the regiment moved forward across the ravine and into a meadow that swept up an incline toward a line of forest and brush. It was from behind that thick green edge that the enemy began to pour a torrent of fire down on us.

As far as I knew, none of us had been in battle before and we took our cues about which direction to run based on the direction of those next to us. Like a school of fish, if one turned, the others did. If one was hit and fell, those at his side fell, too. Or at least that was what I did. I jumped over two men who just a moment before had been running by my side, and I lay behind them with my head down. I remember the deafening noise, blinding smoke, and terrible burning in my throat. For a long time I simply pressed my face into the sour earth and tried to disappear between bodies. This was war? Even when I dared to lift my head and to look up the hill, I couldn't see the enemy for the smoke. There was a gun nearby and I grabbed it, a warrior at last. I aimed up the hill, pulled the trigger, and the gun seemed to explode in my hands. Thrilled, I aimed again toward the smoke at the top of the hill, but this time when I pulled the trigger, nothing happened. I realized I needed to load it again, and I didn't know how.

I rolled onto my back and looked up at the blue sky and pretty puffs of cloud. Invisible bullets whizzed by just above my face. If I lifted my head, I'd be dead. But how could I die like this, after everything I'd hoped and dreamed? How was it possible that it could all end—that the light could go out? On a hillside in Virginia just miles from where my mother was, or had been? I turned to look behind me, down the hill, and what I saw was more blue sky touched by a line of trees, and closer, an officer on horseback, his sword out and mouth agape. Yet before the sound from that mouth had time to reach my ears, some invisible power blew the top half of his body away. The bewildered bay mare, her load suddenly lightened, wandered toward me, her head speckled with blood. I put my head down and closed my eyes and wept uncontrollably—not for the half man, of course, but for my paralyzed self. I might have lain blubbering like that until I died, but when I chanced to open my eyes again, I saw the mare's hooves not two feet from my face. I tilted my head to look up, and there she stood amid the whizzing bullets, still speckled with blood and staring at me as though patiently waiting for me to get control of myself and mount her.

With the full purpose of beating a cowardly retreat, I leaped for her bridle and pushed the lower half of the officer's body out of the saddle, climbed on and galloped away from the guns.

The idea was not an original one. A general panic had developed and the great body of the federal army, of which the Irish Zouaves were only a part, began to mysteriously roll back.

Mysteriously, for who can say why such things happen? What faerie dust causes ideas to suddenly take hold in a group of men? Or in most of us, anyway. For it was during this general retreat that I saw the famous Cornelius O'Keefe for the first time. I didn't recognize him for who he was. Not right away. I only saw a man on horseback charging the enemy, and I was on horseback retreating, and we galloped toward each other. I was mainly interested in his sword, which he had raised and looked likely to cut me with. But before I could veer away, both our horses were shot out from under us. We tumbled over their falling bodies, facedown into the grass.

I stood quickly, barely shaken, and was about to continue my retreat on foot when I noticed him senseless on the field before me. Gripped by sudden shame, I reached down and grasped him by the back of the collar, jerked him up and across my back, and immediately collapsed to one knee under his weight. At this moment I might have let him fall because there were hundreds of bodies in the grass around us and who would have noticed one more? But I had committed myself thus far to his safety, and so by the time the notion to drop him and run emerged, I had an equally strong picture of myself as a hero—a character right out of my very own dreams. So amid all this death and chaos I continued what I'd begun. I struggled to my feet and carried him a few hundred yards beyond the range of the batteries. I rolled him off me and onto the shady stream bank where an eternity ago I'd taken a brief rest. There, kneeling over him, watching his blue eyes open again into consciousness, I recognized his famous face from the many drawings that accompanied the old newspapers I'd read in Nancy's room.

What are the chances that my first hour of battle I'd see the brave Irish revolutionary whose speeches first inspired me to war? And what cruel irony would have me see him just as I'd begun to retreat?

"Who are you?" he asked me. He look stunned and confused. I could not speak. I did not know if he recognized me as the coward who'd been retreating as he charged. I wish now I'd had sufficient wits about me to quote some of his very own words: *Never, I repeat it, never was there a cause more sacred, nor one more great, nor one more urgent* . . . But exertion had taken my breath, and a guilty conscience turned my dry mouth even drier.

Convinced that I was mad or dumb—or as I later learned, something even stranger—he stood first, and then bent at the waist and reached for my hand and helped me to my feet. When I was standing, he did something odd. He reached out and touched my hair above my left ear. He let his fingers linger there for a moment while he blinked and looked at my face and then into my eyes, from one to the other. My hat was long gone up the hill somewhere, and my skin bronzed from my journey.

"You're a different one, aren't ye?"

Maybe I shook my head. Or nodded. I know I resisted the temptation to pull away, and then, strangely, resisted the temptation to lean against his hand.

"You saved my life," he said.

Is that what I had done? Saved his life? The great O'Keefe of the Sword?

"I came to find my mother," I said.

He heard my accent, tilted his head, puzzled. "What are ye, anyway?"

"A long story," I said.

He smiled wearily. "Indeed. Aren't we all? And even longer, thanks to your bravery."

From behind me somebody shouted his name and he let drop his hand from my hair. "Colonel!" said the voice, closer, just as a riderless horse galloped past, sending up a spray of silver water from the stream at our feet. O'Keefe stepped ahead of me and allowed himself to be pulled by another officer, who led him through the knee-deep water to the far side. His head swiveled back to stare at me, though, and we looked at each other until I had to step aside to let pass a wagon piled with wounded men. The wagon got mired in the mud, and I put my hands on the buckboard to help push it up the steep far side, and when I dropped my hands, red with blood, O'Keefe had moved even higher up the bank, surrounded by other officers.

The retreat had grown suddenly crowded. Soon I was walking in a forest among hundreds of men dressed in burned rags, a few still wearing the red-feathered hats of the Zouaves. Smoke wafted in front us, above us, and the sun paled and disappeared. The sound of the shelling quieted, then grew again, and we limped and walked and ran and talked to ourselves, but we stayed ahead of the explosions and eventually they faded into the distance. A hee-hawing donkey with a broken foreleg hopped like a rabbit past us, then back again, and then past us again. We heard the echo of its hee-haw long into the day. I fell back slightly, separated still farther from O'Keefe, and soon I couldn't walk any farther or faster. I wasn't the only one, so there in the part of the forest where I had slept so briefly the night before, I lay down to sleep in a small clearing surrounded by hundreds of other exhausted soldiers.

Smoky night came fast. There was no moon and high clouds blocked the stars. I held my hand in front of my face and saw nothing. I curled up in a ball and shivered. Around me I heard men coughing, talking quietly, snoring, and the occasional cry of the wounded where they'd fallen during the retreat. On a distant ridge I heard gathering wind, and then its descent into the valley. Why not? My mother on the darkest nights claimed to be able to hear the last breaths of the dying in the wind.

How many? I asked, in awe of what she could hear with only one ear.

All of them, child.

The day had given me my first real scrape with violent death and I cannot say I liked it, or my response to it. Yet in my exhaustion even the cold embrace of the earth felt as sweet as any bed I have ever lain on. I was hungry and thirsty, too, but even those discomforts seemed singed by terror. Is this what it felt like to be a warrior? To live so close to death as to be numbed?

I tried to imagine Colonel O'Keefe's courage as he was charging when the rest of us were retreating—and his courage those many years before, looking death in the eye in an English court.

"My Lord," I found myself saying into the darkness, making my accent as Irish as I could. *"This is our first offense, but not our last."* I paused and breathed. I could hear the wind approaching, but it hadn't come into our little clearing just yet, and my voice had turned the night as silent as it was dark. I continued, louder, and imagined I was speaking to a white-wigged judge, to a courtroom, to my country.

"If you will be easy with us this once," I said, *"we promise on our word as Irish gentlemen, to try to do better next time!"*

And then something happened that I didn't expect. From all around me the floor of the clearing came alive with cheers. "Hip-hip hooray!" somebody shouted. And then others joined him. "Hip-hip hooray! Hip-hip hooray!"

Despite the sudden arrival of a cold wind, I was warmed by the unexpected camaraderie of my nameless mates. My mother was out there still, somebody's slave, and I had no intention of abandoning her. But the war had touched me—struck me, more like—and one day of battle had taught me my limitations. I needed to learn to use a gun, for one thing. And not run away at the first opportunity. I resolved the next morning to find Colonel O'Keefe and persuade him—different as I was—to let me join what was left of this Irish brigade and become an official soldier.

I WOKE BEFORE DAWN in the midst of a sound too big for human ears. Shells exploded all around me and the waves of their fury shook my body to its core. My brain felt addled by the concussions, and for the second day in a row, glorious war had me pressing my body madly into the loose soil lest my pitiful flesh be torn asunder. I don't know that I have suffered a more terrifying hour than I did that morning, waiting for sunrise as though light would save me. It didn't. But it did reveal in brightening shades of pink and orange and yellow a ground pockmarked with craters, littered with shattered trees and broken wagons and body parts—what was left of my comrades, the Irish Zouaves.

None of the living were anywhere in sight, so even after the shelling paused I didn't know which way to run. I could hear shouting and gunshots in all directions, so I waited and watched as frightened and wounded horses suddenly galloped into the broken clearing. They were followed by stumbling soldiers, their blue shirts or pants stained with blood and soil. I worked my way on my belly through the cratered clearing and then along a charred wood to the edge of what had been a cornfield, but now the stalks lay flattened and shredded by rifle fire. Black smoke of burning trees and fields created a choking haze. I lay keeping my mouth near the soil so I could better breathe, but suddenly noticed the ground was muddy with blood. As though to free myself from the bleeding earth, I crawled as fast as I could down a slope to a stream where I lay for a time in the shallow, cool water. I drank the water to wash the ashes from my mouth and the taste brought me back to Sweet Grass, to the flesh and earth smells of the cabin, and I thought what a foolish boy I was to get into such a mess. I would have been glad to see my mother coming after me right then, to put her arms around me and protect me.

But hadn't I come home so I could rescue her? What was happening to me? What kind of man was I?

The contest raged around me, and it seemed I could hear nothing but one unending, rolling explosion. I would have run but didn't know which way to go. I would have fought, but even if I had found a gun, I didn't know how to use it, or even which way to shoot. So I slid up out

of the stream and sat leaning against a tree, shivering, the most woebe-
gone eighteen-year-old in the world. I sat like that for I don't know
how long, feeling sorry for myself, and watching the bushes on the far
bank shiver and sway in the breeze until I realized that it wasn't only
breeze but bullets that made them dance so prettily against the blue
sky. I looked down to my feet and noticed the stream I'd bathed in
had turned red with blood, and then, suddenly, I was no longer alone.
There were soldiers on each side of me shooting their guns over the
bank and into the corn. One was a boy named Gibbs—don't ask me
how I knew his name, he must have told me, although I have no recollection of speaking to him, only of being next to him in that spot when
a ball crashed through his brain and ended the battle for him. Without
the very minor assistance of two others, who had been wounded in op-
posite legs and so leaned against each other for balance, I picked up
Gibbs and carried him up the bank and laid him behind a fallen tree.
I don't know why I did that. He was dead and I was no safer behind
the fallen tree. In fact, I sat for a long time fascinated by the sound of
balls hitting the wood just above my head and thinking how that trunk
would make a good lead mine someday. I took my coat off and I laid it
over Gibbs's broken head. I'm still not sure to this day whether that
was an act of respect or disgust. I know I had forgotten about my papers and gold coins sewn into the coat's lining, and so left it there while
the sound of increased gunfire persuaded me to crawl back down to
the edge of the water. I huddled in tall grass and again transported myself out of the horrendous noise of the shelling, and the smoke, and the
sound of whizzing bullets, to a more peaceful place. Perhaps to the
bank of a Maryland run where my mother and my father went to picnic
and make love. I looked up at the trees swaying in a breeze above my
head and I thought, Why not? Where else would the last exhalations
of the dying go?

Suddenly a company of rebel soldiers charged past me shooting and howling madly. I closed my eyes and one of them tripped on me and then rolled to lie beside me, and I could feel him rest his rifle over my hip and use my body to steady his gun. I'm sure I was red with blood from Gibbs's head, and he was using me as cover to shoot over, which naturally put me in an uncomfortably dangerous place, so I raised my head and looked at him, and he looked over his rifle barrel, and I thought he was going to jump out of his skin with fright. Funny thing. Balls flying by, dead men scattered over the field, exploding shells causing an inferno of sound and fury, and one dead man lifts his head, and that's what scares the rebel so badly he runs off.

I lay there alone again. All the rebels had disappeared. Retreated with him? Had I perhaps caused a panic? Yet the shelling increased its fury—flying bombs marching across the field above me and then marching back again, throwing dirt and rock and wood splinters. Certain I'd die at any moment, I closed my eyes and imagined that soon I'd see my father again, and I tried in vain to think of what I'd tell him.

And then, magically, the shelling stopped.

In the silence that followed I could hear the gurgle of water over pebbles as the stream turned at the base of the bank. I opened my eyes and looked again at the little bush, its branches stripped of leaves and still. I breathed deeply and carefully, becoming aware of every part of my body. The noise had been so painful that it wasn't until this silence that I realized I was okay. That there was nothing wrong with my body. I wasn't wounded, or even bruised. I felt an immense lightness, as though I'd been given new life, new birth, and I could do anything, be anybody. I thought of my coat then, with my papers and my money, and lifted my head to try to see where I'd left Gibbs.

Suddenly I heard shouting: *Down, get down! Down!* I ducked but the shouting continued. Curious, I slowly peeked over the bank and across the field. The fallen tree, Gibbs's body, and my coat were nowhere to be seen. They'd been swallowed by a crater. I was about to crawl over the bank and try to make my way there, but was stopped by more shouts from a different part of the field: *Who is he? Down, get down! He's crazy!*

Panicked, I almost lay down again, but something caught my eye. From out of the gloom of the fading light—had the entire day passed already?—appeared the shape of a man walking across the field. More shouts, more warnings. But the form kept coming, a shadow against the lighter sky to the west, and when he passed me I could see he was an old white man with a long blond beard and a modest twinkle in his eyes, as though he were amused by a child or a private joke. For a moment I was tempted to think of him as a shade and not a man—the ghost of my father, perhaps—but he was clearly of flesh, white flesh covered with dust and dirt and nothing else. Naked as the day he was born, large mole or small wound on his left hip, penis shrunken into its nest, he walked past me, past all of us, unfazed by our warnings.

Suddenly a last shell exploded near him and tossed dirt and rock high in the air. He disappeared for a moment, but when the earth settled the old man was still walking upright, and just as he was about to pass the clearing where the cluster of the shells had been hitting heaviest—I am sure every living man in that field was watching him by now, although no longer yelling—he sat down on a stump and crossed his legs and closed his eyes as though praying or remembering something good. Behind him that terrible day died in an ecstasy of color across the sky—orange, red, pink, purple—but we kept our eyes on the old man, his face just as pleasant as could be.

Then it got dark, and I couldn't see him anymore. Through the night the groans of the dying rolled across the field. Men called for their mothers or fathers or lovers or wives, and eerie shadows of soldiers—rebel and Yankee alike—began to move across the clearing to search for the wounded and dig hasty graves for the dead. To this day I do not know why I didn't get up and walk away. Perhaps that was my plan when I slid on my belly across the broken ground to the crater that had consumed Gibbs's body, and my coat, and my papers, and my money. I searched in vain until I grew discouraged and exhausted, and was pulled by the sound of gurgling water back to the bloody run, where I drank until I'd had enough. I lay in the grass to rest. The ground felt good under my back and very soon I slept as deeply as I had in a long time.

In the morning I opened my eyes and looked up and seeming to hang from the blue sky above me was the head and face of a very young rebel soldier squinting down the long barrel of his rifle at me. I thought of my papers, and my money, and was about to say something, but the soldier lowered the barrel of the rifle and pressed it painfully into my mouth.

Another soldier appeared next to him holding a shovel.

"Look here, Burt," the one with the rifle said. "Think this nigger can dig?"

WHEN MY FATHER FREED ME, he used his five fingers to tell me what he knew about life—We *all suffer, We are all going to die, We are not in control, We do not live for ourselves,* and *We are free.* He assumed I already understood the first two. He was wrong. The only one I understood as a boy was the one he had the most difficulty understanding as a man: *We are not in control.*

As far as suffering went, I knew *I* did—but *others? Everybody?* I wasn't so sure.

Now, as a man, a slave again, property of the Army of Northern Virginia, this trick of separating my suffering from that of others was a trick I could no longer perform. In addition to burial detail after battles, there were weeks, sometimes months, during which we stayed in camp hauling water, cutting wood, and tending livestock. In this diseased country, we got sick and took care of one another. We had diarrhea. We caught fevers that made our bones burn. Coughed constantly. Our gums turned black and our teeth loosened. Even if we suffered from none of these ailments—if all had gone well that day and we'd scraped together enough sorghum, roasted acorns, and black beans to fill our shrunken bellies, we might have a tiny sliver on our smallest toe that would throb and grow, and turn red, and fester, and make every step a misery.

Because we marched, too. Or walked. Or straggled behind the soldiers along rough and dusty roads beneath a broiling August sun. Messengers flew fly back and forth on horseback. The column halted mysteriously for five minutes, or five hours, a long way from water. In the distance we'd hear a drumbeat. Somebody was marching somewhere, but not us. Then we'd move again, carrying our heavy loads over mountains and across muddy rivers—on past villages and farms, where we'd tarry only long enough to steal green corn from the field.

We never passed anywhere near Centreville, or even a farm family by the name of Simpson. Nevertheless, I'd scan the territory looking, always looking. Sometimes I'd fool myself into thinking that around the next bend in the road I'd see her. She'd be standing alongside the column waiting with her hands on her hips, as she sometimes stood when she was impatient, and when she saw me, she'd shake her head as though she'd been waiting too long, just too long, and shame on me. But she'd smile and spread her arms to welcome me home anyway. I could work myself up picturing her like that, and the rising joy in my heart would lighten my step. I imagined the thrill of an imminent reunion sometimes as often as twice a day. I got pretty good at it, and when I was low and tired and hurting I could ride that feeling for a while, float for just a ways on the sweet happiness of my make-believe.

Yet always before the road turned, a nagging fear began to pull me down again. How would she even recognize me? I wasn't seven anymore, and my clothes were rags, and most days a thick covering of trail mud or dust had settled on my hair, eyebrows, and thin beard. I imagined telling her who I was, and I imagined her not believing me. I'd yell her name, and she, in fear, would duck back off the road to hide as most women did when our column passed. I imagined chasing her into the brush and losing her again for good.

Even if I did find her, and even if she knew me, what could I do? I was no longer a free man with papers and money to buy her freedom. I was a Nigger Digger. I was a marching slave.

So as I'd round the corner and see nothing but dust and a line of men stretching as far as the eye could see, instead of the crash of despair, sometimes what I'd feel was relief.

When it rained we got wet all the way through. We'd halt in the evening and try to make fire with green wood. Even if the rain stopped the ground would be cold, and so we wouldn't sleep, and we'd have to get up and stand over the smoky fire, which would choke us. Up and down through a night like that, either shivering or coughing—maybe shaking with ague.

And the next day marching again. All of us, black and white. All of us, feet bloody. All of us.

We all suffer.

We are all going to die.

And when we died, we'd bury one another. The way it worked was this: after a battle, each unit searched for its own dead. If the dead were known, they were buried with wooden crosses over their graves, and as often as not these graves were dug by the dead man's friends. The unidentified dead were tossed into mass graves, which was what we dug, the Nigger Diggers. It was our job. We had no choice—it was the only thing to do—but it was also the decent thing to do.

As a boy in London, I'd pulled dead bodies in from the cold water, rifled through their clothing, and unsentimentally cast them back out. So of course I knew people died—those particular people bloated from river water, for instance—but I'd easily been able to separate their fate from anything that could possibly happen to me. Not anymore. Now each dead body I buried was mine. And that a man, black or white, should die without a living witness, be disfigured or forgotten in battle and be buried in a strange place—far from home, by people he didn't know, alongside men he didn't know, in a place that would never be visited—this, of course, was my nightmare. Some nights I'd lie on the ground filled with the loneliness I imagined would be mine if I died alone and were buried with the unknown dead. How I longed for day on those nights, so at the very least someone would see me die, if I died.

Not that I would have gotten my own grave. We always threw the slave bodies into mass graves along with all of the unidentified dead, even if we knew them. But we paused as we did so. We bowed our heads and said the dead man's name, then together breathed the smell of death as we commenced to cover the bodies.

I can still smell the dead in the fresh wind, even as it races across a thousand miles of grass. Still feel the dead *and* hear the dead. But shoulder to shoulder with the horror of those days is this memory, too: often as I stepped over the contorted and bloated bodies, as I carried them in litters and dug grave after grave, often at such times I would feel in my own living person bursts of new strength and vigor, and the world would suddenly strike me as beautiful.

Sunlight on a green shoot of grass could make my blood pound wildly in my temples. The gurgle of water over rocks might bring tears to my eyes. And a lone yellow leaf swaying in the faint fall breeze threatened to break my heart.

Oh, the mystery!

The first few times this happened, I felt confusion and shame, but then gradually I began to believe that our living constitutions are actually heartened by inhaling with gusto an atmosphere choked with the final exhalations of dying men.

That's my theory, anyway, and when you spend two years in the fields of the dead, such theories can be peristaltic.

Early in the morning we'd walk to the place of battle, collect the unidentified dead and lay them out in rows of fifty or one hundred. Alongside the piles of bodies, we spent the day, or a succession of days, digging trenches about seven feet wide and three feet deep. If it was hot, the bodies would be bloated and black before we got them in the ground. I had a couple of partners, one named Crow-boy and the other Saturn, and Saturn's mother had been a midwife, so he'd seen a lot of babies born, and he said even nigger babies were born white, and now he could see that dead white men turned black as ink, so everybody was born white and everybody died a nigger, and if it weren't for the in-between we'd all be one big loving family.

"Just like yours," he'd say to me.

So not infrequently, we even laughed while we worked. Oh, happy slaves!

IF I LEARNED KEENLY my father's first two lessons during these years—and I had already mastered *We are not in control*—what about the last two? What about *We do not live for ourselves* and *We are free?*

Ironically, in slavery I began to feel the full weight of their truth as well. For although we were not legally free, we were free to take care of one another, or not. We were free to live for others, or not. And for the most part, we did. Because we wanted to survive, and to choose the other way was to choose death.

Some did go that way. Halfheartedly wandering off—not to freedom but to be ridden down and shot. Left to rot in the sun or mud.

Even on the worst nights, when we had nothing to eat, no prospects but to suffer, no hope but that we would not die before the sun came up, we could usually get a fire going and heat water and make tea from tree bark—from slippery elm, dogwood, willow. Although I suspect the bark did little more than flavor our putrid water, we imagined those teas did great things for us, sustained our wounded insides and outsides, and I suppose they did—because sharing them was what really saved us. Sitting near each other in the dark over meager flames. One blanket over our shoulders, passing back and forth a curse, a laugh, a cup.

I was able to get extra food occasionally, as my ability to write began to be whispered among the troops and so those who could not write used me to write letters. It had to be done discreetly, as a Nigger Digger wasn't supposed to know how to write, but rather than get me in trouble, the soldiers protected me. They searched for me late at night and supplied me with paper and a writing instrument and dictated by candlelight. Afterward they sent me back to my camp with a handful of acorns or a piece of pilot bread, or a fist-sized sack of coffee ground in a pail under a musket butt—and sometimes salt pork, or a chunk of fresh wild meat that we'd eat all at once—or in winter we'd let it freeze and carry it in our packs for days and cut off pieces with our knives to thaw and cook over a fire.

Writing letters gave me glimpses of the private longings, loves, and despair of my masters. As unique as each individual might be, I could see we were all made of the same stuff. *All men are created equal.* It amazed me to know those words had been written by a slave owner, and not because a slave owner couldn't *believe* them. My father had. But without the intimate glimpses that only a slave can have of his master, how could a slave owner *ever know?*

"Dear Dad," one homesick letter-writer said, "I've marched most the whole world I suspect since I left but I have not yet seen anyplace like our sweet good home."

"Mother," said a miserable dying soldier, "I am ever hopeful to see your face again but illness has visited and gives no sign of departing, and so prospects of our reunion grow dimmer each day."

"Lover," wrote a man to his wife, "in the morning I think of your face and body and you give me courage to open my eyes, and in the evening I think of your face and body and you give me the calm I need to close them again."

And a boy-turned-war-poet had me write his uncle, "We've been giving the Yankees fiery hell, of that I am sure, but they seem no less inclined to give it back. We toss misery their way and they toss it ours, and there's no bottom to that well, which is why this fight has no end that any of us can see except on the last red-sky evening the last starving one of ours kills the last starving one of theirs or, God forbid, the other way around."

THE SECOND TIME I saw Colonel O'Keefe and the Irish brigade was a year and a half after I'd seen him the first time. It was December, and we were camped on a height above a town full of Yankees. It was cold, and I remember we had but two blankets for three of us, Saturn, Crow-boy, me. We all lay on one blanket and covered ourselves with the other. Provided we all lay in the same position, we were covered snugly enough, but if one took a different position from the other two, the blankets failed to accommodate. It amused us to sometimes adopt a military tone, so when one of us wished for a change he woke the others and announced his purpose, and a command to turn right or left was given, and we all made the move promptly and without disorder.

When we woke that morning the air rippled with the promise of battle, but because we had control of the heights, the officers did not expect a full-on assault. Nevertheless, that was what happened, and the result was a fearful carnage as the artillery began to pound the Yanks as soon as they left the village and began to cross the field.

Those that survived the first shelling regrouped and began to charge toward the stone fence behind which we waited. They took a storm of rebel lead. A cloud of smoke shut out the scene for a moment, and then rising revealed only sad and scattered fragments of the original Yankee formations recoiling from the attack. It was then I noticed each soldier wore a sprig of green in his cap, and heard it shouted along the line that this was the famous Irish brigade under the command of Colonel O'Keefe

They regrouped at the base of the hill, and again their mounted (and then unmounted) Colonel led them up into the fury of rebel guns. A third and fourth time they charged, and a third and fourth time they were driven back. Watching them fall like a thousand blades of grass before a swinging scythe, I felt sorrow not only for the soldiers who littered the field but for myself. Since the day of my capture, I'd clung to the notion that if I had only found the Irish brigade after my first battle, I would not be a Nigger Digger but a free man fighting a *good fight*.

But sometime during that long day of battle I lost even that great notion. For as I watched countless soldiers follow their leader beyond all limits of bravery up that hill—a fifth time, a sixth—fresh-faced boys who had awoken that morning in love with their lives, boys who loved their comrades, loved their parents and their memories of their green island home, boys who had awoken that morning singing thousand-year-old songs, boys who dreamed of the promise of a woman and the promise of the free world—as I watched wave after wave of running boys fall openmouthed to their deaths behind the great O'Keefe of the Sword, I lost the last trace of belief in such a thing as a *good fight*.

Rarely are we given such clear glimpses of our fate should we have been able to carry out our best intentions, and there, in the sparkling light of day, I could see that if I'd joined the Union Army and become a warrior, rather than being a hero who freed my mother and the country itself, I'd be a dead man.

And yet . . . and yet . . . A letter I would write for a soldier that evening said it best: "Why, my darling," he had me write, "such was their bravery that we forgot they were fighting us and even as we fired away until our guns glowed red with heat, cheer after cheer at their fearlessness went up along our lines."

The battle was followed by another night of freezing sleet and wind, and the field crawled with looters taking what arms and clothing they could off the sprig-hatted bodies piled in some places three deep. Saturn foraged two more blankets, and four pairs of socks, and he shared his haul with me and Crow-boy. We shivered together until the sleet stopped and a frost settled, and when we woke the sun had lifted and blazed a pretty glaze across one of the most distressing sights I had ever seen. Which was when it occurred to me that although the world does not love us, we do still mostly love the world.

Oh, the mystery!

For how else could we endure it? How else could we ever blink awake and lift our blankets to look out at such a scene of slaughter, and be grateful?

ONLY ONCE DID I write a letter for an officer. I had been called to his canvas hut at winter camp, so when I arrived I knocked. Thinking I heard a response, I opened the door and stepped in. The lantern was lit, but nobody was there. I should have turned and left, come back later, but it was warm inside, and he'd plastered about his walls pictures cut from illustrated periodicals. And not just any pictures. These were colored fashion plates from a ladies' magazine. As we rarely saw women, these images of attractive women in various modes of attire were highly prized. Although I'd seen them from a distance, I'd never been alone with them, never been able to go up to each one and study them carefully.

I lingered for a long time looking at the pictures. Standing in the warm room studying the beautiful women, the tops of their necks, their arms, and the tops of their bosoms bared to the flickering lantern light, I felt myself aroused. I slipped my hand under the waistband of my pants and tried to push myself down, which only aggravated my trouble. I listened. It was late at night, and I could hear nothing beyond the thin walls of the hut. I studied the pictures, felt my breath speed up, and so, keeping my hand inside my pants, quickly gratified myself. Shaken with the climax, I dropped to my knees at the foot of the officer's cot. I was in that position when I heard the canvas flap pull back on the entrance behind me.

Footsteps. I closed my eyes. It was the officer himself. I could tell by the loud way he breathed. He saw me kneeling and assumed I was praying. His step, the sound of his step, indicated a respect—but still he was shocked to see me here. He stood over me and didn't speak, but I knew he was waiting until I finished with my pretend prayer. I mumbled *amen* but I couldn't get my mind off the smear on the back of my hand which now lay across the blanket on his cot. Reluctantly I stood up. The rain began to fall and grew loud on the canvas roof. The captain sat down on his cot, right on top of where I'd wiped my hand. It would be on his pants now.

"Thanks for your prayers, nigger," he said.

He then directed me to the paper and pen and dictated a letter to his wife full of tenderness and humility (depicting himself with much less courage than he was known to actually possess). When he finished, and I handed him the letter, I believe he felt embarrassed by what he'd revealed, and also by the fact that he was an officer and could not write, and I believe that was why he did what he did next.

"Take your shirt off and bend over and hold your ankles with your hands."

"Excuse me, suh?" I said.

He had taken off his belt and doubled it over his fist. "You heard me, boy."

I looked at him swinging the belt around his fist one way, and then the other, not quite believing what I was seeing. I had never been beaten before and couldn't believe I was going to be beaten now.

"Never let me see you in here alone again, you hear?"

"Yessuh," I said. But I'd only come in because I'd thought he was here, I explained. The lantern was lit and I thought I heard him say come in, so when I found he wasn't there, I waited.

He looked at me as though I hadn't spoken. He said, "Do what I told you to do."

I did. I took my shirt off. I bent down and gripped my ankles.

"This is so you'll remember," he said, and he brought the belt down and the sharp buckle landed with a stinging pain across my back. Panic and helplessness raced wildly in my blood. I stood up straight and he kicked me in the back of the legs but I wouldn't go down again.

"Grab your ankles, boy," he said.

I stayed standing, and there was a pause, and I thought naively that

I had won, and that he was going to let me go with just that one blow. Then I felt the cold touch of steel below my left ear—his pistol.

"Boy," he said. "You have done me the favor of writing me a letter, and I will reward you with food. But you have come into my quarters when I was not here, and taken the liberty of kneeling down and praying to whatever nigger god you think you can pray to, and so now I am taking the liberty of striping your back—a liberty, by the way, that thousands of men have fought and died for."

I stayed standing.

"Do you hear me?" I heard him ask.

I did, but I didn't budge. I wasn't trying to be brave or even stubborn. I was curious, really. I only wanted to hear what he had to say, so I stood waiting and listening to the rain on the tent roof. The notion that this army was killing and dying for liberty—the liberty to beat other human beings—struck me as amusing.

"You smiling, boy?"

"No, suh," I said.

I heard the click as he cocked the pistol, then his voice, slow, clear. "If you do not bend over again, I will shoot you in the head and you will die without ever seeing the sun rise again. Do you hear me?"

Outside, lightning flashed, lighting the tent through the canvas, followed by an immediate explosion of thunder that startled me half out of my skin and just as suddenly ended my curious streak. I did what he said. I bent over and grabbed my ankles and waited. The next blow landed and my flesh stung as though someone were burning me with flame. The third landed and I didn't know how I would be able to endure any more. I believe I even began to whimper like a child, and I hated with more hate than I had ever hated. Yet whom did I hate? My tormentor, sure, but I hated myself even more. A fourth landed. Then and a fifth and sixth, each cutting a stripe out of my back with the sharp buckle. As terrible as it was, the pain was less humiliating than my willful crouching beneath his belt, my complicity. Staying crouched in order to live. To avoid getting shot. Was I even as brave as my tormentor? Did he crouch in order to avoid getting shot? No! In the heat of battle, I'd seen him ride back and forth, bullets and shells flying past him, as he waved his sword and urged his troops on. To be whipped was painful and humiliating, but to be whipped by somebody braver than you was the worst of it.

Suddenly I stood again and the whipping stopped. I turned to face my tormentor standing beneath the hanging lantern. In one hand he had the belt, the bloody buckle dangling beneath his fist. And in the other hand he held the pistol aimed at my eyes. Lightning flashed again, followed by another rip of thunder. Wind flapped the canvas and shook down a splatter of rain from the tree branches.

"Excuse me, suh," I said, "but I best be leaving."

"I'll shoot you," he said.

I do not know why I laughed. Perhaps you'll think I felt suddenly certain he was not going to kill me—or that when I looked into the depths of the pistol barrel I saw no fate more frightening than what I'd been living. But neither of those explanations would be accurate or true. For the second time in my life I walked away from a man pointing a pistol at me. I'd walked away from the men on the side of the road because of shame and stubbornness and anger. But I walked away from this man because I understood something in the perfect clarity of that second flash of lighting. I understood that I was alive. I understood that I might die at any moment. And I understood, in a way I'd never understood before, that I was free.

I walked away because I could.

The captain was breathing heavily, his face shiny with sweat, and it seems to me he even twisted slightly out of politeness to accommodate my passing, turned to watch me open the door, for suddenly I was standing shirtless and bloody in a light drizzle. That was when the first jolt of terror shot up my spine. I turned quickly, expecting to see the flash from his pistol, but instead I caught a glimpse of the captain, still gripping both the pistol and the belt, collapsed backward in exhaustion across his cot.

Then the door dropped shut and it was dark and I was alone. A combination of cold rain and burning pain, not to mention the crashing drop of whatever wild courage had driven me to do what I did, suddenly weakened my knees. I stumbled in the dark and fell. I picked myself up and stumbled again, but caught myself on another tent. "Hey!" came an angry voice from inside. I righted myself and wobbled off. Lightning ripped the sky so close I could smell it, and the thunder blast sent me reeling backward until I almost fell down again. Would have, probably, if I hadn't felt her, suddenly. First just the warmth of her body seemed to surround me, then her flesh, her thigh high against my shoulder so I leaned that way. "Mama?" *Stand up, child*, she said, and dangled her fingers in my filthy hair. *You'll be better soon*, she said, and then she began to sing a hymn I had long forgotten. I caught my balance against her but my breathing seized up as I began to sob. *Don't cry, Jimmy*, she said, and I only cried harder.

"I hate him," I hissed. "I hate all of them!"

She let her fingers move from my head to my neck and then gently washed the wounds with rain water. I was afraid to look up because I knew she wasn't there, couldn't be, certainly not so large. But I felt her, and I leaned on her, and I listened to her, and she helped me make it back through the rain and lightning to the lean-to where I slept with my companions.

THE WAY MY SLAVERY ended marked me and deserves to be told in some detail if the rest of my story is to make sense at all. Because even these years later, way out here on the wild belly of this continent, I have not been able to abandon completely the notion of civilized law—the notion of men and women aspiring to be divine. Indeed we all suffer and indeed we all going to die—so what else is there but despair unless we strive to find some meaning and dignity in it all? Some long-lost mother who can help you home on a cold, bloody night, and sing so beautifully of the Holy Ghost that you know in all of your painful bones that the Holy Ghost must be near.

It had been almost two years since my capture and it would be two more years until the end of the war, but one spring day the unit to which I had been assigned as property, after a week of retreating under relentless Yankee attacks, was finally overrun and scattered to the four winds.

We fled north in the rain. Saturn was sick, so I told Crow-boy to go on ahead while we took refuge in a barn, where we were discovered early the next morning by the farmer and his wife. They pressed pitchforks to our necks and locked us in a root cellar with shackles around our ankles. I had never worn shackles before, never felt their clamp and cut and weight on my flesh, and maybe it did something to my head. Or to more than that. To my sense of myself as a man. If I could have found something to cut with, I would have cut off my legs to free myself from the iron that bound me. But there was nothing but darkness and a line of daylight under the door, and so I sat holding Saturn and listening to him moan for water, and felt the earth groan as it was pummeled by shells. Something burned nearby, and the smoke burned our eyes and nostrils. Three days chained in the cellar. Three days hungry and thirsty and certain at any moment that the grumbling earth would swallow us whole, bury us alive, or cure us in smoke, chained in our grave. I went past terror, I'm sure. Terror is exhausting, and I bore as much of it as I could until I grew too tired to be afraid anymore. I sat and held Saturn's head and listened to him moan and held him because he was warm, and I was cold, and the sound of his moaning combined with my rocking put me in a trance that made the worst of my hunger and thirst bearable, or endurable. For I don't know that I *bore* anything—only endured. When the story I am going to tell you is told, you might believe I'm trying to excuse myself, trying to explain why the normal moral constraints of humanity did not apply to me. But in fact I'd argue that the normal moral constraints applied to me as strongly and clearly and truly as they might apply to anybody—and that it was precisely the remaining shreds of my humanity that allowed me to do what I would soon do.

I don't know. When you look back at your life, even if it is a short one, there are a lot of questions that you can only invent answers to. You can say, I am a monster, or you can invent a way in which your monstrous behavior could be looked at as human. Or you can do as I am trying to do, and say that monstrous *is* human and human *is* monstrous, among other things. And it is precisely the monstrous part of us that compels us to invent the notions of decency and civilization. A man who bought and sold human beings wrote that all men are created equal.

It started when I heard shooting at close range, and then Yankee voices shouting, and then, sure enough, the door of the cellar banged open, blinding me.

As my eyes adjusted, I saw the boots, and the dust motes in the light, and then I was pulled out, and stood blinking in the sun, the irons left on. Saturn, too, but he couldn't stand. I bent to lift him up, and struggled to get his arm around my shoulder, and like that we both stood.

The Yankee captain had dark brown eyes and a face that looked as if it had been squeezed in a vice when he was a child. Long and thin, a hatchet face, with whiskers hanging downward from his chin to his collar. He was with a group of maybe five or six Yankees wearing torn blue coats and blue hats and leather boots, which nobody in our army had worn in a while, unless of course they'd pulled them off a dead Yankee.

"Chained niggers?" the Yankee captain asked me, putting spaces between the words as if I were a foreigner.

I nodded. Maybe I couldn't talk. My tongue was swollen with thirst and I could barely keep my eyes open in the bright light. Saturn was in worse shape. He couldn't even nod. The fever had taken his mind, and I don't know how much he was even able to understand. The sun was very bright and hot, and the air reeked of unburied bodies. In the front yard of a mostly burned house sat a boy, eight or nine, and his little sister, maybe two.

"Fetch the niggers some water," the captain said, and the soldier standing with the boy poked him with his rifle, and the boy got up without changing expressions and went to a rain barrel and brought me over a gourd of cool water. I drank it carefully, holding it in my mouth for a long time before swallowing. My eyes watered with happiness. I finished the water and handed the empty gourd back to the boy, his hands white as milk and his expressionless, trying-to-be-brave face covered with freckles and smudged with dirt.

The Yankee captain spat, and then, as if performing the most intricate and delicate of maneuvers, he used the toe of his boot to tap the saliva into the dust.

"You know where the key to them chains is at?" he asked the boy.

"Yessir," the boy said, and one of the soldiers followed him into the barn. A moment later they came out with the key. The boy squatted and opened the lock on my right foot, pulled the chain through, and unclamped the shackle on each foot.

"You must have seen that done."

The boy stood up straight. "Put on and took off both," he said.

His little sister remained in the shade of the yard, but she was crying now because she was alone with the filthy soldier who wouldn't let her follow her brother.

"Them's your mama and papa?" The Yankee captain pointed to the two bloated bodies in the yard near the smoldering house.

"They is," the boy said. "Some Yanks come through a few days ago and kilt 'em. All the rebs is scattered."

"Who put these men in the cellar?" the captain asked.

The boy looked at me. His eyes were flat and gray and he had a serious expression—an old expression. No folly or longing. "I ain't never seen these niggers. Our'n run off some time ago."

"Who put you in the cellar?" the captain asked me.

I nodded toward the boy's dead parents.

The Yankee captain asked me what I'd been doing here. I pointed to the water gourd again, and was brought more water. I drank deeper this time and helped Saturn drink, too, but most of it spilled out of his mouth. I asked if we could sit, because Saturn couldn't stand without me holding him up. The captain nodded. I told him that until our regiment was scattered, our job among other things was to bury rebel soldiers.

The corners of the captain's mouth twitched. "Plenty work for you, then."

I sat and Saturn lay at my side in the shade, at least. I don't know how much he was aware of what was going on. He seemed pleased to get the shackles off his ankles, and he'd tried to drink from the water gourd, but that was about all he showed interest in. The wind picked up and sent a cloud of smoke past us from the smoldering house. A puffy cloud drifted along the length of the barn roof. In the mow, a dog started barking and was quickly shot. As loud and unexpected as the gunshot was, the little boy didn't even flinch. His sister kept crying on the lawn, saying *me-me* over and over again, and finally the boy turned and yelled, "Shut yer hole!" but she only cried louder.

The Yankee captain inhaled sharply through his teeth, and his mouth twitched again. When you have been under the absolute power of other men, you learn to study their every movement. You watch for the telltale dart of the eye, the barely turned hand. You look for signs that they are hatching something that will make your life more miserable.

He looked at me and considered something. I looked back and waited.

"This war kilt my daddy," the captain said, working the words over with his mouth and then letting each come out individually wrapped, so to speak. "And my brother," he said. "And my son. But I ain't feeling sorry, no sir, because I've done a lot of killing myself, lost count long ago, and now I don't know nothing else anymore. The Lord tells us to turn the other cheek, but that don't hardly make sense when rebs is shooting at you."

He looked at the boy, licked his lips, and then wiped his chin with the back of his hand. His eyes, past the dark of his cheek and under the dark of his hair, were strangely flat and calm. I remember thinking, Whatever he's going to do, he's already thought of it.

"Like I said," he continued, "the rebs took all I got and then some, and before it's over, they'll sure enough take me, too."

A murder of crows flew overhead and landed in the yard willow and on the ground next to the bodies. The little girl squealed as a few of them walked over on top of her parents. I waited. The captain squinted at the crows, at the girl, and then at me. I could tell he enjoyed the suspense he was creating. Even the little boy was listening.

"Get a shovel," the captain said to me, nodding at the dead bodies on the grass, "and do what you know how to do."

And so I did. I stood up and right there in the green lawn of what had been the big white house but was now simply a brick chimney rising out of a pile of smoking embers, I dug a grave. The smoke passed in welcome wisps that covered the smell of the three-day old corpses. Saturn lay in the shade, shivering, his eyes rolled back in their sockets. The little girl and the boy squatted next to him and watched me dig, and a soldier dozed so soundly behind them that flies crawled on his face.

"Got a blanket for my friend there?" I asked.

"Banks!" the captain yelled, and the soldier sleeping by the children woke up. "Fetch a blanket for the sick nigger," he said, and so Banks did. I watched as he went into the barn and came back with a wool horse blanket and laid it over Saturn, who didn't seem to notice.

I dug for hours and only paused long enough to drink more water from the gourd and eat two hard biscuits one of the soldiers brought me. The soil was soft with few rocks and I made good progress. The captain had disappeared while I was digging, but near dusk he reappeared next to me and took a look into the grave.

"Deep enough," he said, and looked me up and down.

I looked over at Saturn, who wasn't shivering anymore. He lay curled under the blanket, still as a rock. Banks, who was squatting next to him, noticed me looking and said, "He might be dead."

"Might be, or is?" the captain asked.

Banks felt Saturn's head and neck, then he stood up, tipped his hat back.

"Well?" the captain asked.

"Is," Banks said.

The captain looked at me with about as much emotion as if we'd been watching a horse eat hay. "Take the blanket back, then," he said.

Banks started to pull it off Saturn, but I said, "No, let him keep it."

The captain, Banks, and the boy all turned to look at me and I endured their curious gaze for a long time without speaking. Finally the captain nodded at Banks, who let go of the blanket, and sat down again in the shade.

Smoke from the house wafted between us and the captain lifted his hand sharply to point toward the bodies of the children's parents. "Throw them in there first," he said, and so I put the shovel down and walked over and pulled the bodies by their shoulders, one by one, and lowered them into the grave. The boy and the girl crept over and peered down to watch. The little girl had stopped crying hours ago. Her pink dress was torn and she held the fringe and sucked her thumb. The boy eyed me suspiciously.

"You gonna bury 'em?" he asked.

"That's what the captain wants," I said.

"They'd want that," the boy said.

"To be buried together?" I said.

"They fought day and night," he said. "Leastways now they's peaceful."

In the grave, the bodies lay stiffly on top of one another. I jumped in and arranged the woman on the man's chest, so they looked more comfortable. I climbed out of the grave and picked up the shovel and was about to start filling but the captain raised his hand to stop me.

"You want to be a free man?" the captain asked me.

"I am a free man," I said, surprising even myself.

His brown eyes narrowed. "You told me you been a slave."

I rested on my shovel. "I am a free man who was enslaved by the Army of Northern Virginia," I said. "I haven't been a slave since I was seven, when my father freed me."

He blinked, and again his mouth twitched—a smile? He made me stand there for a long time before he said, "Okay, *free man,* or whatever you are, I found you in a cellar with chains on, ain't that correct?"

I said it was.

"And them chains ain't on you now, are they?"

I said they were not, and I was grateful for that.

Smoke from the embers drifted between us and the captain's nostrils flared. "I never owned your kind," he said. "And until this war started, I never saw more than one of you my entire life. He poled upriver and got off at the landing and came by the lane into town and I thought he looked like a walking turd."

He let that sit for a minute, watching me, but I waited while he swallowed and then finally continued. "Then this here war starts and I have to fight and kill and lose everything I ever held precious so your kind can go free. My mama used to tell me, *Sterling Joseph, now don't you run off and be bitter. You get back here and give your mama a hug.*" He spat and again pressed it delicately into the dust with the toe of his boot, pulled his boot back, narrowed his eyes and considered for a moment his work.

"Daddy had a little store and little farm, and I did my share on those places, but I was the only man I knew who taught his own self to read, and so in the evening I taught my neighbors, too. I try to keep my hand in teaching. These boys I been fighting with'll tell you I'm always thinking of ways we can learn. Learning's what's kept us alive so far. I'm not saying it'll save us."

Here he paused and nodded toward Saturn, who still looked to me as though he were asleep. Past his body, across the darkening field beyond, a sweeping cloud in the west had turned purple, and the thin line on the horizon held the last pink and red of the day. I leaned on my shovel and breathed quietly and recalled the weight of Saturn's head on my lap as I'd held him shivering in the dark of the cellar.

"So before you go wandering off without your chains, *free man*," he said, "I want you to get a little bit of the feeling. I mean, there's been lots of killing, and I been doing my share, that's for sure."

At that the captain blinked again, and one corner of his mouth turned up, and suddenly I realized that hissing inhalation was his laugh. That quirky little joyless expression, accompanied by a sharp breath and absolutely nothing but flatness in his eyes. I leaned on my shovel and inhaled the smoke from the smoldering house and I knew something was going to happen, but I figured it would be something miserable, something that would pass. I was wrong, and since then I've come to understand that evil announces itself in such gestures of banality as that flat little laugh. Human gestures that say, *This is all quite normal—just like any other day.* Which is true, because what I am going to describe does happen every day, somewhere. When it happens where you are—when you actually participate—it is tempting to look up at the heavens and feel as if you have been misled—both about the nature of the world and the nature of yourself.

But if you are honest you know you have not been misled by anybody except yourself. Not really. Ever since you were a child and imagined monsters, you knew there were monsters. Natural as breathing, common as birdsong, close as your own skin. I heard whippoorwills in the trees, peepers down by the creek. Darkness had come on heavy now, the stars were out, and the orange and red embers glowed under the burned wreckage of the house.

I coughed in the smoke and the captain waited until I finished before he asked, "You saw the way that little boy already knew where the key to open the shackles was kept?"

I nodded, leaned on my shovel.

"And so if that boy already knows how to unlock them, don't you suppose he also knows how to lock them up again?"

I said I supposed he did.

"Well, then, I'm going to make you a proposition, *free man*," he said. "The way I see it you got a choice—a choice like any other living free man. Which is more than I got, because I'm in this here army and I'm already dead. The lead ball that's gonna kill me has already been made and is being toted by some reb right now as we speak. I'm a dead man and I can't help no more what I'm bound to do, but you're still living and so I'm asking you if you want to walk away from here without your chains on, or you want to go back in the cellar like we found you and your dead friend?"

I said I wanted to walk away.

"Because this here boy can put them chains back on as easily as take them off, can't you, boy?"

The boy looked at me. He sat on the edge of the grave with his sister's head in his lap. His eyes were wide and scared, but when he heard the captain talking about him, he looked up and nodded.

"See, that's the problem," the captain said, shaking his head. "That's 'actly the problem. It means the germ of sin is deep, and that little girl with her head on his lap, she's seen it all, too, and she too knows how to lock up another human being, and that's not the kind of thing anybody has a right to know. Because that's the kind of thing that took my pa's life, and my brother's life, and my own boy's life, and before this war is over it'll take my life, too."

The girl stopped crying and lifted her head and blinked her shiny eyes. The breeze had changed and the smoke from the house got heavier and she coughed. I dared to look at the captain in the reflected light from the glowing red embers. His hatchet face contracted as though he were about to cough, too, but he shook off the urge.

"Oh, I hate 'em," the captain said. "More than a person oughta hate anything. But there it is. I do hate 'em. The little ones just like the big ones. I hate how they made us fight, and they made us fight for you people, who we never did care nothing for. Who I never did one thing for or against. So I'm askin' you, *free man.* I've done my part for you and your people. Now you do your part for me."

I looked at the children at the edge of the grave and I listened to the crickets and the little girl began to cry again.

"Hardy!" the captain called to the soldier nearest to the little girl. "Grab that girl."

Hardy stood up and grabbed the girl by the back of the pink dress, and she squealed and screamed, and he held her like that, dangling from his big hand, kicking and screaming, and stood next to the grave.

"Toss her in," the captain said.

Hardy did, and she disappeared into the grave with a little squeal and the scuffing sound of her body landing on the corpses of her parents.

"Now the boy."

Hardy had to chase the boy, but he got him and held him by his shirt while the boy silently windmilled his fists.

"Little reb," the captain said, as though mildly entertained by the boy's futile fight.

The girl in the grave said *me-me* again, and I realized she was trying to say *Jimmy,* and that was the boy's name. *Me-me.* Jimmy. He suddenly stopped fighting. Hardy lifted him and dropped him into the grave, where he scurried up next to his sister and the two of them squatted next to their dead parents' heads.

"Start shoveling, *free man,*" the captain said, and I felt Banks's gun touch my back and quickly withdraw. Still I almost lost my balance in my terror. I could hear the breathing of the whimpering children in the hole. I looked up at the stars and closed my eyes and tried to feel their cold light on my face, but again I felt the gun barrel touch my back. Very gently, like a kiss, it sent waves of feeling down my body through my legs and feet, and then back up, exploding the top of my skull.

"Bury them dead parents and them two live young'uns or Banks'll have to shoot 'em both and Hardy'll have to bury the whole family, but not before we drag that boy out again and make him lock you back up in the cellar with your dead friend. Do this last order from a white man with a gun, and as far as me and Mr. Lincoln are concerned, you won't be a free man chained up starving to death in a cellar and thinking about eating your friend, but a free man walking."

Even as I listened to his words I felt a numbness growing. I looked at Saturn lying dead with the blanket over him under a tree as though asleep and tried to remember holding his head on my lap and tried to remember his animated face and the sound of his laughter but could not.

"A bitter choice," the captain said behind me. "But a clear one."

As clear as the sky—and to this day I don't know if I spoke the words, or if I heard the captain say them to me, but the next thing I heard was that sharp inhalation that was the captain's laugh as my shovel blade sliced the soil under my foot. I felt the smooth handle in my hands, and the weight of the earth as I lifted the shovelful, and I heard the sound of the falling earth on the bodies, and the children's whimpering grew louder. I imagined the boy still holding his sister's head in his lap but I didn't look. I threw dirt into the other side of the grave as though I hadn't really made my choice. Yet I had, indeed I had. And it wasn't the gun aimed at my back that had made the choice for me, either. I had already walked away from two white men aiming guns at me, and although I don't believe I would have survived this time, I knew I was a free man and I could do as I pleased. So I did. I looked at my dead friend under a blanket, and I thought about the feel of the shackles around my ankles, and I threw another shovelful, and another, and then suddenly the whimpering in the grave turned to a scrambling and shrieking, and Banks jumped down into the grave with the struggling children. I turned away for a moment while he did something that caused him to cuss viciously and then the children to get quiet. I could hear that, how quiet they were. I listened very carefully for their breathing as I tossed in another shovelful, and another. I tossed in more soil and rocks, and except for the sound of me working I could have sworn it was as silent as a Virginia night ever gets in June. The whippoorwills, the peepers, the crickets. And the sound of my breathing, my shovel, my heart. For some reason I was paying close attention to the sound of my heart, which again felt broken to me. But what could that mean? *Felt broken?* It must have been whole enough, for I filled that grave as fast as I could.

Hardy and Banks had retreated into the shadows but the Yankee captain stood behind me and I could feel his eyes on my every move. In some ways I can still feel him there. Maybe I should blame him for giving me such an evil choice, but I don't. His logic was infallible—if he had to kill so that I could be free, why shouldn't I? And at least he was still curious, even after all he'd been through, still looking for something to feel. I could hear him behind me and wondered if watching this horror he'd devised gave him something to grieve. Who knows? The grave was silent and the children dead and it was too dark to see any tears. I know I didn't shed any. Not until quite a while later—and then, as too often is the case, I couldn't be sure I wasn't crying for myself.

"Jimmy," I said when I finished burying the family. I was alone and I stood for a moment over the grave under a clear sky bright with stars.

"Jimmy," I said again.

I was thirsty so I walked to the rain barrel and dipped the gourd and drank. I stared for a while at the still red embers glowing under the ashes of the house, and then back at the eastern sky, where I could see the crescent moon beginning to rise. The Yankees had all gone to sleep in the dark barn. I considered setting it on fire but was already feeling sick from the smoke from the house. The water tasted cool, and good, and helped wash the ash taste from my mouth.

My stomach growled and I wondered when I'd eat again. I wondered when I'd be able to sleep. And then I didn't wonder anymore. I walked back across the yard and picked up my shovel and began to dig one more grave for Saturn. By midmorning I was finished.

"Saturn," I said, tamping down the black soil on his grave. For some reason now I could recall his laugh but not his face. I closed my eyes but saw only darkness.

"Saturn," I said again.

I dropped the shovel there and stepped carefully around the children's grave, keeping my eyes on the gray sky above the barn. The Yankees had cleared out hours ago but they'd left me some hard biscuits and salt pork next to the rain barrel. I ate myself full and drank deeply from the water gourd, and although I wanted nothing more than to lie down and sleep, I forced myself to walk away. I put the smoldering house and cursed graves behind me and crossed a trampled cornfield into the shade of a grazed woodlot.

Free man walking, I said to myself, disappearing for a time into the forest.

BOOK TWO

. . . Me miserable! Which way shall I fly
Infinite wrath and infinite despair?
—John Milton, *Paradise Lost*

GOLD

MY JOURNEY THAT BEGAN over a freshly filled grave in a Virginia farmyard might have taken me anywhere. I was, as you might imagine, an ambivalent free man—my own master, certainly, but not necessarily one I cared to serve. The Union was using Negro soldiers by then, so I was free to fight as either the son of my mother or, if I cut my hair and cleaned myself up, the son of my father. I chose neither.

If my shackles were gone, so were my illusions. The sword, I now knew, would not make the world a better place—only a bloodier one. And in the wake of this war, finding my mother seemed ludicrous and painful. Ludicrous because of the luck that would be required to find her moving in endless streams of refugees from one unknown place to another. And painful because after all I'd been through, after what I'd just done to those two children, what would I say to her when I put my arms around her and felt hers around me? How could I look her in the eye?

I took a new name, Freeman Walker. It was the name of the experience—the name of my choice to avoid shackles. As Freeman Walker, I walked away. If freedom had given me no other options, it had given me this one. I was free to take the next step. And the next. And although night had me lying in the palm of the past, gazing at shiny eyes staring downward from heaven or upward from the grave, sunrise seduced me onward into the future.

But what good is freedom without hope or purpose? I wasn't sure. I didn't know. I couldn't think about it. I'd find out.

I walked north with remnants of grief-stricken farm families stumbling away from their burned fields, with deserters and former slaves, eyes glazed with fatigue and hunger, moving relentlessly through gullies and along the edges of forests. We filled the rural pikes and spilled into the streets of northern cities. We crowded inns and markets and saloons and whorehouses. Everyone a traveler, we breathed each other's air, used each other's words, and saw the same sky and land and light. We absorbed enough of each other so that even our deepest wounds began to merge into the one big shared story of suffering and endurance.

We all suffer. We are all going to die.

We were the chaff of a harvest bigger than any of us had ever imagined. We were dust drifting in a gale. We were men and women walking of our own accord from a place we didn't know anymore toward a place we'd never been.

We are not in control. We are free.

Within minutes of leaving that Virginia farm, a knee-high black-and-white cow dog started following me. I'd never been fond of dogs. Perhaps not since as a toddler I'd seen that slave mauled on the porch of the house at Sweet Grass. I knew what dogs did to bodies on the battlefield, too, and so thought of them as slinking vultures. For a day or two I ignored this one, hoping he'd go away, but whenever I'd turn, there he'd be, about ten steps back. His panting face grinned like a fool's; his long-haired tail looped up like feathers in the hat of a French swordsman. I'd stop, he'd stop. I'd walk, he'd walk. I'd yell at him to go away, he'd stand still and turn his head slightly to the side as though he were listening to something else. I wondered if he was mad, and suspected hunger would drive him to steal from me if I had anything to steal. I slept uncomfortably, knowing he was out there. In the morning I'd see him looking at me from a distance. I'd throw rocks at him, but he'd only scurry to the side, loop back around, and look at me again, his eyes beckoning before he looked to the side and pretended to be interested in anything but me.

After about a week of being followed and trying in vain to scare him off, I tried again to ignore him. I walked through a thick forest all day without once looking back. My hope was that he'd grow bored and move on, and maybe he would have if before lying down to sleep that evening curiosity hadn't gotten the best of me.

I didn't see him at first. I was on the edge of a blond meadow now darkened by the shadows of dusk, and it seemed suddenly immense, and empty, and I was alone. Where could he have gone? Rather than relief when I couldn't see him, I felt oddly panicked. I stepped up onto a log so I could see better in the dying light, and I looked this way and that way, and just when I began to feel my heart heavy with new loneliness, I saw him again. He was sitting about fifty feet away in the tall grass, his pink tongue hanging out the side of his mouth, and his sparkling eyes—one pale blue and one brown. When he saw me looking at him, he quickly looked away. And then, as if to show me where he was going to stay the night, he walked slowly toward a bush, turned a few tight circles, and curled up to sleep.

The next morning, when I got up, he was sitting in the same place where he'd slept, watching and waiting. His unmatched eyes blinked good-morning.

That day I relented and stopped shouting at him, or throwing stones, and that evening I tossed him the bones of a partridge I'd managed to kill with a stick. He wouldn't come near me. Or the bones. I had to back away a good ten steps before he'd even approach the food, and then he walked toward it very slowly and stood over it and looked from side to side but not at it. Only when I turned and pretended to be occupied with something else did he deign to eat.

Soon he was walking at my heels, and then at my side, and whatever food I had I shared with him, and whatever warmth he had on a chilly night he shared with me, and for the first time in my life I was the beneficiary of a dog's love—which like God's is unearned, and therefore full of grace. The difference is that while we suppose God cares if we've buried living children, a dog, we know, does not.

BUT MAYBE GOD DOESN'T care, either. Because one evening during our first week together, Dog and I straggled hungrily upon a deserted farmstead at night. There were no livestock outside and the fallow fields were choked with weeds. I found an ax outside the door and stepped inside holding it high. We searched the house just to be certain we were alone, and then we sat on the floor together and by the light of the full moon through a broken kitchen window feasted on old ham and moldy cheese. Or I did. Dog took his chunk of ham back around the corner into the dark pantry. When I was full I followed him to see what more food there was to carry. In the dark I filled a gunnysack with potatoes from a hamper against the back wall and hefted the bag over my shoulder. The ham and cheese filled my stomach but gave me a craving for water. Dog, crowded by me in the pantry, got up to carry his ham to some other place, and suddenly he was under my feet in the dark and I tripped on him. I reached and grabbed a shelf, but heavy with the potatoes over my shoulder I fell anyway, pulling the shelf and everything that was on it down with me. Pots and pans clattered on the floor, as did chunks of plaster from the wall. I took the full impact of the fall on my elbow and I rolled onto my back, writhing in pain. When I managed to sit up, half in the kitchen and half out, I could see that I was surrounded by potatoes from my sack, pots and pans from the shelf, bits of plaster from the wall, and something else that gleamed in the sweep of moonlight across the floor. Coins? I slid out my hand and gathered a few of them, picked one up and held it close but couldn't see clearly what it was. My hand started shaking anyway, and I remember I steadied it by doing something Mr. Perry had taught me to do when robbing the dead. I bit down on the coin. I remember the taste of metal and the way saliva filled my mouth and the slight give of the gold between my teeth. I swept my hands around me on the floor and gathered more. More than my shaking hands could hold, so I started putting them in the sack with the potatoes.

My elbow throbbed. I paused and listened. An owl hooted outside the house. I thought I heard a floorboard creak. I did hear a floorboard creak, and suddenly my stomach was in my throat. I spun around and saw Dog by the stove, settling with his hunk of ham.

I filled my sack and started to get up, but when I pushed up with my sore arm, I lost my balance again under the weight and stumbled and dropped the sack and a half-dozen potatoes rolled out across the floor. I wanted to flee right then, but forced myself to stay still for an-other moment and listen. I felt sure there was somebody else in the house. Ghosts, probably. I could hear breathing, and I thought of the children in their graves, and I was afraid it might be them. Yet as I lis-tened carefully, all I heard for sure was my own breathing, my own heartbeat.

I lowered myself to my knees, gathered the potatoes as though they were the last of the coins, and carefully this time swung the sack over my shoulder before fleeing into the bright night.

SO EITHER GOD DIDN'T care what I'd done, or after watching me suffer through some bad years, He simply figured I was due. That was what *I* thought, anyway, as I sprinted across that moonlit yard with a sack of treasure bouncing on my shoulder. We create our Creator to accord with our own circumstance, don't we? When we want justice, we make God just. And when we want mercy, we make Him merciful, too.

I thought of the Yankee captain and his God of experience. The way we would come together, he seemed to be saying—the way we would finally be equal was for me to feel what he felt, for me to know what he knew.

Yet he hadn't volunteered to feel my shackles on his ankles, had he?

No, but he had volunteered to die. All men are created equal, endowed by their Creator with a tendency to kill and to die. . . .

Oh, the mystery! Sometimes it was enough to weaken my legs. Luckily I suddenly had so much money that I didn't need theology for long. Freeman Walker was not only a free man, but a rich one. I was a free man walking with gold in my pockets and a dog at my side. For the first time in two years I was free from want, free from hunger and physical misery. I had a new suit made for me in Washington, got my hair cut short, and wore a *civ'lized* new top hat tipped at a jaunty angle. I could have ridden in carriages or trains, but like my father I preferred to walk, and so walk I did, tarrying at every roadhouse and buying drinks and meals for my fellow travelers. And plenty for myself as well. I was in Philadelphia during the battle of Gettysburg, but I was drunk for those three days, and the news of another battle, no matter the scope, was not news. The Army of Northern Virginia was moving south again, and that was the news.

I went north again, feeling freer with every step. I was richer than I had ever been except when I had come to America to buy my mother and set her free. Yet I felt freer now because I had no such goal. Without the weight of that ambition, I could do anything, go anywhere.

In New York City, recently ravaged by riots and the bloody killings of dozens of Negroes, I rented a room and blithely walked each day through the crowded bar districts, eating and drinking and dancing myself into joyful oblivion. I read in the paper that Colonel O'Keefe had not only survived the massacre of his Irish brigade but was in the city recruiting volunteers to form another. For a fleeting moment I considered going to hear him speak—what could he possibly say to get men to follow him into the slaughter of the war? I couldn't imagine. Still, I might have gone, for a flicker of curiosity about him remained. . . . Then a companion grabbed my arm and off we went to the taverns instead.

But my fortune was not a true fortune and soon it began to run low. After such a spree, I didn't like the feel of my lightened pockets. Gold had given me wings that had lifted me for those short weeks beyond race, beyond history, free from sorrow, free from care, free from my earthly wants and sins toward the heat of the sun. I determined I would use what I had left to accumulate more than I could ever spend. The newspapers were full of reports of a massive gold strike in the Great Western Territory, so I used most of the money I had left to buy passage on a ship to San Francisco. I tried to hold myself together during the two weeks until the ship's departure by concentrating on all the gold I'd dig from the mountains of the West, but without the diversion of spending money, the nights were too quiet and lonely. Freedom without purpose or hope was bearable—but only with distraction. And suddenly I was too often alone. Sometimes I thought about my mother, where she might be, and in order to console myself for not looking for her, I reasoned that she no longer needed my heroics. Since the Emancipation Proclamation, she could no longer be bought, and she was already free.

I walked on broken sidewalks past broken buildings. I stepped through the rivers of sewage in the street and through swarms of tiny insects that descended in the evening and made me wave my hands in front of my face to keep from breathing them. Block after block through open windows I heard the endless coughing of children, little lungs gasping for air, and I began to hear something else, too. One night it seemed to approach from the side and fall in just behind me. I heard its ragged breathing and turned, and Dog turned, too. I looked for the source of the sound and Dog stood patiently with his pink tongue hanging out and his eyes laughing. Could he hear it, too? The last breaths of dying children?

I covered my ears as I walked but still heard the little girl say *me-me* again. Heard them both struggle to escape their grave.

Suddenly I wanted to toss myself under a trolley or carriage. To run screaming up a stairway to the top of a building and jump off. I remembered the attraction of the freezing Thames after I received the news that my mother had been sold. But that felt like fleeing, like an unseen hand driving me, while this felt more like one pulling me—gleefully!—toward my own silent death.

It took all of my strength to resist and make it back to my room that night, where I lay alone in the dark and listened to a church bell toll down the block. Then silence. And then as clear as that bell, I heard the breathing again, heard what I'd refused to hear that night in Virginia. The gasping sounds of children dying underground.

Desperate, I dashed out of my room and around the corner into a stairwell, intending to climb to the roof for one last escape. But running full speed in the dark stairway, I collided with a wiry young woman as black as the night. She fell, bumping her head on the stairs. I helped her up, and then back to her room.

I know there are plenty of respectable people who would never believe something good could visit the union of a murderer and a prostitute, and perhaps you won't believe it either. Nevertheless, in those last days waiting for the ship, in a tiny end room in a row of rooms tucked up a muddy alley not far from the East River, on a filthy mattress we shared with insects of all kinds, biting and otherwise, a candle burning only rarely, Junie offered a glimpse of goodness. And it was close, and I hope to think it warmed both of us.

She saw the scars on my back and I saw how any quick movement of my hands caused her to flinch, and besides the gold coins I gave her—and when they ran out, I gave her my dog—that was all we needed from one another. Over and over we mingled our bodies, and in all those many times she reflected back to me no disgust or even exhaustion. Perhaps I was simply missing it. I do know that she treated me with kindness—so much in fact that I couldn't fully feel it until I was away from her on the ship heading south. The sky early one morning grew pale blue from horizon to horizon, and I felt the warm breeze on my skin, and I thought I could smell her skin again in the air. For the second time in my short life—since my first acquaintance with suicidal despair on the banks of the Thames—a woman had saved me from self-destruction. That they both happened to be prostitutes seemed as relevant and incomprehensible as rest of the mysteries with which I had become acquainted. All I knew was that if it had not been for Junie, for her ink-black eyes and plum-blue skin, for the honey feel of her mouth, for the sour smell of her sweat and earth smell of her sex, I would not have lived the last days I needed to live before I got on the ship and sailed away. The demons would have grabbed me. Even if I had managed to keep myself from jumping off the roof of the building the night I met her—without motion, and with little treasure left to spend—the emptiness in waiting would have swallowed me whole.

YET EVEN ON BOARD SHIP, sailing south, the furies followed. I avoided the heat and torment of my cabin by rising early and walking on deck. Except to take breaks for necessities, I walked on through the heat of the afternoon and into the evening, and sometimes late into the night. From bow to stern and back again, from beam to beam. I knew if I went back to my cabin too soon, before exhaustion promised immediate sleep, my night would be haunted. With ghosts of battle. Smells of the root cellar and the cut of shackles. And worst of all, silence—because in silence I heard nothing but my own breathing, which quickly became the intolerable gasps of Jimmy and his sister in their grave. More than once I ran up to the deck in the middle of the night fully determined to toss myself overboard, but by the time I felt the air on my face, heard the waves and the sails flapping overhead, the strain of the mast, before I took those few steps to the rail, I lost the urgency and turned. I slowed, and began to pace again—for hours, until exhaustion overtook me.

Such episodes left me shaken and uncertain. For although I might have been able to save myself that night . . . what about the next?

One evening while walking back and forth on the deck, I passed a man who stood by the starboard rail and gazed out at the horizon. He was dressed well—a black overcoat, *civilized* boots, *civilized* hat—but seemed unusually agitated. He kept shifting his weight from one foot to the other, and he gripped the rail with such intensity he might have been trying to break it off.

As I passed him, he said, "Sir," and I paused. He turned slightly, as though he hadn't seen me, and perhaps wasn't even speaking to me. But there I was. Stopped, waiting. He cleared his throat.

"Would you happen to have a light?" he asked.

I did, and I waited as he withdrew his pipe from his pocket and filled the bowl with tobacco. His hands were shaking terribly. I lit a match and held it to his pipe. The seas were fair, and we eyed each other. He was a white man, and although my hat had blown off the first evening on the ship, my hair was still short and my skin paler after my weeks in New York.

I was about to resume walking when he said, "Stay with me here a moment, will you?"

He wasn't looking at me when he spoke. He was facing out at the sea again, his top hat pulled low over his forehead and the tops of his ears in order to keep it on in the wind. He held the pipe stem between his teeth and kept his hands on the rail so they were no longer shaking.

"Certainly," I said. I put my own hands on the rail to hold myself steady. The sun had set, and the fair colors darkened, and just now the first star appeared. The man moved closer to me, and without speaking slid his hand along the wooden rail until it was just inches from mine. And then his hand, the side of it, was touching mine. I didn't know what to do. I hesitated, and then I slid my hand away, but only slightly. He moved his until the side of it touched mine again. All this time we were looking out at the darkening sea. The wind had picked up and behind us sailors shouted orders at one another.

I kept my hand still for as long as I could stand it. I could hear the man breathing—he was my age, but he sounded old. I could smell his unbathed flesh. From our position there at the rail, it seemed I could see the edge of the world. I could feel its immensity spreading out in all directions bigger than my mind could hold. And it was all outside me, all out there—except the one square inch in that universe where the side of his hand touched mine.

I held on like that for as long as I could, and then I stepped away from him.

The next night he was there again. I did not want to stop and talk to him, but I did. I think perhaps I was just very lonely and tired of my fear of the rail—of jumping over the rail—fear I'd forgotten about yesterday. As awkward as that moment had been, the distraction had been a relief from my own madness.

I stood next to him and we both looked out to sea. The waves were bigger today, the wind harder. We both held the rail but he did not touch my hand today. He did not move it near. Without looking, he simply said, "Circumstances pushed me to this end, but I had a good mother."

I did not know how to respond to that. I didn't have to. He continued, "She shucked corn, spun and wove wool, knitted stockings and caps, sewed clothes, and made shoes. She made soap from lye and candles from tallow and beeswax and every year, with magnificent regularity, she gave birth to a child. I was the last one, and she didn't live long enough to care for me, so I was raised from the time I was six by my brothers and sisters. When the war started, I was happy and grateful to light out for glory like everybody else."

A long pause followed this little speech—or accounting. The higher seas had made me a little sick to my stomach and I was afraid, briefly, that my response to whatever he said might be to vomit. Out of the corner of my eye I watched him lift his hand and, shaking, strike a match in a vain attempt to light his pipe. I watched him try three or four times before I turned to help him and used my hands to shield the wind. The light turned his face yellow.

"Heading out to the gold mines, then?" I said.

"Turns out," he said, finishing his story, "I didn't much care for glory."

He smoked his pipe, and savored it especially. When he inhaled, the coal lit his face, and for just that moment he seemed to relax. He held the smoke in his lungs and then exhaled. Although I was not a smoker, I envied him the pleasure he seemed to be taking. We stood side by side until it was completely dark, and then, when his pipe was out, and I was ready again to resume my walking, he bent over and took off his boots. First one, then the other—tall black boots, good leather. He handed each boot to me as he removed it. Then he took off his top hat and overcoat and handed them to me, too.

"These are fine pieces of clothing," he said. "As fine as I've ever owned in my life."

He stood only in his black pantaloons and his white cotton shirt. The wind picked up and swept his hair back off his forehead, which had a long dark scar along the hairline. With my arms full of his clothing, perhaps I should have anticipated what came next. But I watched him with more curiosity than anticipation as he lifted one leg over the rail, then the other.

"Put on the hat," he said, and I did. He looked at me approvingly. "It's been a pleasure," he said, and before I could answer, before I could drop the boots and jacket and attempt to grab him, he vanished overboard. Dropped out of sight. No yell, no sound except the splash. When I looked over the rail at the churning sea, I saw his arm as white as a fish belly lift once above the surface and then slip out of sight for good.

I yelled, "Man overboard!" I yelled until I'd gathered a crowd. I held out his boots and jacket as proof. I pointed to the spot where he would have gone down, even as it got farther and farther away, even as we turned the big ship back, I kept pointing. But a single spot is hard to be sure of on the moving surface of the sea, most especially at night, and by the time we'd doubled back, I wasn't sure anymore where it was he had been. I knew only what everyone else gathered on the rail could clearly see—wherever he'd been, he was not there now.

From that moment on and for the rest of the voyage—although still haunted by the silence of my cabin, still driven to pace the deck—I had one new certainty: I knew I would not throw myself overboard if I happened to pause. My unnamed friend had done it for me.

AND I HAD STILL more helpers along the way. In San Francisco— a city so cold and foggy I barely saw it during the week I was there—a maiden lady wearing a short gray wool skirt, high-laced boots, white stockings, and large straw hat begged to join our group of immigrants preparing to traipse across a thousand miles of mountains and desert to a booming little gold camp in the heart of the Rockies that had become known as Last Best Chance City.

Her purpose, she told us outright, was to find a mate. All we needed to know was could she walk? Could she work? She could, and more, apparently, for she found a husband from our group shortly after her arrival, and they married just two weeks into our journey. Francis Smith, the groom, owned a wagon and team of oxen, and the newlyweds went into the wagon for private sleeping arrangements. A few hours later the adults in camp surrounded the wagon, the women on the tongue and the men pushing behind, and we drove it well out ahead on the trail, a half mile, almost, and left it there, retreating back toward camp shouting and singing and skipping.

Sometimes I still think of the couple in the wagon, the wild ride, the voices close through the canvas, and then the wagon stopping, finally, and the sound of our voices retreating fainter and fainter, and then growing quiet completely. I like to think they clung to each other for dear life, surrounded by so much silence and space and darkness. I like to think they were brave and joyous on that night.

Because less than a month after her Sierra wedding, while we all stood waiting for a ferry raft to cross a river, deliver its cargo, and then shuttle back for more of us—back and forth all day—the bride stood with seven women and me, and she pointed at the tiny ferry on the big blue river, and she said, "See that man with the red hat on? With our wagon on the raft? Well, that is Mr. Smith, my husband!"

We all knew who her husband was, and so I assume she was thinking out loud, trying to put into words and make real what had happened to her so quickly and appeared to have brought her so much happiness.

But just then, just as she said it, just as all of our eyes located the red hat bobbing downstream on the distant raft, the raft struck a snag, tipped, and turned under. That fast. As fast as it takes to read these words. There was the red hat—a dot on the blue sky and blue water— and then there was nothing. We watched the water for what seemed like minutes waiting for the hat to come up again, for something red to pop up to the surface. We ran downstream and stood and watched and watched but Mr. Smith never reappeared. Mrs. Smith continued to search the river surface with her eyes wide and unbelieving. Almost smiling, but with both panic and horror just below the surface of her voice, she said, "He was right out there, was he not?"

"He was," I said, for she was holding my arm.

"I saw his red hat!"

"You did," I said, scanning the unendingly blue stretch of water. Others were fanning out even farther downstream, but there was no sign of him or his hat. The raft and wagon had gone under a sweeper and he, perhaps, was trapped there, too.

"Just a moment ago," she said. "We all saw him."

"Yes," I said.

"You saw him, didn't you?" she said, and squeezed my arm so tightly I had to resist the impulse to pull away.

"I did," I said. "I saw him. He was right there."

———————

SO I AVOIDED SINKING by watching others do it for me. And I kept my balance by watching others do that, too. For just a half day from the river where Mrs. Smith had gripped my arm so tightly, we came upon a woman standing by a fresh grave. Mrs. Warner wore a red calico frock, a pair of moccasins of black buffalo hide, and a hat of braided bullrushes trimmed with white, red, and pink ribbon. It was as though, lacking black, she'd dressed up in her fanciest clothes to bury her husband, whom she'd lost to cholera after just six hours' illness. She still had five sons and a daughter—the oldest but fifteen years of age and the youngest a nursing babe of six months—all packed into one wagon with numerous boxes of tea, which I assume she meant to sell in the mining camp. We invited her to join our group that afternoon, and she nodded with slow dignity and said, *Much obliged,* and sat up on the wagon seat, took the reins in hand, her knees spread under her dress, and clucked her tongue to get the oxen started.

I walked alongside her for a while. She said she'd never driven the wagon before, and I told her she looked like a natural teamster. She paused at the compliment and looked me over. It wasn't exactly true. What she looked like was a long-legged, featherless hen. With her nostrils pinched close together and her eyes hardened to keep the grief and fear from spilling out, she did a fair imitation of somebody else. Of anybody else. Just like the rest of us. Which was good enough to keep the wheels rolling and the children alive. Good enough to keep under her skin whatever wild beans jumped crazy in her blood.

"You look like a Negro," she said.

I told her I was half, and she nodded, glanced from one eye to the other, pursed her lips and said, "From that side, it's plain."

After a few days, the recently widowed Mrs. Smith joined the recently widowed Mrs. Warner on the wagon seat, and together they traveled toward Last Best Chance City. And except for the fact that Mrs. Smith was younger, they took on the same look and were often mistaken for sisters.

WHEN CHOLERA HIT OUR GROUP, I avoided digging graves. I panicked at even the idea of standing next to an open grave with a shovel in my hand, much less lowering the body or, God forbid, filling the grave again. Nevertheless, some men had to do it, so while I tended livestock or cut and hauled wood for fire, I'd watch them tromp off with shovels over their shoulders, the bravest of the brave. Exhausted after a day of travel, they'd find a place near camp and dig as deep as they could in that rocky soil, as deep as they had the hands and back to dig. One, two, sometimes three a night. They used no markers, as everybody knew we'd never return for a visit on this immense plain, and we were told the natives would dig up the corpses to steal clothes.

One night we camped on the edge of a wide, deep river, across a shallow creek from a camp of natives. We'd sent part of our group upstream and part downstream to look for a place to ford or enough timber to build a ferry. A few of us who were left waded the creek to visit some of the filthiest human beings I had ever seen. Not only did their skin and hair appear as if they had not bathed in a year, they were gathering a meal of some of the strangest things I'd ever seen eaten. I'd heard that natives ate the raw organs of their prey, but these were eating grasshoppers, and I even saw an old woman turn over a rock, pluck up a white grub and swallow it with as much relish as if it had been a juicy dumpling.

Apparently they'd been hit by cholera as well, because they were preparing a funeral. And for the first time in my life that evening I witnessed the cremation of a corpse, which despite my own private torment still seemed an improper way to dispose of a body. While the fire was being lit, the widow screeched in a frenzy, twisting her body, spinning round and round. Then she crawled to the fire and daubed her face and hair with pitch and cut her bare breasts with a knife so the blood ran in streams down her belly. After that, she commenced to howl, spin, and howl some more. As distressing as this was at first, eventually it became downright monotonous, and I crossed the creek back to our camp.

That night I lay down to sleep but couldn't for the keening that went on until morning. Our scouting parties did not return the next day, so we listened to the grieving woman through most of a second night as well. Finally the madness ceased—we were told—because the last vestige of the body had been burned.

I laid my head down in the silence of the third night on a bunched-up pair of canvas pants. Above me the stars were hidden by a new veil of smoke that had spread to fill the wide valley from a distant forest fire. But I couldn't help but feel as though I were breathing the ashes of the dead from across the creek.

Oh, the mystery! I thought, yet the words were an incomplete mask for my confusion and fear.

All men are created equal, said my father's civilized law. Except for the *merciless Indian savages, whose known rule of warfare is an undistinguished destruction of all ages, sexes, and conditions.*

But where was Jefferson now, this man who had aspired to be divine? Decayed in the same Virginia soil his words had turned to a bloody bog, both a grave and a cradle, by a war more ferocious than any war had ever been. And by me.

On the last day I'd seen my father, he'd told me he used to think civilization moved westward until he'd been to the jungles of Mississippi to visit his brother and seen the horrors of what men do to others when there's nothing to stop them.

Where was my father now? Escaped from his diseased country. Dissolved at the bottom of the sea. I missed him terribly, and I envied him.

And Mr. Collins? I couldn't even see his face anymore, so deeply had it disappeared into the mystery.

Mr. Perry? I didn't *want* to see his face, but it appeared unbidden before my eyes—his *bright new creature* like a grotesque jack-o'-lantern glowing in the murky darkness of a western sky.

So lying on my back on the rocky edge of the Great Western Territory, I closed my eyes and distracted myself from the sound of my own breathing by imagining again a gilded future, a carriage and four, a castle on a hill, a blue-sky day of material bounty, where things such as words and the faces of their flawed and blood-soaked authors would be meaningless. Where the natives would sleep quietly on their side of the river and the dead would stay buried and not waft after us like spirits. I used all of my willpower to conjure again the gold I'd pull from the bosom of the earth, and the mountains of pillows I'd buy to comfort my head in such weird darkness.

LIKE THAT, THEN, the strangeness of the land and the strangeness of our journey created new ways of thinking even before we arrived at our destination. In familiar places, we live between lines. Lines between rich and poor, between theirs and ours, between the known and unknown. But out here, as travelers, we could see the world in its true nature, a place without boundaries, a vast seething hot world of fluidity. A liquid world. And to keep our heads above water, to stay sane, we kept our minds on the practical. I wore my hat because of the sun, not because I was trying to disguise my mother's blood. My hair had grown woolly again, and if anybody noticed—of course they did, *It's plain!*—they didn't seem to care. Out here we were pilgrims equalized by the task of the journey. Who would dare draw a line between the ex-slave with yellow skin and one green eye and the free Vermont farmer with olive skin and eyes the color of coffee? Who could tell the canal man's bastard son from the scion of a wealthy New York family? And the Yankee deserter hunted deer side by side with the rebel deserter and became fast friends. It took the same amount of steps to cross the land, the same amount of suffering. Everybody's stomach needed to be filled at the end of the day. Everybody needed protection from the sun and rain.

The land itself—more than any of us had ever seen—stunned us with its sheer size. Rivers roared out of naked mountains, grew larger and faster and turned endlessly through canyons that led to the infinite sea. Other rivers spread across the salt plain and grew smaller and smaller, until their last drop of water had risen from their powder bed and disappeared into the air. We walked for days through fields of boulders as though a mountain had crumbled and left only its bones. We crossed grassy meadows, and the shoulders of mountains, and the crags between peaks. We were made small by the land, humbled by it, turned into ants crossing a sandy plain.

But the land also made us giants, because simply by putting one foot in front of the other we could walk to the sky!

None of us had ever seen as much open land and we all felt as if it were ours. Why not? To whom did it belong? The natives? Not by any standard of ownership any of us had ever known. For if natives owned it simply because they had been born on it, because they took their sustenance from it, and because it lay scattered with the charred bones of their ancestors, then we—all of us—owned the land we had come from. Which we did not. And if the natives owned it by wandering through it, then we owned it as well. For weren't we true nomads? Didn't we move day after day, relentlessly pushing onward toward our good dream—and away from our bad one?

Sometimes we saw lone travelers, going in both directions, and they always fascinated me, perhaps because I knew I would not have been able to make such a long journey alone. One evening a Dutchman arrived in our camp pushing a wheelbarrow that held all of his possessions and despite our offers of shelter and fire, he slept on the bare ground in the open air, ate raw meat for his supper, and the next morning began up the trail before us. A child who watched him walk ahead of us until he was just a dot on the land asked, "Won't he be all wore out when he gets to the camps?"

Or the Negro woman I saw walking toward us through the heat and the dust carrying a small cast-iron stove on her head with her provisions and a blanket piled on top it. We watched her appear as an apparition and grow larger and larger. When she was near, she looked at me out of the corner of her eye and without pause said, "You ain't he, is you?"

I turned around, for she was already by me and passing the line of our group. "Who's *he?*" I asked, but she didn't answer. I was breathless catching up to her. "Who's *he?*" I repeated. I could see the blue-black skin on the side of her neck shiny with sweat. If she was a ghost, she didn't smell like one. The stove on her head began to tilt, so she straightened it with her hand.

"Why are you carrying that heavy stove?" I asked.

Still no answer. We were walking back past the long line of our train, but my fellow travelers had disappeared from my vision. I was looking only at her.

"Where are you going?"

This time she laughed, and her laughter filled me with sorrow because it was aimed at me and reduced me to a child.

"Well you ain't *she,* is you!" I shouted.

I didn't expect an answer but out of the corner of her mouth she answered, "Honey, I ain't been *she* in a long time, but I aim to be again!" Which was when I let her get a few steps ahead, and watched her woman shape move as a woman shape moves. Her neck was wide and strong, and spread out to her shoulders, and her black arms swung with each step. Below her too-short calico dress her black calves disappeared into dusty men's boots laced up over her ankles. I stopped and stood and watched her walk down the hill we had just walked up. Before I turned and began again to walk in the direction I'd been going when I first saw her, I became aware again of the train of our group, wagons, riders, but mostly walkers streaming past me up the steep trail. I looked at their faces burned by heat, covered with dust. Ghostly faces strained by grief and fatigue, eyes aimed downward at the trail, oblivious to me, oblivious to her.

Then she was gone, and I turned and joined them.

IT WAS A BREATHING, cackling stink, Last Best Chance City—an open keg, a heap of slop, a decomposed pig. It was gumbo on your boot soles getting heavier with each step, the smell of shit and beans, of roast buffalo and horse piss—a belch, a sonata, an explosion of vice and language—a place of dead strangers floating daily down the river, live good fellows, earnest evil—a place where every day there was spectacle in the street—something to pay for, something to see for free, and something to pretend not to notice. It was America in all her mad glory: Swedes, Irish, Jews, Italians, Bohemians, English, German, African, Chinese, Mexican, and native—all of us greedy, yearning, sweating, hiding, longing, hoping. We were full and drunk, yet thirstier and hungrier than we'd ever been in our lives. We wanted freedom and we missed our chains. We were wealthy sons and lost daughters, deserters, heroes, cowards, killers, thieves and ex-slaves and slave traders. We wrapped up our fears in optimism, buried our guilt in sentimentality. We were miners, freighters, tree-cutters, butchers, teamsters, gamblers, beggars, hurdy-gurdy girls, and outlaws. Wives, husbands, daughters, sons. We ran boardinghouses, laundries, kitchens, a half-dozen stores carrying provisions and hardware, a jewelry shop, two bakeries, a gunsmith, a butcher shop, five hotels, and gin mills too many to count.

By nightfall on a Saturday the street would be filled with staggering miners. They drank joy juice, brave maker, black and tan, red disturbance, forty rods, skull bend, apache tears, lamp oil, white mule, tiger spit, who shot john, tangle leg, blue rain, tarantula juice, panther piss, and Mormon valley tan. They gambled on fighting cocks, on horse and mule races, on mule and bear fights, on bull rides, on boxing matches and card games. In the saloons they'd break each other's heads. They'd bite and gouge, and with the blood barely dried, they'd share a drink and take turns with a whore.

The first Saturday night I was there, a man killed another in a fight, but the legal defense was made—and successfully, too—that some necks are so fragile a man cannot be held responsible for breaking them.

On the hitching posts outside the Sighing Bones, every knave with a knife carved the name of some faraway girl who'd come to symbolize all his long life left behind. Including the language he used to know. And all of the desires and crimes that from a distance seemed quaint or holy and best approached drunk. The roughest of the toughs would sit and sing and cry and dig initials into the posts that soon wore out with carving, broke down and burned, only to be replaced by new ones. Each dawn then seemed to mark the arrival of an uncarved future— and each night the close of a cluttered, sentimentalized, and soon burned past.

Of course optimism is easier with gold. So is innocence and a degree of harmony. Gold was something that all of us with our varied pasts and peculiar dreams could agree upon: having it made us rich, and not having it made us determined to get it.

Having it drove us mad, not having it drove us madder.

How far would we all have come to get it? Twice as far? Three times as far? Around the world? The Chinese did.

I would have walked forever. But I didn't have to. Gold lay in the gravel of Cricket Creek as it made a wide S-turn around the town and descended gradually into a narrow canyon. It lay up the gulches that fed the stream, in the mud of its banks, and in the fissures between rocks under the mud. Gold glittered in our sluice boxes and pans. Filled our bags and pockets. It trickled down into the cracks between the boards on the one-block-long sidewalk outside the Sighing Bones Saloon and the Dead Dog Hotel. It filled cubbies in family homes, boxes and bags and cans tucked behind logs or buried in sod roofs. It sprinkled into the sawdust and dirt floors of the tacked-together stores. You could see it in the makeup and dresses of the hurdy-gurdy girls, in the righteous brows of the good fellows and their wives. It glittered in the eyes of the gamblers, on the wet lips and tears of the drunks, in the shine on the pistols and knives of the thieves.

We all found it—and for a while it colored our dreams and glared blindingly in the skies of our nightmares. Some worked steadily on steady-paying claims, some moved from one claim to another in a fierce and determined and often futile effort to find more. Some people took it from the ground, and others took it from them—at the general store, the gambling table, the barroom, the dance hall, the bedroom, or on a dark and lonely trail at the point of a gun. Some of us grew fabulously rich, and some grew only a little bit rich, but all of us grew rich for a while.

THE AFTERNOON WE ARRIVED I helped the two widows with six children and one on the way—Widow Warner and Widow Smith—set up camp. Within minutes we'd pounded stakes into the ground and sent the children off to fetch water, and soon we had a fire going and the water heating and together they began washing their faces. First one bent over the basin and then the other. I refilled the basin three times with fresh water before either woman had made the slightest change in the color of her skin. Then we commenced on the children. The little ones first while the older ones went off for more firewood and to trade tea for food, and then the older ones bathed themselves while the women began cooking. Before the end of the evening we had twenty-five miners under the canvas eating beans and oxen meat, stewed apples and Dutch cheese, hard sea biscuits, bacon, rice, coffee, and black bread sprinkled with dead mosquitoes. All the scraps went into a pot and they called it stew and charged a dollar apiece, and that was the first of thousands of meals they would make together as the canvas tent stretched from their wagons grew with my help to a tiny board shelter in the coming winter months, and then into a two-story boardinghouse with bushels of gold flakes stowed in the wood box, under beds, and in cupboards.

I filed for a claim just a couple hundred yards from town and lived out of a lean-to that first cold season on boiled wheat and peas when I wasn't eating better with the widows. As soon as the frost broke in the spring, I began work on my claim. I was a patient miner, and my hands and back were strong. I knew how to use a shovel, and I was content to get rich one day at a time. In the evening I waited until the sun went down and I hid my new flakes with my growing stores in the earth around my shack. I took pleasure in seeing my treasure grow. What did I want? I wanted more.

I did not gamble, drink, or visit whores. I found sanity and a feeling of false security in the movement of my body, the strength of my limbs, and the reasonless accumulation of gold flakes. The present, although physically grueling, was so pleasant that I rarely thought about the future anymore, or even why I was doing what I was doing. I was getting rich, and I was being left alone. I didn't have to pretend to be anything I wasn't—I let my hair grow. I was a Negro and I was a white man, I was both, I was neither. I woke early in the mornings and took pleasure making my coffee and drinking it as the sun came up over the eastern peaks. I took pleasure in my bread. I did not know how I deserved such simple pleasure and at times felt overcome with nausea-free gratitude. The horrors of my past took on the meaning of recalled nightmares—sad things that could not be denied but somehow also added to the bright preciousness of my daily physical existence.

By the end of my first year in Last Best Chance City, I had begun to think that true freedom was possible only with gold. Mining it and accumulating it kept my body occupied and my stomach full, and allowed me to live as I pleased. I didn't need to spend as I had in New York to feel it lift me on its wings. As long as I was eating, working, saving, I felt free. Free from having to be this or that. Free to do nothing. Or because in my case *nothing* was too frightening, free to keep digging, keep accumulating. I dug, sluiced, bagged, and guarded. I'd been a slave twice, and a workhouse boy for a good chunk in between. I knew how to work all day long. But this didn't feel like work. This was for nobody but myself, and I liked it. My father told me we do not live for ourselves, but I was finding it quite pleasurable—perhaps even necessary. Dig the gravel and flush it through sluices. Pick out the gold. Simple enough. Glittering, valuable gold. Some days a lot. Some days a little. Easy enough. My mind rested, my body strained but in comprehensible ways. I understood calluses and sore bones. I understood causes and effects. I moved this earth with this pick and this shovel. I nailed these boards with this hammer. I ran water through this ditch, that box, and shoveled this much gravel. Tons and tons of gravel. Remember how good I must have been with a shovel! Imagine it. To watch me, to watch any of us with a shovel in our hands, was to watch a craftsman, an artist. Such grace. Such economy of movement. Such precision with the steel blade as it sliced again and again into the dirt of my gulch off Cricket Creek. Breath in, breath out. I felt the sap of this free life pulsing through my veins and wondered joyously at how such good fortune had come to me.

Oh, the mystery!

And if that wasn't enough, didn't the sky bring new air every day? High clouds or low? Blue sky or rain? Snow? Didn't eagles and ospreys and geese and ducks ride the high wind like acrobats? Like angels? Didn't songbirds gather in the brush across the creek and swallows nest in the cliff past the row of cottonwoods? Didn't they weave pretty patterns in the evening sky?

Indeed they did. And at night when I lay down to sleep I listened to the breeze in the cottonwoods and the water in the creek. I could hear neighbors singing or shouting out to one another. I could hear barking dogs, roosters, drunken hoots and the jangle of piano from the Sighing Bones Saloon. I closed my eyes in the darkness and felt myself grow small on my cot, tiny, vulnerable, but safe. I slept and ate and worked, and the sound of demon breathing faded with each ounce of gold I mined.

But it never went away, not completely, and if the truth be told, sometimes I'd lie in bed and wonder why I was alive—why me and not Saturn? Why me and not the soldier Gibbs? Why me and not the Yankee captain's father, and brother, and son? What had they died for? Why had Jimmy and his sister died? So I could live? So I could merely breathe?

Breathe in, breathe out.

Because I needed to be free?

We are free!

Free from sorrow, free from care?

Not quite. It seemed that despite my best efforts, I couldn't hold it all in without some sort of redemptive dream—at least not for long, and not happily.

So again I began to think about my mother. Where was she? What was she doing? Did she need me? But instead of imagining I'd someday leave here to find her—to rescue her from her lonely misery—my new fantastic notion of redemption required only that I use my growing wealth to pay others to find her and bring her here where she might live happily ever after in a castle I'd have built for her. The good thing about this plan was that it required that I do nothing more than what I was doing. Mine gold. Accumulate flakes. Pass from one day to the next. I didn't even have to try to find her—not until I had so much gold that there would be nothing she might ask for that I could possibly deny.

How much gold was that? More.

SO ALONE ON MY CLAIM I could walk a thin line of my own making between hope and despair. Sometimes, however, I needed to go into town, which required a different set of tricks. For there, in the course of a single afternoon, I might shake hands with a former rebel general, a preacher, a doctor, an Italian count, a con man—and maybe all in the same person!—who'd just the day before been acquitted of murder by bribing the witnesses against him. I might decline the honor, but how could one murderer refuse another's hand? We were all far from home and getting rich. And didn't we all believe in good intentions? Didn't we all believe in the right of a free citizen to invent himself again and again, and to be treated to a drink, and to buy back? You bet we did. And didn't we all look solemn and feel tingles in our bones when we read the president's speech, almost six months after he'd given it, at Gettysburg? Didn't we nod our heads and blink back tears when he resolved that in this nation dedicated to the proposition that all men are created equal, the dead shall not have died in vain?

We did.

For didn't we all agree it would be a terrible thing to die in vain?

We did.

So to refuse to shake hands with a fellow mortal would be to deny a great principle: *All men are created equal.* Or, *Nobody's no worse than nobody else.*

Yet beyond our gilded innocence, this was how it really worked: For white men, stealing was punished by whipping and banishment, and I watched one day with impressive (to me, anyway) passivity while three white men were tied to a bridge and whipped for stealing flour. Impressive because only the excessive sweat on my temples and brow betrayed the internal tear caused by each snap of the whip.

Another day a Chinaman was hung for horse thievery. I didn't watch. Nor did I watch the next day, when they hung a Mexican for a similar crime.

The third day both horses were found up in the hills.

"So we were wrong," the judge said by way of excuse. "But we ain't always wrong, and that chink and greaser are lucky they ain't been hanged sooner, the way I see it, for some other crime they didn't do."

If I hadn't found so comfortable the groove of my obsession with gold, I might have considered that a warning. And if I hadn't fooled myself into thinking that I was no longer either just a Negro or just a white man, I might have made a simple extrapolation and so avoided my fate. But alas, who can avoid his fate?

That fall, the rest of the Chinese were chased off their claims for good, and most miners agreed it was a good thing, as the Chinese had become altogether too plentiful.

And the Mexicans, after they struck a big vein on a rich flat below town, had to be run off by a mob of toughs who worked the ground themselves, and out of a forty-foot claim took almost a quarter of a million dollars.

All men are created equal. (Except for the chinks, of course, and the greasers, and the . . .)

When the light is too bright, we close our eyes. I stayed on my claim and clung to the new illusion that had grown with my buried treasure: if I minded my own business, others would mind theirs. With gold I would be safe. With gold I could be everything I wanted to be, and everything I could never be, and all of it together sometime in the glorious future.

BUT SOMETIME BEFORE CHRISTMAS that second winter, an event took place that would have far-ranging effects on our glorious future. A townsman named Heck Thompson had a not-uncommon winter hobby of drinking himself into a stupor and cuffing his native wife back and forth across his cabin until they both passed out. On the night in question, however, she either faked passing out or awoke sooner than usual and ran off.

It being as cold as it was, and there being an encampment of natives just across the gulch, a cluster of tepees along Stinking Creek below town, she didn't run far. When Heck woke in the morning, he knew where she was and he went after her. But a couple of big men, her cousins or uncles, came out of the tepees and chased him away. He crossed the gulch and went to the Sighing Bones and drank all day, and when night came again he got his rifle out of his cabin and walked over behind the woodpile. He pushed the snow off the top so he could rest the barrel on a piece of split pine, and he stood aiming for a while in the general direction of the native camp.

Then he thought better of it. He lifted his face from the gunstock, his rifle from the woodpile, and walked toward the livery. He went in the back door and climbed up into the mow, where it was warmer, and he could lie down. He poked his barrel through a hay hole. He looked over the sights through the moonlight and aimed into the silver tepees.

Calmly, then, he began to shoot.

It was not unusual for me to hear gunshots coming from town as I lay in my cot at night. But these were different. These were not the rambunctious pistol-shooting of rowdies, or even an angry murder in a saloon. This was the methodical and cold-blooded rhythm of assassination. Ker-*bam!* With enough time between for the shooter to recover his aim. Ker-*bam!* The sound of each shot bounced off the distant hills and came back an echo. I got up and went to the door and opened it, felt the immediate chill of the winter air on my legs. The shooting had paused and there was no sound at all in the gulch. Only the silence of dread. And winter. Maybe a little wind in the trees. Maybe the trickle of water under the ice in the creek. While I listened, Heck was apparently reloading, because suddenly another shot rang out. Ker-*bam!*

I dressed and ran through the snow over the low rise to where I could see town. From there I heard a woman scream across Stinking Creek. Another shot, and another woman screamed, raising the hair on the back of my neck. Another shot. A horse whinnied, dogs barked, and a child cried. Then more shouting and screams, and soon in the light from a waning moon I could see natives running from tepee to tepee. Ker-*bam!*

In the street below, a crowd of men converged on the livery shouting, *This way! In the mow!* Across the gulch in the native camp all hell had hatched, and the wailing and weeping had become a din. Folks on the town side of the gulch had begun to run around crazily, too, with their guns drawn ready to pour more lead down toward the native camp should any shots come up this way. But only more wailing and more weeping came from below—grief over what we later learned to be the death of a lame boy, a baby, and two women.

Then a voice loud and clear from across the gulch. "A man's been shot, a man's been shot in the savage camp!" Meaning, of course, a white man.

Surrounded by the mob in the street, Thompson surrendered his rifle, and as I walked closer in the snow, I could hear him say, as clearly as if he had been standing next to me, "He ain't had no business being over there once it got dark in the first place."

That would be a good enough defense to keep his neck free from a noose, but for the sake of his own protection, Thompson spent that night, and the next, in jail.

Town was quiet for a few days as the massacre sank in. The dead white man, an unknown loner ("Recently Arrived, Recently Departed," the newspaper called him), was stored in a coffin to be buried in the spring. Thompson was taken out of the jail, put on his horse, and banished from the Territory. And one moonless night before the end of a week, the natives packed up and left. Where there had always been a collection of three dozen tepees across Stinking Creek from Last Best Chance City, there was now only a field of trampled snow, stained—you could see, if you walked the bench as I did that morning—with pools of darkened blood.

A day went by. Two days. A week. During the isolation of winter in a wilderness mining camp, the active mind turns uncertainty to dread. Dread grows to threat—and then to dreaded certainty. A rumor spread that the angry natives had joined with their wild brethren over the mountains, where the combined massive force waited until spring to run the entire white population out of the Territory. People in Last

Best Chance City gathered around woodstoves in cabins and stores and saloons, and they talked, and the rumor grew, because like all good rumors it was based on inarguable facts: The natives were out there still, were they not?

And we were still here, far from home, in a big land we did not know.

SO WE HUDDLED TOGETHER, trying to make ourselves as invisible as sheep pressing their heads toward the center of a tight flock. I know I did. But as much as I might have considered myself just like everybody else, my mother, it seemed, was still too near me—in the color of my left eye, in the slight breadth of my nose and lips, and in the texture of my hair as it grew.

It's plain.

Late one evening toward the end of that winter, a group of hooded thieves showed up at my shack and relieved me of the burden of my illusions. They also took my gold—even almost all of my hidden treasure, which they located as though they'd been spying on me for months. When I dared to try to split the back of one of their heads with my shovel, I was promptly set on horseback with my wrists tied behind my back and a rope around my neck.

"My crime?"

"Bein' a nigger with gold," one of the hoods replied.

I sat on the horse and watched stars blink coldly in the sky above the rock wall on the other side of the creek. I listened to the water rush around the corner and through a shallow stretch of boulders where only yesterday there had been ice. I swallowed and felt the noose scratchy on my bare neck.

"But now I no longer have my gold," I said. "You've taken it."

He didn't say anything for a moment, just lifted his hood enough to spit tobacco. "I have," I heard him say, "taken your gold. So now you're just a nigger again, or close enough." And with that, he slapped the horse's rump and the rope tightened, and I struggled in horror as my neck took my weight and I thought my head would pop off like the head of a dandelion. But it didn't—and the next thing I remember I was on the ground with my face in the gravel and the gravel in my mouth, and my ankle burning like crazy, and a tight rope still squeezing my neck.

With all of my willpower I lay on the ground as though unconscious, even though my ankle made me want to scream in pain. Apparently imagining my neck to be broken, my tormentors cussed the rotted rope but left me where I lay, facedown at the start of a mountain blizzard. I'm sure they assumed that even if I wasn't quite dead, I'd soon freeze to death. I tried to catch my breath but the rope was still too tight to breathe freely, so after I was sure they were gone, I rubbed it on the ground to loosen it. I lay gasping for a minute or two trying to feel grateful that I was still alive but the raging pain in my ankle caused me to look down to the end of my leg, and what I saw almost made me vomit. My foot was turned a quarter turn toward the inside.

Snowflakes swirled in the cold air. I blinked back tears and writhed and rolled toward my cabin. I remembered how my mother had come to help me after the rebel officer had whipped me in his tent, and I hoped she'd do the same this time. Maybe she did, because somehow I freed my hands and was able to at least lift myself off the ground and crawl. Once inside, I managed to get a fire going—so maybe she helped with that, too, for I thought of her bent over the stove every day before I got out of bed, how she talked to the flame, coaxed it. And maybe she was there when I sat down on the edge of my bed and managed, somehow, to begin to turn my foot, thinking I had to splint it to make it heal straight. I got it partway turned before I mercifully passed out, so maybe that was her, too.

FOR THE NEXT FEW WEEKS, while the town dug out from foot after foot of snow, I holed up in my cabin healing crookedly. I might have died then but for the kindness of the Widows Smith and Warner. Daily they brought me food and kept me supplied with wood and news.

I was not the only victim of theft in Last Best Chance City, Widow Smith told me while changing my bedding. She was the younger of the two, and the movement made her face flush pink and her bosom expand as she breathed. "So thank the good Lord a Committee for Safety and Decency has been formed."

"Truer words, truer words," said Widow Warner. She dropped an armload of wood on the floor in front of the stove.

I looked from one to the other. "A *what* has been formed?"

"The Committee is kind of a hail-fellow-well-met social club," Widow Warner explained. She'd fattened up a bit since arriving and looked much less chicken-like than I remembered. "They've begun to meet at our boardinghouse in the evening. They're a society of good citizens, so all new arrivals, after being checked out and accepted as proper, will be invited to become members and take direct responsibility for defending the order of the Territory against malefactors."

The door of the cabin was open and the sun shone brightly on the melting snow. I was sitting on a stool while Widow Smith was fluffing my bedding. I liked the way the cabin smelled with these two women in it. Widow Warner had bent over in front of the stove. Widow Smith had bent over the bed to smooth the quilt. I looked from one to the other. When the fire was lit, Widow Warner stood up and rested a sooty hand on her hip.

"What this all means, Freeman," she said, "is that the Committee will be enforcing law in this lawless place."

"Things are changing, thank the good Lord," Widow Smith said, to which Widow Warner added again, "Truer words, truer words."

And things did change. In the coming weeks the songbirds came back, and the snow melted in the bright sun, and the creek ran high with wild water. Also, my right ankle healed crookedly; my foot turned well inward, and although I had a little bit of gold left that the thieves had not taken, I'd gone from rich to poor, from healthy to crippled.

To stave off the blues, I began to limp around town with a crutch and learn things. One thing I learned was what a camel looked like—a combination buffalo and chicken. Six of them arrived in town to haul freight two hundred miles north to the steamboat landing. They could carry four times what a mule could, and showed their stuff in an exhibition by carrying ten children at a time up and down Mountain Street, where most every horse that saw them ran away. The resulting chaos, along with the fact that Widow Warner's oldest girl was pitched off headfirst, stopped the show. She wasn't hurt badly, but after that the animals were kept out of town, where somebody soon mistook them for elk and shot them all.

Another thing I learned was with no police force and no functioning courts, the Committee had become our shadow government, and the widows' boardinghouse our sometime capitol. Pink-faced good fellows gathered there in the evening to act as unofficial claims judges, sheriffs, and deputies. They controlled the rights to run a stagecoach line, to collect bridge and ferry tolls, and to dock a riverboat. All roads leading in and out of the Territory came under the control of the Committee, and when the Washington-appointed governor attempted to convene a legislature for the purpose of taking legal control of these byways, two representatives were mysteriously hung by the neck over the two principal trails leading into the capital. Their blackening, bird-pecked bodies had an inhibiting effect on the efforts of the remaining legislators to arrive.

Then the corrupt territorial judge was run off and for a two-week stretch, every sunrise lit a new body hanging from a T-shaped gallows on the western edge of town. At first I was pleased to imagine that many of the dead had been my robbers and would-be killers. But soon there were others. The town was producing gold that the Union needed for its war efforts—so the killings were associated with the righteousness of war and many of the newly strangled were indeed rebel sympathizers. Yet many were not. The Committee for Safety and Decency, that hail-fellow-well-met social club, had expanded its list of victims to include people who had never been a threat to the peace of the Territory, much less to the Union. An obnoxious but harmless drunk. A loudmouth. A gambler.

The popularity of the Committee only grew. Nothing like bodies hanging willy-nilly to bring out the nodding heads. But I wasn't any braver. After a while all I could do when I saw an occasional body hanging pink in the new dawn was avert my glance, and hope that whatever finger was choosing souls to take, that finger would avoid me.

BY SUMMER WE LEARNED that the war had ended in the East, that Lincoln had been murdered, and that the millions of slaves still held as slaves had walked free—including, somewhere, maybe, my mother. I didn't even know if she lived, much less where, and I wallowed in my failed effort to rescue her, and in all my shattered visions of freedom. I couldn't work a shovel anymore, and without physical activity I slouched still deeper into self-pity. In order to avoid the haunting sounds of my own breathing while alone in my cabin, I began to visit the Sighing Bones Saloon. I took what became my customary stool at the end of the bar and sipped beer. The hurdy-gurdies sprinkled throughout the crowd wore dresses of bright red and purple and royal blue and turquoise and yellow and pink—colors that without these women I might have forgotten existed.

Yet as melancholy as I felt, and as much *ooh*-ing and *aah*-ing as I got when they first noticed my different colored eyes, I wasn't tempted to take the short walk upstairs. I had very little money left, for one thing, and maybe that was what dropped the scales from my eyes. Because in the late afternoon before the gaslights came up, and before the saloon was filled with tobacco smoke and music, when it was quiet and dark and cool, I sat in my place and saw them all too clearly. They sprawled in various slovenly poses on stools and benches scattered across the filthy floor covered with sawdust and pig dung, resting, quiet, chatting. Because I had never lain with any of them, they began to look at me without recognition, and talk as though I weren't there. They were from Italy, Germany, France, South America, and spoke only a few vulgar words of English, which they masterfully applied to most every subject. The young ones were only girls, but in their faces it seemed I could see the last lingering blush of vigor fade before my eyes. Their future showed clearly in the lost and vacant faces of their older sisters, who lay about them in various shapes and degrees of drunkenness.

So why did I pass my days sober and chaste in such a depressing place? Why didn't I stay at the widows' boardinghouse instead of the saloon? Surrounded by children. Surrounded by love and affection, and the optimism of decent, stout-hearted women?

I don't have an adequate answer. But in the saloon I found an optimism I could believe, and for a while it was an antidote to the very same hopelessness I saw there. For just when I began to feel as blue as the smoke hanging over the entire room, Long John, a man with a purplish nose and a face tied up with a kerchief for the benefit of a perpetual toothache, sat down to play the piano with a grace one could never anticipate by looking at him. Hearing the music, the women became enlivened and sat upright. They tapped their feet and nodded their heads, and I watched the void in their eyes miraculously begin to fill and brighten as though they'd cheated death one more day.

Me, too. For if I could no longer believe in a glorious future, I could believe in one more day. One more day.

Then one blue-sky afternoon I ran out of gold. I went into the Sighing Bones and couldn't even get a beer to sip—or pay for what I'd already sipped—so a Wisconsin tough named Schmidt picked me up by the collar, called me a freeloading nigger, and tossed me out the front door into the muddy street. I lay for a moment on my back and looked at the larch and cottonwood yellowed already with autumn. I felt cold wind blow from the north up the gulch, and I began to believe that my own last chance had ceased to be. The maternal bond ruptured by slavery would not be made whole again by love or war or gold, so maybe this was it. If the world called my mother a nigger, finally, in the end, I would be a nigger, too.

To assist in this new career, I assumed a more humble demeanor and become a pathetic presence on the street. In the coming weeks I'd live off the droppings of miners feeling flush with new wealth. My clothes would became rags. And whereas for the most part I'd spoken in my natural English accent, I now affected the drawl of the plantation. I came home again to my diseased country, and I embraced my mother as I hadn't been able to since I was a child.

If we are free to pursue happiness, we are free to fail to find it. Free to surrender.

I didn't lynch myself. I didn't cause the rope—or my leg—to break.

We are not in control.

But I was free to spend myself broke in the Sighing Bones, free to avoid the restorative powers of widows or prostitutes, free to abandon my shack for the cool mud on the side of the road, where I slept freely with dogs and drunks. Free to fight for scraps of food and tossed coins.

We all suffer.

But you know that already.

One night outside the Sighing Bones, I won a scramble with two others for a gold piece and held it in my sweaty palm close to my heart.

We do not live for ourselves.

But we can certainly die that way.

We are all going to die.

You know that, too. Of course you do.

Free to live, free to die. Free from sorrow, free from care.

We are free.

To give up the fight.

When in the course of human events it becomes necessary to dissolve the bonds . . .

Despite my hunger, I freely gave the gold to a tall half-breed I knew only as Belly.

"Here," I said. "Be free."

Belly took the coin and strode off, and I lay back down on the ground listening to the piano in the saloon, the shouts and stomps of dancers, and the cackles of female laughter. Burying my face in the cool mud to escape a late-season torment of mosquitoes, I thought of how this very dirt spread thinly across the wide arch of the continent and covered poor Jimmy and his little sister in their Virginia grave. I thought of Saturn, too, and of the thousands and thousands of unnamed dead. I pressed my face still deeper, struggled to breathe, and like that found not only some of the same comfort of invisibility I'd discovered on the battlefield, but also a moment of wild joy anticipating how the coming winter would erase me, finally, from this sad earth.

HEROES

WHEN THE NEWS ARRIVED that Colonel Cornelius O'Keefe, newly appointed territorial secretary, had crossed the territorial border, still eight days' ride from town, the official governor, who hadn't shown his bewhiskered face in months outside his hotel office, waved his hand at the muddy street and muttered, "This he can have!" Then he climbed into a stagecoach to flee.

The governor's exit turned the approaching Colonel O'Keefe into the acting governor of the Territory, or the Acting One, as the newspapers mockingly called him.

Which—even from my filthy nest of rags half under the steps of the barbershop across the street from the Dead Dog Hotel—bothered me, that sneering tone of theirs. He was a hero, after all. O'Keefe of the Sword, Irish revolutionary and Union Army officer, champion of freedom on two continents, was coming our way—to this territorial capital besieged by the Committee for Safety and Decency, to this cluster of shacks and frozen mud streets swollen with a new migration of war veterans, men tired and bitter and haunted by blood.

As a teenager in London, I'd read his speeches on old yellow newspapers and been filled with courage and the illusion that hot, brilliant war would be my ticket to freedom. On the battlefield, I'd carried the man to safety and dreamed of joining his Irish brigade. As a slave, I'd seen him raise his sword and lead green-sprigged troops up a hill into a barrage of bullets that laid them down like grass in the wind.

If his body had survived that slaughter, what had become of his mind? What had become of his heart? Walking stunned and crazy in New York City, I'd missed an opportunity to hear him speak. But now, here, I had nowhere else to go, nothing else to do except hang on until he got here.

And so a pea of curiosity disturbed my bed of despair. Even before he arrived he began to save me.

Of course I'd heard his enemies' slander that he'd been swallowed by the bottle, and I knew he'd been drummed out of the army by career officers, and I read with dismay the newspaper descriptions of how the handsome Colonel, with that famous feminine flip of hair, graying slightly, had moved humbly down Broadway in the Union victory parade, on foot, in citizen's clothes.

Inside the once solid frame was a vacuum, the newspaper said.

A vacuum? I knew from my own life that if the war didn't kill you outright, it would twist you into a different shape and form, and so who could be surprised if it had turned him, too?

With smarting eyes, the newspaper said. *Soon to be exiled as Secretary of the Great Western Territory,* it said. *A marvelous career at an end.*

An end? Perhaps that was what I was curious to see, how glory ends. To see the final chapter of his fantastic story. What happens in the end to the young Irishman horrified by the sight of his starving countrymen, brave enough to encourage open rebellion against the Queen, strong enough to endure and then to escape his Van Diemen's Land exile, cunning enough to get to America and make his way in the world, handsome enough to marry a society girl, bold enough to become a colonel and fight bravely for the Union, who now finds himself banished once again? What does the wick of once burned glory look like up close?

When he finally appeared that frozen morning in early December of '65, riding into town on his gray mule, I admit I was slightly disappointed. Perhaps even in my little nest of rags, I'd kept enough of a fire going to imagine an entourage. Maybe troops. A flag. But he rode into town unnoticed, I think, except by me, and unaccompanied, unless you happened to be able to see, as I did, the ghosts of ten thousand Irish soldiers straggling along behind him in a sad column that stretched from town across the valley and up over the top of the south pass. Over his right shoulder was slung a broad green worsted belt, and to this a tin canteen was hooked. Underneath the belt was his blue frock coat, which stood in need of a good washing. His sword was encased in a jangling steel scabbard that hung at his heels, and that would have been all the brighter for a little sweet oil and brick dust.

Nevertheless, he dismounted across the street with the gay grandeur of a circus cavalier, stood for a moment looking across the mountain valley already frozen and blanketed in a pall of wood smoke, and then gracefully lifted his drab sombrero. He was a delicately whiskered gentleman, more than forty years old, five feet nine inches, black hair beginning to gray on the sides, pale of face, his eyes sparkling suddenly with what now I can only call the gorgeous glow of lunacy.

"You tend mules?" he said suddenly to the tall trapper named Belly, who'd stepped out of the saloon behind him.

Belly nodded, and so the Colonel gestured toward his gray.

"Destiny needs grain, and water, and rest," he said. "As do I."

I sat up. I watched Belly lead the Colonel's old gray mule toward the livery, and I watched the Colonel walk bow-legged across the street. Before disappearing into the Dead Dog, he tipped his hat to a couple of hurdy-gurdy girls cussing in German as they pried their frozen bloomers off a laundry line they'd strung up that morning in what, given the season, must have been a hopeful mood.

BUT FOR THE OCCASIONAL glimpse of his shape through the window of his hotel room, I did not see the Colonel for another three days. Unfortunately, those three days coincided with a drop in temperature, and I endured the coldest nights of the infant winter. I huddled under a porch near the pitiful embers of my fire, which I kept alive by scraps of wood filched from a pile behind the stable.

I was not in good shape. Half-cured boils on my legs, a headache, mild delirium brought on by fever seasoned with frost on a light blanket—and what I kept imagining to be the rifle-cocking sounds of imminent murder—all this made for restless sleep. But my physical condition was rendered worse by a deteriorating emotional state. I admit to being afraid the Colonel might repeat the pattern of his predecessor, who'd stayed in the hotel for weeks at a stretch, showing his timid red face only occasionally, and only in ways that reassured the Committee that he would be no threat to its authority.

Why I kept my tiny fire going at all remains a mystery. I can only say from this distance that the flickering flames and small red embers had become a metaphor for the last bit of curiosity that remained in me. Why had he not appeared? Was it true that his weakness for the bottle had swallowed him? Was it true that while I lay in the frozen dirt watching my fire glow faintly into the second and even colder night, that whatever hope he'd carried with him by sea, by river, then over the mountains on an old mule was just one of many false hopes, and his was merely the last journey of a man who, like me, would be soon dead?

It seemed likely.

On the third day the temperature dropped still further, and even from under the steps I could see that the shutters to his room remained closed. Footsteps passed, the bootfalls of living men still drawn to the notions of wealth and transformation. Through the cracks beneath the steps I could see the angry pewter sky announcing the snowy certainty of winter. Horses trotted by in the street, wagons rolled, a last stage-coach pulled up from the south, and the frenetic activities of the living seemed pathetic and vain. As night fell men hurried for shelter with long, confident strides, their shoulders thrown back. They talked of tools and work and winter, of good horses, of women and land they'd known long ago and far away, and would someday know again.

Were they stupid? Or blind? The blizzard was coming, and sure, they might survive tonight, but it was only a matter of time before they proved too slow, too old, too weak, too unlucky, too unwhite.

Perhaps they were all insane.

As darkness fell and doors around town slammed closed for the night, I began to imagine that the Colonel was already dead, that he'd been murdered in his room by men threatened not only by the law of his office, but by the courage of his once hot flesh. The streets emptied, my pretty red coals dimmed, and I curled under the steps and imag-ined his body growing colder and colder by the minute. When I drifted to sleep for the first time, I saw the eyes of the children as I had been unable to see them in their grave. The eyes blinked and I leaned closer. They blinked again and I laughed and cried for joy and leaped into the grave to lift them out, thinking they were alive and forgiving me! But as I bent to lift them, their little bodies broke in my hands.

I shuddered myself awake. It was dark and my embers black. I breathed in frozen air, and made a conscious decision not to move, but to let night encroach and cover me like a cold blanket. I cannot say it was unpleasant, for as I drifted to sleep again, I immediately began to feel a warm wind that I believed to be a hypothermic dream. I had heard stories of travelers rescued in blizzards, and they'd described this feeling of absolute comfort even as death had begun to overtake them. My mind wandered back to my life at Sweet Grass. Every day after milking, my mother and I would take the dairy herd down to the stream and the high grass. It was there that my father would visit us, and sometimes he and my mother would walk away and leave me in charge of the cows. I would lie in the shade and pass the afternoon in leisure, glorying in the balm of Maryland summer.

This is how it is going to end, I thought, in that strange way we can be conscious even as we dream. This is how I'll die, a cowherd again, lying in the high grass with a hot wind on my bare skin.

I WOKE TO THE miracle of blue sky visible through the cracks of the barbershop steps, my assumed coffin. I could feel my cramped limbs and stretched my arms and inched my way out. The air was indeed warm, the ground thawed to mud, and the sunshine nearly blinded me. The Colonel's shutters were open but there was no sign of him behind the glass. Horses and wagons filled the street with morning activity. I was covered in dirt, my hair plastered to my head, and although I was convinced I must be invisible, a tall dark man walking toward me in shirtsleeves actually stepped aside to avoid me. He flashed me a broad smile and tossed me a coin.

"G'mornin', Freeman," he said.

I stared at him. How did he know me? Then I recognized him. It was Belly, cleaned up. I started to raise my hand but he'd already strode by me. I bent down to pick up the coin, held it in my hand. Newly minted since the war had ended, the gold glittered in the morning sun. I bit it, tucked it into a pocket, and walked around the corner of the building to do my business, amazed at the smells brought so quickly back with the warm weather. My urine, the filth of the tavern, horse manure and thawing earth. I had not died, after all, and I have to admit that even the sting of my boils, my dry mouth, and my heaving heart were almost a pleasure to bear.

I limped back around to the street and before I even saw him, I heard him. Just a snippet of his voice through the open window, a high-pitched brogue, the words unrecognizable. Then the door of his room flew open and in a moment he was standing on the second-story balcony of the Dead Dog Hotel wearing a blousy white shirt and black trousers, surrounded by three chubby, laughing hurdy-gurdies.

Stunned to be alive, and to see him there, combed and lightly whiskered, I crept closer. The unseasonable warm wind had brought with it the prospect of a few more days sluicing gold before winter hardened the streams to ice, so the street was busy and I dared to dodge horses and wagons to squat against a hitching post where a mangy dog lay sunning itself. On the balcony behind the Colonel, pink-skinned women continued to chat among themselves in German, so for the life of me, I did not know to whom he was speaking.

"One glance," I heard him say, leaning out over the balcony, "and you can see mad ghosts traipsing about the earth too plenty to count." He paused and stared down at the crowd passing in the street, horses, wagons, and busy mortal men with tools. I thought of the army of ghosts that had accompanied him into town, but I hadn't seen them for days. I guessed they'd dispersed to the gulches in search of gold.

"And faeries," he said—and here I noticed his spooky eyes suddenly locked on me—"faeries, though rare, simply stand to reason."

DURING THE NEXT FEW days he appeared always with the women, and sometimes with Belly, on the balcony outside his hotel room lunching on stuffed sausages, hard-boiled eggs, cheese, and garlic. From my place in the ditch across the road I'd watch and listen, my stomach knotted with hunger. Although I never heard the women speak anything but German, and I never heard Belly speak at all, daily I'd hear erupt from the Colonel into the crisp thin air of that unusually warm December week a tantalizing English phrase. Once he cornered the fattest and sweetest-faced young woman, and while she was busy eating as fast as she could, as though the food might be taken away at any moment, he said, "You are eating as if you had trodden on the hungry grass."

Then, with the weariest expression I have ever seen on a face, the face of a man who had buried his share of loved ones, he turned toward the street and said to all of us, or to no one, "The soul cannot live without sorrow."

That week the sky was blue and miners worked and came into town and traded gold flakes for winter supplies. Some got drunk and some entered the Sighing Bones or the Dead Dog and requested time with one or more of the women. For a while there seemed to be a mild curiosity about the Colonel, but it quickly waned as the general opinion, including those of the shadowy men who gathered like me to watch and listen, began to write him off as harmless. He seemed comfortable enough there on the balcony of the hotel surrounded by agreeable women, and so most busy citizens simply lost interest.

I remained rooted to my spot, alert and listening. His occasional words had turned me into a student again, and my days as a curious adolescent came back to me. Once, in the middle of lunch, he suddenly dropped his fork and the sausage impaled on its prongs, eyes flashing, I could have sworn, in my direction, and proclaimed to his uncomprehending circle of feminine companions, "Laws should be enacted that will protect and assist crippled soldiers, because it is not right that they be treated the way the Negro has been treated, thrown out of the house and called *free*."

The women did their nails or braided their hair, or ate his food, and sometimes even laughed at jokes muttered in German. Perhaps they were making fun of him. Most likely they were. But he was unmoved, and his eyes, when I caught a glimpse of them, maintained what I have already described as a gorgeous glow.

When he finished eating, he'd often burp, spread his arms wide, and before retiring back into the room say to no one in particular, "Let us manifest some destiny, shall we?"

ONE AFTERNOON, A WEEK after his arrival, the Colonel left his hotel and stood on a box Belly had fetched for him and set on the street corner. He was dressed in a blue surtout buttoned up and trousers of gray tweed. From under his felt hat, disposed rather theatrically on his head, cascaded a jaunty roll of hair that he was fond of touching from time to time.

"I am Colonel Cornelius O'Keefe," he began, "formerly of the Irish brigades and now the Acting Governor of the Great Western Territory, a responsibility I have shouldered for the purposes of bringing the Law—the shining light of Peace and Freedom—to this Wilderness."

Here he paused, touched his hair, and squinted at the blessed sunshine before continuing. He'd gathered a rough crowd of passersby—miners, merchants, freighters, and drunks. Across the street I could see through cracked blinds the eyes of the more powerful and dangerous community leaders, who, along with a handful of men standing in the shadows of doorways, listened carefully. It was still warm, and a cluster of hurdy-gurdies squatted in the sunshine on the board sidewalk behind him. They'd grown fond of him, it seemed, but the majority of English words they knew were vulgar and as soon as they became satisfied that none of those words was going to be spoken now, they settled in to brush one another's hair.

The Colonel continued, "I am here with the express presidential order to improve conditions in the Territory. To create opportunities for those countrymen of ours who still linger in the squalor of distant cities. The West must fulfill its promise as a place where all can have a stake. For the secret of our nation's industry, the secret of our pluck and our dauntless independence, is that Every Man has a Home and Fireside, and the Civil Peace necessary to enjoy them."

"What are you going to do about the wild natives?" a man yelled from the crowd.

The Colonel paused and thought for a moment. "Wild natives," he said, "I haven't seen." He raised an eyebrow and leaned toward his crowd. "Wild emigrants, however—"

He was interrupted by the spread of general laughter, broken by a high, clear voice from the midst of the crowd. "I've seen 'em, Colonel, and them savages'll take your pretty hair as soon as look at you!"

Maybe it was the reference to his hair, but the Colonel suddenly appeared flustered. He cleared his throat and briefly touched the curl on the side of his head with his right hand. The sun disappeared behind a cloud, and the audience felt the chill of a north wind and grew restless. They had work to do, gold to mine, and the warm week seemed to be coming to an end. Tonight, tomorrow, the next day, it would be winter, and they'd be locked in until spring. They didn't have time to stand and listen to a speech—and besides, if we hadn't seen many wild natives, we *had* seen Committeemen watching from across the street through the blinds of the bank office, from the steps of the livery, and from the doorway of the Sighing Bones Saloon. We *had* seen the parade of bodies that hung from the gallows. And we knew that any loyalty— any interest—in a civic power would be seen as a threat to the Committee's shadow government. This Territory offered newcomers the chance to get rich and to go home again, rich enough to drive a carriage, to buy a farm, and to marry the old sweetheart. Emigrants tolerated whatever they needed to tolerate in order to make that dream come true. But now here was a man, the Colonel, talking about staying for good.

"Dangers," he began, "no doubt abound. And to dangers I have not been a stranger." His voice gained strength with each word. "To help face this one, I've received authorization to raise a militia for the general protection of our settlements. For the enforcement of law, and to ensure that the roads are safe and the commerce fair. It will be most certainly a dangerous expedition—not only for me but also for those brave enough to accompany me."

"Got horses?" somebody shouted.

The Colonel looked confused.

Another voice said, "Guns?"

"What?"

"Do we get rifles and horses?"

The Colonel shook his head and seemed to regain his focus. "No horses, no guns. Not yet."

This answer brought a cascade of jeers. A militia without horses or guns? The Colonel cleared his throat, swallowed, and seemed to settle his weight onto his two feet. "Freedom from the harassment of bullies and tyrants—" he began, and his voice grew steely and bold—"Freedom from harassment by bullies and tyrants is one of the precious gifts Heaven gave to mortals."

"But how much does it pay?" a voice called from across the street.

"Treasures under the earth and beneath the sea cannot compare," the Colonel answered, but his voice was drowned out by shrieks of general amusement. He stood still and boldly waited for the laughter to subside. Then he said simply, "No money in this militia, only honor."

The listeners who had been waiting for an excuse to move on down the street, to get on with their work, began to do just that. Even the gaps in the blinds across the street had snapped shut and the shadowy men in the shadows disappeared. The Colonel, it seemed, would pose no risk. He might talk fancy words, and he might have been authorized to raise a militia, but with no horses, guns, or money, it would be an invisible one. Soon the only listeners left were Belly, three German women, and I. The Colonel looked at me huddled across the street. My hair was matted with mud, my skin covered with dust, my fingernails long and curving. He let his gaze move slowly down the length of me to my crooked foot.

"You," he said.

I nodded.

"You can write," he said. It wasn't a question, but I nodded anyway.

"Belly," he said, "get this man a bath, a good meal, and a suit of clothes fit for a secretary to the governor. I've got letters to dictate."

And with that he looked at the dark gray sky, blinked once or twice, stepped off his box and strode toward the hotel.

I followed, thump-dragging along behind Belly. The women stared at me with the big-eyed stare of children seeing a creature they've never seen before. When I passed them, I winked. They flinched, then giggled nervously—for all of us, I'm sure.

AFTER MY BATH, and after a kind, orange-haired woman named Helga with soft, fat hands clipped my nails and hair and made and applied a stinky poultice for my boils, and after I'd been wrapped in a towel and fed as much roast duck as my grateful (but slightly nauseated) stomach could hold down, and after a new pair of black trousers and a white blouse had been laid out for me to wear in the morning, Helga excused herself to go to work for the evening in the dance hall below, and I was left alone in the room for the first time with Belly.

Half Cherokee and half French—his mother having been lured off the Trail of Tears by his French immigrant father—six foot four inches tall in his bare feet, wide across the chest, smooth of face but with a crop of long straight black hair, he told me he had managed to spend four years hunting and trapping in the Territory and knew it well. Now he was aide-de-camp to the Colonel, his loyalty having been purchased with a commission to the rank of captain in the militia.

"*Invisible* militia," I said.

That made him laugh, but to show he meant no disrespect to his new boss, he said, "The Colonel's a great man, you know! Famous all over the world!"

I told him I knew that.

"And a silver tongue, that's for sure!"

I told him I knew that, too, but was curious about something. Having attained the rank of captain, I asked, was he by any chance receiving captain's pay?

He shrugged and sat down on his bed to remove his boots. "You heard him out there," he said, gesturing toward the street. "He wasn't lying. The government's broke."

"And that gold coin you gave me?"

"For taking care of his mule. He's wild about that mule."

He got the right boot off easily enough, but groaned a few times over the left before he looked up at me. "You mind?"

I limped across the room and gripped his *civilized* boot with my two hands and leaned back and pulled. I could feel his heel begin to lift out of its leather casement, and then, slowly, the boot began to slip off. When it finally did, and I had it in my hand, I couldn't help but recall the incident on board ship when I'd been asked to hold a man's boots. But the recollection was brief, because as Belly's boot came off, his filthy sock was revealed, and I got both nostrils full. I dropped the boot and retreated as quickly as possible to my side of the room.

"The Colonel looks at me," Belly said, "and says he needs a loyal captain but he ain't got no treasure, and he ain't got no livestock or guns, but as acting governor, he says, he does have prospects."

Belly stood and unbuckled his pants and slid them down, stepped out of them where they lay, and then stretched out naked on the bed and spoke toward the ceiling. "I told him I didn't know what that meant, and he says, *As my fortune ripens with thy love, it shall be still thy true love's recomps.* I told him I don't speak Irish. He said that was English, Richard Two. I told him I don't know any Richards, one, two, or three. So he tries to say it plain, he says, *As I rise, Mr. Belly, you will also rise!*"

This made Belly laugh, saying this, lying naked on his back across the room. "Of course I'm thinking of rising," Belly said. "I'm always thinking of *rising.* So I tell the Colonel that if by my service I might put my stake in a broad piece of territorial bottomland . . . well, that would be as good a *recomps* as I could dream on just now."

He laughed again, hearty and unabashed, and when he finished, I asked, "And in the meantime?"

"That's it," he said. "That's the meantime! Or the good time. The food's filling. The bed's warm. And the hurdy-gurdies are mighty friendly to the Colonel's captain!"

With that Belly reached to the wall above his bed and dimmed the lantern until our room went dark. I lay in my bed, the sheets washed and clean, the blankets thick. Through the window I watched the cold stars that until tonight had been my only ceiling, while across the room, Belly lit a pipe and commenced to smoke tobacco, which covered nicely his foot reek. Even if the Colonel's ambition to carve a Code of

Law into a lawless wilderness seemed immense and futile, it was true the food was filling and his bedrooms warm. I kept my eyes fixed on the night sky out the window and cast my mind toward the east. In my comfort, I even dared to think again of my mother, where she might be, and if, as the secretary to the acting governor, I might be able to learn anything.

In the morning I woke to the Colonel gently knocking at our door. "Mr. Walker," he said from the hallway, "I'd like to see you."

I blinked in the light of the day, happy beyond reason at my physical comfort. I lifted my head, and there, with his eyes closed, Belly lay on his back like a crusader on his tomb. The peaceful image was disturbed, however, by a blast of flatulence released with such force that his body rose six inches off the mattress before coming down safely again. He turned his head and winked one sleepy eye at me.

I sat up and pivoted my bare feet to the floor.

"On my way, sir," I said.

I FOUND THE COLONEL in his desk chair with his bare feet raised casually onto the windowsill. When he saw me he lifted his head abruptly, changing his balance, and the chair, which was tilted on two legs, fell backward onto the floor and he with it.

I jumped around the desk to help. He'd bumped his head and looked unconscious, but as I bent to touch him, to grab his hand, his eyes opened suddenly. Up close, he seemed to recognize me, remember me from long ago, but said nothing. He gave me his hand and I helped him up. We righted the chair, and he sat again, red-faced.

"Are you okay, sir?" I asked.

He touched the back of his head quickly with his fingers, then held them out for me to see in the lantern light.

"Blood?" he asked.

"No sir."

"You see," he said, as though he didn't need to explain. "Indeed you *see.*"

See what? I thought better of asking. A nod was sufficient.

"Mr. Walker," he said, and his eyes moved from my brown eye to my green, then back again to the brown one, "you look better today than you did yesterday."

"Thanks to you, sir."

"And you will not find it overly taxing to take dictation and write my letters, and show them to me so that I can sign them?"

"No sir."

He let his eyes linger, and for the first time I let mine drop to the polished wooden floor. I listened to the chickadees outside his window. He'd scattered seeds on the balcony and they'd come close to the glass to eat.

"Do you have any questions?" he asked.

I listened to myself breathe, and to him breathe, too, but I did not take my eyes off the floor. I wanted to ask how he knew I could write. A lump grew in my throat. I wanted to ask if he remembered my cowardly retreat on the battlefield, or how I'd carried him to safety. I wanted to ask what it was like to be the great O'Keefe of the Sword but my mouth had dried like paper and my cheeks filled with blood.

"No sir," I managed. "Only that I am glad for the opportunity to work with the governor in his efforts as the lone government official in this Territory."

He laughed, and I had to glance up to make sure he wasn't laughing at me.

"But I'm no longer alone," he said, or maybe asked, as he dipped his head and smiled at me coyly from under bushy black eyebrows. It was the kind of look that can get a man far down the trail of an adventure, but not deliver him.

When I didn't say anything for a moment, he touched the curl above his ear with nervous, freckled fingers.

"Am I?" he asked.

I cleared my throat. "No sir."

"Good," he said. My reassurance calmed him, and when he spoke again he pronounced each syllable slowly and deliberately. "All right, Mr. Walker, then let's go over what we both know. We know we are surrounded by a citizen organization that has taken to secretly and willy-nilly holding trials and executing citizens." He paused, blinked his blue eyes. "And we know we are surrounded by wilderness. And by natives who may or may not want us here, natives that most of our fellow emigrants believe are less than human."

I felt my face flush and my breath grow suddenly short. He leaned his bare forearms onto the desk and creased his brow as though to gather his thoughts.

"And here's the last thing we know," he said. "Or maybe it's the first. Maybe we know this one in our bones before we even get up in the morning. We know our best efforts to create a fair and just civilization will take us on an unimagined journey."

But I had to stop listening because behind him, on the balcony through the window, the chickadees suddenly flew off and a naked Belly appeared shivering. He bent to knock, and the sound of his knuckles on the glass caused the Colonel to turn around quickly, stand up, and raise the sash.

"Excuse me," Belly said, ducking in. He stood immodestly before us, his privates like two eggs and a hatchling in a black nest of hair. "I thought my clothes were out there drying but somebody must have brought them in already, and the window to our room stuck shut soon as I stepped out."

The Colonel closed the window against the cold as Belly's big, lean body slipped past us and then out the door into the hallway, where we could hear him enter the room next door, my room, his room.

"I believe you already know Captain Felix Belly," the Colonel said. "He told me you were a great help to him in a time of need."

Belly had brought with him a ripe, fleshy odor that lingered even after he was gone. I didn't know what to say to the Colonel. The help I'd given Belly had nothing to do with generosity.

Nevertheless, I must have nodded, for the Colonel dipped his head in a bow. "Then it's my turn to be grateful," he said.

WINTER SETTLED IN WITH a heavy dread. Frozen smoke hung over our bald mountain valley so it was easy for me to imagine that past the glass of my hotel window, concealed by winter's darkness, lay an undersea world or an alien planet, some unkind place where humans are not meant to live, and any out-of-door activity must be performed only after very thorough preparations. This was my third winter here, yet I felt more alien to the place than even the day I arrived. The stark fact that outside waited deadly cold air was a notion I could not get out of my head.

Partly I felt this way because without the Colonel's sanctuary, I knew I would have been dead by now, and my flesh hardened into a frozen earth tomb. But there was an ongoing cause for my dread as well: it wasn't easy to get around in the winter as a cripple. The walk through the snow to the privy each morning was treacherous. So was kicking through the slush after a thaw, or stepping over ruts after the ground froze again. I might have changed my name to Freeman Limper. Or Freeman Faller, so often was I on the ground. The elbow I'd hurt when I'd found gold in the Virginia farmhouse swelled to the size of a small child's head when I fell on it again.

Needless to say, I stayed inside. I drank gallons of tea and wrote stacks of letters, my fingers becoming permanently stained with ink as I took dictation from the Colonel. Before he began, he'd move the wicker rocking chair so he could pace back and forth behind me, for he liked to keep moving, but occasionally he'd pause and place his freckled hands with their stubby fingers on the tall back of the rocker, and he'd stand looking toward the dark window in which I could see the reflection of his face lit by lantern light. He liked to begin at dusk and work into the night. And instead of writing to the Secretary of the Army or the Secretary of War requesting arms authorizations, certificates of commissions, and vouchers to pay for horses, provisions and even uniforms, we wrote to congressmen, to bureaucrats, and to newspaper editors attempting to gain political support for statehood. Sometimes he'd wake me in the middle of the night, wearing only his underwear, carrying his boots that he couldn't stop moving long enough to put on. I'd follow him back into his room and sit down by the woodstove with a pen and ink and paper while he began pacing back and forth, mostly naked, a boot dangling from each hand. As he talked, he'd lift his chin slightly and squint his eyes and describe lush grassland in valleys where I had only seen scattered clumps of buffalo grass, moderate winters while we were locked in a deep freeze, and black soil where I had seen only gravel and gumbo. His words painted a picture of a land scattered with prosperous settlers, vast wheat fields, and innumerable herds of cattle blackening the hills and the riverbanks. He built railroads and then placed villages along them. He stocked warehouses full of goods to be shipped, or recently received. He described lovely hotels decorated with bright flags from all over the world, and dining rooms stocked with the delicacies of the season, fish and fruit and game, and the tinkle of a piano to help enchantingly dissipate the hours.

At any moment he might stop pacing, notice the boots in his hand, and giggle with delight. "I led soldiers on thirty-mile, all-night marches," he said once, "sometimes in the winter, and half of them without shoes."

He said this without bitterness or bluster, but with joy at the unpredictable bounty of the world, as though having known scarcity he could be that much more surprised by the sudden appearance of a pair of polished, *civilized* boots in his hands.

Down he sat, pulling the boots on, grinning as though he were the first man putting on the first pair of boots. He hopped to his feet again, and so continued the peripatetic dictation in his underwear and boots.

One night he stopped, however, and I could see the reflection of his face grow grim. "I've seen enough fighting," he said, "to last until eternity. And have you noticed how I'm trailed everywhere by the dead?"

I might have pretended not to hear, or I might have lied, but he'd charmed me into affection, and the peculiar intimacy of his voice coaxed the truth. "Yes," I said. Whispered. Breathed.

"Aaah," he said.

"I saw them when you came into town."

"Indeed," he said, and before he started pacing again he touched me briefly on the shoulder. It put goose bumps on my skin, and I thought again of our first interview. *You see,* he'd said, *indeed you* see. And then with that peculiar joy, *I am no longer alone!*

Yet on most nights he asked only that I write, and so I did, hunched over the desk dipping and redipping my pen into the ink bottle while he constructed pleasant villas tucked into alpine valleys, complete with balustrades and fountains, and so many lovely things that while I wrote I could almost convince myself that this world already lay just outside the door of this shabby log boarding hotel and dance hall that stank of

French cologne and chamber pots, tobacco, cabbage, garlic and whiskey. I could almost forget this lawless town, this smoky valley, this vast wilderness ruled by terror and greed. If I closed my eyes, I could almost believe in what he called a *fair and just civilization.*

Almost. Because believing in civilization—*civilized law*—required me to do a number of things that were somewhat unlikely. Like hold my nose and suspend disbelief. Or forget most of my life. It's true I'd once cherished the Declaration of Independence, my father's gift. But it's also true that that document—after saying all men are created equal—never bothers to mention the Negro slave, and calls the natives *merciless savages,* an opinion I'd been inclined to share. My point is that I left my ability to believe in civilized law—to believe in it and to sacrifice for it—buried with a family in the bloody soil of a Virginia farm.

Because after I did that, what was possible?

Anything, I supposed. Or nothing. And I hadn't yet decided.

So for the time being, I thought of the Colonel's depiction of civilization as I thought of theater—sometimes farcical, sometimes pathetic, even perhaps beautiful and grand—but always unreal. Yet to the Colonel, as to any great artist, theater was reality. And *civilization,* rather than a word that described a place we had come from—a place lost—or a sentimental whimsy for which horrors had been committed so that they wouldn't have to be committed anymore—*civilization* became a thing still in the process of being imagined. For not only had his vision of the future remained uncorrupted by the horrors of his experience, but the horrors of his experience, of all of our experiences, had become the supporting timbers of his vision.

This was the magic trick that intrigued me. And so I paid careful attention as his tiny room, his dark office, became an art studio in which he painted pictures of cities with wide, clean streets, public universities, museums, and airy cathedrals displaying a grace far surpassing the finest ever built anywhere on earth.

Sometimes, if Belly happened to be passing through the room (for inactivity bored him, and he was ever on the move), he might listen just long enough for his gaze to cloud over. He stood mesmerized by the Colonel's descriptions of places he knew, or thought he knew, and as his confusion grew he shifted his weight from one foot to another and clamped and reclamped his big hands.

"Colonel!" he shouted one day when he could no longer stand it, for he raised his voice when he was uncertain. "Are you thinking of the same Pigeon Falls I'm thinking of?"

The Colonel paused and tilted his chubby face as though he'd heard an unidentifiable sound. Then he said quietly, with a voice trained in reasonable discourse, "Apparently not, Captain."

And once, when hearing the Colonel in a letter to a U.S. senator describe me as "my secretary, the esteemed Dr. Freeman Walker, writer, explorer, social scientist," Belly grinned and shook his long face from side to side and said, "Colonel, I think you got the wrong Freeman!"

ONE AFTERNOON THERE WAS a knock at the Colonel's door, and we were visited by two Committeemen who introduced themselves as Mr. Grundy and Mr. Frank, of the law firm of Grundy, Frank, and Gallagher. Grundy was a large man with a wide neck and face that spread muffin-like from a tight white collar. Frank carried a cane and smelled like eau de toilette. He was shorter than Grundy, thin-necked, with an Adam's apple that looked sharp to the touch.

Immediately after shaking our hands, Grundy excused himself and squeezed the wide bridge of his nose to suppress a sneeze. We all watched and waited, and when the urge had apparently passed, he said, "Excuse me, but the doctor told me if I sneeze, I could die. May we sit?"

I pulled a chair from the dark corner into a shaft of dusty light coming in from the window. Grundy sat and thumped his chest a couple of times with his fist. "Bad heart," he said, and dared a smile.

The Colonel sat in his wicker chair.

I offered Mr. Frank a stool, but he shook his head and took what looked to be his customary position at the arm of Mr. Grundy.

"Tea?" I asked.

"Please," Grundy said. Frank nodded. I left them alone and went down the hall and stairs to the kitchen to get some hot water. My steps made a thump-drag noise on the wooden floor that made me self-conscious. When I came back with the tray, Mr. Grundy was squeezing his nose again. "We," he managed to say, and paused. I put the tea down. The Colonel and I looked at one another, his eyes twinkling in amusement.

"We," Grundy continued, when the danger had apparently passed, "are extending to you, our acting governor and his staff, an invitation to join our cause."

The Colonel kept his mouth taut, although I could tell he wanted to smile. "Let me get this straight," he said, and paused. "You mean we have been voted adequate by a—"

"Voted, no," our guest said. "Not exactly. We make our decisions based on consensus. Any one man can block the entire Committee actions, isn't that right, Frank?"

Frank nodded.

"But we are all good fellows, and so we've never had a blocker."

"Not one that lived, anyway," the Colonel said.

Grundy shook his head. "Fellows like that, fellows that can't seem to get along, tend not to be asked to join, wouldn't you agree, Frank?"

"Indeed," Frank said. It was the first I heard his voice, and it sounded like a squeak. As though painfully aware of that fact, he tapped his cane resolutely.

"I think you will find," Grundy continued, "that the Committee for Safety and Decency is an organization of good men, full of class, so to speak. In fact, we are the best class of people—and you must know the Territory is overrun by those of weaker moral character—lower classes, certainly, as I know you've surely seen the displays of public drunkenness, gunplay, lewd behavior with women of the night. Indeed, not even *of the night,* but *of any old time.* You've seen the public gambling and the association of darker characters who have attempted and in some cases succeeded in making private gains, that is, taken personal advantage, through illegal means, of our lack of laws and—and if you excuse me here, Mr. Acting Governor, but you must admit—the government's inability to enforce the law we do have. Because of all of that, combined with the threat of pagan savages, who lurk at the edge of our vision and impede our travels into the wild country and threaten our homesteaders, whose wild and unnatural instincts cannot be tolerated, our organization of the decent citizens for justice, our Committee, mind you, has dedicated itself to the eradication of evil and vice and paganism, things that in a civilized person such as yourself—in this advanced year of our Lord one thousand eight hundred and sixty six—things which a civilized person such as yourself, Mr. Acting Governor, cannot help but champion."

During this earnest speech, a number of curious things happened. For one, the speech was punctuated by Frank, who, having at last found a means of participating, continued to thrust his cane to the floor as though called upon to dutifully squash bugs. For another, the Colonel pulled from his pocket a flask of whiskey, which he attempted unsuccessfully to uncap. He had a sliver in his hand, and his palm had grown red and sore. He passed the bottle to me. I uncapped it and passed it back to him, and we all watched as he tipped some of its contents into his tea. He looked up from under his bushy eyebrows to our guests and raised the flask slightly as a gesture of invitation.

But before either of our guests had a chance to decline, a shirtless Belly burst into the room wearing a gold garter around the crown of his head. Close behind him, as though in chase, ran the woman whose garter he'd apparently taken. Surprised by the crowd, she stopped and stood perfectly still, her turquoise eyes moving timidly from us to Belly to us again. She wore a gold-trimmed scarlet dress cut especially to feature acres of her bare bosom, which rose and fell as she caught her breath. Belly reclined on the bed and beckoned her to join him. She hesitated, looked confused for a moment, and then let out a high-pitched scream that raised the hair on the back of my neck.

The cause of her distress was a black rooster that had scooted in the door behind her and briefly tangled itself in the folds of her skirt. With a flurry of wings and beak and claw, it managed to untangle itself. I stepped toward the door to guide it out, but instead collided with the woman just as she was turning toward Belly on the bed. I lost my balance when my bent foot came down wrong, and I fell backward onto Mr. Grundy's shoulder and across his right thigh. The woman fell on top of me, shrieking with laughter now, and from somewhere past all of her flesh, I heard Grundy let out a sneeze of unimaginable sound and fury.

If this scene is comic in the telling, it was less so in the living. My elbow was throbbing, and my ankle, too, and when we scrambled quickly to our feet, Grundy's face had turned as red as the woman's dress. We all stared at him, waiting for the fatal effects of the sneeze—would he keel over dead?

He did not.

"Mr. Acting Governor," he managed to say slowly, recovering, "my health necessitates that I be brief. I am asking you to join the Committee and lead an expedition into the Territory east of the mountains in search of wild natives. No need to wait for money and supplies from Washington—for we might all be dead by then! The Committee can guarantee all you need—horses, provisions. And you can be sure there will be no shortage of armed and mounted volunteers. It's your choice, Mr. Acting Governor. We can leave in the early spring with you at the head of the column, or with someone else."

The Colonel's eyes flashed with anger. "Someone else?" he asked.

"Or no one," Grundy said. "If you aren't interested, there are other ways to do it. With a bounty on scalps, entrepreneurs will find their way."

At that the Colonel stood. He approached the sitting Grundy and bent forward at the waist so his face was just inches away. "Are you proposing to open this Territory to the buying and selling of human flesh?"

Grundy looked suddenly amused, and his tiny green eyes seemed to dance between the folds of his overly meaty face. "Human?" he asked.

The Colonel's face turned bright red. He seemed on the verge of exploding with anger, but instead slowly stood up straight and took a step backward. I put myself between him and our visitors.

"As secretary to the Governor," I said, "I can guarantee that your proposal will be put on his agenda and you will receive your answer in good time."

With that I limped toward the open door, and stood to the side while our guests filed out. Grundy led the way into the hallway without a look backward, but Frank paused in front of me and leaned close to whisper in tea-smelling breath, "You might do better with a cane, son."

BEFORE THEY LEFT THE next morning, I listened from the hotel balcony while the Colonel, mounted on his gray mule, Destiny, his sword still in its rusted scabbard, announced to an almost empty street that his own long and bloody career as a warrior had convinced him that he could no longer abide slaughter.

Belly hunched at his side on a little black pony named Bug. His long black hair fell out from under his hat and across the shoulders of his white coat, and his long legs dangled past the stirrups and his boots almost touched the snow. A small cluster of men with scarves pulled up over their faces for warmth leaned against the barbershop across the street. Two children trailing a bone-bag yellow dog walked by carrying bundles of firewood on their shoulders.

"Yes, it is true," the Colonel shouted, as the wind was fierce, "that we may very well meet an early death! And yes, it is true there may indeed be much to fear! But I have been spared death too many times not to have wondered why! And as I made this long journey to the Great Western Territory, I suddenly knew in my mortal bones that if this new place offers us anything, it offers us the promise of peace! But it is a peace we must be brave enough to seek! Our enemy is fear, and our friend is courage! Fear has given us war without end! Courage—and this new Territory—gives us a chance for peace!"

His words and the little puffs of vapor that accompanied them blew away in the wind as soon as they left his mouth. His mule lifted its tail and dropped green manure on the white snow, and then they rode off. I watched their dark figures grow smaller and smaller as they followed the switchback trail up the hillside east out of town. The plan was to try to find this congregation of bloodthirsty natives, to make peace, and so to diminish the fear that would drive the Committee's war of extermination. They entered a cluster of trees, just the two of them, but still I stood outside shivering, determined to see—because they'd need all the help they could get, certainly—and sure enough, when they emerged again to cross a white snow field, just before disappearing over the brow of the mountain, they trailed a long line of mounted ghosts.

While they were away, I kept myself busy writing letters—to "Norton, trader" and to "the Simpson Family" in Centreville, Virginia, and to all the government offices I could think of that might have records concerning the whereabouts, or fate, of my poor mother. In my room writing, I could sometimes conjure the smell of Sweet Grass soil and spring sap. I could hear her laughter mingling with my father's voice and the sound of water running over rocks. But each day when I put away the pen and closed the envelopes with the seal of the Governor of the Great Western Territory, my joy would quickly fade and I'd be alone again, and far from home, in a silent room. Belly and the Colonel were gone a week. Two weeks. More. Were the rumors true? Had they left the Territory altogether? Had they been murdered by natives? Had they left me all alone?

To distract myself, and to escape the dangerous silence, I often crept down the hallway outside our rooms to the stairs where I squatted on the top step to gaze down at the dance hall below. The hurdy-gurdies and their colorful dresses made splashes of mad color throughout the drab crowd. I'd taken to smoking a pipe, as Belly did, and so I sat on the top step whiling away long hours taking vicarious pleasure from the dancing and laughing and drinking below.

Late one afternoon when the light from my window faded from blue to gray and then again to early darkness, the noise from the dance hall grew lively and joyful shouts sounded through the wooden floor of my room. Seeking the usual diversion, I crept down the hallway and squatted on my step, where I could see through the dim lantern light the two barrels supporting a plank that served as the bar. Men in great-coats and greasy hats filled the room, along with at least three dogs, a goat, and even a pig lying asleep under the bar. I knew something was different when I saw that the hurdy-gurdies had pressed themselves up against the far wall like paint. I hadn't time to puzzle, though, for the saloon doors swung open immediately and in walked a squint-eyed, knock-kneed rounder named Meyer with a couple of nearly naked native men on leashes. The natives had apparently sneaked into town and been caught stealing liquor. The crowd roared and made a circle, and the solemn-faced braves paraded around like show horses while a man named McQuirk took bets on what he was calling a Fight-o-Rama. One of the braves was very tall and lean, and the other short and husky, and their wide physical difference gave the impending battle a bull-versus-bear appeal.

With the leashes removed from the men's necks, they moved into the center of the human ring, bare-fisted, dressed only in breechcloths and moccasins. Between them, on a table, stood Meyer with a frowzy red silk kerchief around his neck. His shadow cast by a raised lantern loomed large on the wall and ceiling behind him. He stood coiling the leashes slowly around his right hand until the crowd quieted, and then, in the middle of a baggy face the color of a catfish belly, his lips parted to reveal a pair of orange squirrel teeth. His tongue flicked over the teeth as if to reassure himself that they were still there, and then in a high, piercing voice he announced the rules of the contest.

"Each buck," he said, "will take his turn standing upright, hands at his side, allowing the other to hit him squarely above the waist. Any move to dodge or block a blow will serve only to allow the puncher another swing. The bucks will take turns punching each other, and every solid blow landed will be rewarded with a shot of whiskey to the puncher. The last man standing will win fifty dollars in gold flakes."

Men cheered, placed their final bets, and the human ring expanded and contracted, then expanded again as if the crowd itself were alive and breathing with anticipation.

The tall, lean brave had the first opportunity to punch his brother, and he did, with lanky gusto. The sound of knuckles against cheek sent chills down my spine and I had to look away. When I looked back, the short brave stood blinking, but otherwise seemed to have taken the blow without apparent effect, and the tall native turned and drank his payment, a shot of whiskey. Swallowing, he shook his head and grinned, and stood staring at his wider brother, prepared to accept a blow. By the looks of his crooked nose, this would not be the first time he'd been punched.

The short native landed a powerful uppercut that seemed to lift, or at least to stretch, the tall one upward. When his weight came down again, he was on his heels, and he had to take a step back and his head wobbled. The crowd gasped and cheered as the short one took his shot of whiskey and stoically prepared himself to field a second blow. It was delivered by his tall brother with more precision if less force than the first, and his nose spurted brilliant crimson blood, eliciting a wild cheer from those who'd bet he'd fall first. The tall native drank a second shot of whiskey and, grinningly, prepared to accept another blow, which was delivered by the shorter man. Blood trickled from the tall man's lip.

Like this, then, the fight progressed. Soon each man's face grew swollen and discolored, and the blood dripping from their noses and mouths reddened not only their knuckles and hands, but also their shoulders and chests. And as they got bloodier, they also got drunker, so their punches grew less effective, which served the purpose of drawing out the spectacle and drama. The tall native man would land a blow, and the short one would stagger. Then he would collect himself and send the tall native spinning with a hook to the side of his head. Each man tottered on the verge of falling from the beating and from the whiskey, but at the last possible moment would find the hidden reserve necessary to remain upright and cling to the opportunity to keep drinking and, perhaps, to win fifty dollars.

I wish I could say that while I was witnessing this bloody spectacle, I grew so outraged that I stood up from my crouch on the stairs, stamped my crooked foot, and announced my intention to stop the barbarity or die trying.

But I can't.

For as much as the contest horrified me, I could not avert my eyes, and the longer the fight went on, the more complicit I felt—and the more complicit, the less capable I felt of moving. This was the slippery slope of cowardice and I recognized its intoxicating pull. But there was more to it than that. I'd been in the place of those natives, and I'd felt their debasement, and I loathed everything about me that had put me there. Every cell of our bodies rebels against victimhood and powerlessness, and so when given the chance we leap to the side of the perpetrators. At least that's what I did. Each fresh spray of red blood, every new punch and stagger, was accompanied by lusty cheers, and in hearing these voices, in feeling this warm air and this colored spectacle by lantern light, and finally in smelling the living flesh of a room full of fellow men, I attached my will to that of the crowd.

I hated myself for my cowardice, but cowardice only grows with self-loathing, and so in my downward spiral I even began to cheer. Not for either one of the fighting natives, but for both, and for the undaunted and indefatigable spirit that remained in each—that was what I told myself, anyway. They were human beings, after all, for how else could I feel such admiration? Part of me had begun to believe the rumors about the Colonel and Belly—that they'd never return—and I assumed it was only a matter of time before I was thrown out of the hotel onto the street again. So all of the pity I had to spare I aimed at myself. Me, the poor murderer of children. I looked at the joyful faces of my fellow watchers, willed myself a part of them, of that crowd, and told myself we were also cheering for ourselves, for our own suffering and endurance and depravity—cheering even for our ability to still cheer.

That's the best way I can describe it, or excuse it. Because the fact is I was cheering madly with the rest of them when the doors of the saloon swung open and, accompanied by swirls of snow, the Colonel and Belly stepped inside.

"WHENEVER I SEE INJUSTICE," he said to me the next day by means of explanation, "I can no more not act to stop it than the rays of the sun can fail to warm or those of the moon to dampen."

He lay in my room, with his head on the lap of Helga, the red-haired German woman, who had bandaged his face so absurdly and entirely that only a slit remained for his words to come out and food and drink to go in.

When he and Belly had walked into the saloon the night before, the tall native had just taken a blow that swiveled his jaw and sealed his fate as a man who would die of starvation before spring, a gruesome death caused by his inability to chew food.

The Colonel, wearing a buffalo-skin greatcoat, stood on a chair and raised his voice and sword until all around him had stopped cheering and simply gaped at him. Yellow lantern light played on the underside of his face, and his giant shadow spread across the wall and ceiling.

"As acting governor of the Territory, as a man who has vowed to do all he can to build a fair and just civilization, I hereby announce the end of this fight."

Laughter followed this announcement, and the spectacle of the Colonel on a chair, in his greatcoat, waving his sword, served for a short time as entertainment.

"You going to stop us from having a little fun with the savages?" shouted McQuirk, a stubby, hairy, troll-like man, whose bootlegs sagged to his ankles.

"I am."

Belly tried to play the diplomat. "Sir," he said to the Colonel, "perhaps we should parley with the men tomorrow, when all of this is settled, and all bets have been won or lost accordingly."

The Colonel shook him off. "Heaven hath not created," he shouted, waving his sword about his head, "nor hell seen, any that can frighten me. Like any mortal, I am rationed one square death, but there exists no evil power in all the world that can defeat me."

I, like the crowd, and like the bleeding natives themselves, stared at the figure of the man, roundish, whiskered, dressed in a big buffalo coat and waving a sword that, as sharp as it might have been, seemed quaint in its harmlessness. Hadn't I seen this before?

"How you going to stop us?" somebody yelled.

"With the strength of my arm!" I heard him shout. Then, suddenly, whether he stepped down into the fray or was pulled, I don't know, but the last I saw was the glint of his sword as he disappeared into the mob, which pounced on him, and pummeled him. Belly was also pulled to the floor and buried under kicks and punches, and like that they might have both been murdered had not a good share of their attackers been diverted into a general free-for-all in which everybody punched and kicked and gouged and pulled everybody else's hair.

I ran down the stairs and crept on hands and knees across the sawdust floor through a mayhem of legs in order to aid both of them. I don't know what I was thinking beyond that. I suppose I thought that if they died, I might as well be dead, too. But when I reached them, they weren't dead, and neither was I. So how was I to pull two men through a vicious crowd and up the stairs to safety? I pried one hand under the Colonel's head and shoulders, and clamped the other around Belly's ankle. Then something mysterious happened that I can't explain. I pulled, and they moved. I pulled again, and they moved more. There were feet and legs all around us as the melee continued. There were boots kicking but I wasn't touched. I pulled again, and the two bodies slid behind me as easily as if they had been sleds on ice. And then, suddenly, I could see. Ghosts, dead Irish soldiers, had crowded into the riotous saloon and parted the crowd and hunched over the Colonel and Belly, and helped me pull them across the floor and up the stairs without being noticed. Helped me pull them down the hall and into our dark room and shut the door.

I lit a lantern and looked around but it was just the three of us again. I struggled to get Belly into bed, and then I sat on the floor and cradled the Colonel's bloody head in my now bloody lap. He opened his blue eyes, and stared at me in a way that gave me the shivers.

"Within a few days," he said, "we came upon a—" He coughed blood, and I wiped his cheek with my sleeve.

"It's okay," I said.

"A village," he said, "so expansive it filled the eastern valley to the horizon. As if all of the natives in the entire Territory had come together for the winter. But when they saw us coming, they folded their tents and were suddenly gone. They disappeared into heavy timber. We followed their tracks in the snow. Into the mountains, where the air is thin and clear and very cold. High. Higher than either of us had ever gone before. Past the trees to where the tracks entered a bare talus slope. But they never emerged on the other side. Or on any side. It was as if an entire nation had found a seam in the mountain and, through it, disappeared."

I glanced at Belly. He shrugged. He seemed as puzzled by this story as I was. I looked back to the Colonel.

"We camped up on the edge of that rocky field waiting to see something but we never did. We waited until our hunger grew too strong, and we had to come down again."

"We did get hungry," Belly said.

The Colonel closed his eyes and breathed raggedly through his bloody mouth and nose. Was he dying? Or about to die? In his hand he still gripped his sword, which had broken in the struggle, but now his fingers slowly relaxed. I wiped the sweat from his brow; he opened his eyes and looked at me with a steady, blinking recognition.

"Aaaah, yes," he said, and breathed. "I know you now. Wouldn't you be the faerie that saved me once before?"

I looked at him through sudden tears of joy and guilt. *No,* I wanted to say. *You* are the one who saved *me!* From my frozen grave on the side of the road. From my own paralyzing fear. From the loss of the notion of what heroism might still be possible—

Yet before I could open my mouth, he closed his eyes. Which gave me time to think. *A faerie?* What was that? Was it like a *nigger,* just another box? What's possible? *Nothing?* I swallowed. *Or anything?*

But my uncertainty was fleeting because at that moment as I sat warm and well-fed, my nails clean and trimmed, as I looked at Belly on the bed and the Colonel cradled on my lap—two men I'd just pulled from a mob with the help of Irish ghosts—and in so doing pulled myself from the depraved joy of the bloody Fight-o-Rama—well, being a faerie seemed as good an explanation as any other.

Oh, the mystery!

The Colonel opened his blue eyes with his question yet hanging between us.

"Indeed," I finally said. In this odd life I would be free to believe anything. "I am he."

This time when he closed his eyes, the Colonel smiled slightly, and his body immediately relaxed into sleep.

BOOK THREE

I sound triumphal drums for the dead. . . . I fling through my
 embouchures the loudest and gayest music to them,
Vivas to those who have failed, and to those whose war-vessels
 sank in the sea, and those themselves who sank in the sea,
And to all generals that lost engagements, and all overcome
 heroes, and the numberless unknown heroes equal to the
 greatest heroes known.

—Walt Whitman, *Song of Myself*

MAGIC

THE DAY AFTER THE beating, Belly, bruised and sore, his head
aching from being knocked unconscious, was up and taking care of
himself, but the bandaged Colonel lay still and didn't want me to leave
his side. At first I was nervous—how does a faerie-secretary behave?—
but there were practical things to do which I did with ease, if not faerie
magic. I changed his facial dressings so he could see. I also noticed
a bad puncture—a knife wound—in his biceps that had not been
cleaned, and so I washed that and bandaged it, and nursed him with
tea and sausages and whiskey, and then I sat with him while he took a
nap. He hadn't mentioned anything about calling me a faerie, but if
he'd forgotten, I had not. While he slept, I thought it through. Hadn't
I lived a charmed life?

How many other seven-year-old slave boys had been freed from
slavery by a loving father who'd sent them to England to be
educated?

None that I knew.

And even after my father's death, when I was forced to leave school,
hadn't I been the one boy in the saddlery who was *not* an orphan?
Whose mother existed somewhere, and who I knew loved me?

I was.

And walking this country, hadn't I been given a white man's privilege, simply by wearing a hat? And hadn't the soldier Gibbs taken the ball to the head while I, sitting next him, did not? And hadn't it been Saturn, not I, who died of fever just minutes after his shackles were removed?

True, all true.

Why did I run into Junie in that dark New York stairway on my way to leap off the roof? Why did the gentleman on the ship jump overboard and not me? Why Mr. Smith in the river? And even though I'd been left a cripple, had I ever met another man who survived his own hanging?

I had not.

But perhaps even more to the point: Why did Miss Crinkle die when I hoped she'd die? And why did my father drown at sea right after I told God I'd give up *anything* to be delivered from fever and isolation?

For a long time I had understood these mysteries as manifestations of divine justice and my own selfish prayers. Or simply as mysteries.

So why not faerie magic?

I sat by the Colonel's bedside and I closed my eyes and wondered how many hundreds and thousands of shovelfuls of hard dirt I had dug and tossed back onto bodies in graves, how many dead I had buried and how few I remembered. I dared not look into the grave after Hardy put the children there. I refused to hear their breathing after Banks jumped in to quiet them. The stars blinked out that night in Virginia—part of my sky had gone dark and I'd been afraid to look up ever since. But in the growing darkness of our quiet room, with the Colonel lying on a bed in front of me, I listened to his breath, and I listened to my own, and suddenly I wasn't so afraid anymore. I breathed in—breathed in the horror, felt it fill me, and breathed it out. I breathed it in again, felt it fill me, and breathed it out.

Did the Yankee captain decide I needed to bury the rebel children—or did I make that decision?

Breathe in, breathe out.

Through the rectangular window above the Colonel's bed I could see stars blinking like eyes in the frozen night, and I felt the weight of shame begin to magically lift from my heart. Not because I believed my choice was anything but brutal—nor that I'd been forgiven—but because without the anesthesia of self-pity, I felt more poignantly than ever the true horror of what I had done.

I shuddered in anguish. What I had *done,* not what had happened to me. I buried living children with my own hands. Then I walked free with my own legs. Walked away because I was free. Because my father said so. Because he read it in the Declaration of Independence. Which I learned to read. Especially the part about the right to pursue happiness, which I could see now (suddenly! brightly!) I'd been afraid to do. For hadn't I used my shame to keep happiness at bay? Hadn't I wallowed in my suffering, real as it might have been, in order to justify my selfish prayers?

I tucked my legs under me on the soft chair next to the Colonel's bed. Breathe in, breathe out.

We do the best we can do. But then, suddenly, things had magically changed. First when the Colonel stood on a chair surrounded by a mob and announced an end to the brutal fight, an end to my own free fall. And then that moment on the floor of my room, saved by Irish ghosts, the Colonel's bloody head on my lap, when a question emerged that I'd never dared ask until the Colonel had unwittingly given me an explanation.

How else might I explain my good fortune?

I was a man, certainly, but couldn't I be a faerie, too? I was a Negro and white man, a slave and free man, lover and killer both. Indeed.

Faeries, the Colonel had said from the balcony that first afternoon, *faeries stand to reason.*

But what exactly was a faerie?

Ghosts were spirits of dead mortals that held grudges and passions, and often visited their former lives. The ghosts of the Irish brigade had parted the crowd in the bar and helped me pull Belly and the Colonel to safety. But faeries were different. They were creatures that lived in a world separate but parallel to the world of mortals. They passed back and forth from one side to the other through places in which the worlds intersect. Their dealings with mortals were often chance meetings, and often, for the mortals, dangerous. I'd heard it said when a man died young that the faeries must have loved him too much.

So it was clear. *It stood to reason.* More than a few I'd loved had died. And hadn't I passed back and forth from one side—of the ocean, of the street, of the racial divide, of the grave, of the continent, of the line between poverty and wealth, hope and despair—to the other?

One morning I languished underground with shackles around my ankles, and by evening of the same day I had buried the innocents. One day I was hungry and alone, and the next I walked over the same ground, treasure in my pocket, accompanied by a happy-faced dog.

When the Colonel woke in the morning after that long night, I adjusted the pillow under his head so he could look past the ferns of frost on the glass to the pink sky over our smoky town. I prepared paper and ink in case he wanted to dictate but he only mumbled something I couldn't understand and reached for my hand and closed his eyes again. I closed my eyes, too, and thought of my father's words: *It will take becoming a man to learn this one: We do not live for ourselves.*

"Stay with me, Mr. Walker." He squeezed my fingers.

Becoming a man. Becoming a faerie. It felt as if the gates to my soul had opened and the world, much bigger than I had previously imagined, flooded in. I filled with possibilities. I was free. For good as well as evil, hilarious as well as grim. I determined to learn the Colonel's magic—how he used the horrors of the past to gird his beautiful vision of the future—and perhaps I'd already begun.

"Have we any word from Washington on statehood?" he asked. "Any new recruits in the battle of free civilization over timid respectability, bold law over the terror of safety?"

I told him no, but it was still winter, and much of the mail had been delayed by heavy snow.

EVERY MORNING HELGA AND I changed the Colonel's dressings in his bedroom while he sat stoically and endured the discomfort. His head and face healed quickly, so soon we were only tending his arm. He'd sit up in bed and we'd gently unwrap the cloth from his shoulder only to see in the light from the window spreading colors around the wound. Helga would come in with a basin of soapy water and I'd rinse the wound, dab it dry, and then rewrap it with a clean rag. Helga would wash the dirty rags and hang them to dry downstairs over the stove. I did not know a lot about infection, but by the smell of this one I knew the Colonel was on the edge of losing his battle. If gangrene bloomed, it would mean the beginning of death. I tried to have faith, and if I still prayed, I would have prayed, but instead I used all of my faerie magic to clean and bandage the wound as well as I could while the Colonel looked out the window and kept his face calm. He'd breathe deeply through his nose, nod his appreciation, and sometimes grip my hand tightly in pain.

My magic worked. Before the smell that I knew to be a forebearer of death became real, it was gone. The blooming color deep under the skin faded and we both knew he was going to get better. As he began to heal, he began to talk again. I'd sit by his bedside in candlelight, or by day in the bright wash of sunlight though the window, and listen while he recounted to me often and with stunning clarity a life in which he had repeatedly failed to succeed at the great goals for which he strove. After the defeat of the Young Irish Rebellion, he journeyed to Van Diemen's Land, where he'd been banished by the Queen of England. There he married a woman. They had a son, who died, and his wife soon followed the boy to her grave. His failure to love her adequately haunted him still.

"They were near me," he said, "yet I couldn't see them. I was blinded by my own past, by my defeat in Ireland. Then, suddenly, they were gone."

In his grief, he escaped on a ship to New York City, a place teeming with his ragged countrymen. He used his celebrity to build a short career as a star lecturer. When that faded, he bought a newspaper but couldn't turn a profit. He fell in love with a society girl, and they married. He studied law but because he was unable to sit still long enough to establish a reputation and gain clients, he never earned enough to support her and their marriage foundered. He told of the shame this caused him, and so he fled to Central America, wrote travel pieces, and tried in vain to negotiate the rights to build a canal through Costa Rica. This would be his great success, he thought, and make his fortune, but the war between the states erupted and all negotiations ceased. He returned again to New York, penniless, and was offered a commission in the Union Army because he could successfully recruit Irish soldiers. He fought bravely and honorably, but despite his best efforts on the battlefield, he was drummed out of the service by career officers and forced to finish the war as a civilian.

In short, two decades of wandering in search of fame and fortune in the most remote corners of the globe had brought him no fortune and only a tarnished portion of fame.

And his luck here in the Territory did not appear to be changing.

"Two roads to greatness," he said one morning, "are gold and the sword. I've tried both, and failed, and failed again. And so I have been reborn under another star. And regardless of how things turn out, I now know of what I am made, and must undaunted continue to follow the path of righteousness."

Did I remember, he asked, the gentlemen who had visited us and asked us to join the Committee for Safety and Decency?

I said I did.

And did I remember Mr. Grundy's appeal to respectability?

I nodded, and helped him sit up in bed. The gray light from the window made his face look pale and sad.

"The most dangerous evils of the world," he said, "show themselves as the respectable activities of respectable people. There are cultures where it is perfectly respectable to eat other human beings, do you know that?"

I told him I'd heard as much.

"And there are cultures where the starving are left to die because respectable people think it is always better to let nature take its course than to help the weak, do you know that?"

I told him I did.

"And cultures where it is respectable to get on your horse or in your boat, cross the wilderness or the sea to a foreign land, rape the native women, kill the men and children, and bring the booty back home to your family, do you know that?"

I looked toward the window and the street below.

"And cultures where respectable people buy and sell other human beings and separate mothers from children, and husbands from wives?"

I nodded.

"And cultures that take eager girls to the top of pyramids and cut out their hearts and let their blood be a sacrifice to the god of corn?"

I'd read that.

"And cultures that march tens of thousands of eager boys across a battlefield to slaughter in a single day and consider it a necessary sacrifice for freedom? Have you heard of that kind of respectability, too?"

I stared at his blue eyes and swallowed. "Yes," I said.

"So why," he asked, "do we think of respectability as a virtue?"

I shook my head.

"For years," he said, "I strove for respectability. I wanted success that the world recognized as success. I wanted to make money, to have a position; I gloried in my fame. Being an Irish revolutionary in this country is a glamorous thing. Women's eyes shone when they looked at me. Men admired me, envied me. I was invited to the club, given a seat as the guest of honor. And I lived that way for a number of years in New York. A kind of roving honored guest. But never a regular, respectable member. That's what I wanted to be. And that's what I could never be. They wanted me to inspire them with tales. The army wanted me because I could bring my countrymen into the fight for the Union, Irishmen they could then slaughter. I could give rousing speeches that unleashed the courage of thousands of Irish hearts in the Union cause. I did that, and watched those Irish hearts pump their last blood into American soil. And when there was no more Irish blood to be spilled, the club of Union officers had me discharged. I never got credit for unleashing the storm that was the Irish Zouaves. And then, as if to get rid of me, to stop my pestering—although it has been the best thing that ever happened to me—I was dispatched here to this far-flung Territory as the lone representative of the federal government. To a Territory ruled by respectable thugs."

He laughed sadly. I'd begun to comb his hair, and red-haired Helga had come into the room and was standing behind me. I could feel the warmth of her body without even turning around. The Colonel's eyes brightened when he saw her watching.

"Here we can fight back, Dr. Walker. Here we can make our stand." And he turned to look up at me with the most vulnerable look in his eye, as though he wanted me to know, however it all ended, that his hopes were high hopes and his dreams were dreams such as good men dream.

Helga stepped between us to take the comb from my hand and continue with his hair. Her eyebrows were richly penciled, and her complexion suggested cream and roses. She wore a loose and low-cut calico dress that displayed to best advantage necklaces of colored beads lying across her bosom. She brushed carefully around the side of his head, taking special care with the black curl knotted above his ear. Out the open window the chickadees gathered on the sill. A warm wind had blown into the valley and we were getting a late-winter thaw. Dogs barked, even roosters crowed. Women yelled at children, and children called out each other's names, and men yelled at women and women yelled back at men, and everybody yelled at mules, and mules brayed and ravens cackled, and when he was done splitting wood, Long John began to play the piano in the Sighing Bones. In contrast to the dance tunes he played later, this time of day he played classics.

The Colonel closed his eyes as he listened. "I can feel it breaking my heart even as it lifts me to heaven, dear friends, don't you?"

"Ya, ya," Helga said, wiping a tear off his cheek with her big broad thumb.

BELLY GREW RESTLESS DURING the Colonel's convalescence, so he took to rising early and taking long hunting trips. One afternoon when he returned, his long black hair had been shaved off, and his bald pate stuck obscenely up through the hole of his bear-fur cape. He told the Colonel he'd grown tired of picking lice but he said something different to me. The Committee had set up a camp three days' ride from town in a place called Bloody Bend. No organized militia had been formed, but the hunting of natives had begun by small bands of murderous freelancers, who were arriving at Bloody Bend daily with scalps for bounty. He reported that a more fearsome stink hole he'd never seen in his life.

"If my hair were not gone," he said, "I'm sure I would have been separated from my topknot days ago."

To mitigate the effect of our gruesome secret, we commenced to drink heavily, and Belly cooked us all an ambrosial dinner of elk steaks. Attended by the Baden-Baden Princesses, as the Colonel had begun to call Helga and her sisters, the dinner took on the feel of a Roman bacchanal. The Christians were being tossed to the lions, but we had good food and good drink, which we savored all the more for what we knew we would eventually have to confront when the Colonel fully recovered.

I sat next to Helga and listened politely while the Colonel, his stab wound mostly healed and facial bandages long removed, described his ascent to the summit of a Costa Rican volcano.

"Green and glorious as the valley of Cartago is, the valley of Orosi surpasses it. Gazing from the bold brow of Paraiso to the raging waters far below, then up again to the mountains until the eye aches with their immensity, we ascend the steep and winding road."

Seated on either side of him, Greta and Gussy, whose English, if not their manners, had improved daily, began a discussion about the degrees of intimacy demanded by different sexual positions. The more intimate the position, the more difficult to do with a stranger.

"The gentle horses pick their steps with care," the Colonel said, "as though they know that stargazers and wonder-seekers sit on their backs."

Gussy and Greta had found a point of disagreement concerning what position they considered more intimate, and began shouting over the Colonel's head. Sometimes in German and sometimes in crude English, they argued vociferously for their respective points of view. As interested as I was in the Colonel's volcano story, the graphic details of the sexual activities described to support each sister's arguments were too compelling to ignore. Gussy stood up, and with an unlit candle as a phallus began an attempt to prove her point, albeit with her clothes mostly on.

The Colonel remained oblivious, and while Belly roared with laughter and shy Helga blushed, he calmly refilled his whiskey glass and began a description of his arrival at the summit. "On the brink of the crater in the predawn darkness, I felt as though I had been spirited from the living world and now stood in the very presence of Creation."

"That is *nothing*," Greta said, referring to the act her sister graphically demonstrated. "*That* I do with a gorilla!"

Without daring even so much as a glance at one another for fear we would blush or giggle, Helga and I looked down at our food. I liked breathing her scent when she was close, and soon I dared to look at where her left hand lay on the tablecloth next to her plate. I stared at the chubby white fingers and scarlet nails and used all of my faerie magic to get her to slide her hand over the edge of the table.

She did.

And lower it to my lap.

That, too.

Where she quickly learned that, faerie or not, I was a man in flesh.

"Gazing into the crater," the Colonel continued, "I watched a crack open and begin to leak fiery steam, although only steps away grew oaks big enough to prove that a hundred years had elapsed since the last eruption."

I placed no further demands on Helga. I didn't have to. It had been a long time since I'd felt the nimble touch of a woman's fingers, and it didn't take long.

"The dawn grew brighter," the Colonel continued, "and colors and fancies grew like a wild throbbing sea across the sky."

I caught my breath and rocked my chair back onto two legs. I don't know how long I managed to balance like that, gasping with my eyes closed, but the world disappeared while I was held suspended in Helga's dear hand. Finally I felt it passing and I rocked forward again.

"A home in a strange peace," I heard the Colonel say, "though frightfully far away."

When I opened my eyes again, Gussy and Greta and Belly had begun a retreat from the room, apparently to do research. The Colonel was watching them go.

"In order to be chaste," he said, "a man must first give in to his desires. In order to fast, a man must eat."

Helga had skillfully wrapped my dash of cream in a linen napkin, which she neatly tucked onto her lap. For the rest of the dinner she rewarded my timid glances with reassuring smiles.

THE NEXT MORNING, the newly bald Belly roused me early. My head ached and my mouth felt dry as dirt, but there stood the big-framed chap, dressed and ready. I got out of bed, and in the dim light from the window, I felt him watch me limp across the room and pour myself some water from a pitcher.

"Can you ride?" he asked.

I drank the glass of water.

"Where?"

"When the Colonel learns what's going on, he's going to want to go there and shut it down. We have to think of a strategy to keep him from such madness."

"Where?" I said again.

"Bloody Bend," he said.

Within the hour we were mounted. I was on Destiny, and Belly rode Bug, the little black mare. It was early spring and the snow slushy. We followed the trail south out of town just as the sun was coming up. The switchbacked trail took us over the lip of the mountain and down into a valley. To distract myself from the horror of our destination, I asked Belly questions about what we were seeing. He knew the country well, but was insecure when I asked questions, and so he responded as though he were a schoolboy and I was the master. For instance, I might say, "What tree is this?" To which he'd respond, "I know it, I know it! It is a fir!"

"What kind of fir?"

"A true fir!" he'd say. "A fir of the finest class! A tall, green-topped, well-bred fir!"

We'd ride in silence for a while, and then, if only to distract myself further, I might say, "And this? What bird is this?"

"I know it!" he'd reply. "A bird! A bluish bird!"

"A blue bird?"

He knew I had some schooling, and so tried hard to impress me with his subtle distinctions. "No," he'd say, "not exactly blue. Blue-ish. Distinctly bluish!"

After a while this became tedious and we rode in silence. The path evened out and became easy to travel. The ascents were gradual and the descents neither steep nor slippery. On the south slopes the snow had melted, and on the north slopes it was patchy. An hour before sundown we crossed a beautiful stream—a sparkling succession of little falls that caught the lower branches of the trees on its bank, and there we halted and built our camp for the night.

My legs throbbed from riding all day, but we feared an evening snowstorm and so cut uprights and rafters and peeled off strips of bark to tie them together. We planted six posts with the prongs up to receive the cross-ties supporting the roof. We spread an India-rubber blanket on the floor, then other warmer blankets over this, along with our saddlebags stuffed with socks and flannel drawers to serve as pillows. Our wet shoes and clothing we hung over a stick tied above the fire pit to dry, and after a while the iron pot was emptied of rice and elk meat and the last pipe smoked, and we stretched ourselves in our blankets and for a few moments listened to both the wind in the trees and the water in the creek.

Into this solitude, Belly let out a tremendous belch, which he followed with a somber soliloquy on our destination. Bloody Bend, he said, was a couple of dozen tents and hastily built cabins on the far shore of a stream that made a horseshoe bend through a canyon. Last week, as he'd approached it, he noticed its citizens had been leaving their shit on the trail that followed the riverbank. Before he crossed into camp, he could see quite of few of those same fine citizens lying on their backs in the sunshine, or facedown in the mud, and his first thought was that fever—smallpox, perhaps—had been ravaging the camp. He paused and stayed hidden in the trees. What he saw next terrified him. A group of men rode into town with stacks of scalps on the backs of their mounts bundled together by the hair. In the course of an hour, he watched three such groups ride past him, grim-faced and similarly loaded, and saw them take their bounty into a tent and emerge with money to buy whiskey, or whatever gruesome concoction was being sold by the bucket from barrels on the back of a wagon.

"It was then, there, in that grove of trees, that I cut my hair off," he said.

I felt him move and knew he was palming his bald head. My hair was long and woolly. I hadn't cut it in a long time. He must have read my mind, for the next thing he said was, "Nobody's buying Negro hair."

"I'm glad," I said. It had begun to snow and I could see the flakes drifting past the black shadows of pines. "But what are we supposed to do when we get there?"

He didn't answer at first. We both lay looking at the snow falling.

"I just thought you needed to have a look," he said finally.

"Why?"

He waited for a while, and I listened to the stream running, and the branches bending and dipping, and then I heard him say, "I don't know. He trusts you. Maybe you can explain."

"Explain what?"

"That if we try to stop them—just the three of us, I mean—they'll kill us."

For most of the night I lay awake with a ball of dread in my stomach. I stared up at the falling snow and wondered what good was magic if I couldn't even get a good night's sleep. I listened to the stream running nearby, and Belly roll over, roll over, and roll over again. When he finally lay still he began to snore like a champion. It wasn't until just before dawn that he stopped and I finally closed my eyes and heard rain begin to fall. I managed to sleep briefly while Belly packed most of our gear and got our mounts ready to go.

BUT THAT DAY WE never made it to Bloody Bend. Two things happened that caused me to successfully test my faerie powers and send us safely and heroically back to Last Best Chance City.

A steady, cold rain was falling by daybreak, so we went without breakfast and headed out onto the merciless damp trail, on which we had to dismount often. The loosened earth and slushy snow made for poor traction, and the rain and wind beat the branches against us, and lightning made our mounts reel. But by noon the storm had ended. The sun came out and steam rose from our wet clothing and the necks of our mounts as we descended a south-facing slope to a river. As we approached the bank, we heard a woman scream. We paused. Belly tilted his head and furrowed his brow.

We heard another scream and looked upstream. Belly pointed to the top of the cliff across the current. A coyote, ears upright and pricking the blue sky, stood on the edge of the precipice and looked downstream at something that was hidden from us by the bend.

"That way," Belly said, and we worked our mounts through the shallow water. At first the sound of the voice seemed to diminish as we approached the bend and I wondered if the coyote had been playing a trick on us. But soon the intensity and volume of the screaming grew and we knew we were going in the right direction. We increased our speed. When we got to the curve we saw a wagon tipped over in the middle of the fastest, deepest part of the blue-green water, and washed against the branches of a recently fallen fir tree. The current held the wagon against the straining branches of the horizontal tree and was pressing it relentlessly underwater.

The woman's head and clothing were wet and her face looked blue with a chill. Still, she animated when she saw us and screamed again. The sound of the water, the cool of the shade, and the frenetic screaming gave me the shivers.

"Have no fear!" Belly shouted to her, doing his best imitation of our boss. "We are the captain and secretary of the acting governor of the Territory, and we will have you out of danger as soon as we can!"

The woman looked at us through wide, wet eyes, across a vast white forehead and soaking mounds of hair. Swallows darted back and forth over her doomed head as if they wanted to watch the drama, or they imagined she would suddenly leap from her precarious perch, swim across the river, and steal eggs from their nests.

Belly worked his mount as far out into the river upstream as he dared. He wanted to get himself into a secure position from which he could toss a rope down to the woman. She could grab hold, and then he'd pull her back upstream out of the branches of the snag and then sideways to shore. But the current pushed against Bug's flanks and the water level rose with each step. I watched helplessly from the bank as she picked her way out between rocks, picking up a hoof and placing it carefully, sometimes trying two or three times before finding a spot under the torrent on which she could safely put her weight. By the time the water had risen to just under her stomach, she had to stop.

Belly began to swing the rope above his head as the wagon on which the women stood dropped even lower, entrenching itself in the submerged branches of the sweeper. The women screamed and Belly tossed the rope. The current pulled it straight downstream and yet the end of it dangled just shy of her reach. He looked over at me.

"What?" I shouted.

He tipped back his hat and moved sideways in the water, one careful step after another. If Bug stepped into a hole, and her chest lowered to catch the surface of the moving water, then mare and man would be swept downstream directly into the wagon, where mare, man, and woman all would be drawn under the sweeper to their deaths. I tried to look hard, to see the man, to see the mare, the water splashing around them, the spires of fir trees climbing the bank behind them toward a marvelous blue sky. No sign of help. No sign of ghosts to the rescue. I looked at Belly's magnificent body bent in struggle with his horse, his rope, and I wanted to remember every detail because I knew it might be gone in an instant.

I focused all of my power on him, on his horse, on the rope.

Belly tossed the loop again and this time the woman dove to grab it. For a terrifying moment she was submerged but suddenly she was on the surface again, her arms through the loop, whitewater churning around her head and face and her dress billowing out behind her. She had it!

Belly wrapped the end of the rope to the pommel of his saddle and leaned back in his stirrups to help offset the new weight. Bug stiffened and I focused on her to give her the strength she needed. She lifted a hoof to take a step, but her other three hooves started to slip, and she quickly put her fourth hoof down again.

I refocused my efforts. Bug readjusted her weight, and lifted a hoof again—this time she didn't slip—and took a step back. Carefully she lifted another, and another. The woman was screaming wildly, her shouts mixing with the crash of waves around her face and head. The wagon had submerged completely and the water under the snag bubbled and churned. Step by careful step, with my help, Bug worked herself, and Belly, and the woman toward shore.

When they got close enough, I stepped out into the freezing river over slippery rocks and grabbed the rope, worked my way hand over hand to the loop, and helped the woman to shore. As we emerged from the water, I discovered to my amazement that she'd been mostly undressed by the river. With too much to cover, she chose to cover only her face with her hands. I limped to my mount and unwrapped a blanket. With my back turned she must have stripped herself of what remained of her wet clothing, because when I returned to wrap her shivering shoulders in wool, she was completely naked and blue, her face once again hidden behind her hands. I got Belly's blanket, and put that around her, too, and only then did she dare a peek of tearful gratitude through her fingers.

WE STARTED A FIRE on the riverbank for warmth and when she dried off and warmed up sufficiently, Miss Colleen, as we came to know her, told us she lived in a mining camp just a few short miles from here, where she ran a boardinghouse. Tomorrow was her wedding day, she said, and she'd been trying to cross the river to bring back a preacher, but now, oh my, who would marry her and her sweetheart?

Belly told her I would. He said I was Dr. Freeman Walker, secretary to the governor of the Great Western Territory, and in the absence of other authority could perform weddings.

I didn't believe this was true, but Miss Colleen looked at me with such joy that I couldn't deny it. In fact, I must have nodded, for she gratefully threw herself into my arms and covered my neck with kisses. She pulled back momentarily and touched my hair with her hands. "Are you a Negro?" she asked, as though delighted by the possibility, but before I could answer, she'd begun looking from my left eye to my right eye, then back again.

"Look at your adorable eyes!" she said, and resumed her hugging and kissing.

Only when she'd sufficiently spent herself on admiration and appreciation did she pull back and think to hold the blankets more modestly around her. She dipped her head, blushed, and said she would be pleased to host us at her boardinghouse if we would allow her to keep the blankets for the journey, and perhaps ride one of the horses by herself?

Belly let her ride Bug. He walked alongside and we made our way through aromatic woods along the banks of the sea-green river. At the end of the day we ascended a hazy mountain slope into an isolated mining camp, tents, cabins, smoke, the smell of meat, and Miss Colleen directed us to a dusty log-cabin inn, where we were greeted by the presumed groom, an unfriendly-looking dwarf whose nose appeared to have been broken so many times that it resembled a piece of putty flattened to his face. His name was Epstein and he showed us our room and then escorted Miss Colleen behind a door guarding her private chamber. We didn't see either of them again for the rest of the night.

Without food, then, we lay awake on flea-pocked stretchers choking with smoke from the stove. Outside barked curs galled with hunger, and every time I almost fell asleep I'd wake to a cock crowing just outside the door. It seemed to me that all the plagues of the world had been summoned that night. We should have burned the place to the ground. It was an overwhelming desire that had to be resisted. Instead we spent much of the night huddled under ponchos in the open doorway, where we could at least breathe fresh air. Yet when it began to rain again we were forced to share even that narrow space with dogs.

In the morning, Miss Colleen emerged from her room looking greatly refreshed. After our infernal night, her face was a reminder of the startling beauty sometimes offered by the world.

Belly bowed and said he was glad to see she was feeling better this morning.

She laughed and put her finger to her lips. "Better, yes," she whispered, "but now my dear little man is sleeping, and he certainly deserves his rest." She paused; her cheeks pinked and she fanned herself. "Perhaps I ought not to have allowed myself to be seduced by a Southerner—especially since my dear brother lost his life to a rebel bullet. But all of us must endure, and that little man of mine certainly knows how to help soften the hardships of womanhood."

Here again she paused, giving us a moment to consider her meaning. She continued to fan herself and when she spoke next her voice had risen well above a whisper.

"Blessed be the day it became my good fortune to be his," she said, and gestured for us to sit, so we did. "And blessed be this day, the day of our wedding!"

We watched then as she made us a meal of buggy hotcakes and bitter coffee. While we were engaged with breakfast, Epstein emerged from the bedroom, stretched, and leaned against the doorframe . He was shirtless, lemon-colored, and more friendly-looking than he had been the night before. But I could see by the way he bit his lower lip that he had something he wanted to say.

Finally he spoke, and his words seemed to surprise even him: "Captain," he said to Belly, "are you authorized to make arrests?"

"I am," he said.

"Will you arrest me, then?" He stepped forward and put his hands up. "I am the notorious Robber of the Field, and I am turning myself in to your good offices."

WHY EPSTEIN WANTED TO be arrested by us on this, his wedding day, became clear in the darkened doorway behind us. Two men I recognized as good fellows from the Committee for Safety and Decency stood with drawn pistols cocked and pointing squarely at him. One was a red-faced, creased-browed schoolmaster from Last Best Chance City named Chamberlain. The other was a hunter named Burke, who wore *civilized* boots to his knees, spurs, and fringed buckskin leggings. I'd once spent a long afternoon drinking with him at the Dead Dog, during which he'd never ceased speaking of the time when he'd commanded the Moline Grenadiers in their raids against Black Hawk—or the time he'd been elected major of the brigade—or when he'd torn his way through miles of cacti and stone to lay siege to Chapultepec—or the evening he'd parleyed peace with the president of Bolivia or dined with the governor of California.

"Epstein," he said this morning from the doorway of our humble inn.

Epstein nodded. The nostrils of his misshapen nose whitened. Miss Colleen sighed and began to weep over the stove. Belly stood up from his meal and positioned himself in front of the pointed pistols.

"Lower your guns," he said. "For the Robber of the Field is in our custody."

Nether man lowered his gun. Belly ignored this fact. Inspired by his bravery—and also by Miss Colleen's tears—I stood up next to Belly.

"And besides," I said, "I, Secretary Walker, have been enlisted to perform a wedding. You two fine men for decency and respectability wouldn't stand in the way of Mr. Epstein and Miss Colleen making their union legitimate in the eyes of God and society, would you?"

Chamberlain looked me over. "Do you have any idea what crimes this Jew has committed?"

I had never heard of the Robber of the Field, or of his crimes, but I knew my own crimes, and I knew the crimes of men like Chamberlain and Burke, so I nodded. "I do," I said.

"He's our prisoner, anyway," Belly said.

As if on cue, both Burke and Chamberlain cocked their pistols.

"Sit down," Chamberlain said.

Belly and I did. Miss Colleen, however, threw herself on the floor and clasped her hands together. "Please," she said. "Please allow us to be married!" Tears fell unashamedly down her smooth cheek and dripped to the floor. Then she turned to her lover, stood up, and lifted him to her bosom and caressed his hair and kissed his face, and although his feet were not even on the ground, he looked every bit her equal in ardor. This went on for what seemed like too long. Finally, just to stop it, Chamberlain said to me, "Okay, marry 'em. Then we'll hang him."

Miss Colleen cried even harder at hearing this, but bent to set her groom down and retreated to her chamber to prepare. While she was gone, I arranged the furniture so that the groom was standing at the head of an aisle. Chamberlain kept his pistol pointing at Belly, who'd slumped in his seat in despair. Burke stepped around behind the groom to tie his hands behind his back and his ankles together. When he was satisfied the prisoner was bound well enough, he lifted him up and perched him precariously on a chair at the head of the aisle. I took my place next to the groom and he began to tell me the sad and pathetic story of his life. Through flooded eyes, he told how his father and mother were French-born, and he himself was born in Virginia but his father died when he was still a babe at his mother's breast. When she was strong enough, his dear mother scraped together a little money and they moved to Richmond. There she took in washing and was getting on well enough when all of a sudden he took it into his head to join William Walker's mercenary army, having heard it was carrying the day down in Nicaragua. Somehow or other he contrived to get down there, believing that from then on he'd have only the best of living.

"I was not a day in Nicaragua before I wished I was home again," he said. "But it was too late to turn back and I had to make the most of my wild whim—so I roughed it out and fought as bravely as I could in every battle from the burning of Granada down to the last assault at Rivas. Sharpshooting is my specialty, and from high in the branches of a tree, I killed many a man whose exact features were unknown to me. Oh, the horror I witnessed! The horror I was a part of!"

I used my handkerchief to dry his cheeks and wipe his flattened nose.

"Alas," he continued, "after the surrender of Walker to General Cañas, I was struck with fever at Punta Arenas, where I'd been brought as a prisoner of war, with several of my comrades. When I recovered my health, I managed to sneak out of the prison hospital in a sack full of bloody rags, after which I stowed away in a barrel on board a ship bound for San Francisco. I've been here since '62, and at first I dug gold, all I could. I did all right, but my back doesn't work like a tall man's back, so I thought my future lay in something else. It was then and only then I turned to crime."

Here again I took the liberty of drying the bound man's tears, which were still flowing freely.

"I beg you now to spare this poor man's life," he said.

Burke touched his pistol to the groom's temple. "Shut up now," he said, "and for exactly one hour I will."

So we waited in silence, choking in the smoke from the stove and listening to the rain on the roof.

Finally Miss Colleen emerged from her room wearing a yellow cotton dress, simple but clean and chaste, a matching piece of fabric holding back her black hair. Her red eyes gave proof that the tears had not stopped coming, even as she dressed. And when she stood before me next to her fiancé, her flow of tears thickened.

"Shall I do the long version?" I asked, "Or shall I be brief and to the point?"

"The long version," said the tearful bride.

So I asked the congregation to be seated. Burke and Chamberlain both sat down, their guns still raised and pointing at Belly and the groom, respectively.

"I will not begin until the guns are uncocked and set down," I said.

Burke looked at Chamberlain, who shrugged, and both did as I said, laying their pistols on their laps.

"The sun and the moon," I said, noticing that Chamberlain's gun was just an arm's length from Belly. I cleared my throat and began again. "The sun and the moon are the man and the woman, your life and yours, and they are traveling and ever traveling through the skies." I paused and tried to catch Belly's eye, but there was no need, for I could see he was thinking the same thing I was thinking. "You are each," I continued, "what God made for the other. He made your life and your life and all of our lives before the beginning of the world. He made them that they might go through the world, up and down, like the two best dancers that dance together one way, and then another, up and down the long floor of the dance hall, fresh and laughing, when all the rest are tired out and leaning against the wall."

I went on and on with this nonsense, my mind racing, looking for an opportunity to cause a distraction that would give Belly a chance to grab Chamberlain's gun. I extolled the virtues of married life through the ages, and praised the wonders of sanctified carnal relations through many long-past times and far-flung places, at which point Miss Colleen, seemingly on the verge of losing her balance, reached for and took the tied-together hands of her groom.

"Switch to the short version," Chamberlain said.

"Indeed," I said, and I proceeded to ask the betrothed the required questions, and they answered appropriately, and then with a magic word I pronounced them husband and wife.

What followed was a long kiss that we watched with awe. On and on they kissed, drunk with each other and oblivious to us and the rest of the world. A rooster crowing in the open doorway shook them from their entanglement, and, I believe, might have been all that saved the rest of us from witnessing a full-scale consummation of their new marriage.

Afterward Miss Colleen, now Mrs. Epstein, begged to be allowed to prepare for us a small celebratory repast of reheated beans. Without waiting for an answer from Chamberlain or Burke, she wrapped an apron around her waist and busied herself over the smoky stove. That's when something happened that I can only ascribe to faerie magic.

Bursting through the partially open doorway came the same black rooster with a bright red comb that had crowed just a moment ago, only this time he was mounted on the back of a panicked yellow dog. The rooster dug its leg spurs into the skin of the dog's back, cackled madly, and flapped its wings. The dog ran circles in our midst, yelping, bucking, snapping vainly over its shoulder. We all took a step back and stared at the spectacle.

"Goodness!" Mrs. Epstein said, turning from the stove to kick the moving dog. She flailed and missed, flailed and missed again, but this time connected squarely with Chamberlain's shin. Perhaps she was trying to do just that. For he whooped in pain, and Belly made a dive for his pistol. Before Chamberlain could recover, Belly had the pistol in his hands, and he rolled across the floor behind the spinning dog and fired twice. The first shot dropped Burke where he stood and the second did the same to Chamberlain.

Both men lay bleeding at our feet now but we hardly noticed because the dog was still leaping and turning in midair, and yelping and whining and snapping—and still the rooster hung on.

Mrs. Epstein stepped over the two dying men and kept after the dog, kicking and shouting until it was completely out the doorway and into the yard, where we watched as the mad rodeo continued. We marveled at the sight, and also at the velocity of the rock thrown by Mrs. Epstein, and at the hollow sound of it against the feathered side of the rooster. The rock knocked him off, and he ran away as fast as his two bloody feet could carry him.

The dog, suddenly relived of her crazy burden, sat down to try to lick herself clean, while we—the still living—collapsed into our chairs with laughter. Our faces flushed, we looked at each other and at the two dying men who'd so recently held us hostage, astonished at our magic new freedom.

All except Epstein. He remained standing with his feet tied together and his hands behind his back in that absurd position on top of the chair where he had just become a husband to his wife.

"I'm your prisoner now," he said to Belly.

"I suppose so," Belly said.

WE WERE BACK IN the city not more than a week—Belly given an immediate governor's pardon for the shooting—when I realized that a curious thing had happened to me since I'd become a faerie. I had been magically freed from my latest preoccupation with my mother. Since I had been back, I had neither written a letter nor gone across the street to check for answers to my earlier inquiries. I walked more easily—floated?—despite my limp. To look at the post office or watch the stagecoach arriving from the south no longer meant the onset of a melancholy mix of longing and disappointment when I invariably learned there was no letter for me. It wasn't that I never thought about her. I did, but with so much else going on, knowing her fate seemed less urgent.

For one, the Colonel had learned about the scalp market at Bloody Bend and was already talking about making a foray to close it down. When Belly told him it would be suicide with just the three of us, the Colonel took to spending his afternoons in the field below town drilling his Invisible Militia. Invisible to everybody but him and me. He wore an absurdly tall turkey-feather hat that Helga had made him, and an amber cloak with four crude stars sewn across the back, and he pranced back and forth across the field on Destiny's back, shouting orders and waving his broken sword.

To everyone else he looked like a madman. Only I could see the thousands of ghostly soldiers who followed at his beck and call.

So that was one distraction. The other was the upcoming trial of Epstein—for guess who had been appointed judge?

I was also the jailer.

I woke at dawn and dressed quickly to the sound of Belly's snoring. In the still pale light I tiptoed in my crooked way down the silent hallway to the stairs overlooking the dance hall. There I greeted the yellow cat and sometimes paused to pet him. I liked the view I had from the stairs through the window above the door to the street. I liked the tawny color of the dust, the shadows growing through the ruts, and dawn paling and pinking the sky. I put the cat down and got bread from the saloon pantry and walked the two blocks to the jail. It was late spring, and frosty in the mornings, and Epstein stirred on his straw tick when he heard me. I looked in at the dirt floor, the dark log walls. The room itself was barely six feet by six feet. I lowered myself to one knee and quietly slid a water pitcher between the bars, balancing the bread on top. Before I could turn to go, he moaned and opened an eye.

"Where does a man shit in this jail?" he asked.

I walked around back to find the old gold pan. When I came back, he was leaning up against the bars with his privates aiming toward the street, urinating. A horseman rode by, eyeing him curiously from under a black, broad-brimmed hat.

"Never seen one before, eh, drifter?" yelled the Robber of the Field.

The rider had a black scarf over his face and the collar of his jacket turned up. He reined in his horse and paused. "A runt like you, you mean?"

Short as he was, Epstein's piss made a high golden arc that muddied the dust a good twelve feet out from the bars. "No," he said. "A shooter like mine."

The horseman took a squint-eyed look. "Ain't hardly visible to the naked eye."

"Say thanks to God it ain't bigger," Epstein said. "'Cause if it were, I'd joust you to the ground!"

The rider's eyes—for that was all you could see of his face under his hat, over his scarf—his eyes sparked with amusement. "Lot of time for dreaming in there, eh, little man?"

"And after I knocked you off her," Epstein said, "I'd have my way with your mare!"

The horseman lifted his scarf to spit over his horse's neck, then he let the scarf fall back down again. "Aw, shucks, little man," he said. "If this old slut warmed to you, you'd be welcome to her. Nobody ever said or will say that John L. Crockett stood in the way of love."

"I'd take her if she warmed or not," Epstein said, finishing his business and tucking himself back in. "What I'm talking about wouldn't have nothing to do with love."

The rider narrowed his eyes. "Are you telling me you'd take Belle here against her will?"

The Robber of the Field nodded.

"Just fer spite?"

The Robber held the bars with both hands and nodded again.

"Are you that *mean?*" the rider said.

The prisoner squinted into the new sunshine. "I am."

John L. Crockett shook his head, whistled between his teeth in amazement. He patted his mare's neck and squeezed her gently with both legs to get her moving again. "Well, that *would* rile me some," he said. Then he turned, and for the first time we could see his mare's rump, and the four long black tails hanging where there should have been just one.

"Hey," Epstein shouted. "What's all that?"

The rider paused again, looked back over his shoulder. "These'n?" He gestured toward the extra black tails with his chin. "Them's scalps," he said. "The blood dries like glue so they stick fast and look like extra tails. And so pretty you wouldn't know which one to lift, now, would you?"

A too-thin boy with a round head and cropped yellow hair ran out from the house across the street and pointed at the horse's many tails and laughed a crazy laugh, like a string of singing hiccups. The rider looked at the boy coldly from up high, squeezed his horse's flanks and passed, but the boy followed after him, pointing and laughing his not-quite-sane hiccupping laugh. We watched and listened to the macabre spectacle as the tall horsemen, his many-tailed mare, and the lanky, laughing boy moved slowly down the block.

"What kind of inferno we come to here?" Epstein mumbled, after they'd finally turned the corner. He took the pan through the bars and retreated back into the shadows of the tiny jail for privacy.

While I waited, I watched a robin land on the peak of the house across the street and a woman step out onto the wooden porch and toss a bucket of water into the street. She paused when she noticed me leaning back against the log wall of the jail. She pushed a loose strand of hair off her forehead, nodded good-morning, and retreated back to the door, where a miserably filthy, knee-high child with a rag blanket wrapped around him stood waiting for her. I could hear the robin sing and smell wood smoke from the breakfast fires around town and the first sounds of men's voices shouting at livestock. A skinny black dog loped by about half sideways after a furry brown bitch. A white chicken poked out from behind the house across the street. A rooster crowed and a sudden breeze lifted dust from the road and carried the unpleasant scent of Epstein's private business my way. When I turned, there was the gold pan slid out under the bars. I took it and held my breath walking out behind the jail to the privy, where I dumped its load and returned the empty pan to Epstein.

"I passed me another miserable night," he said. "The bugs and the cold! And just when I got to sleep, someone standing in the dark where you are says to me, real slow and scary, he says, *How long you think before we come for you, Epstein? Tonight? Tomorrow?* I told him I had a fair trial coming up next week and that made him laugh. He said, *No, Jew-freak, how long before you feel the rope? You and that half-breed, Belly?*"

I felt dread tighten my stomach and asked if he needed another blanket. I also reminded him that his wife was supposed to be here later today or tomorrow.

"Bless her," he said. "But what's to become of me? I suppose I'll be strung up and never be with her again! Oh, I know they say there's nothing to do in jail, but I can feel my time already swollen with feeling sorry for myself!"

Again I didn't know what to say. If freedom was the ability to change shape, well, I was certainly free. Freeman Walker, filler of chamber pots, emptier of chamber pots. Doctor, minister, faerie, jailer, judge. Yet I couldn't shake the hard little ball in my belly. Couldn't make it go away. Maybe that's just what freedom felt like, given the facts and all, a hard little ball of dread.

First fact: seeing as how he had already admitted his guilt in numerous robberies, Epstein would be found guilty.

Second fact: I'd sentence him to banishment from the Territory. Where he and his dear wife might have a chance at a happy, long life together.

Third fact, which I didn't care to dwell on: Epstein might very well be dead before he even had a chance to be banished.

Fourth fact: Belly, too?

Maybe it was my faerie power, but the fact that none of those facts had happened yet didn't make them feel any less factual.

I turned to walk back to the hotel and paused in the weedy lot behind the hotel. While I relieved myself, I dared to look up at the windows of the room where Helga lived. I caught a glimpse of her by the window, and ashamed, turned away. I finished up and went into the hotel, limped up the stairs, and then slowly down the hall, where I heard her feet on the floor behind the door of her room. Just a shuffle, so I knew she was there. I slowed and slid my feet so she'd know I was passing. I only wanted to drag out this odd little moment, she on her side of the door and me on mine. But she must have been impatient with my step, or wondered if I had passed already, because suddenly her door opened and I could see the silhouette of her head, and the pale light on her face as she turned to look at me. Her expression betrayed embarrassment, both at her impatience and at her rumpled look, which I found so endearing my knees weakened. She froze with her head out the door, afraid to pull back, and I raised my left hand just enough to touch her chin, just to graze the middle knuckle of my forefinger softly over her chin and her cheek. What I wanted was for her to know that the sight of her face flooded me with fondness. She sighed without pulling back, and her cheeks turned pink. Charmed by her blush, I caught my breath and put my hand on the wall to balance myself. I had fallen in love with her, no doubt, and I knew I would have taken her then and there if she hadn't moved suddenly aside, opened the door wider, and let step past her a thin-faced young man with six inches of beard dangling from his chin like Spanish moss.

He assumed I was next, for he winked as he stepped by me. So fervently did I loathe him at that moment, I wanted to chase him down the hall and jump on his back, or wait until he got to the stairs and then push him to his death.

But then he did something that stopped me in my tracks. He began to whistle while he walked down the hallway. It was one of those full-throated whistles that can break your heart and magically free you from murderous thoughts. I swallowed hard and stood listening to the whistle even after the boy had gone out the front door into the street.

When I looked back at Helga, she raised her eyebrows as though to beckon me but I knew I couldn't endure it. Now that the doors had opened to my heart, I felt everything. I felt too much. I wanted her. Then I wanted to kill the boy. And now I stood weak-kneed from his whistle.

"Pardon me," I said, and limped past her down the hall to my room.

SUMMER WAS THE TRUE start of the new year in the Territory. The aspen and cottonwood had leafed out fully and the creek no longer roared with snowmelt. The days grew longer and hotter, and as soon as the sun came up in the morning flies began buzzing on the windows. When he wasn't drilling his Invisible Militia, the Colonel was pacing his room giving me a primer on the law. He said that the Rule of Law must be able to defeat the Rule of Power. He said power is greedy and afraid. Greedy for more, and afraid of losing what it has. Power, he said, takes whatever it wants—whatever it can. Power's cloak is "respectability," but its only loyalty is to itself.

Law, on the other hand, he explained, is a human invention based on conjured principles of fairness, decency, reason, and compassion— the loyalty of one citizen to another, one human being to another. In other words, he said, the basis of law is the belief in something we can only imagine. An idea of justice, say, or fairness. An idea of compassion.

"But how do we know what justice is?" I asked. "Or fairness?"

"We can't know justice until we have seen injustice," he said, "and the same with fairness. And one needn't wander long on this wide earth before he sees either. And so we are moved to feel compassion, which we cannot feel without imagination. And hope becomes our very best magic."

He'd paused by the window and pulled back the drapes to look for and see—indeed, even I could see the flicker of their cooking fires on the bench across the creek—his Invisible Militia.

"Hope and imagination," he said, "are the beginnings of the triumph of bold justice over mean respectability. They are the first steps away from the terror of safety onto the risky but joyful freedom trail."

"What about Belly?" I asked him.

"What about him?"

As the Colonel paced from the window to the door and back again, I told him what I'd heard from Epstein. I was seated, and the Colonel paused behind me. Then he stepped around in front of me, touched the curl above his ear, and smiled to reassure me.

"Soon we'll be on our way—you, Belly, and I—and our Invisible Militia!—on our way to Bloody Bend to do the work we were put on earth to do!"

"They won't let us stop them," I said.

He gave me a look that stabbed my heart. Was he a child? Did he really expect success? Such disappointment! Such sadness in his lunatic blue eyes! He put his freckled hand on my shoulder and I resisted with all of my might the urge to slip out from under its weight.

"We'll see," he said.

"They'll kill us!" I said, surprised at my sudden anger.

"They might."

"So what's the purpose?"

He walked to the window and parted the drapes. "Perhaps it's natural for the strong to prey on the weak. But it's also natural for human beings to imagine otherwise. And to act in accordance with what we have imagined."

"What I imagine," I said, "is that they'll kill us."

Here he turned and from across the room gave me the same look he'd given me from his bed when I'd tended his wounds—an almost too vulnerable yearning to be understood.

"They might," he said, "but they won't stop us from living free while we're alive, will they?"

We are free. We are not in control.

THE TRIAL TOOK PLACE in the Sighing Bones dance hall and saloon. To distinguish me as the judge, the Colonel had taken one of Greta's hats, a purple one adorned with tassels and clusters of beads designed to look like grapes, and cut out the crown so it would expand enough to fit around my skull. The result was that my hair stuck out through the slits at comic angles.

The Colonel had added ostrich feathers to his already absurdly large turkey-feather hat, making a grandiose display that he occasionally had to balance with his hand. The hats, he said, were to show people that once the trial began, we were not simply men, but men charged with the grand office of upholding the law. We were magicians, conjuring the Unseen. Men—even faeries—charged with such a job always dress differently, he said. The native tribes had medicine men, who wore all manner of ornament to set them apart from the average hunter. In England, men such as us wore powdered wigs and robes, and in the East, they wore black robes, and here, well, we'd wear outstanding hats.

I sat down on a raised stool pulled up behind the bar, and the Colonel sat in the corner. It had been years since there'd been an official (or even a public) trial in Last Best Chance City, and the courtroom overflowed until a crowd formed in the street and faces were pressed up to the windows. The crowd jeered when the defendant was brought in the back door with his wrists bound and his legs shackled. Mrs. Epstein sat in the front row and stood when he came in. She fanned herself and wobbled as though she might faint. Epstein, wearing a lime-green silk shirt and a pair of black serge pants, took a seat at a table next to his attorney, Captain Belly. How strange for me to now sit in judgment of the man I'd been taking care of for the past few weeks. And how strange to bend down before him this morning in his cell and put the shackles around each ankle. I remembered the Yankee captain's words about the boy, Jimmy, and how he knew how to put shackles on a man, and how that knowledge alone was enough to show that he was vermin who should be exterminated from the earth.

So it was with some humility that I looked out at the scene before me. Humility for my role as judge, and for my ability to perform it well. But I was given a gavel to hammer for order, and a glass of water, to which Belly (who for some reason had been allowed to dress normally) was kind enough to add a bit of whiskey. The room was thick with cigar smoke, and the day was sunny, so the yellow sunshine illuminated smoky stripes that shone in through the windows and cracks in the wall. Men and pigs and dogs milled around together, and occasionally one of the men would kick at one of the pigs or dogs, and there would be a general commotion, a squeal or painful bark, and the crowd laughed as the animal skirted away through other men's legs. A rooster perched on the windowsill and crowed loudly, and somebody shouted, "Indeed, but could you repeat that for the record?" and the cock crowed again.

I took another sip of my water and pounded my gavel. Perhaps my appearance was just absurd enough to give me authority. Or the gavel itself was magic. In any case, suddenly the room fell silent. All eyes locked on me and my big hat and wooden hammer. I swallowed hard and announced the charges: armed robberies too numerous to count.

Everybody sat down—or those who could—and like that the trial began. For all its buildup, it went surprisingly fast. A series of witnesses all gave testimony that Epstein had robbed them, but he hadn't taken all of their money, only about half, and sometimes less. The defendant himself interrupted each witness to say, "That's right! I did it! But I only needed a little something. I tried to be an honest man, but frankly wasn't very good at it!"

Every time he said this, his wife's face paled and her bosom heaved, and she touched the corners of her eyes with a white handkerchief.

Finally the last witness for the prosecution finished his testimony and I asked Belly or his client if they had any witness to call in their defense. Belly called Epstein, who when asked to take the oath, said simply, "I don't know about God, but nobody has lied about anything yet today and I'm not going to start."

Then he sat down and with his head just barely visible over the table, he made this statement: "When I was a boy, I wanted to be a good and honest man, indeed I did. But after Nicaragua it was hard to get a grip on that notion. After all, in just one battle I shot eighteen men while hiding in the branches of a mango tree. Eighteen men. Lots of soldiers don't count, but I did. I do. I count everything. It's just the way I am. For instance, I know that to kill those men I used twenty-one bullets. That's all. And I know how many folks are in this courtroom— ninety-six, and I know how many hours I've been in that jail—two hundred and twelve, and I know how many I robbed—thirty-two. It's just the way I was made, same as being a midget, part of my nature. I could hide well, too, stay still as a rock for hours on end. And shoot, of course. Also part of my nature, that I know. But I don't know who I killed, their names or what they loved, or even a very good reason as to why. I know they couldn't even see where the bullets was coming from. One moment they'd be walking along joking with their *compañeros* and the next they'd be lying dead in the road. After quite a few of those—I could tell you the exact number but I won't. It's more than I like to admit. Anyway, after quite a few of those I had to start asking myself: *Is this what a good and honest man does? Travel halfway across the globe so he can hide in a tree and shoot passersby?*"

The courtroom erupted and I pounded the gavel for quiet. Epstein shrugged, looked at Belly, and then looked at me. "I did the best I could after that," he said. "But it would have been downright dishonest for me to have pretended to be a good and honest man anymore, don't you think?"

Again the courtroom erupted with voices. I pounded the magic gavel and dismissed the jury to deliberate. They filed up the stairs with a full bottle of the best whiskey, and stayed up there just long enough to empty it. Then they filed back down again.

"We have made up our minds, Your Honor," said the foreman of the jury. "We find the defendant, Jean-Jean Epstein, otherwise known as the Robber of the Field, guilty of robbery more times than any of us could keep track of, although he himself said the number was thirty-two."

I banged my gavel and waited for quiet. When all eyes were on me, I asked the defendant to stand. He did, but his head barely cleared the table. I asked him to get back up on his stool so as to be better seen. Belly helped him up, and when all seemed ready and proper, I began. First I told the defendant I was impressed by his story. I told him that many of us had experienced—and perpetrated—horrors in the war. And we were familiar with the struggle to know ourselves again afterward. I told him that I was impressed by how witness after witness had testified that he'd never stolen as much as he could have stolen, and how his obvious compassion for his victims had forced him to work much harder than you'd think a real thief would want to work. Nevertheless, I said, he was obviously a bad man, though not so bad as many I'd known. He was also a good man, though not as good as some. So with all that in mind, I announced, I was going to show leniency. Rather than hang him—and here I looked at the Colonel, who nodded approvingly—I would use the authority invested in me as appointed judge to sentence Jean-Jean Epstein to banishment.

There was a brief uproar in the courtroom, which I quieted again with my magic gavel. I looked the prisoner in the eye and told him he had until sunset tomorrow to ride out of town and never be seen again within the boundaries of the Great Western Territory.

After sentencing, the courtroom quickly turned back into a bar. The crowd began ordering drinks, and Long John began to play the piano, and the hurdy-gurdy girls filed down the stairway. Helga's orange hair was neatly banded and gathered in a tasteful ornamental net, with a roll and gold tassels at the side. When she saw me, her nervous hands clasped across her middle, and then one shot upward and fixed her handsome brooch in its place, and the other touched her neck and hair and then flitted from one glistening earring to the other. Over her shoulder the head of a dance partner appeared, piercing eyes under a wide felt hat, and a cigar moving up and down in the corner of his mouth like a lever. It was the scalp hunter I'd seen, John L. Crockett. His clean white hand reached for hers, and turned her, and she didn't look back to me again.

I sat on my stool for a long time watching them dance until the prisoner, still shackled, and his wife began to shout my name. Remembering myself, I slipped out of my chair, and I got down on my knees as little Jimmy had gotten down on his knees in front of me, and I used my key to remove his chains.

Epstein nodded his gratitude. He stood and stretched and walked up to the bar for a drink.

I carried the shackles out of the barroom and up the stairs. I didn't know what to do with them, so I dragged them down to the end of the hall and opened the window and dropped them into a watery ditch, then tossed the key as far as I could into the grassy meadow.

AFTER THE PARTY THAT night, after we celebrated our magic to our limits and beyond, Epstein retired to his room with his wobbly wife—this time in the hotel itself—and Belly and I retired to ours, and we expected to sleep soundly and wake comfortably—perhaps an absurd expectation. And perhaps it was only mine. For ever since his pardon, Belly had slept with a six-shooter in his hand.

Nevertheless, a peaceful sleep was our hope and it was mostly accomplished. We both slept through the night but for a small disturbance that seemed nothing at the time, seemed in fact a drunken dream. Epstein's voice in the street—or was it the hallway?

Boys, let me go and I'll dance away!

Too late now.

Then Epstein's voice as calm as could be: *Then poor me,* he said. *I reckon I'll have to stand it.*

Stand what? I might have awoken if there'd been more alarm in his voice. We both might have. But the dream ended with the dull sound of a drop outside my window, and I woke in the morning to Belly standing naked in the dawn looking out at the street. Naked except for the pistol dangling from his hand.

"What's out there?"

"Dead man for breakfast."

"What?" I sat up.

"The midget's lynched."

"I thought it was a dream."

Belly looked at me, confused.

I got myself to the window and parted the drapes. The morning sky was pinking in the east, but on a hastily constructed gallows (using the barber pole across the street and the movable steps I'd once used for shelter) hung the dark silhouette of Epstein's little body. He was hanging by the neck, his hands bound behind his back. His wife had collapsed in sadness beneath him in the dirt.

I dressed quickly and went out to cut him down. His wife wouldn't look at me. She stayed on the ground and made a ball of quivering flesh and tears. I climbed the barber pole to reach the rope with my knife. I tried not to look at the top of his hatless head while I worked my dull knife back and forth across the rope, back and forth until the body fell and crumpled on the ground next to his wife. She leaped to cover him with kisses, despite his foulness.

I slid off the scaffold and was standing over the lifeless body by the time the first passerby nodded in my direction. Soon a small crowd had gathered, and although I insisted on digging the grave, I needed help carrying the little body to the graveyard.

A newspaper editorial later that day would call the execution "a good and honest hanging for a not-so-good-or-honest man." The writer would argue that "the Negro Judge's sentence of banishment went against the opinion of the majority of good citizens, who recognized the little Jew's malevolence beyond his incompetence. And because the Negro Judge's judgment violated the will of the majority, it could be construed as *tyranny,* and, as Mr. Jefferson had advised in the Declaration of Independence, the people had the right to *alter or abolish it,* which they have done."

Three men I didn't know helped carry the body. Another ran to get me a pickax and shovel. While I dug that blue-sky morning, Mrs. Epstein laid her man out on the ground and undressed him and cleaned him, and dressed him again. Belly brought me some tea and hard rolls and spelled me for a while. The ground was rocky and the going slow. I finished up and Belly rolled Epstein into a blanket and lowered him.

"Jean-Jean Epstein," I said, looking down into the first grave I'd dug since that night in Virginia. His little body appeared even smaller wrapped in a black blanket at the bottom of the grave—yet think of all it had contained when alive! Like me. Born white, die black. A little body at the bottom of a grave. Like mine. Put the shackles on, take them off.

"Jean-Jean Epstein," I said again. His wife jumped in and threw herself on top of her husband and urged me to bury them both. I refused. Breathe in, breathe out. Nor would I look away.

Belly jumped down and struggled with her. She kicked his shins and pummeled his shoulders with her tiny fists. I listened to the sharp suck of her breath before he finally subdued her and lifted her out of the grave.

I tossed in a shovelful of dirt and rock. Breathe in. My crooked foot hurt and the shovel handle had bit the flesh of my secretary hands and formed blisters at the base of my thumbs. Breathe out. I was a grave-digger again. A grave-filler, too. I felt a breeze touch the sweat on the back of my neck and cool my skin. Somebody's last breath. I was a faerie, preacher, jailer, judge. I was a coward but was learning I could also be brave.

I slid the shovel into the clumps of soil at my feet. Breathe in, breathe out. I tossed in another shovelful, and another, and another, until the little body began to disappear from view.

If freedom is the magical ability to change shape, well, I figured I must be as free as any man could be.

BUT NOT QUITE—NOT YET. For one long week after the lynching, I woke from an early-evening nap to the sound of the Laughing

Boy following another scalp hunter through town. It had become an almost daily occurrence, this haunting laughter like the sound of a loon that woke me from a dreamless sleep into a shivering nightmare. On this day I sat up as usual and limped to the table to pour myself a glass of water from the pitcher when I saw in the dim light still coming through the window an envelope on my bedside table. Belly must have brought it while I slept. On it was written *Jimmy Gates Freeman Walker, Secretary to the Acting Governor, Last Best Chance City, Great Western Territories.*

I'd signed all of my letters *Freeman Walker,* so only a letter that had found its way to her would use the name *Jimmy* as well. I picked it up and felt its weight and lifted it to my nose to smell the paper. I closed my eyes and used all of my magic to make it say what I wanted it to say but I couldn't even conjure an image of my mother's face, much less the words. The room was growing darker by the minute. I lit the yellow lantern on the dresser, and out the window the sky blooming stars disappeared. I sat down with my feet up on the sill and looked at my right foot turned inward, that leg skinnier. I held the envelope in my hands for as long as I could without opening it and tried to believe, but I couldn't. It was the end of a hot summer, and the evening before we were to leave on the Colonel's mad foray to Bloody Bend, so perhaps it was dread that finally stripped me of my powers.

I thumbed open the envelope and unfolded the letter.

Written in a man's hand, it said, "Jennyveeve Gates, born in 1818 a slave in Maryland, has recently passed away from illness and been buried outside Niagara, New York. Before her death, she had been living near the great waterfall, in a mill, and had been made aware of your inquiry in her last days, and died happy, knowing her son was alive and thinking of her. Her last words were that she was looking forward to further communications between yourself and herself."

I couldn't read the signature; the ink was smeared. I stood trying to catch my breath until I figured it futile, so I tried faerie magic to make time go backward. Why not? I carefully refolded the letter and put it back inside the envelope, *envelope the inside back it put.* I blew out the lantern and got up from the chair, *chair the from up got and lantern the out blew.* I went over to my bed and put the envelope back on the table and lay down and closed my eyes, *eyes my closed and down lay I.* I tried to imagine that when I opened my eyes again, things would be different. I tried to curse my father for sending me to school to learn to read such words, but even as I cursed him, I felt the falseness of my anger. Through the paper-thin wall that separated me from the Colonel's room, I could hear Helga laughing. On the other side I could hear Mrs. Epstein sobbing for her dead husband. Downstairs Long John played on the piano music to dance to.

I kept my eyes closed and felt a hard little ball in my stomach begin to soften and dissolve. Behind my eyelids my mother's face suddenly appeared as clear as I'd been able to see it in years. I opened my eyes and closed them again, and she was still there, looking at me, her love child, her loved child. And then I felt her lift. I felt the weight of her as I had carried her since I'd first closed the cabin door rise off my chest and float upward toward the gray ceiling and magically beyond, rise through the pall of this smoky town and higher still, where it burst into the clear summer sky and filled a dark part of the heaven with stars.

She lifted, and I felt a freedom I'd never felt before, a lightness, almost unbearably pleasant.

Then I was truly alone. Mad with grief and suddenly unafraid, I wept as I'd never wept before.

MADNESS

"LAST CALL," THE COLONEL announced, mounted on the back of Destiny, to a street full of miners and merchants and teamsters, and ladies with children, a busy crowd passing with hardly a curious glance. "Last call to join in our efforts to carve a Code of Law into a Lawless Land."

It was a drizzly September morning, and the Colonel had insisted we wear makeshift uniforms patched together with every gaudy piece of fabric the Baden-Baden Princesses had been able to find. Captain Belly wore his bearskin cape pinned with bright yellow strips of fabric, a blue sleeve, a long green stocking on one leg, and a long purple stocking on the other. On his head was an oversized beaver-fur cap with a tin star on the front. I was dressed similarly, although not being an officer, I had not the star. Our clothes were soggy, and our horses' ears lay back, and although by late morning the sun was trying to come out, the streets of the capital had turned to mud. We were off to Bloody Bend, and if that weren't ambitious enough, we had recently learned from the War Department that a steamboat full of arms to be used as protection from wild natives was headed upriver into the Territory. The Colonel wanted to be at Cut Bank Landing to receive the steamboat and destroy the arms before they could fall into the Committee's hands.

"Where's the rest of the militia?" shouted a sallow lad who was part of a small crowd gathered around a pen of fighting cocks.

The Colonel sat up straight in the saddle. He wore the same absurdly large feathered hat he'd worn at the trial, the same amber cloak marked with four uneven blue stars. This morning, however, he'd added a cluster of buttons the Baden-Baden Princesses had collected from the clothing of clients, pinned them to his chest, and insisted they were medals for valor.

"Are you a dark boy?" he asked, meaning a blind one

The lad blinked, confused, and looked at me. "I don't believe *I* am," he said.

The small crowd of gamblers laughed and the Colonel's face twitched with anger. "Then what do you see?"

The lad smirked. Here was a question he could answer. "I see the mad cock of Killarney," he said. "I see his bald half-breed captain and his nigger secretary dressed up like clowns."

This caused even more laughter, but the boy turned his pock-scarred face back to the roosters and the last exchange of bets. He staked a fistful of gold on a little red cock with good spunk to beat a big yellow.

Angry at the boy, I couldn't help but test my faerie magic to see if there was any left. So I focused on the rooster—something I'd seemed to have some luck with in the past. I watched the boy drop him into a storm of wings. A spring, a tussle, a blur of feathers—I was trying to envision the red one dead, of course, but just as quickly as I did, the fight ended and the yellow rooster lay in a pool of blood.

The boy gathered up his red bird and fistfuls of gold until he'd filled his pouch with his winnings. Then he shot me a malevolent grin as though he knew I'd been trying to make him lose.

The Colonel commenced to ride Destiny one more time up and down the muddy street waving his broken sword and announcing to

all who would listen that we were off to rid the Territory of crime, cor-
ruption, and terror, and to protect the natives from slaughter.

"Who will join us?"

Nobody did. Nobody paid attention. Even Helga, Gussy, and
Greta, standing on the hotel balcony, had taken to laughing and ex-
changing catcalls with the passersby below. Belly had told me the night
before that I should ride south out of the Territory alone. Banish myself—take the trail that Epstein didn't get a chance to take. Or ride
west to run the boardinghouse with Epstein's widow, who within a
short time, he predicted, would agree to have me for a replacement.

Nobody would bother me, he said. I could still live a long life.

"You mean because she loved a dwarf," I said, "she'd love a cripple, too?"

He looked hurt. "No," he said. And he explained that he didn't
have my options to escape the Colonel's madness. If he stayed behind
or rode off, it would be only a matter of hours or days before he was
lynched for the shooting of Chamberlain and Burke.

"Ride to San Francisco!" he whispered that morning on the street,
still urging me to make my break. "Get out of here while you
still can!"

He was right, of course. I was free to flee. But for what? If there was
one thing I'd learned in my short life it was this: there is no true safety,
no way to avoid suffering and death. Gibbs sat behind the same tree
where I sat, and he took a bullet to the head. Saturn moaned with fever
for two days and died within an hour after his shackles came off. The
little boy Jimmy and his sister might have lived good lives before the
war rolled up onto their farm, burned their house, and killed their parents—and all that before they even met the Yankee captain or me.

What is it Mr. Perry had said? "Happiness is but an illusion that
lasts precisely until savages emerge from the wood to slay your pretty
wife."

We all suffer; we are all going to die.

I'd been a slave. I'd been a killer. I'd been lynched. Now I was an orphan. What more could happen in my allotted time?

We are not in control.

The grieving native woman I'd seen on the way west had covered herself with pitch, cut her breasts, and let the blood run down her belly. Me? I wore purple and yellow sleeves and stockings and an oversized fur hat dangling long yellow strips of fabric. But I was a free man, and what that meant to me on this sloppy morning was that I did not have to run from fear. I was free to love, and to do what I needed to do, what I wanted to do. And what I wanted and needed on this day was to follow the Colonel, stay with him, do my best for him. I wanted to see how his mad scheme played in the world. I wanted to follow not only the man who'd built castles for me since I was a boy, but the man who had given my life back when I'd been ready to let it go, the man who had saved me.

We do not live for ourselves.

He rode Destiny, Belly rode Bug, and I sat on a fat little black gelding given to me as a gesture of kindness by the widows Smith and Warner. They'd bought it the day before and did not know its name. The Colonel lifted his arm and cast a loving look over what I imagined to be a long line of mounted ghost soldiers stretching all the way through town and out of it again, winding in double file across the valley behind us and up and over the hill. But I couldn't see them anymore—hadn't seen them in days, actually—which combined with my lack of magic gave me some discomfort.

Was this *my* madness, then, to follow the mad Colonel?

I supposed it was—and I held that notion gently but firmly, as perhaps one of my last remaining reasonable thoughts. *This is my madness. Oh, the mystery.* Gently but firmly, I lifted the reins and squeezed my horse to follow Colonel O'Keefe and Captain Belly out of town.

———

THE RIDE THAT FIRST morning was difficult. Our mounts kept slipping on the trail and the awkward silence was finally broken when Belly said, "Sir, Bloody Bend is a fearful place."

The Colonel let that sit for while. While we rode under dripping pine boughs up the steep slope of a mountain, Belly continued, "They won't let us ride into camp and shut down the market. Just the three of us, you know, and me the only one armed."

The Colonel straightened himself in his saddle. Destiny flicked his tail. "There you are wrong, Captain. Our troops form an Invisible Militia and they are more powerful because of it."

The wind picked up slightly and from the heights the air felt suddenly colder.

Belly said, "But if it's *invisible,* how can it help us?"

"The wind is invisible," the Colonel said.

"With all due respect, Colonel," Belly answered, "the wind moves the trees. The wind I can feel on my skin."

"Your point, Captain?" the Colonel asked.

Belly cleared his throat. "What sign is there that our militia has passed?"

"It follows us," the Colonel said, "and when we have moved, it has moved. And when we rest, it rests. Look at what we do, and you know what it is doing, too. Lose your faith, and the militia will surely scatter. Keep your resolve strong, march onward, and you can be certain the dead are close behind."

Belly merely shrugged. We rode in silence for a while. I glanced behind us again and still could not see the column of dead Irishmen. Had I lost faith?

"Colonel, with all due respect, I might be able to believe that some magic power had made them disappear, if I had ever seen them."

"Have you ever been in battle, Captain Belly?"

"Yessir, just once."

"Well, then you know it is rarely what is seen that marks the battle's outcome," the Colonel said. "It is what is unseen. What is it that makes a man charge into withering gunfire against all odds? Or compels entire armies to turn on their heels? Can anyone see what is in the soldier's mind and heart as he responds heroically or cowardly, or as he lies in a patch of bloody ragweed to die?"

Here he paused and contemplated for just a moment the common belief that ragweed is sacred to faeries.

"Excuse the unfortunate image, Judge Walker," he said.

I nodded but remained silent.

Belly did not. "I've never once even heard of an *Invisible Militia,* as you put it—nor have, I believe, our enemies. So I don't know how an Invisible Militia will be of much help if those we're arresting can't see it!"

The three of us rode across a steep slope thick with fir and jack pine. I felt my horse moving between my tired legs and listened to the chirping birds that seemed to accompany us from treetop to treetop.

Finally the Colonel answered. "You tell me what you've never heard," he said to Belly. "And you tell me what you don't believe, and what you don't know, and what you don't see. Is there anything you do believe?"

"I believe this mission is doomed," Belly said, and paused as though waiting for the Colonel to scold him. When that didn't happen, he took a deep breath and continued. "I believe they'll kill us all before they let us shut down their bloody business. And even if by some miracle we manage to march into Bloody Bend and arrest everybody involved, a new Bloody Bend will open up within weeks. The Committee's got a lot of money. And if it's buying scalps, regular folks is going to be selling. That's the story around here. There ain't no story bigger than buying and selling."

Our saddles squeaked and our horses breathed and we listened to the fall of their hooves on the trail, smelled their flesh and manure, and our own sweat under the folds of our heavy capes. We reached the last switchback and began to ascend the ridgeline into a new drizzle. The gray clouds got lower and darker and ahead it looked like snow. Finally I could hear the Colonel's high voice erupt from the slot formed by the raised collar of his greatcoat beneath his amber cloak and tall feathered hat. He spoke as though he were a making a speech to an audience that remained hidden just ahead on the trail behind the ghostly clouds.

"Ours is not a story of *regular* folks," he began. "For if the world had only regular folks with regular natures, where would the world be? Where would be its valor, its heroism, its faith? When life passes in easy routine, then the regular natures and the regular men sow the seed and gather the harvest and grow rich and dream that all society should be made only of such as they. But in the strange economy of this world, all natures have their uses. And when there is evil at the doorstep, indeed evil in the parlor of our homes, the least regular among us must act. Men like you, Captain Belly. Men often frowned at by their more regular neighbors. Men whose weaknesses and temptations their respectable neighbors have never known. Men whose character their respectable neighbors will never comprehend. So if the good regular people of this Territory continue to buy and sell human scalps, Captain Belly, men like you and I and Judge Walker will continue to try to stop them. Sometimes life is complicated and sometimes it is simple. Tell me, Captain Belly, faced with such clear evil, is there something else you think we should do?"

No answer from Belly, and as we climbed the drizzle turned to snow. We hunched down against the wind. I pulled my hat low and tucked my face into my collar and stared out through the slit at the Colonel's yellow cape and blue stars, but soon his shoulders were covered with snow. Next I tried to watch Destiny's round rear end just off the nose of my gelding, but soon even that began to dissolve in the blizzard.

We halted near the top of the pass in the lee of a cliff, where the shape of a man on foot appeared on the snowy trail ahead of us. The shape revealed itself to be an old native man wrapped in a blanket. Frightened when he saw us, he pulled from his blanket two skinned rabbits, which he seemed to be offering in exchange for his life. The Colonel shouted that we meant no harm but his words blew away in the swirling wind. The native man dropped the rabbits in the snow and hurried past us, disappearing down our hoofprint trail.

Belly dismounted and picked up the rabbits and hung them from his saddle before we continued down the other side of the pass. The Colonel and I stayed mounted, but to be safe, Belly led his horse on the narrow, snow-covered trail. We hadn't gone far when even this precaution failed. His mare lost her footing, pitched forward, and did a full somersault before popping to her feet again down the snowy slope on the edge of a thick growth of lodgepole pines, apparently without injury. Seeing this, Destiny refused to take another step, so we dismounted and decided to set up camp where we were. We built a lean-to in the trees and soon Belly had a fire going. We cooked the rabbits, ate our fill, smoked our pipes, and then lay together under common blankets for warmth.

Whether it was the native's vengeance for what he assumed to be a payment for his life or a more banal reason, the rabbit did not sit well with us and we passed a bad night running from our warm nest through the snow to shit. First me, then the Colonel, and then Belly. Then all of us at once and each in our turn, again and again.

In the morning we huddled together weak and dry-mouthed under our blankets. The yellow sun rose into a deep blue sky and the temperature rose steadily. The new snow glistened as it melted and water dripped from the branches above us into our nest. We lay shivering under the damp blankets until finally Belly got up to start a fire. He made us weak tea and as the day wore on our cramps grew less frequent. By nightfall they were gone.

On the second morning so was most of the snow. Feeling better, we packed our mounts and headed down the mountain. It was perhaps a sign of my improved health and general outlook, and also the particular movement of the saddle between my legs as we rode downslope, that I dallied with the memory of Mrs. Epstein, wet and naked under her blankets, her arms around me and her kisses on my neck. That the last I'd seen her she was mad with grief and trying to throw herself into her husband's grave didn't seem to matter. It had been too long since I'd been with a woman.

We wound down the mountainside through a lodgepole forest, and little birds leaped from tree branch to tree branch alongside the trail, and in the warm valley we tarried to let our horses and mule graze and, as the Colonel suggested, to allow the Invisible Militia to catch up. I lay on my back in the dry grass, and the person of my fantasy changed to Helga and her nimble hands and the extravagant necklaces splashed across her bosom. I laid my coat over my lap to keep private my arousal, which even on a glorious day like this surprised me with its duration. I looked up at the puffs of cloud moving across the blue sky and felt the sun warm my face and chest. I closed my eyes, listened to the trickle of water all around me. *Sometimes life is complicated and sometimes it is simple.* I heard a hawk whistle up high in the canyon and the last thing I heard before falling asleep was the sound of Belly snoring next to me.

———

THE NEXT MORNING THE sun shone steadily and the day grew hot. By the time we got to the river I intended to bathe, but stepping close to the riverbank we found ourselves face-to-face with two startled native men and a boy squatting around a dying fire.

"Greetings, pilgrims!" the Colonel said, and dismounted. We all did.

Seeing no weapons, for Belly's pistol was tucked in his belt under his jacket, the men and boy took in our strange attire without expression or comment and generously made a space for us in their circle. The oldest fellow, having nothing on him but a red blanket, was shortening sticks of firewood against his knee. His grandson, a skeleton of a boy in a sooty smock, gathered the broken pieces and stacked them while the son of the old man—a middle-aged fellow in another red blanket—sat on his haunches smoking a pipe. He kindly passed it to me, and when it went out Belly produced tobacco to fill it again. I took another smoke and passed the pipe around the circle, and as we were so engaged the Colonel began to describe with language the natives showed no ability to understand the golden days in store for them among the treasure-veined mountains of the Territory. He spoke of bonhomie between the races and the practicality of trail fellowship, and while he was doing so Belly stepped into the river with a line produced from his pocket and bugs he'd picked from under rocks, and he began to fish.

Within half an hour the three generations of Natives, who surely when they first saw us must have wondered if they were doomed, now were merely dumbstruck by the Colonel's interminable speech. Soon Belly was back with a dozen trout. Giving a multitude of orders to himself, it seemed, for neither I nor the Colonel nor the family of natives budged from our rest, Belly gutted the fish and rebuilt the fire. Bear cape off, purple and green leggings soaked with river water, blue sleeves rolled tightly up above the elbows, big hands mottled with fish blood and glossy with slime, he was something to see. We all watched as he stuck the fish on green limbs and dangled them over the fire to cook.

After we'd eaten I thought about slipping downstream to bathe but the air cooled suddenly when the sun set over the mountain. Soon the stars had lit up the sky and we arranged our bedding. Before lying down the Colonel bade a good-night to the Invisible Militia, which, judging by the direction he faced when he spoke, had spread out along the river's edge.

All six of us curled close to the fire to sleep, which I did soundly until dawn, when my ears beheld the panicked voices of men on the river. I opened my eyes to see that a fog had settled heavily on the water. The shouting grew closer until sudden ghostly forms appeared: two men stood upright on the water with apparently nothing under them. How did they stay up? They drifted closer, shouting and cursing, and finally they jumped onto dry land with the enthusiasm becoming men who'd just a moment before feared drowning.

Behind them in the river a small log raft rose up from under the tea-brown water and revealed itself as the sunken platform on which they'd stood.

The two men looked startled, for at their feet lay the six of us. One of them had the pocked face of a pirate, and he wasted no time pulling a pistol from his waist and aiming it at the three natives, who were fully conscious now and not ignorant of the bad dream into which they'd awoken.

"These are the buggers we've been trailing!" the pirate said.

His partner had very small, sharp black eyes that made him look the more dangerous of the two, even though he hadn't yet drawn his gun.

He might have been a lawyer in the past, or a preacher, for when he opened his mouth to speak he talked with the clear enunciation of a man accustomed to making himself heard.

"We're on our way to the gold fields," he said—and then as though to explain his partner's pistol—"but first we're earning a little stake selling hair."

"Nobody is buying or selling scalps," the Colonel said, sitting up and blinking at our visitors.

The lawyer-preacher smiled. His tongue flicked over his tobacco-stained incisors. "We just came from Bloody Bend," he said, "and folks are certainly doing just that."

"Not if I have anything to do with it." The Colonel stood up and, except for his hat, he was still fully dressed in his uniform of the day before.

The two intruders took a moment to look him over. "What are these?" the pirate asked, pointing to the cluster of buttons pinned onto the Colonel's jacket.

"Medals," the Colonel said.

The pirate flashed a hard-bitten little grin. "For what?"

"Valor," I said, sitting up in my bed.

Intrigued, the lawyer-preacher stepped forward and bowed slightly to the Colonel. "And what good hero, may I ask, do we have the good fortune of meeting?"

"I am Colonel Cornelius O'Keefe, the acting governor of the Territory, and I am here to enforce the Rule of Law in this lawless land. This is my captain. And this is my judge and secretary."

Belly and I stood up and our guests took a long look at our brightly colored sleeves and stockings. I winked. First my brown eye, then my green one. "Our Invisible Militia is camped downstream along this grassy meadow all the way to the distant cliffs," I said.

The two men looked across the empty meadow, then back to us. "These men are crazy," the pirate said, but he kept his pistol aimed at the natives, who remained seated.

"Nonsense," the lawyer-preacher said, and turned to the Colonel. "Mr. Acting Governor, I am honored to meet you and your men. And despite the time we've invested in chasing these savages, we do respect the Rule of Law and we wouldn't dream of taking what is obviously now your property."

"These men are not my property," the Colonel said, "and we would not dream of separating them from their hair."

"Well, *we* would," the pirate said. "In fact, we've been dreaming little else for days!"

"These men and their boy have caused no harm," the Colonel said.

"That might be true," the lawyer-preacher said. "And it might not. None of that is our business, nor is it our place to judge. But I would hazard a guess that if you don't take their scalps, somebody else will."

The Colonel set himself squarely over his stocking feet and said again, "Not if I have anything to do with it."

The lawyer-preacher seemed both intrigued and entertained. Again he dipped his head humbly before speaking. "I don't question your sincerity, Mr. Acting Governor. And your medals are certainly proof of your valor. So I won't be so impolite as to assume that it makes any difference that you don't have a gun and we have several."

Saying this, he pulled his own pistol out from under his coat. But he didn't point it. He just let it dangle in his hand.

"On the contrary," the lawyer-preacher said, "we'll stick with philosophy like two civilized men. First of all, wouldn't you agree, Mr. Acting Governor, that it is the pluck and industry of men that have built the great and beautiful institutions of our nation—the museums and theaters and universities, the courtrooms and capitals, the churches and markets and factories—that we would like to see duplicated here in the Great Western Territory?"

The Colonel blinked his blue eyes and touched the bed-flattened curl on the side of his head. I assumed he was thinking of the many letters he had composed describing just such a world. "I would," he said.

"And wouldn't you agree that it is through this same pluck and industry and free commerce between citizens that we hope to build a society in which principles of law and fairness are held dear?"

Again the Colonel blinked, and again he answered, "I would."

The lawyer-preacher tilted his hat back and smiled. "I thought so, Mr. Acting Governor. Because it is obvious in your bearing, in your manner, and in your—" Here he pointed to the cluster of buttons on the Colonel's coat—"again, in your *valor,* that you are a man who believes not only in what *is,* but in what is *possible.*"

"I do," the Colonel said. "For what is possible *is!* And what can be imagined *is!* And both of those are as real and as true as that rock here, or those trees across the river."

The lawyer-preacher gestured with his pistol to the empty meadow. "And the Invisible Militia?"

"Indeed."

"And this family of natives?"

"Yes," the Colonel said.

"So there seems little question, Mr. Acting Governor, that this is a Territory blessed with vast resources, both seen and unseen."

"It is."

"And so doesn't it follow, Mr. Governor, that it is a good man's duty to look for and use those resources for the benefit of himself and his loved ones?"

"And for the benefit of others," the Colonel said.

"Of course," the lawyer-preacher said. "A good man's duty to Christian charity goes without saying. But before he can do for others less fortunate, don't you believe it is that good man's duty to get as much value for his resources and labor as the market will pay?"

"That's fair," the Colonel said.

"Then don't you suppose that if you are not going to take advantage of this resource squatting meekly at your feet, then you are doing an injustice by denying others their right and duty to get a benefit from their good hard work of trailing this family for the past week?"

Here the oldest native man, the grandfather, did us all a favor and interrupted this dark dialectic by beginning to hum in a high, quivering voice, and then to enunciate words in queer song.

"What's this craziness?" the pirate asked. "Some kind of witch chant?"

The boy and his father quickly joined the grandfather in singing, and we all stared at them and listened. All except Belly, who used that moment of distraction to reach behind his back and, quick as a blink, pull out a revolver with his right hand and began fanning the trigger with his left. But the gun didn't shoot. Instead, it clicked, clicked, and clicked again as the hammer fell back onto one empty chamber after another.

Belly looked at the revolver in his hand as if it had betrayed him. "My bullets," he said.

The pirate began to laugh but stopped suddenly when the lawyer-preacher raised his pistol and pointed it at Belly. Suddenly it was very quiet except for the voices of the natives still singing their song.

"I took the bullets," the Colonel said, his blue eyes glowing. "Ours is a different way."

"Ours ain't," the pirate said, and with that, he took one quick step forward and landed his heavy boot sharply into Belly's crotch. Belly doubled over and went down hard. The Colonel leaped immediately to his aid, and the pirate kicked him in the ribs. I hoped to join the fray, but at that particular moment felt the lawyer-preacher touch the back of my neck with his pistol. It was a feeling I had not forgotten, so for an awful instant I stood still and cowardly while the pirate kicked away at the two men at his feet. Behind me I could still hear the three generations of natives singing their death song, which I like to think would have finally moved me to act if the man with the gun had not momentarily removed the barrel from the back of my neck before bringing it down firmly on my skull. I felt a hot explosion in my brain, and then nothing.

WE WOKE SOMETIME LATER, sat up, and rubbing our lumps and bruises we took in the horrendous scene between us. The three generations of natives lay next to the cold campfire as though sleeping, each with a hole in his chest, and each with a pink and bloody pate where his hair should have been. Also, our mounts were gone. And Belly's bulletless revolver. But we were alive—a fact the Colonel immediately ascribed to the heroism of the Invisible Militia.

"They must have chased them off," he said.

"Good God," Belly said. "I can't believe you took my bullets."

"We are alive to fight another day," the Colonel said.

"Fight who? Fight how?"

I had a terrible headache. Belly struggled to stand straight because of the kick to his groin and the Colonel must have broken some ribs, for he grimaced when he spoke.

"Follow me," he said, but he moaned when he tried to get up, and so sat back down again.

Belly and I hauled the two men and a boy up on the bench. The fog had burned off and we found ourselves in a beautiful canyon surrounded by yellow and red cliffs and steep draws choked with fir trees. Lacking a shovel to dig, or soil to dig into, we buried the poor family under rocks. We did the sad job without conversation or the pretense of prayer. While I put the last of the rocks on top of the dead boy, Belly started back to the river, leaving me briefly alone, but he changed his mind and tarried ahead of me under a grove of yellow cottonwood. He seemed to have something on his mind, something he could no longer contain, and he fell in with my slow pace.

"Look," he said, and he pulled from his pocket a bent dollar coin he told me he'd kept since Shiloh. He let me hold it in my hand. "I was the only one from my town's group of volunteers to survive the first charge. Every single one of them was shot down or blowed up and naturally I wondered why. Not so much at the time, though. Mainly what I did the rest of the battle was charge like a wild man at every rebel gun I saw, figuring I'd . . ."

I turned the bent coin this way and that in my hand. It looked as though it had stopped a bullet, or even two. We walked a few more steps. He stepped quickly around a log and then paused to let me limp up alongside him again. His face was creased with confusion.

"No, I wasn't *figuring*. I was *hoping* I'd die like all of my friends, every single one of them."

The poignant smell of cottonwood sap, the wide circle of an eagle's glide under the clear blue sky—all of that, combined with the last exhales of the dying, made even my good leg weak with longing. There was a slight breeze, just enough to cool my sweat. But still my head pounded where I'd been hit.

"After that fight," he said, "I walked away from the war. And the whole way out here to the Territory, every step, I'm thinking, *Why why why?*"

I fingered the coin, half afraid Belly was going to ask me something I couldn't answer, or even pretend to answer. But he didn't, and when we got to the riverbank the Colonel was struggling to walk through high grass. He had put on his tall feather hat and he occasionally had to touch it with his hand. "Follow me!" he shouted, grimacing toward the empty meadow, "and we'll march away from here into the great wide open of our righteous endeavor!"

"I can't believe you took my bullets," Belly said.

The Colonel turned from the meadow. "Shooting people is madness," he said.

"So is not shooting them!" Belly said. "So is shouting at a bunch of ghosts!"

The two considered one another for a moment, then Belly turned to me. I dropped the coin back into his palm. "Good metal," he said quietly. "That's what I believe in. Coins. Bullets."

"And luck, too?" I asked.

He shrugged and dropped the bent coin back into his chest pocket.

THE LOG RAFT DIDN'T quite hold our weight, so as we drifted from shore, spun one way and then another, the river rose to cover our shoes and ankles. Belly and I gripped poles to push and also to balance ourselves as the raft picked up speed in the flood. Our knuckles whitened as the raft bumped a snag, spun, freed itself, then bumped a rock and spun the other way. We gained speed on our way downstream. We could see the fir-covered slope of the far bank, yet no matter how hard we poled, we seemed to get no closer.

The Colonel stood calmly between us, his blue eyes glowing beneath his tall feather hat. "Here we are, companions, after our long and checkered lives, drifting on the flood!"

Another bump, and the Colonel grimaced but maintained his balance, one hand on my shoulder and the other on his hat. And then, as if to rid his mind of the horrible scene we'd just left, he said, "Imagine, if you will, traveling down this river and passing friendly native camps dotting the choicest spots on the banks, stopping at each one and sharing a good meal and fellowship."

I couldn't help but think of the fat grubs I'd seen the native women eating on my way to the Territory, but not for long, as our partially submerged raft hit another rock, and another, and spun three times in succession before Belly and I managed to halt our rotation. As we drifted farther downstream I could hear the pounding of big water ahead. We poled toward the far bank but the current had picked up speed and the crashing grew louder, and louder, and then suddenly we saw it. Not fifty yards away the broad river narrowed toward two black boulders the size of houses and a white spray hovered over the gap where the green water disappeared between them. I could feel the Colonel's fingers tighten into my shoulders, hear his voice tight with pain as he continued his speechifying. "Imagine a great steamboat shrieking and blowing against the green volume of this huge river!" he shouted, and Belly and I began poling with all of our might. We spun slightly, and poled, and poled again. The roar of falling water grew so loud it sent surges of strength and terror through my body. I could see the bank ahead, just upstream from the boulders, smooth and almost sandy, and I could hear Belly shouting as he coordinated his strokes with mine and we were able, finally, to make progress with each push. Our lives had come down to this race between the approaching cascade and the approaching bank of the river. In about ten seconds of utter exertion and terror, reaching with the pole, pushing, reaching, pushing, everything was forgotten but this race.

We laid into the last couple of strokes before the log raft hit the river bottom a couple of feet from shore and just ten feet shy of the falls. The sudden stop forced us all forward and we leaped off the raft onto the bank. I fell, of course, and so did the Colonel, but we sat up in time to see the log raft surface without our weight, rotate off the gravel, drift downstream and over the great white drop between boulders. I watched it fall twenty feet into a churning pool of whitewater.

Sitting, the Colonel continued his painful speechifying over the tremendous sound of the falls. "Imagine arriving here at a city built on this bank," he shouted. "Imagine the facades of fine hotels and warehouses. The bell towers, the theaters, and the freshly whitewashed official residences surrounded by a bright display of flags, and in the finest restaurants chefs preparing the delicacies of the season: fish, fruit, and game."

With that he whistled loudly to signal the Invisible Militia to follow on horseback across the deluge. The effort left him cringing and holding his chest, yet looking across the water with awe.

I tried to imagine what he was seeing and hearing: the water alive with hundreds of splashing hooves, the shouts of dead Irishmen as they slid off the backs of their mounts when the water rose to cover everything but their heads and hats, and the flaring nostrils of hundreds of horses and mules racing our way. As the water grew shallow again, their dripping bodies emerged and stumbled up and over and between rocks, and even over the roar of the falls I would hear the splash of hooves as the men and beasts arrived safely onto the near bank at last, a wild chaos turned suddenly precious by pinpoints of sunshine that made drips and splashes sparkle like soda water.

But I couldn't see them. I glanced at Belly, who like me had been staring at the river and the falls from under his starred beaver hat. I could tell by the frown on his face that he was trying to see something, too, but he gave it up with a sudden shake of his head.

"Madness!" I heard him shout over the sound of water.

———

FOR THE NEXT TWO miles the trail to Bloody Bend wound through a forest in which a fire had raged a few weeks before. Some trees had been reduced to heaps of muddy ash into which we slipped from time to time, blackening our colorful clothing. Other trees made charred masts fifty feet tall which a gust might snap and topple at any time. Slowly and carefully we made our way up the slope, our ears filled with the roar of the falls in the canyon below. Finally we came out on top, cleared the burned forest, and crossed an open bench for most of the day. In this type of walking—painful limping, actually— I might have lagged well behind, but the Colonel, plagued as he was not only by his broken ribs but by corns, had taken off his boots and slung them over his shoulder, and so had to walk barefoot and gingerly.

Taking mercy on us, Belly halted in the late afternoon on the edge of a meadow in which we could curl our hungry and exhausted, ash-covered bodies under heaps of dry grass to sleep for the night.

In the morning we were up before light and on a rocky trail we descended switchback after switchback though a cedar and hemlock forest. By noon the forest thinned sufficiently for us to see the narrow valley below. Clustered in a horseshoe canyon on the far shore of a stream were a couple of dozen tents and cabins. From the heights, through a veil of autumn yellow larch, Bloody Bend looked almost pretty.

Closer, we could smell it: first the riverbank like the tidal flats of the Thames decorated with shit, and then the corrupt sweetness and too-heavy air of decaying flesh. We walked three abreast into town, our strange and colorful outfits covered with mud and ash and pieces of dried grass from our beds. Sweat dripped down from under our hats and streaked our dirty faces. We walked slowly past a scattering of drunken men lying on the side of the road, and the Colonel raised his hand in greeting and dipped his high-hatted head.

"Hail, citizens," he said, "I have come as the acting governor of the Great Western Territory to bring the Light of Law to this dark valley."

A few of our hosts sat up and stared mutely at the Colonel as though they were hearing Arabic. Encouraged by their movement, the Colonel continued, "We are here to rescue you and make this land safe for civilized behavior!"

The drunkards blinked and lay back down again. We were just another cluster of passing ghosts. Finally we were greeted by a man who introduced himself as Kerr. He had a scar that ran from his forehead across one of his eyes and down his cheek.

"With all mighty reverence and respectful acknowledgment of your wise personages and esteemable escorts," Kerr began in an oddly official manner that raised his voice an octave, turned his scar bright red, and sent his brown eyes circling as though in search of even more unnatural words, "I am the fair constabulary of this fair commune, and this is my honed factotum, O'Brien."

O'Brien, a tall thin man with a face compressed as if by a horse's hoof, decades ago, let fly a gob of blood-colored tobacco juice from between his cluster of twisted teeth, licked his wormy lips, and said, "Follow me!"

So we followed the two men past the squalor of bone-bag dogs eating carrion, and more citizens sleeping in the mud. We paused in front of a buffalo-skin lodge. O'Brien pulled back the flap and we ducked into a tight, foul-smelling place where we were forced to squat in the dark before somebody lit a candle. The Colonel had to remove his hat in order to duck under the flap and once inside he struggled to put it on again. It hurt him to lift his arms above his head so I sat behind him and straightened the hat while he cleared his throat to speak.

"It is evident to me," the Colonel began, "that the commerce of this town is based on hunting natives, and the buying and selling of their redskin scalps."

Kerr seemed to be listening but answered as though he weren't. "We are most gratified and grateful," he began, his voice still affecting a high, official-sounding twang, "to have made our acquaintance, and you yours, and of course for this opportunity to parley." Here he stopped, coughed, and began again. "What I mean to say," he continued, "is that gratitude or nigh, we certainly would have preferred to have made our preference, that is, our choice an alternate, if an alternate choice or option or manner of commercial sustenance had been made available. Preferring, of course, an activity of commerce more in accordance with, as my dear mother used to say, *our better natures,* we—"

His scar paled and he waved a fly from his face and called for tea. A boy delivered it through the flap. Pinch-faced O'Brien leaned forward and poured four glasses, and spat. I felt suddenly nauseated—and grateful for the tea.

Kerr raised a finger as though he was going to pick up the thread of his odd, abandoned sentence, but thought better of it and began again. "Being official men of the official world, with due recognizance and compredibility based on due diligence of experience utilized to stand firmly on firm factual determination—" He cleared his throat—"and supposition, of course, have dutifully observed that this Territory is a dangerous place!"

Pleased with this phrase, Kerr raised a finger and said it again, louder. *"This Territory is a dangerous place!"*

"Indeed," the Colonel said. "Indeed it is. And so we are here as official representatives of the government to close down these operations."

Kerr cradled his cup of tea with two hands as though to use it for balance. He sipped, then lowered the cup slowly to its saucer. Again as though the Colonel hadn't spoken, he continued, "If these natives call for our pity, it is only because they have been rendered powerless by our merciless assault on their persons in general and topknots in particular, if you will. For you can be sure that if the native element had bigger guns than we ourselves are presently equipped, then they would be doing the killing and we would be doing the dying."

He paused for a breath and O'Brien sent another stream of tobacco juice over his shoulder into a dark part of the lodge. I tried to swallow my rising nausea but felt my mouth begin to flood with saliva.

"So given the general choice of this or that," Kerr continued, "I have chosen *this* as preferable to *that,* heat to cold, shall we say, quick to slow, or the better of the two situations and paradigms, the most favorable and enjoyable one of which results in me sitting here with you, and the other resulting in me somewhere else, dead."

O'Brien punctuated this speech with another spit.

I looked away, closed my eyes, tried to breathe deeply. I heard the Colonel clear his throat and put his teacup down. "What the natives would do if they had bigger guns is not my concern. We have our traditions and they have theirs. One of ours is the Rule of Law. And so we shall accord ourselves with its intent toward justice. Therefore, I declare this scalp market officially closed, and I state my intent to arrest every man woman and child who continues in this activity or dares to resist my enforcement of the law."

I was amazed not only that the Colonel had followed Kerr's contorted logic and syntax, but at the sanity and clarity of his response. I kept my eyes closed and felt my nausea begin to abate. I could smell whiskey and heard the sounds of men milling outside the tent. Belly nudged me—did he think I'd fallen asleep?—and I opened my eyes to see in the flickering candlelight Kerr's head tilted and brow creased as though imitating the look of one deeply possessed by thought—yet the effect was more like a dog hearing a distant whistle.

"Grateful is what we should feel," Kerr began, "for God put our mothers in this world to be deflowered and to give bloody birth to us. And if he wanted us to live in some other world, that's I suppose where he would have put our mothers, too. But He didn't, and we're here, through no choice of our own, and so irregardless, don't you agree?"

O'Brien twitched and I was afraid he was going to spit again. My stomach turned and began to rise. I stood to pull back the buffalo-skin flap. Even the grim scene outside was a relief from the foul air of the lodge. The hills had grayed under a descending afternoon fog. The boy who'd brought our tea sat across the muddy path looking at me blankly. Behind him lay a pile of scalps that I hadn't noticed when we'd come in. Had they just arrived? Fresh product? They didn't smell fresh.

Suddenly two guns appeared in front of my face, and the men holding the guns backed me into the lodge again.

"Civilization," the Colonel was saying as I sat, "calls on us to comport ourselves with laws above and beyond the law of the jungle. Civilization requires self-restraint. And in a world that is not inclined that way, we are forced to act positively for justice, or to actively resist injustice. There is no other way."

We looked at our host. He leaned forward and for the first time spoke without the odd, artificial affectation in his voice. "May birds eat their last stinking carcasses," he whispered, his brown eyes suddenly hard and fixed on the Colonel, "for *civilization* will grow only as the native ceases to be."

Deputy O'Brien punctuated this horror with yet another blood-colored stream of tobacco juice, which was just too much for me to bear. I bent sideways to vomit.

"Dang sure!" O'Brien said, and giggled.

I wiped my mouth with my purple ash-tasting sleeve. Through watery eyes I could see the lodge flap had been pulled back.

WE WERE TAKEN TO a squat building in the draw behind the main barracks and locked in. I lay with my head against the dry log walls and struggled to smell the old wood rather than the reek from the street. I tasted vomit and craved water, and listened to the wind in the tops of the trees up the hill and thought of that hill, and the one beyond, and the one beyond that, and the moon rising somewhere in stillness. I had a feeling for the size of this country that put an emptiness inside my stomach that grew and grew and eventually swallowed me. I thought of my father telling me the Declaration of Independence was civilized law, written by men aspiring to be divine, and thought of how it described *merciless savages whose known rule of warfare is an undistinguishable destruction of all ages, sexes and conditions,* and I wondered how, if those were divine words, how would God describe the men who'd slaughtered the family of natives we'd seen only yesterday? And the men who, judging by the amount of scalps coming into camp, had slaughtered hundreds of families across the Territory?

We were given no food or water that day, and as night fell we lay listening to the howling wind without letup and my mouth was dry and my tongue thick, and my stomach knotted in hunger. We clung to each other for warmth and I heard the Colonel whisper fiercely but couldn't understand his words, as though the passion of a great internal debate had spilled up and out of him and into the storm. I must have fallen asleep, for I dreamed the wind had come in the cracks of the cabin and filled me with its wild madness. Once I woke and needed to urinate but had trouble getting my balance with the swirling wind, it seemed now, *inside* my head. I held on to the log walls and made my way to the corner and there relieved myself of precious water. When I lay down again, I thought of God putting our mothers where he'd put our mothers to give birth to us, and what we could possibly know of his intentions. Mine he'd put in a tiny cabin along a moist river bottom in Maryland, where human beings with white skin owned human beings with dark skin, and worked them, or sold them, or did with them as they pleased for pleasure or profit. Belly's mother had been forced to leave her home and marched halfway across the country, her family dying along the trail like so many oxen left in the desert. The native grandfather, father, and son we'd met and shared a trout dinner with had each a mother, of course. Had God put those women in this world to give birth to baby boys who would grow up and be shot and scalped along a riverbank, their bodies buried by strangers under rocks, to make room for civilization?

The words seemed suddenly comical—and I laughed but couldn't even hear my own voice above the wind.

I woke again at dawn to dead quiet and a mouse crawling over my shin. I felt it pause as though wondering if it should walk up my leg or not. I lay as still as I could and waited for it to make up its mind. Finally it did, and it hopped off my foot and onto the ground. I could see its shiny black eyes in the growing light and I slowly lifted my boot and brought it down with such force as to deny the mouse even the briefest of squeaks before its body was crushed under the heel.

BY MIDMORNING THE WIND had begun again. We'd been given water, and some dried meat, so were more comfortable in that regard, but the big blow rattled the door of our jail and made the roof moan. The Colonel had sat up and found his feathered hat, bent and broken, and tried to fix it while I watched through a crack in the wall a crowd of men haul two naked lodgepole pines and try to plant them in the ground, connect them with a crosspiece, and then drape the crosspiece with a rope, which blew in the wind until the men finally used a hooked pole to grab it and pull it down so they could tie a noose.

With his hat back on, the Colonel strode from corner to corner in our tiny cell ordering his own release. Occasionally he'd stoop to peer out through a crack in the wall and shout orders to his Invisible Militia. Then he'd stand, and feeling my eyes on him, he'd say, "Have no fear! Our comrades have the enemies surrounded!"

To stay out of his way, I limped along behind him, and in each pass of the small cabin we stepped over Belly, the big-framed chap, who stayed horizontal and tried his best to find restless sleep.

By evening, with the wind still roaring in the canyon like a captive beast, Kerr knocked on the door. His eyes were bloodshot and he wobbled before us with an unlit candle in hand. The Colonel demanded to know why the gallows was being built. Kerr stepped into the cell stinking of whiskey and motioned for the door to be shut behind him. When it had been, he squatted and gestured for us to squat with him. I lit his candle, and in its glow could see by the gymnastics of his eyes that he was about to foray into another mad speech.

"Hanging you posthaste we conceived the notion of last night," he began, "but dismissed it because the Colonel is the acting governor of the Territory, and a decent gallows nor proper trial by which we might be held to account had neither been built nor executed—standards, I am talking about—for trials and gallows decent and proper by which future generations or the powers back East, or both, might render judgment upon us negatively." He took a long slow breath and continued. "So while battling the tempest some of our good citizens have been completing the former, others of were conducting the latter, the trial, that is, and during the procedure of the aforementioned proceeding, while there was compelling testimony given in favor of banishment, the conclusion was quickly reached that you would never leave the Territory but would merely wander indefinitely and speechify as is your wont, and thus and therefore make us sorry that hang you we chose not."

It was dark in the cell except for a candle that lit Kerr's face from below and made his busy eyes look sunken, his scar paled. Here I imagined his deputy spitting, and despite the dire meaning of Kerr's speech, I felt glad he'd come alone.

"So we've decided to hang you in the morning," he said, clear as day, and for just the second time his voice made the sudden descent from a high official whine to the voice of the simple man squatting in front of us. "All three of you. For crimes against commerce. And if it is any comfort at all, it will be a civilized hanging."

"A what?" I couldn't help it. I'd heard him but I wanted to hear him again.

He didn't hear me, though. Just as I spoke the wind roared even harder and poured through the cracks of the log walls of our jail and shook the door. I'd been hung before and survived, but had no illusions that might happen again. The Colonel, too, had been almost hung, sentenced to be hung, only to have his sentence commuted at the last minute by the Queen. There probably weren't many people who'd lived long past hearing their second death sentence. I had been locked up before, in the root cellar on that Virginia farm, and I must say there was a peculiar unnaturalness to it. Or naturalness, perhaps, because it puts a person in intimate touch with the law above all laws. At that moment I noticed the door of the cell must not have been properly latched from the outside because the wind had blown it ever so slightly ajar, and without even a moment of hesitation I lunged forward onto Kerr's shoulders and wrapped my forearm under his chin and squeezed his neck. The candle flickered out and we struggled in the dark. He was a strong man, and he could lift me up and twist, but all that did was transfer all of my weight to his throat. I remember it was while I was hanging with his neck levered between my forearms that lightning suddenly lit the cabin followed by a blast of thunder that seemed to lift the roof. He spun like a bull with a man on his back, but I hung on because I knew if he shook me off, he'd kill me—and also because I knew I had him in a way that kept him from being able to cry out. Just outside the door stood a man with a gun, and if he heard anything, our game was over.

Belly brought both fists down on Kerr's head. I felt him collapse beneath me, but I maintained my mad and murderous grip on his neck and throat until I knew he was dead. Belly helped me to my feet, and the three of us rushed toward the door. Before I could even get outside, I heard Belly crumple the guard with a rock across the back of his head. He took the man's rifle, and then we were all out on the street of that strange camp, sharing the dark with stumbling drunks and a warm swirling wind. I was limping, of course, so moved easily like the wobbly citizens of that fair city. A dog barked, then another one, and soon it seemed fifty curs must be barking in our area of the camp. Roosters crowed. I heard a man cuss at the top of his lungs at his woman or his dog. No rain was falling, but occasionally lightning flashed and we could see the outline of trees against the sky and we raced to get there.

Then we were on the edge of camp, past the last tent, and into the trees, I limping and the hatless Colonel gasping from the pain in his chest, and both of us trying to keep up with the sprinting Belly.

More thunder and lightning and the trees seemed to do a mad dance around us as we hurried through the woods. After a few hundred yards, the dancing trees ended, and I could see Belly's outline against the sky as he stepped out into a small meadow. Suddenly he crouched and raised his rifle to aim, which was when a single gunshot cracked through the sound of wind and we watched our friend drop his rifle and grasp his neck and fall to the ground.

I ran to drag him—heavy! heavy!—weeping—where were the ghosts to help?—back into the thick of the woods. Bullets ripped the air and splintered the bark of trees around us. The Colonel stood behind me oblivious. The thought of losing him, too, of losing both of them, gave me strength beyond myself, and I ducked down and dragged Belly still deeper into the forest, where I collapsed, finally, and felt his dead weight in my arms. His bloody neck drained on my lap. I hunched over and put my ear on his nose and mouth—no sound of gurgling breath. The Colonel had followed and stood above me, breathing heavily and straining with the pain it caused.

"This way," he said, and reached to put a hand under my arm. We were far enough back into the woods that the bullets couldn't reach us, but the shooting was getting closer. "Felix Belly," I said, and I let his bald head slide wet off my lap. The Colonel helped me stand and we headed uphill toward a sky lit suddenly bright again with lightning.

WE FLED WILD AND grieved through the thick of the trees. Wind and almost constant thunder masked our sound. The shooting grew more distant as we climbed to the top of a ridge. On the other side the wind slowed and we could hear a river, and no shooting at all. I worked my way ahead of the Colonel down a steep hill, and then across a talus slope, using hands as well as feet, from one rock to another toward the trees a hundred yards away. Below us the river hissed against cliffs. We could hear the yipping of a coyote and then nothing. More yipping, and then nothing but our own breathing and the slide of the rocks under our hands.

I waited just inside the shadow of the forest until the Colonel joined me, and we stepped off the last rocks, rubbing our scraped palms against our sashes and wraps and odd clothing. We began to work our way past low branches and over fallen logs. We moved quickly for a crippled young man and an old one with broken ribs. Near the river we surprised a beast and the explosion of sound caused me to turn and knock into the Colonel. The two of us fell down and lay in a pile of pained and panicked flesh while we listened to the hooves beat a fast retreat up the slope.

"Our militia!" the Colonel said.

"A moose," I said.

I rolled off him onto my knees. The river was in front of us. We could see the inky black reflection of the sky in its surface.

"This way," I said, and we made our way through thick brush upstream along the bank. After about a hundred yards, the river widened and presumably grew shallow. But halfway across, wading waist deep ahead of me, the Colonel suddenly stepped into a hole and all I could see over the shiny water was his hatless head drifting downstream. Then I was in the hole, too, and both of us were awash on the cold current.

At least I could swim. The Colonel splashed inadequately so I caught up and took his hand and shouted to relax and hang on. I could see the trees on the far bank sliding past us. We had crossed most of the way before the hole, so the trees were close. I held on to the Colonel and kicked my legs. I felt his iron grip on my arm, but his body lay back and let me pull him.

The river here was surprisingly peaceful for all its speed and power. Terribly cold, too. We moved swiftly downstream listening to each other gasp for breath. The Colonel moaned in pain from his broken ribs.

For the second time that night I imagined I was going to die. Past the terror of being washed into and under a sweeper was the sudden realization that it would not be such a bad way to go compared to hanging. Or getting shot in the neck like poor Belly. Into the quiet black water. Into the silence and deep freeze of death. I imagined seeing the stars fade as I slipped underwater into blackness—and in my grief, I might have done just that.

"Help me, please!" It was the Colonel's voice, like a child's, and it shook me from my dangerous lethargy. Suddenly panicky, I pulled the Colonel's hand as hard as I could. I pulled and kicked until I felt rocks under my feet, and the two of us were standing and scrambling toward shore. Dripping and cold, we emerged from the water, the poor Colonel doubled over in pain.

"I would not have made it without your help," he said.

"Nor I without yours."

But I don't think either of us was thinking of ourselves, not really—for at that moment neither of us cared much that we'd rescued each other. In fact, we both might have preferred otherwise. We crouched and shivered and held one another, mad survivors, and wept for the friend we'd neither saved nor buried.

THE FIRST FEW DAYS on our way to Cut Bank Landing, the mornings were cool and shady in the forest and the afternoons hot, the air smelling of warm pine needles, and we were lucky enough to kill with rocks or sticks a squirrel, a raccoon, a grouse, a camp robber. Springs formed creeks that turned and fell and pooled among boulders, and we got down on our hands and knees to drink, felt the water cover our faces and fill our bellies with weight.

The days passed, and our feet inside our boots rubbed raw and every step gave us pain. My knee above my twisted foot grew sore and swollen. The Colonel held his arm across his tender torso as though cradling a baby. Our plan was to take possession of the steamboat bringing guns and ammunition upriver, take possession in the name of the official government of the Great Western Territory. The guns had been sent by Washington to be used to arm a militia in the war against the natives. Daily I'd ask him, and daily the Colonel would describe to me how he'd order his Invisible Militia to set the boat on fire and cut it loose. He described how we'd sit together on the bank and sip a refreshing drink while we watched colorful flames and spectacular benign explosions soar high into the prairie sky and double themselves on the quiet black water.

He said we'd sit like that all night and watch as the boat drifted back whence it had come.

I can't say I was crazy enough to believe this would happen, but as I had in the past, I used the heat of his mad dream to keep me warm during the cold and hungry evenings.

Three, four, five days passed with little more than mouthfuls of berries. We either didn't see anything to kill, or missed our throws when we did. I rolled over a log and ate grubs like the old native woman I'd seen on the gold trail. They weren't dumplings, but they weren't so bad, either. Nevertheless, my hunger grew. I began to think about what I would sacrifice for an elk roast. Seven days. Eight. Would I sell myself to slavery again? None of us know what we'll do to eat until we've been hungry. Is that why I'd buried the children? Is that why I'd killed Kerr? For food? Or freedom? I couldn't remember anymore—was there a difference? I wanted to ask my father, but he was probably too long dead to remember—and when I looked at the Colonel's face I saw only the same awful nothingness that was overcoming me.

One hot afternoon after we'd broken out onto the plains, we found a dead horse not too badly decomposed and we cut it up and ate from it. The rancid meat tasted like the best elk we'd ever eaten, but our stomachs had grown tight with hunger and we threw up. In the morning we ate more. We threw that up, too, and in the evening of the second day, we ate some more. We stayed by the carcass of that horse chasing off vultures and wolves with rocks and gorging ourselves for three days, until the meat had grown too putrid and our bellies stayed full.

Then we moved northward again. The Colonel had abandoned his jacket and lost his turkey-feather hat, but he still wore his blue shawl with the yellow stars. I still had my jacket but carried it during the heat of the day. I used my purple and blue sleeves and green stockings to wrap around our heads as protection from the sun.

"When we get to the steamboat landing," I said, "they might shoot us as Turks."

We walked along in silence contemplating that.

"We are unconventionally attired," the Colonel said, "but exceptionally so. And therefore, should anyone see us, they'll know us as the leaders of the Invisible Militia, and as representatives of justice and peace."

"You think they'll know all that?" I asked.

"I do," he said.

Good enough, I thought. If the Colonel was indeed mad—mad with love for all of the living and all of the dead—this must be one of those times—hard, hungry, dry, bloody, and heavy with grief—when madness is just what's needed to take the next step, and the next.

WE LIMPED ACROSS THE hot grasshopper flats above Cut Bank Landing at midday. The evening before we'd dropped and slept without fire or food, or water, and by now our tongues had grown too fat and dry to form words. The air smelled of dried grass, and the late-September sun shone so hot that even our weathered skin burned. To make things even more unpleasant, the Colonel had been stricken with diarrhea. Over and over again I'd step ahead to give him some privacy but the act of squatting caused him terrible pain in his ribs and I'd hear him moan even as I heard his bowels emptying on the hard plain.

We straggled over a final hill and saw in the distance the bright strip of river glittering in the sun. Settled down on the near shore was Cut Bank Landing, shanties clustered in gumbo dust. We heard dogs and roosters and the sound of hammering. The children came out to see us approach, apparitions of something they'd never seen before, and they parted for us, and when the Colonel had to stop and squat they stared silently.

We walked into town between wooden buildings bent from winter winds, across rutted streets where the gumbo had creased around wagon wheels with the last rain and folded into deep hard ruts. My feet were sore and bloody in my boots and the Colonel looked like death itself. Even his sunburned face had turned as pale as the bleached land. On the way to the water, we passed clusters of ragged men, drunk in the shade of scattered cottonwood trees, who out of curiosity joined the crowd of children already following us to the river. The Colonel couldn't speak but I could tell by the way he held his purple and blue turbaned head high and raised his hand to greet our growing entourage that he thought these ragged people had gathered to welcome us. I could see their intentions were different. Most were curious to see the mad colonel and his nigger secretary. They'd heard we were coming. They expected us. And in a town full of odd-looking people, the Colonel with his blue cape with yellow stars, and both of us with our colorful turbans, were the strangest of the strange.

We passed a station where scalps were laid out in the sun to dry, and a station where butchered buffalo and beef hung in the shade covered with flies, and an open saloon on the street, where more men picked up bottles of rotgut and joined our entourage. The town smelled of sweat and shit and alcohol, and wood smoke from the steamers, two of them parked, one getting its boiler going again. We scanned the names on the stacks, looking for the *Jackson,* but it wasn't there. Our thirst drove us down to the riverbank, past another cluster of men who'd been unloading a boat, and one of them said the first clear words we'd heard since we'd come into town: "There he goes."

The Colonel was the first to the river and he knelt on the bank and he dipped his hands in the water and splashed the water on his face. I knelt next to him, my knees sinking into the mud. I splashed my face first, just to feel the cool wetness. I licked my lips and splashed and licked again, and then cupped water in my hands and raised it to my mouth and sucked water out of my palms. The coolness burned my throat. I took another sip and held the water in my mouth, which felt like a leather pouch. I held it there, held it, feeling some trickle down my throat and some overflow out of my mouth and over my lips and down my chin. The Colonel leaned all the way forward and submerged his face. He held it under for a long time and finally came up for air, breathing loudly, and spitting water in a fat, arcing stream. His blue cape had darkened with moisture and his purple and blue turban had begun to unwrap. Mine, too, as I dipped my face under the water and drank what I dared and cleaned what seemed to be a bushel of dust from my hair. I came up for a breath and licked my lips and felt my stomach revolt from the gulps of water. The children laughed at our antics. The Colonel used his hand to splash the boldest of the boys, who stepped down into the water and splashed him back. I used my cupped hands to throw water at the boy, and then his friend stepped in and kicked water at me, and then suddenly, as if somebody had given a signal, the entire riverbank came alive with splashing children. Even some of the men jumped joyfully into the river to splash each other or simply to wallow in the shallows to escape the heat.

We were thus engaged when one of the men who'd been unloading the nearby boat told us that the acting governor, and His Honor the judge and secretary, were invited to take some refuge from the sun in the back of Nelson's store. Mr. Nelson had some blackberry wine that he wanted to share, particularly with the acting governor, who he'd been given to understand was suffering from illness.

Nelson was a hook-nosed one-eyed man who'd met the Colonel during the war, and his store was a tiny shack along the main street. He greeted the Colonel warmly with a New England accent and dipped our cups in an open cask of blackberry wine. He said he hoped the wine and cheese would help the Colonel shake off his disorder, and if not, well, it was good anyway, was it not? We agreed, and while Nelson tended to customers in the front of the store, we sat on a cot in the back with the door open and stared at the dry bench above town through watery waves of heat.

The Colonel leaned over and whispered into my ear, "They're camped up there."

I blinked and didn't ask who. The crowd of boys that had followed us down to the river had gathered out by the bushes, and stared at us taking our repose. We sipped and nibbled on cheese and refilled our cups and sipped and nibbled some more. Once the Colonel had to make a dash to the privy, a hole in the ground partially surrounded by a wooden fence. He came back more pale-faced than ever, but eagerly raised his cup.

"To the unimaginable journey," he said, before drinking deeply. "Didn't I warn you months ago?"

He had, and I nodded, and we both drank again. The afternoon had taken on that unreal quality of rest after a great exertion. From our seats in the shade the world outside looked so bright it seemed an impossible and uninhabitable place, and I could not quite believe we had been out there for weeks until this moment, finally, until this moment of rest and wine and shade obliterated all of it—the hunger and thirst and exposure—into an alcohol-induced dreamland. It was silent except for the buzzing flies and the occasional slap as we killed one.

A steamboat horn broke our reverie, followed by the arrival of its captain, who appeared in the doorway, begged our pardon, and helped himself to Mr. Nelson's wine. He sat down on a stool and introduced himself as Captain Angelo Duke, and told us the steamboat carrying the guns from the East was still downstream but should arrive in a few days.

"In the meantime," he said, "You and the judge are free to stay in one of the staterooms on my boat, the *El Dorado*."

The Colonel accepted the offer but his face clouded over and he leaned forward and whispered, "They are after me, you know."

Puzzled, Captain Duke looked at the Colonel, at me, then back again to the Colonel.

"They've been waiting for me." The Colonel lifted his small hand and waved it in a circle. "All of them!"

"Who?" the captain asked.

A bony dog wandered in and sniffed the air. "The Committee," I said.

The captain looked genuinely concerned. His forehead creased and he lowered his voice. "I just arrived here two days ago, Governor, and in this strange place I can't say I know who's who, much less who's waiting for whom. I do know, however, that the stateroom I am offering is secure, that the door locks, and that nobody will be allowed to board without your permission. And when the *Jackson* arrives with your guns—and there's gold on that boat, too, for pay—you'll have these same scroungers begging to join you in whatever the hell it is you're doing."

The dog turned to slink off when I made a move to kick it.

ON BOARD THE *El Dorado,* we were given new linen shirts and shorts and wool trousers and slippers for our sore feet, and told supper would be ready in an hour. I lay on my bed in the stateroom and tried in vain to nap. The Colonel paced restlessly across the room and back again to the window, where he'd pause occasionally to look out at the river.

Beyond the smell of our dinner cooking and my incessant salivating, what kept me awake was the notion that I stood alone on the threshold of a door opening into an unknown and unimagined world. I had passed through many such doors in my short life and in order to embolden myself I was tempted to count them. The doors of my mother's cabin and my father's carriage. The door into and out of my cabin on board the ship to England. The door out of isolation with Miss Bridget. The door into Mr. Perry's saddlery with nothing, and the door out of Le Chat's apartment with gold. The door of the confederate officer's shack where I'd gone to write a letter—and walked out with my back colored with bloody stripes and a gun to my head. Lots of doors. I could go on and on with the doors without even counting the figurative doors—out of slavery, into slavery, and out again. From hope to despair and back to hope. Out of the womb. Out of another womb. Out of yet another.

From boyhood to manhood to orphanhood.

But the fearlessness I'd felt after losing my mother was gone. When I closed my eyes I could no longer see her face. I could barely remember Belly's. I lined up the dead I had known going all the way back to Miss Crinkle and they formed a long line of bodies but all of their faces were gone, dissolved by soil or the sea. My father. Saturn. Jimmy and his sister. The dead I'd loved, the dead I'd killed, the dead I'd buried. Where had they gone? And why did I suddenly miss them so?

Yet if I felt abandoned by the dead, something else was rising up to take their places. While the Colonel paced, I felt it in the room as clearly as I felt the mattress against my body, pressing upward, pressing with a weight exactly equal to mine.

Don't move, I whispered to myself with every breath. *Don't move, hold it down!*

Needless to say, I was still awake when we were called to supper, which was to be served in the dining room for the officers. The evening light flooded across the floor from the western windows, and the doors on both sides stood propped open to let through the gentle river breeze. I had a headache from the afternoon, and I think the Colonel did, too, for finding ourselves alone before a splendidly set table for four, we quickly filled our cups from a carafe of red wine.

We waited like that, standing, sipping, and alone, while the staff spread the table with platters of roast buffalo and potatoes, with heaps of bacon and butter, and with bowls of fruit preserves for the bread. A tall man with long blond hair and matching mustache breezed into the room and announced to the Colonel that Captain Duke had been taken ill unexpectedly, so that he, the captain's first mate, Mr. Benjamin Dodge, would be our lone host.

Then he took one look at me—at my hair and my eye—and his face paled. There was an awkward moment, during which we hovered behind our chairs without sitting. He coughed, cleared his throat, and appeared on the verge of gesturing for us to sit but did not.

"Forgive me," he said, "but I'm a newcomer here and I didn't know."

"Didn't know what?" the Colonel asked.

Mr. Dodge's glanced at me again and his pale face pinked. "Sir," he said to the Colonel, "may we speak in private?"

"This is as private as it gets with me," the Colonel said.

To give the suffering man as much of what he asked for as I could, I walked to the window and looked over the river at the wide sky beginning to darken over the eastern plains.

"Mr. Acting Governor," he began, "despite your eminence, I believe I am going to have to . . ."

I stood waiting. I could guess by his accent and his manners what he was about to say.

"Sir," Mr. Dodge began again, "I don't believe I ever shared a table with a—with a *Negro,* and I don't believe my good and respectable mother would forgive me if I did so now."

So hungry was I, and so bothered by this delay, I was prepared to fill my plate and take it onto the deck, but when I turned to do just that the Colonel gestured for me to stay where I stood.

"Eat where your good and respectable mother would have you, Mr. Dodge," the Colonel said, "and don't eat where you won't."

A confused smile flickered like a shadow across the first mate's face. "Pardon me?"

"If you take issue with our company, or if you feel our company would offend those who are perpetually with you in spirit, you are free to eat outside," the Colonel said.

"With all due respect, Mr. Acting Governor," Mr. Dodge said, still blushing, "it is not *your* company to which I take exception."

The smell of the food filled my mouth with saliva, which I was forced to swallow. I was beginning to want to spit, or to vomit, or to run outside and do both over the rail, but the Colonel gave me a look that glued me to my spot and miraculously dried my mouth.

"Sir," he said, looking back to Mr. Dodge, "permit me to be more blunt. This young man is the secretary to the governor of the Great Western Territory, and the territorial judge. He is also, I believe, either a faerie or one of those blessed mortals that the faeries favor, for he has used his powers to save my life four times that I know of."

Mr. Dodge opened his mouth to speak but the Colonel closed it again by merely lifting his hand.

"He has also killed for my benefit, Mr. Dodge. Did you know that? Slight as he is, and with his bare hands. We have crossed a lot of country to arrive here and we have eaten very little. Both of us are weak, and I, personally, am ill."

Mr. Dodge looked at the floor.

"So I eat where he eats. He eats where I eat. Just a few days ago, that was on the fireless prairie with our hands full of putrid horse meat. Now good fortune has delivered us this heavenly bounty."

Mr. Dodge nodded.

"You are free to join us or not," the Colonel said.

Mr. Dodge took one step backward, dipped his head as if to humbly apologize, and then pivoted and walked out of the room, leaving us to our feast, which we ate with less joy than such a feast deserves. Because despite the food and the wine, and despite the pleasantly cool air and the purple and pink sky out the window to the west, we weren't quite alone. Brooding silently in the two empty chairs sat the only companions left to us, our fearful hunger and our rising sense of doom.

ON THE WAY BACK to our cabin after supper, I stood by the rail and looked down into the dark river moving beneath us. I heard the Colonel cough at my side. We were weary from the journey, and the meat and wine in our stomachs brought a dreaminess to our minds that seemed to muffle the sound of the drunken howling coming from the saloon.

"What a flood," I remember the Colonel saying. "The thoughts it brings to mind are a terror!"

I assumed he was thinking about his near drowning the night we'd escaped Bloody Bend, the night Belly had been shot. I reached for his sleeve. "This way," I said, and we retreated to our cabin.

I did not sleep for hours. I know I listened to the Colonel snore, and I know I heard him get up numerous times to empty his bowels out on deck. I know that in the sound of his footsteps I felt a terrible certainty that had nothing whatsoever to do with the reason for his wakefulness, and I know I must have fallen asleep, for I woke to the sound of a splash.

Not a big splash. Not one that should have awoken me. I was inside the cabin, after all. How could I have heard it? But I did. And it shook me out of dreamland.

"Man overboard!" I shouted, recognizing the sound even before I got out bed. "Man overboard!"

On deck somebody had a lantern and hung it over the rail. The yellow light reflected up off the moving black water. Beyond the yellow circle the night was even darker.

"The Colonel?" the man at the rail asked. "Has he gone over?"

"Yes," I said.

"How do you know?"

I breathed deeply. I did, I just did. The air felt suddenly cold and I shivered. More men arrived at the rail and shouted into the darkness, but we heard nothing come back from the water.

"He's fallen," said a voice to my right.

"Or pushed," said another.

"Slipped."

"Drunk."

"Murdered, surely."

"He can't swim," I said, and walked toward the stern. Away from the lantern light the starry sky came into focus. Had men from town come right to his bunk and taken him and thrown him in? Wouldn't he have screamed? Or had they waited for him to come out on deck, as they knew he would to relieve himself, and then pushed him, tilted him, watched as his body tipped over the edge and was swallowed by a splash? Perhaps the white smudge of his face rose once to the surface as he kicked and gulped for air. Or one arm like a fish rising, and then sinking forever beneath the surface. I remembered his helpless weight in the river as I pulled him to shore that night, and how on shore he'd sat down like a terrified child spitting water between his knees, his black hair matted against his skull.

"Where's the nigger?" I heard somebody shout in the darkness.

I limped down the plank off the boat onto the dock and then along the landing wearing only my shorts.

"That way!"

I stumbled over ropes and crates and scanned the surface of the water for anything that might be the Colonel. Barefoot in the mud I splashed madly downstream along the bank, falling, getting up, falling again. I could hear my pursuers behind me but I called his name anyway and listened for a response from the river. I ran farther, and called louder, for I don't know how long, searching the smooth black water, scrambling as best I could with my crooked foot and no shoes. I thought of my father, and of the man with the top hat who'd jumped off the ship, and Mrs. Smith's red-hatted husband, and now the Colonel, who might simply have slipped while shitting.

The shouts of my pursuers got louder and closer, and suddenly I was wading knee-deep in the water, not so cold out here on the prairie. Then I was waist-deep, and as I watched my pursuers appear along the shore, I lay quietly back and floated with only my face above the surface. My mother had taught me to swim, and I remembered her saying if I filled my lungs with air and relaxed, I could stay up with little effort, so that was what I did. My pursuers were not twenty feet away, but even when I could see they were looking right at me they couldn't see my dark face on the dark water.

"Never!" I shouted, making my voice like the Colonel's, his brogue, his high pitch. *"Never, I repeat it, never was there a cause more sacred, nor one more great, nor one more urgent!"*

I saw the flash of a gun, heard the explosion, and felt the splash of water near my body where the bullet struck. I wanted to laugh and shout again and actually bit my tongue to keep from doing so. I might have let myself sink, and roll and swim under the surface to put some distance between me and the shooter, but I enjoyed watching the scurrying and stumbling along the bank through the willows. The second shot wasn't even close. The current had pulled me quietly away toward the center of the river, and only then did I roll over and swim. I dove into the darkness until my hands hit the muddy bottom, and then I rolled over and let myself float up toward the surface again. I lay like that stroking quietly and stared at the stars in the wide sky over the high bluffs and listened as the voices of my pursuers faded to silence.

By the time I dragged myself shivering to shore I was miles below town and the sky in the east was already brightening with dawn. I wiped the dripping water off my skin with my hands and curled up for warmth in the high grass. Just before I slept, I saw something move on the far shore. At first I thought it might be an elk, but when I sat up and looked closer I could see through the mist rising off the river the vague outline of a ghostly horse and rider. Another rode over the bluff and down beside the first, followed by two more. And so they came, two by two to the river's edge, where they spread out until the ghosts of thousands of mounted Irishman lined the bank.

I blinked and shivered and stood up. They weren't there long. Downstream the sun had come up, yellow and fiery red, and it began to burn off the mist. And as the mist disappeared the soldiers filed up the bluff and over again in the direction from which they had come. Near the end of the column I heard a familiar mule braying, and then I finally saw him, straggling well behind on Destiny's back, the humble shape of the Colonel, dressed as I had first seen him out here in the Territory, his broad green belt and blue frock coat. I stood and waved but he was struggling with his sword, trying to get it in or out of its rusty scabbard. He was met on top of the bluff by a ghost I recognized as Belly, his hair long again, his naked chest gleaming in the morning light.

Then they were gone—all of them—and I stood alone for a long time and when I couldn't bear the silence anymore I shouted the Colonel's name. My voice raced across the river and back again.

Don't leave me! I shouted.

I stared at the line between bluff and sky over which the column had vanished.

Please! I yelled, this time with all the wind that was in me, all that I had been or known or done or hoped for, *please please please!* until the sound became a song I had no more voice to sing. Then I lay back again in the grass and slept.

WHEN I WOKE MY cheek was pressed against the muddy ground, and a few feet from my forehead coiled a rattlesnake. Its tongue flicked in and out of its mouth, and its eyes made two black oil drops on each side of a yellow-black head shaped by hard, clean lines. The head rose and lowered and moved from side to side, and the rattle was a blur. I lay perfectly still, feeling the sound fill my stomach with fear. I felt dried blood on my face and sunshine on my back, and for a moment it was only me and the snake on earth—and then, before I could blink, the snake slithered off and it was only me.

I sat up and remembered Belly and the Colonel's ghosts, and I bent toward the river to see my face but only saw my shadow. I dipped my hands and drank water from my cupped palms. For a moment I thought about how I might be drinking water that had drowned the Colonel, but what did that matter? We have in us all that ever was, Mr. Collins used to say. In every breath we take is a part of the conquering hero who drove his chariot into Rome, and a part of the slave who rode behind him, tapped him on the shoulder, and whispered, "Glory is fleeting."

The sun was high already. I let my eyes scan the river all the way to the other side and the bright bare hills rising east onto the prairie. I stood and waded out into the current and felt the water cool my body. The body of my unnamed African relatives and my unnamed English relatives, and the body of Caesar himself, and of Caesar's slave. All of them here, and all of them invisible. My body submerged to the knees. I shivered but felt the sun warm on my shoulders and the top of my head. I felt the press of the current against my thighs and waist. The bottom was muddy and my bare feet sank into it. I leaned forward across the water, stretching toward the far bank, and began to swim again. Somewhere out here in the water his life had passed from his flesh and this water had passed into his lungs and then out again. I lay out and felt the water splash over my face.

On the far side I walked up the bluff in the tracks of the Invisible Militia. I stood dripping and breathing and feeling clean and new. I climbed up onto the bench above the river and began to walk across what appeared to be a limitless expanse of land.

I walked toward the east. After a few hours I veered southward, then westward, and soon came to the conclusion that on this vast grassland it didn't matter which way I went. Right, left, right, left. These things I knew: my feet on the earth. The sky, the wind, the ground. Thump-drag, I limped. I wore the white cotton shorts that Captain Duke had given me to cover my body, but no shirt, no hat, and no shoes. My feet hurt but so did most of the rest of me.

Night came and the temperature dropped fast and I fell asleep exhausted on the grass where I had taken my last step of the day. It was cold and I had no way to make a fire. I felt the earth under my body and stared at the heavens and watched waves of wild color explode from the northern horizon and fill half the sky. I breathed deeply the descending autumn air and curled as tightly as I could for warmth. It was possible I'd freeze to death by morning and who would know? Who would care? For the first time in my life there would be no living person to mourn my death. I dreamed I was walking to oblivion. I walked and walked on the wide plains, limped and limped, invisible to myself, invisible to God. Nothing but sky and land and cold fire in the sky, and so strong was the sadness in my dream that it took all of my strength to keep from throwing myself on my face and screaming madly for a witch doctor.

And then I was screaming, just as I had on the bank of the river, only this time I was screaming at the lunatic blue eyes of the Colonel, which had merged and grown and become the sky.

See me! I shouted. *Don't let me disappear!*

I woke in the morning and sat up and swallowed. My dry throat was sore, but thank goodness for daylight because the pity I'd felt for myself in the dark had almost killed me. Little puffs of cloud made moving shadows across a tawny grassland. My knee hurt and my feet were raw but I stood to walk. Which way? The only way I knew, first one foot, then the other. Always avoiding as best I could the prickly pear. Along a muddy little creek (which I gladly drank from) I found a stick

I could use for snakes, and also for a cane. I thought of my pursuers from the river, and how they'd return to the landing and say I had disappeared. Surely drowned. I thought of my schoolmates at Hodgson Academy and how I had stood on the carriage and waved like a hero until I'd disappeared behind the trees. I paused on the top of a rise and looked this way and that, and for a moment wasn't sure which way to go. I had disappeared under the petting hand of Mr. Perry, hadn't I? Disappeared over the lip of the grave to Jimmy and his little sister. Disappeared to my mother and grandmother, and to all of my forefathers on the plains of Africa—could they ever have imagined? Could I?

Perhaps I was the last man on earth.

We hold these truths to be invisible. All men are created invisible. Endowed by their invisible Creator with certain invisible rights. For years invisible words had circled the sky of my boyish dreams like invisible eagles. Yet only now, today—as I walked as a man across the wide belly of the world with nowhere to go and no reason to get there—only now did the words begin to feel true. I felt in my sore flesh what my mind had never been able to hold. Freedom brings no promises—not of long life, nor healthy life, nor happy life. Freedom isn't power, because power can be lost and is always limited. *We are not in control.* Freedom doesn't come when your flesh-and-blood father gives you papers and puts you on a boat, or your first adopted father makes you his pet, or your second a killer, your third a faerie and a judge. You can't get it from documents or armies or gold and it isn't a gift from a hero any more than are your hands or feet. But it does live in your body—in the flesh-and-bone cells of your very being, in your lust and in your hunger, in your longing to love and to be loved, and even in your desire to kill. As hard as we may try to give it away, it is always there. We are free, all of us, all the time—for as long as we breathe—free to our invisible core whether we be slaves or kings. To choose right or wrong. To close the door or to open it. To be true or false. Ignore or not ignore. Love or not. Bury the children or die refusing.

I had made all the choices and walked away, and made new ones, and here I was still walking, limping, still free. You can hear me if you can't see me: *Thump* (my good foot)—*drag* (my crooked one). *Here.* Not *there* yet—or not anymore. Only *here.* Jimmy. James Gates. Jimmy Gates. Freeman Walker. Son, student, pet, warrior, slave, killer, miner, victim, nigger, secretary, faerie, judge . . .

This way, I thought, and it was while I was limping matter-of-factly down the broad and grassy hill—just about when I figured myself through with magic and madness—that a cloud shadow passed over me briefly and I felt touched by a wild, unexpected joy.

Now what?

Anything!

Out here the air was so dry that even very distant objects grew quickly clear. Yet out here there was nobody left to see me, nobody left to name me but me.

EPILOGUE

ONCE AGAIN, HOWEVER, I was wrong. For the next few days I was followed by wolves. They appeared in front of me and then suddenly disappeared to circle around behind me. And more than once I saw native men painted with colors and adorned with feathers pop up from breaks to watch me limp past. I could see doom in their faces—so I looked away and kept walking. Thump-drag.

I walked under a sky bigger than my mind could ever be. Clouds moved across it, and high V's of geese. The only thing between me and that far pointed butte was more sky shivering in heat. It might take two days to get there. And when I did, then what?

A swarm of locusts moved in and covered the land. I ate them and followed them and slept among them. When they finally flew off I lay on my belly from sunrise to sunset, to sunrise again, waiting to club a rabbit when it came out of its hole. And I did. I crushed his skull with one blow and even cooked him in a fire I made with hot coals I found at a recently abandoned campsite.

That was today or yesterday or perhaps tomorrow. Time became a dream of the precarious, and always dangerous, *now*.

One morning I heard the rumble of unending thunder. I looked for storm clouds but saw none. Perhaps I was imagining the sound. For it seemed to be more of a groaning of the earth than a groaning from the sky. I let my eyes drift along the fine unending horizon, and from the north grew a dark and thickening line. One moment grasses swayed as far as the eye could see and the next the grass was being covered by what looked like a pool of molasses that seemed to be sliding down a tilted plain toward me. Above it rose dust that formed a cloud as big as a storm. The earth shook beneath my feet. The earth shook beneath the growing rumble of a million hooves. Buffalo.

Not far away the plains broke into small cliffs and badlands. I hobbled that way and ducked over the lip where I could no longer see the approaching herd. But I could still hear it and the rumbling of hooves grew louder. I knew that when the buffalo came into the breaks they'd flow between the cliffs like water, and unless I found a place to hide they'd trample me into the dust.

While I scanned the low rock walls for a crevasse, the first black-faced buffalo appeared over the little rise, followed by another and another, and soon a running mass filled the draw and headed right for me. I ducked behind a loose boulder and then saw a narrow cave a short sprint away, just wide enough. I hobbled over as fast as I could and slipped in sideways. The walls of the rock vibrated on each side of me, but all I could do was stand and wait, and look out the narrow opening at the buffalo beginning to pass not three feet away. Below I could see where the draw squeezed still narrower, and there somebody had set up two pikes with their butt ends in the ground and stone tips pointed in the direction of the running buffalo.

I watched with fascination as the first animal barreled through that opening. He was a young male, and when he saw the pikes he tried to stop, but another was on his heels and piled into him. Then another came and another after it, and soon the gap filled with buffalo, and the running herd split as water flows around a dam.

The rock vibrated against my skin and I smelled the dust and the mass of beasts passing. Only then did I begin to be aware that I was not the only person in this narrow cave.

I slowly turned my head and what I saw first were the bright whites of her eyes, and then, as my eyes adjusted, her broad forehead and the scabbed wound where the tip of her nose should have been. She clenched her jaw. In her fist she held the handle of a knife. I held up my hand to show her I meant no harm, but she pointed the blade toward me and we stood that way for a long time while the herd passed. I tried not to stare at her face but had nothing else to look at. If she was no longer beautiful, her eyes still shone with cunning and courage. I watched her look from my right eye to my left, then to my hair and the scars on my bare back, which she could see as I was standing sideways in the cave.

When the last buffalo passed, I slid out into the dusty light and she followed me with her knife. The pikes in the opening had impaled two young buffalo. She began cutting one of them open. I squatted a short distance away and watched as she pulled from its chest the bloody liver and with two hands lifted it to her face to eat. I watched her pretty eyes close as she chewed, and when she finally lowered the dripping organ, her round face was wet with blood and her mouth full of raw liver. She took more bites, devouring half the giant organ, and handed what remained to me. I felt it wet and warm in my hands, and I bowed to her, and then I ate the rest of it.

The wind blew and when she was finished gutting and skinning the animals she used her knife and flint to start a fire with the sticks and brush I gathered. She kept the knife in her hand even as she sat down on her side and I sat down on my side. After a while it got cold, and I watched her get up and go over to where she'd put the two bloody buffalo skins. She dragged one back and laid it over her body, hair on the inside. I went to get the other. I walked well around her on my way back to the fire and lay down under the skin. I liked the smell of the wet flesh, and I liked the smell of the fire, and from the other side I could hear her breathing through her scabbed nose. The wind blew and in the wind I could smell an old sadness that I didn't need to name. I wondered if she could smell anything. The last thing I thought before I let myself fall asleep was how shortly—maybe even the very next day—I would be turning twenty-four years old, the same age as my parents when I was born.

I woke in the middle of the night to see that she'd crept over to my side of the fire and now knelt over me with her knife. I caught her wrist as she brought it down, and we struggled until I pried the knife away from her, and she scrambled over to her bundle, where she kept a forked deer antler. Now we each had a weapon locked in our fists. Across the red embers we studied every inch of one another.

Things got better after that first night. It was a short, fierce courtship, and I won't go into the details except to say that when the sun dried the dew from our robes, we ate again, and again before the next vaporous night, and again the morning after that. No toast with marmalade, but the effect was the same. Air and light, the wonders of having a body, a picnic. She'd been banished from her tribe and I from mine—and from the deep well of sadness springs joy. From the depths of madness . . . something *civilized?* I don't know—we're still working on that. And I feel as if I've said enough already. If you're curious, though, we're still here. Come looking where the wind drops down the east slope of the mountains and races forever across the plains and grass grows all the way to the sky. If you can't see us at first, don't be discouraged. We'll be here for a long, long time.

AUTHOR'S NOTE

This story is a fiction, and as such readers can be assured they'll learn nothing about African American slavery, nineteenth-century London, the Civil War, Native Americans, or the gold fields of the American West that they can rely on to be factual. Nevertheless, I could not have written *Freeman Walker* without the information, ideas, images, and phrases found in the following books. To their authors, whose plums I've plucked to make my poor punch, thank you.

Memoirs of Gen. Thomas Francis Meagher, by Michael Cavanagh, The Messenger Press, 1892; *Thomas Francis Meagher: An Irish Revolutionary in America,* Robert G. Athearn, University of Colorado Press, 1949; *Mythologies,* William Butler Yates, Macmillan Publishing Co., 1959; *Saloons of the Old West,* Richard Erdoes, Alfred A. Knopf, 1979; *Women's Diaries of the Westward Journeys,* Lillian Schlissel, Schocken Books Inc., 1982; *The Diary of a Forty-niner,* edited by Chauncey L. Canfield, Turtle Point Press, 1992; *The Boys' War: Confederate and Union Soldiers Talk about the Civil War,* Jim Murphy, Clarion Books, 1993; *In Pursuit of the Nez Perces,* General O. O. Howard, Duncan McDonald, and Chief Joseph, Mountain Meadow Press, 1993; *Vigilantes of Montana,* Thomas J. Dimsdale, The Globe Pequot Press, 2003; *A Decent, Orderly Lynching,* Frederick Allen, University of Oklahoma Press, Norman, 2004.

In particular, I'm indebted to Thomas Francis Meagher, whose speeches and *Harper's Magazine* travel articles (some written under the pseudonym Col. Cornelius O'Keefe) I've plundered like a pirate in a mostly futile attempt to give this story a bit of the magic of his most remarkable world.

—D. A. C.